I Will Forget This Feeling Someday

WRITTEN BY
Yoru Sumino

TRANSLATION BY
Diana Taylor

Airship

Seven Seas Entertainment

The following novel was produced in collaboration between the author and The Back Horn from the earliest planning stages. Please enjoy this novel along with the EP from The Back Horn, *Kono Kimochi mo Itsuka Wasureru* (released October 19, 2020), a work of mutual inspiration that crosses the boundaries of book and music.

*L*IFE, IT SEEMS, is a horribly dull thing.

The fact that every single adult always says that their teen years were the best time of their life is proof of that simple fact. To think that one day I'm supposed to look back on these meaningless days with reverence, with jealousy—with the notion that I'll never rise any higher than the place where I currently stand—is a tragedy.

I'd always assumed that everyone around me was burdened by a similar sense of dread, but it seems that is not the case. Every last person manages to find some kind of fulfillment, some kind of consolation in their own way, whether in reading books, listening to music, playing sports, or pouring themselves into their studies.

By following certain basic rules and acquiring certain basic abilities and generally avoiding any extreme hardship, I've been able to survive. Food tastes good, and sleep feels great, but no matter what I do, it's all boring.

It's all so very, very boring.

Every morning I eat breakfast, go to school, walk into my assigned classroom, and sit in my assigned seat. I never share any particularly meaningful exchanges with anyone. I don't make friends, and I don't offend anyone. I just sit at my desk, waiting for the time to pass me by.

Any stimulation makes the boredom all the more apparent. When you wriggle your body, the pain resonates. As long as you remain still, you can get by just being there. All I do is gaze upon the boredom that sits in the back of my mind.

I raise my eyes, taking a quick glance around me. There is not a single special soul amongst the gathering of thirty unremarkable children in this classroom. Every last one of them is dull—myself included. What sets me apart from them is that I am always keenly aware of just how boring I am. The rest of them live with the illusion that life is a colorful, many splendored thing and that they themselves are special. And every one of them grates on me equally.

I find myself at a loss. I feel a swell of anger both for my own aimless self and for those who feel no such confusion. And yet it seems that these days, when all I can do is curse my own dullness, are supposed to be the height of my life.

Give me a break.

Seriously... Someone, please take my feelings away from me and take me away from this pointless place.

—✳—

I used to read a lot of books in my spare time when I had nothing else to do. Thanks to this, I accumulated a lot of useless knowledge, but I didn't reap much more from it than that. Specialized books and nonfiction aside, the stories thought up by others gave me no hope whatsoever.

"Suzuki, please read from line five until the next paragraph."

"Okay."

As the teacher instructed, I stood up, language arts text in hand, and read the indicated passage aloud. There was no point in rebelling: Whenever I saw the self-styled delinquents in my class complaining about what a pain in the ass this sort of thing was, it struck me all the more how absolutely clueless they were. If you think something's a pain, then just do as you're told. Going with the flow is the easiest way to keep time marching on. If you elect not to skip school or if there's some reason you have to attend, this is your only means of alleviating the tedium. Or if it isn't *actually* a pain, and you just think you can deal with your boredom by having someone fuss over you, then you're truly the lowest of the low.

The sooner you sit for your lesson, the sooner it's over.

Four lessons before lunch—just sitting there and listening to someone talk is enough to make you hungry, so every day you go to the cafeteria and eat. You pick an empty chair and sit down in it, putting whatever you happened to pick up that day in your mouth. You force yourself to eat a meal that's never *quite* what you were hoping for.

After lunch, you return to the classroom without much

dawdling. When you take your seat, the others around you distance themselves. To be frank, this is a blessing. There's nothing good about actively getting involved with others.

And then, just like in the morning, you suffer through the tedium of boredom. Usually, you're successful.

"Hey, Suzuki."

Today, however, I was interrupted. Tanaka, the girl who sat in front of me, was sitting sideways in her chair, looking at me through dull eyes. A straw ran between her mouth and a juice box.

"What do you do for fun?"

Piss off, I thought. Both for asking blunt questions for no real reason and for acting like her life was somehow so much more special than mine.

"Nothing really."

"Quit being so pissy and answer the question. What d'you do after school?"

"Go running."

"With *who*? You aren't in any clubs, right?"

"Alone."

"What, you some kinda athlete?"

"No."

"That's *obvious*, idiot. Why don't you find something funner to do? Just lookin' at your gloomy face glaring at your desk all the time really gets me down, y'know."

Mind your own business. I'm not even bothering you. Why are you so concerned about other people's feelings? If I were to bother striking up a conversation with my boring classmates who seemed to measure their own worth by how buddy-buddy they could get with random people, it'd just add to my own tedium.

"Fun doesn't exist."

"...Jeez, that's dark."

I choked back the sigh that I was about to let out at the way her face twisted up at my statement. I had no intention of recklessly making enemies in my class. Not only would it be tedious, but it would also be incredibly annoying.

"I mean, you're not wrong that it's boring out here. I can't wait to get out of this hicksville, y'know what I mean?"

What a vapid opinion—endlessly so.

It didn't matter if we lived in the middle of nowhere or in the heart of the city. It only took an hour to get to the city by car or train, maybe two at most. A completely trivial amount of time. Exactly what could either of us accomplish in such a short span? Both of us were boring people, regardless of our location.

I looked away—there was no point in conversing with her further. Tanaka, however, still seemed intent on using me as a means of killing time and pretended to mutter to herself, fishing for a reaction. "Oh, our class's resident dark cloud, the girls' rep, is back." She looked toward the back of the classroom as she spoke, loud enough that it was clear she was making no attempts to hide it. I knew without looking who it was that she was referring to. "You ever talk to her, Suzuki? Y'know, as a fellow stick in the mud?"

What would it take to satisfy her? There were so many pointless questions in the world.

"I mean, not really."

"I bet you two could get along. You're both always staring at your desks, so maybe you could talk about what kind of desktops look the nicest!"

I hated people who laughed at their own jokes.

Fellow sticks in the mud. I was aware that from the outside, Saitou—who had probably just entered the classroom—and me appeared to be the same sort of person, but that didn't make it a meaningful point of connection.

Having finally gotten her fill of talking at me, Tanaka vanished, leaving me to sit quietly until lunch break was over. I was in charge of cleaning the classroom this week. Wipe down the floors and blackboard well enough, line up the desks reasonably, things like that. Cleanup is necessary when there's no one else around to do it for you. Performing tasks that one was not expected to derive enjoyment out of in the first place was an easy thing for me and put me far more at ease than even our midday break.

After that, I made it through fifth and sixth periods, said my farewells, and headed home with no lingering attachments. My classmates remained for a few moments in the classroom, some of them nervous about upcoming club activities, most of them relieved at the feeling of freedom. As a result, only I and one other classmate left the room without wasting any time.

Sometimes the pattern of which one of us ended up staring at the other's back on the way out flipped, but not once had we ever interacted as we made our way down the hall. Our enrollment numbers were close, however, so whichever of us arrived at the shoe lockers second always had to wait for the other to finish changing their shoes before they could leave.

Today, Saitou arrived at the lockers first. I waited quietly as she donned her shoes in no particular hurry. Almost every day we shared these few moments together, sometimes with our positions reversed. Never once had we spoken. After Saitou left, not speaking a word or even turning back to look at me, I changed my shoes as well.

Would you really think that Saitou and I were two peas in a pod? I'm sure that whatever was inside of her was no more than a few tenths of a millimeter different from the boringness that lies in anyone else. Being lucky enough to have someone in the same class who you could share your feelings with and who'd come to your rescue would never happen—at least not to a worthless human being like me.

Fate, miracles, outstanding moments—none of them are real.

"Oh, Kaya! Welcome home!"

My mother was on the way out when I arrived at home. She was dressed all in black.

"Hey there."

"Glad I caught you in time. I'm going out for a bit. I don't think you ever met her, but your grandpa's younger sister passed away. They're having a wake for her. Could you let your brother know?"

"All right."

"I'll be home late, but I left some dinner for you in the fridge. Make sure you eat, okay? There's some snacks too!"

"Okay."

"I'll be back before your birthday."

"'Kay. Don't get caught."

After seeing my mother off, I climbed to the second floor of our very average house and dropped my bag off in my similarly average room. I changed out of my uniform and into some sweats, went back downstairs, and then opened the fridge to find a box of doughnuts. *Won't they be cold...?* I wondered as I took the box out and opened it, selecting the doughnut that looked like it contained the most calories. I needed plenty of energy for running, after all.

I sat at the living room table in the middle of the quiet house and nibbled on the doughnut. Ours was the sort of household you'd find anywhere—right about now, my father was out working hard to put food on the table, and my older brother was giving his all to his university classes in the morning and a part-time job in the afternoon. With my mother gone, there was no soul here but me right now. The three of them lived average lives, all seeming to go about their days with some measure of happiness—all the while spouting to me, the youngest, about how your teenage years are the best time of your life as though they'd just resigned themselves to their lousy existences.

Something suddenly occurring to me, I stood up and turned on the radio in the corner of the living room. My mother usually had the radio playing while she was doing her housework, so it was normally on when I got home. Having been raised in such an environment, it was easier to ignore any unwanted noises with the radio on than while sitting in silence. When I turned it on, there was news about the war playing. There'd been a lot of that lately.

The doughnut had sucked up all the moisture from my mouth, so I went to the fridge, poured myself a glass of milk, and gulped it down. It was probably owing to my lifelong fondness for milk that I'd grown a little taller than average. Unfortunately, I had no interest in playing any sports for which my height would be beneficial.

Food was delicious because I was hungry. Eating was necessary to survive. There are likely those who believe that a boring life is not worth living. Death by suicide, however, was not currently an option even on my radar. I had the typical fear of death. But, more importantly, dying now would still be *boring*. If I ended myself, jerks like my seat neighbor Tanaka would just say "I knew he'd do it" before moving on with their dull lives.

It would be completely pointless.

After waiting thirty minutes for the food to digest, I turned off the radio, put on my running shoes, and headed out. First I did some stretching in front of the house, then I started walking, gradually picking up speed as I headed towards the mountains in my usual routine. I didn't have a goal or any specific plans in mind. I was simply training my body in case anything ever happened. But I couldn't say it wasn't a little bit exhilarating.

As I ran, I alternated between periods of thinking and periods where there was not a thought in my brain. When I was thinking, my thoughts were primarily occupied with how I could escape from these days of doldrum. Ever since junior high, I would spend my runs imagining conducting myself like the delinquents did, or dropping in unannounced on club activities, or living my life to the sound of music. I would keep that up until I was disappointed in myself, thinking, "Is that all?" Then I would once again start running and think some more. Again and again. This time, surely, I would *do* something.

In the coldest days of winter, my runs felt as though I were putting myself through some sort of intense club training, but now that it was the latter half of February, more and more days were a comfortable temperature for running.

I supposed I would run for about an hour—down the usual back road, to the tower I used as a landmark, and then back. On the way back, already breathing heavily, I cut through a forest en route to my final stretch. The unpaved road eventually gave way to crumbling asphalt, at the end of which was a single lone bus stop. That was the actual goal of my run.

Affixed to the bus stop sign, which was browning and rusted from disuse, was a timetable for a bus that would never come no matter how long I waited for it. Beside it was a probably unnecessary prefab structure which served as a shelter, of which I would slide open the door and take a seat on the bench.

By the time my breath had steadied and my heart rate had settled, there were no sounds in the shelter besides the chirping of birds outside. Not a single car drove down the asphalt road before me, largely because some years back, a nice new road that circumnavigated this forest was paved, so no one used this route anymore.

The biggest reason that I used this spot as my goal was how abandoned it was. Even though I could not fully explain why, I hated seeing people when I'd just finished running. It just made me feel *weird*. There was nothing particularly off-putting about seeing someone mid-run, or when they were just setting out, but finishing a run was a moment that I wanted to keep to myself.

The next most important reason—which was probably just my own imagination or something—was that this was the only place where I could actually daydream. I felt like sitting here, all alone, was the only time I could allow myself wild fancies, like the idea that a strange bus might show up here one day and take me somewhere far away. I knew that such a fantasy would never come true. I knew that I was just as stupid for sitting here in my delusions as the vapid people in my class who consoled themselves with such things. That was why I only did this here, in private. This was the only place where it was permitted. The only place where, twice a day, I could truly be alone.

I wondered if everyone had a place where they could daydream.

Well, other people probably didn't need something like that.

I sat there until my sweat began to dry, standing up once my thoughts had put themselves back in order. Then I left the shelter to once again become acquainted with my boring, everyday self. There was not a single soul to my left or right along the strange, twisting asphalt path.

After about a thirty minute walk, I returned home to see that my brother was finally back. We exchanged a hollow greeting in the living room before I conveyed the message from our mother.

"Hold up, wasn't your birthday today, Kaya?"

"Tomorrow."

There was no point in being defiant towards a family that was in no way lacking—other than their dullness. Leaving him with that one-word answer, I headed up to my room to change. I stayed there until dinner researching mountain climbing, which had occurred to me during my run as a potential next challenge for myself. I always thought of the sports that involved competing against other people, or against the records that others had set, as pointless for all but those who would make their marks on history—but having nature as my opponent might not be so bad. If I saw something with my own two eyes that I couldn't see in my normal life, perhaps that would awaken something within me. Though there was a strong possibility that I might see some beautiful sight and just think to myself, *Is that all?*

Just as I was reading an article online about a monk who had climbed to a mountain summit that no one had ever reached before, my stomach started to rumble. I went downstairs and ate the dinner my mother had prepared, savoring it well enough, before sharing another pointless exchange with my brother and returning to my room. My parents used to worry about how much time I spent holed up in my room, but that didn't seem to concern them as much lately. They knew by now that I had a set after-dinner routine.

After spending another hour or so looking up the necessary equipment for mountain climbing, I once more changed into my sweats. Then I descended the stairs and headed for the living room, where my brother still sat.

"I'm going out."

"'Kay, try not to get caught."

Ignoring his flat reply, I went to the front door and put on my shoes. Sure enough, it was chilly outside. Still, it was fairly comfortable considering that not long ago I'd had to bundle up before heading out at night. I started out once more in the same direction I had run earlier that evening. I'm sure my family assumed that my nightly runs were somewhere with good visibility, but that was not the case. Ever since I realized that spending too much time in my room would attract unwanted attention, I started wasting a lot of time just wandering around in the dark, hoping to avoid any family reunions.

The speed at which I ran at night was not the only difference from my earlier run. This time, I headed directly for the bus stop. I did not pass through the forest, instead walking leisurely down the dimly lit asphalt road. While I was still around inhabited homes, I didn't have to think about much as I walked. But I had to be more careful as it grew darker, the scenery around me changing to streetlights that stood farther and farther apart, empty houses, and the occasional passing bicycle. I wore a glowing band around my wrist to keep myself from getting run over, but if I spaced out, I might just take a tumble into a field or a rice paddy. If I did, there was no telling when someone might pass by who could help me.

Still, it was a route I took almost every day, so I once again arrived at the forest without issue. As I walked along the darkened asphalt, streetlights looking down upon me, the bus stop came into view.

Though the bus stop was situated at the exact darkest point in the space between streetlights, it was still lit by the moon, though nothing else. After all, there was no need to have a light for a bus that never came. Beyond the sliding door of the shelter was what looked to be a switch for a fluorescent light, but I had never tried turning it on. I had no idea if it would even work.

The shelter blocked the wind from getting in, so in winter, it was warmer in here than outside. I shut the door and sat down upon the bench that I could only assume was still there. I crossed my legs, then removed my wristband and put it in my pocket. In the darkness, the light was only a distraction.

Pitch-black darkness.

It would be hard to describe the shelter in that moment any other way. Outside was slightly brighter, which made this place seem like a completely different existence from the dull world surrounding it.

Here was the only place where I was permitted to dream. Twice a day, this was the only time I was allowed to be my own boring self.

I closed my eyes, waiting for the special something that might come for me someday.

— * —

There was a reason that this bus stop, no longer in use, had not been removed—a strange legend that was passed down in this little town. Structures that fell into disuse were always left alone for a while, undemolished. Why? Because abandoned places might still be in use by our ancestors—they might still be needed by those who came down from the afterlife. Here and there in this town, old houses stood eerily empty.

The origins of the legend and the reason it persisted until the present day were irrelevant. But it was thanks to this ridiculous fairy tale that, day after day, I had a solitary place to relax.

In that relaxation, however, I grew careless. At some point, I had fallen asleep within the shelter. This wasn't the first time I dozed off, but I wondered if it was due to the temperature getting warmer or if it was simply because I hadn't gotten much sleep the night before.

At any rate, upon waking, I was shocked at myself for falling asleep, and even more shocked when I took out my phone and checked the time. I was now officially sixteen years old.

I had a number of missed calls and texts from my mother, who must have gotten home from the wake. The texts were part concern, part lecture. Only half lying, I replied that I had taken a break on a bench in the park and fallen asleep, and that I would be home soon.

The dark and quiet of the shelter, darker and quieter still now that it was late at night, gave me a strange, hazy sensation, as though I were still asleep.

I felt my breath getting a bit out of sync with my body and

steadied it. I'd said I would be heading right home, but I still needed a bit of time to prepare myself to step from my dream world back into the outside. I had to align my rhythm with that of beyond the shelter walls. I breathed slowly, and after a while, I could feel my body acclimating itself to the real world.

I stood up and took a few steps to shake off the motes of darkness clinging to my body, then reached for the handle of the sliding door.

"Where is it you always go?"

There was a voice.

My hand flew from the handle, the door rattling in its wake. I had breathed in too suddenly. Pain coursed through my lungs. My heart was beating as loud as a drum.

In a momentary panic, I wobbled back in the darkness, placing my hands against the wall. It felt coarse to the touch, and something—maybe dust or fragments of the wall itself—fluttered to the ground.

Calm down, I silently told myself. I breathed out and back in again.

What *was* that?

I'd heard a voice. A voice that came from my right—perhaps a female voice.

It had to be my imagination, didn't it? I probably was still half dreaming.

"Today, I've learned that you sleep too."

Just as I was thinking this, I heard the voice again, more clearly. A husky female voice. I felt electricity run down my spine.

Where was it coming from?

The first thing that came to mind was a ghost, no thanks to the legends I had heard so often they were practically drilled into my brain. I couldn't imagine a better setting for such an encounter than an ancient bus stop late at night. Still, I had my doubts. Why would a spirit appear right now, all of a sudden, when they had never done so before? Plus, how could a person as normal as *me* ever hear the voice of a ghost?

The next thing to occur to me was that perhaps someone had snuck in here while I was asleep. But why?

I put my all into steadying my breath and heart rate. I wondered if I should turn around. I stood at a crossroads. If I turned around now, would some danger befall me? I was scared and nervous, but I came to a decision quickly.

Was I stupid? Was I *really* that big of an idiot? This was nothing to worry about. There was only one correct choice here.

I realized that this was what I thought about every day. I'd been waiting for this. I came to this dilapidated bus stop every single night, nauseated at my own vapid self, because I was waiting for a moment like this one to arrive.

And finally, the moment had come, without fanfare.

That was all.

At the very least, I needed to verify what was happening. I didn't know how I'd be able to live with myself if I let the moment pass without doing at least that much. I took another deep breath in and then breathed out for just as long.

A plethora of dreadful premonitions ran through my head. Truth be told, I was frozen in place. Slowly, gradually enough that this person or thing would not notice, I turned around.

There, in the dark...was not a humanlike form. Nor an animal-like form. Yet, *something* was there, though I didn't know what exactly it was.

I squinted.

In the darkness floated a small form, or perhaps *forms*, glowing with faint green light.

There were no light sources within this shelter, which meant that whatever was floating here shone with their own light.

There were two a few dozen centimeters above the bench. Just above the seat of the bench were ten more. And near the ground there were nine—or rather ten again—as two of them merely looked to be overlapping. The two up top were different in form from the other twenty. They moved differently as well. The top two were almost elliptical in shape—a bit like almonds, one beside the other. Now and then they disappeared at the same time. The others were rather small and round. They wriggled about almost systematically, like insects.

Were *these* what had spoken to me?

I stood there watching, but the little lights did not appear to mean me any harm. I gathered up my courage and drew nearer.

"What's the matter?"

I felt goosebumps rise on my skin as the same voice sounded again. My feet stopped in place. The voice was coming from right in front of me. It was clearly responding directly to my actions.

These were words with meaning. Were these things capable of conversation?

I swallowed hard and decided to try speaking back myself.

My words faltered.

"Who's...speaking?"

There was a reaction to the sound of my voice. I heard something like a person inhaling. Then, the twenty small orbs began to wriggle, the upper ten shifting upwards into a line. The two lights at the top grew larger than before, changing from ellipses into almost perfect circles.

"How?"

The female voice sounded surprised. The two top lights blinked off and on in repetition, like a traffic light changing. I stood there in silence, unable to reply as I did not understand the question. Again, I heard the sound of someone inhaling.

"You...can hear me...?"

"...I can."

The two top lights grew even larger. Half of the twenty smaller lights, the ten up top, moved up closer to the top two in a line.

"Why now?"

Again and again the top lights flickered. *Blink, blink. Blink, blink.*

"Are you...alive?" the voice asked.

"I-I am, are you?"

"I'm still alive."

The conversation was progressing. I supposed it was asking if I was alive because it thought I might be a ghost. On my end, I had no idea whether this thing made only of light that was speaking to me was an organism or not, but apparently it was also alive. I figured I should at least ask what sort of life-form it was.

"Where are you?" I asked.

"Where?"

Right here, the voice seemed to say. But where?

"Are you...a bug or something?"

"A bug? I'm a person."

No matter how you diced it, that did not look like a person. The lights stretched and wriggled.

"You don't...look like a person," I said honestly. The voice grew quiet. I wondered if I had made it unhappy, but it seemed to be thinking.

"You do look like a person to me though," it said.

"Well, that's because I am one."

"How do I look to you?"

I explained it exactly as I saw it: two elliptical lights, about the height of my chest, with ten small, connected lights just above the seat of the bench, and ten similarly sized lights near the ground.

"I see."

I could not have imagined what sort of reaction I would get to this, but there was a sense of acceptance to the voice. Then, the two top lights drifted simultaneously up and down.

"What you're seeing are my eyes and nails."

"Eyes and...your nails?"

I reflexively gasped at the absurd reply. Once more I stared.

Now that I took a closer look, I could almost see variations within the light of the top two shapes, like sclera and pupils. Was the momentary vanishing blinking? Growing larger as the eyes grew wider? Was the vertical motion nodding?

The two groups of ten lights were hands and feet?

Working off of the assumption that these were eyes and nails, that would mean that the rest of their body was invisible in the darkness. Judging by their posture, they were probably sitting. Was this an invisible person or something? When I posed the question to them, however, they immediately replied, "No, I'm just a normal person." Exactly what about this was *normal*? I still didn't know if they even *were* a person.

"I am surprised that you can hear my voice too," they muttered, forgoing any explanation of why I could only see their eyes and nails. I thought hard about this.

"Could you...always hear my voice...?"

"Yeah."

The lights meant to be eyes drifted up and down. Another nod, I supposed.

"Up until yesterday, I could hear your voice, but no matter what I said, you could never ××××."

"Wha...?"

The words cut out partway through. They were drowned out by some sort of interference, like the noise you hear when a radio frequency doesn't quite match up.

"I was surprised that you could suddenly ×××× all of a sudden today."

Once again there was that sound, like television static. Judging by the context, the incomprehensible word was probably the same sort of word as before.

"And now I can suddenly hear you..."

At my earnest reply, the girl—wait, was it all right for me to call her a girl? The voice sounded female anyway, so—in front of me said, with reasonable suspicion, "I wonder why..."

"Just before, you called me an invisible person... So nothing besides my eyes and nails looks ×××× to you?"

"Nothing but the glowing parts."

I pointed, and the two upper lights moved downward. "I see..." I heard her mutter in some sort of understanding. Because I could not see where her mouth was, her voice came suddenly, and it was tricky to catch her meaning. Then, there was that noise again.

"Do you have any body parts besides the glowing parts?"

"Of *course* I do."

I was unsure if I should believe that, but if I did choose to believe her, I couldn't help but start to imagine the hazy outline of the rest of her form, if what I could see were her eyes and nails. Judging by the placement of her eyes, the length of her arms and legs would not be at all unnatural for a human.

"I can see *your* body ×××× though," she said.

There it was again.

"My body looks...what? I didn't quite catch you."

"××-××."

It seemed like she was sounding the word out, but I still couldn't hear it. What on earth was that noise?

"Clearly. Distinctly... Does that make sense?"

"Ah, yeah, I can understand those. There was just a part I couldn't make out. Um, so anyway, I can only see your eyes and nails, but you're saying you can see my whole body?"

"Yeah. Even before you could hear my voice. I always just thought you were a dead person, the way you'd appear here and then disappear without doing anything. I would try talking to you, but I never got any reply. That's why I was so surprised before."

For a long moment, the eye lights went out. I could tell that she was more at ease than I was.

"So why is it I can only see your eyes and nails?"

If I was to believe all that she said, then this was a bizarre inequality.

"...I mean, I guess it makes sense if you think about it. In a dark place like this, you *would* only be able to see the parts that are glowing. Honestly, it's weirder to me that I can see *all* of you."

"Dark..."

No, that wasn't it. Though it was faint, beyond her eyes and nails I could still see the wall and bench. There was clearly no body there. I offered a proposal.

"What if I turned on a light?"

"Lights are forbidden."

"Forbidden? By *who*?"

"The government, obviously. Guess you don't know about ✕✕✕✕✕."

There's a lot I'd like to ask you, she started to say, when the lights that were apparently her eyes went wide and turned to me.

"Oh."

The girl, who had seemed quite calm until now, suddenly sounded frightful. Judging from her glowing nails, her hands moved slowly up beside her eyes. She looked as though she was covering her ears.

"That's the siren. I've gotta go."

I didn't hear any siren. I turned my focus to beyond the walls but heard nothing from outside the shelter.

"Goodbye."

All I heard was an abrupt word of parting.

"Huh?!"

"I have to go. I'm still alive."

"Hold on, what? Wait!"

A parting as sudden as our meeting. Though I still knew nothing, felt nothing, understood nothing, I was immediately terrified that this special thing was going to leave me.

"You don't have to go, though," she said calmly.

"I, uh, no, I mean that doesn't matter."

She sounded like a worried parent.

"I don't know where you came from or where you're going, though. If you are alive, I'm sure we can meet here again."

Was that really true? Or was this special moment going to end here, never to occur in my life ever again? I began to imagine going back to my boring everyday life, day after day after day with nothing but a sense of premonition, and I shuddered.

The girl made of only eyes and nails, not seeming to share my concerns, stood up, at least as far as I could judge by seeing the position of her eyes shift. "Goodbye," she said once more. From the movement of her nails, I could see her walk towards the wall opposite where I was standing, disappearing just before she would have collided. Or rather, the lights of her eyes and nails simply went out, gone. Nothing more.

"Hey!"

I called out, but there was no reply. I called out once more again, but of course there was still nothing. Had she left, or was she simply ignoring me? Regardless, it seemed the conversation stopped here. There was probably no point in saying anything else. The only thing I could do was leave.

Now, just as I'd always assumed I was, I stood alone in the bus shelter. Just before her departure, there were two things that I was able to determine, or rather, to suppose: First off, judging by the height of her eyes, she was probably no different in height from the average human woman, perhaps about 160 centimeters—though if there was any strange elongation from her forehead upward, I would have no idea. Second, though I could not see the rest of her body, it probably did exist, just as she said. When she stood up and it appeared that she was turning around, one of her eye lights went out of view. That probably meant that she had a head and that the one eye had been hidden by the angle she was facing.

Once more, the bus shelter was dark and quiet. Left alone in the simple prefab structure, I was thrown into a sense of disarray, of anxiety. My pulse shamelessly began to quicken in a much different way than it did when I was exercising.

It had only been a few short minutes. What had I just experienced?

What had happened to me?

For a while I stood frozen and dazed, vividly replaying what I had just witnessed again and again in my head. I kept questioning it: Had that really happened? I had no idea. Maybe it was just a dream, though how horrid it would be if that were true. At the same time though, I had to wonder: Could my own boring subconscious really come up with a being with such a fantastical appearance? A creature that looked like a human, invisible but for her nails and eyes?

What the *heck*? What the heck was *that*? What in the heck had just unfolded before my own two eyes?!

I was not ready to allow myself to feel any reckless joy. I had no idea if there would even be a next time. She'd said that we would meet again, but I had no proof of that. Even if I truly had encountered this girl, if this was to be our only meeting, then it was no better than a dream.

Regardless, I knew that just standing around there forever would gain me nothing. If what she said to me was true, then perhaps if I came back the next day something might happen again.

And, if in fact this was a dream, if it truly *was*, then I needed to wake up so that I could recognize that fact. I couldn't linger in this dream of something special forever. I steeled myself and made up my mind to exit the shelter.

I put my hand on the handle and slid open the door. When I stepped outside, I was buffeted by a cold wind, but it did not awaken me.

I was still standing in my own normal world. Though, while I knew that it was too soon, *far* too soon to be happy, for a few seconds I merely stood there, wearing an expression that I would never show to anyone else.

I could not sleep a wink after that. The next morning, when I went to the living room, I received another lecture, same as I had when I returned home, along with birthday congratulations.

As I did every other morning, I ate my breakfast to the sound of the radio, changed my clothes, and rode my bike to school. It had been a while since I'd pulled an all-nighter, but for some reason I wasn't that tired—maybe the daily exercise was paying off. Besides, if I did get tired, I could just take a nap during one of our breaks.

Something special had happened last night. And yet my daily life was unchanged. As though my emotions were plain on my face, Tanaka gave me what could only be described as a look of indifference as we passed each other on the way from the bike racks to the main entrance. Even still, she greeted me with a "Yo!" as if she didn't mind wasting her own boring energy on a boring guy like me.

"Mm."

"What're you poutin' for?"

"I'm not."

A lie. A flat-out, bold-faced lie.

"You *definitely* are. With a face like that, the girls'll be throwin' themselves at you!"

That'd be nice. But of course, I'd never say that aloud.

"I mean, whatever."

"That's what happens with good-looking guys...!"

When I couldn't come up with anything to reply to this meaningless opinion, Tanaka made herself scarce. When I got to the classroom, she was raucously bragging and showing off pictures of her dog to another classmate.

Normally, I would just spend the rest of our arrival time gazing around in boredom, but today was different. Now I had the girl from the bus shelter to think about. Maybe she really was a ghost. There were plenty of legends about them in this town. She might have only said that she was alive because she didn't realize she was dead. Or maybe she was an alien, or some other kind of unknown life-form—not that a woman made only of lights had ever appeared in any of the stories or accounts I had read.

I considered a number of different possibilities about her true identity based on what I knew. I honestly had no idea if I would ever even see her again, but it was still a departure from my pointless everyday life. Spending these few moments thinking about something special was not a waste of time. Thinking in and of itself was not pointless until it became so.

The most important thing to consider was this: Should I meet this girl again, and how could I utilize this encounter to make my life into something special? Meeting a non-human being only once was not enough for me to live a special life going forward. What would make it meaningful was what might happen next, such as if she could share some knowledge or information with me that only she knew, which I could apply to my own life in the future. I even had the fleeting thought that if she was a ghost, perhaps she could show me a glimpse of the afterlife, but that was a little *too* out of the box.

What mattered most to me was that I saw her again.

That day, I sat through my classes as usual, making Saitou wait her turn at the shoe lockers this time, and set out running—as always—the moment I got home. The only way I was going to encounter that girl was by going to the bus stop, so there was no point in deviating from my usual routine.

I ran my normal route before ending up at the bus stop. It was as deserted as ever, the shelter lit by the evening sun refracting off the asphalt and not giving the slightest vibe that any ghosts might emerge from it. I sat quietly within it as I always did, but nothing special occurred. Perhaps she really wouldn't appear until after dark, or maybe she was already there, and it was simply too bright out for me to see her still. In case it was the latter, I tried striking up a conversation, but there was no reply. No matter what I did, I received no response, and waited there until just before dinner time before I decided to head home.

Today, my family was celebrating my birthday, and as a gift, I received a wristwatch that would monitor my heart rate while running. I had never really paid attention to stuff like that while running before, but I *had* heard that maintaining your heart rate while running was good for building fitness, so I decided to put it to use.

I ate my dinner and then set out for my walk, as I always did. My mother chided me and reminded me not to go falling asleep in the park again, but I was already fully set on using the same lie today when I set foot out the door. Even if she didn't show up, I was going to wait there until the clock struck midnight. There was a chance that she might only appear in the dead of night, after all.

I arrived at the shelter once again. There was no one there. I sat in my usual spot, quietly awaiting her. I wondered how she would appear—if she did at all. Yesterday she had been sitting to my right when I was facing the sliding door, at the farthest spot from the entrance. Perhaps she would come walking in from somewhere, the opposite direction from which she had left the night before.

I had not slept enough, but I wasn't tired. As I patiently awaited her, wide awake, finally midnight came. Though I was reluctant to do so, I decided to head back home. Naturally, my fears had accumulated over the course of the night—how strong the possibility was that the previous night had been only a dream, that another encounter with this girl might never come again.

My life followed the exact same pattern the next day.

And the day after that.

And yet, she did not again appear at my side.

I was anxious, and though I was well aware that my impatience would get me nowhere, I felt a prickling sensation all throughout my body. As if it was obvious to those around me that I was much more irritable than usual, Tanaka hadn't started up with me at any point in the past few days.

It felt like I was being struck by a fit of some illness. I tried to will myself out of my anxiety, but the feeling of my skin crawling was going nowhere, present as ever. I knew that the only way I would be able to escape this was by meeting her again. If not, I would probably spend the rest of my life visiting this bus stop, the sensation never leaving me.

What a terrible life that would be.

I spent another day hoping that she would be there, half resigned that she would not, heading to the bus stop as I always did when evening came, opening and shutting the door of the shelter futilely.

"Looks like we meet again."

At that voice and the sight of the faint lights, the prickling in my body swelled in one dramatic moment to a fever pitch and then vanished as though it had never been. I felt so horribly at ease that I thought I might cry.

"I'm so glad to see you...!"

I almost thought the words had come out of my mouth, but in fact they had been hers.

"There're so many things I've been wanting to ask you," she said.

"Me too. I've wanted to ask you some stuff, so..."

I sat down, a bit shaken that I said something so sappy in my own elation. She only replied with a simple "Yeah..." in her usual husky voice.

"I actually thought you'd only be here at later hours," I said, checking my watch to see it was not even 8 p.m. yet.

"It's not always the same time. Plus, there are a lot of ×××××, so I figured it might be a while before we could see each other again."

As I once more heard that strange noise, I knew for certain that this day was connected to the other, that it had not been a dream.

"Sorry, a lot of... What was that again? I couldn't hear you."

"'Safe houses.' How about that?"

"Ah, yeah."

"I wonder why you can't understand certain words. Maybe it's a lack of knowledge or something."

What a rude way to put it.

"No, I mean, it's not just that they're words I've never heard before, I literally can't hear them. It's like they're buried under some kind of *shhhhh* sound."

"Curiouser and curiouser..."

The girl, who as before was made up only of her eyes and nails, lined up her ten fingernails around what I supposed would be her lower abdomen if she were a human, moving them back and forth. Maybe she was scratching her knees. Speaking of curious things, perhaps it was even more odd that I could simply accept someone who looked like this enough to have a conversation with them. Of course, standing around there forever was going to get me no closer to my goal, so I had to force myself to accept what I saw in front of me.

"First off," I said, "there's something I'd like to establish."

I figured it was best to start off with the simplest question, putting aside whether or not the person I was conversing with actually existed in this world. There was no telling how much time I had, so I needed to hurry up and get to the point.

"*Who* are you?"

It was a stupid sounding question, but the girl just laughed.

Thinking about it, I actually couldn't remember the last time I had actually been interested enough in another person to want to know about them.

"Me? Well, what do you want to know about me?"

"Um, like, assuming you're a person, what gender are you?"

"Female. And you're male I presume?"

Apparently "she" *had* been the right pronoun for her.

"Yep. How old?"

"You mean how many years has it been since I was born?"

"Yeah. I'm sixteen by the way."

"I'm a bit older. I'm eighteen now."

So she was a third year in high school—or maybe even a university student. Though, if she was a ghost and that had only been her age when she was alive, there was no telling how old she actually would be now. For a fraction of a second, I wondered if I should be speaking more formally to her, but I put that aside and continued questioning the owner of this voice that sounded a bit husky for her age.

"What's your name? I'm Suzuki Kaya."

"Su-zu-ki-ka-ya. Sounds strange. I'm ×××××××××××××××."

My ears were assailed by a static noise longer than any before.

"Sorry, I couldn't make out your name."

I apologized, thinking this might annoy her, but she didn't seem bothered. Though it might have shown in her nose and mouth and eyebrows, which I could not see.

"Guess my name's a no-go either. That's rather inconvenient."

I supposed so.

"Why don't you decide, then? If there's some universal name that you might have for a woman, you can call me that. Anything's fine."

"Universal?"

"I mean that you can really just call me whatever, y'know."

It occurred to me that this girl might have an odd way of thinking. Regardless of whether she was a ghost, it was one thing to say that you didn't care what someone else was called, but much different not to care about one's own name.

"Also, is that name Suzukikaya just your personal name? You don't have a family name?"

"Oh, uh, Suzuki's my surname, so I guess you'd call that my family name. Kaya is my personal name."

"Oh, Kaya, that's shorter and much easier to say. Weird though. Are you from another country, Kaya?"

Suddenly being called by my first name by someone I had barely interacted with felt almost like a violation. More importantly, though...

"Another country? This is Japan."

"Jappan...?"

"Japan."

"Jappan...?"

This was getting us nowhere.

"Um, that's the name of this country."

Never did I think the day would come when I'd have to explain to someone that the name of this country was Japan while I stood upon its shores. Putting beside my own bewilderment at this bizarre experience, however, the girl's glowing eyes opened wide.

"The name of this country? You're saying that's the country we're in right now?"

What a strange question.

"That's right."

"What could *that* mean?" she asked, moving her eyes and nails as though in thought, before saying with her unseen mouth, "The name of the country that *I'm* in anyway is, well, it's called ××××××××××."

Another word I could not hear.

"Couldn't hear it, hmm?" she confirmed.

I wondered if she could tell that from my expression, which would mean that she really could see me clearly, even here in the dark. I gave an earnest nod. She then nodded as well (judging by the movement of her eyes) and muttered, "I see. Guess there's a lot I need to think about here."

"...Such as?"

"First off, Kaya, I need to tell you that I have never heard of a country called Jappan, and moreover, I don't think such a country even exists in the world I'm in. Probably."

"Wha...?"

Didn't exist? But we were in Japan *right now*. As I seriously considered this incomprehensible thing she was telling me, she suddenly let out a loud, "Oh!"

"It's the siren," she explained. "I have to go. Didn't have much time today, huh?"

She had mentioned something similar before.

"What siren?"

"The one that means it's over up top."

I looked reflexively upward. It was faint in the dark, but all I could make out was the rusting, dusty ceiling.

"What's over?"

"Right, of course you wouldn't know. The ×××××."

I knew that she wasn't making fun of me, but the way she phrased it really sounded like she was. She then made a move that looked like she was standing up.

"Hey, wait a sec."

"'War.' Do you understand that?"

"Huh?"

I stopped myself from reaching out pointlessly into the void.

"I'll explain more next time I see you, but I've gotta go now. I think we..." the girl, the girl whose name I had not yet decided, began, then turned toward the wall and said, "...might not be in the same world."

And then she disappeared.

— ✳ —

I yet again grew impatient, but I was handling the wait better than I had the first time. I now knew for certain that there was a chance we might see each other again. As I waited, I thought again and again about the meaning behind the mysterious girl's words. She lived in a different world where there was a war going on, and Japan did not exist. What could that mean? I didn't understand it, but I had to consider that it was true, even with my limited knowledge. I wondered if it had anything to do with the war I had been hearing so much about lately.

Right, and more importantly, what was up with all that static? It was like a radio receiver suddenly going out of focus.

"Somethin' is up with you, Suzuki-kun..." Tanaka, who was already at her desk, began when I entered the classroom and took my own assigned seat.

"Hm?"

"Don't usually see you playin' with your phone. Didn't even realize you had one. Whatcha doin'?"

"It's got nothing to do with you."

Never in a million years would I exchange contact information with Tanaka.

"Tch, I wasn't assuming that it did...?"

If it doesn't concern her, then why is she asking about it? I thought, but of course I couldn't say that, so I just let it go. If Tanaka wanted to waste her life being a busybody poking at things that she had no interest or investment in, then she was free to do so. *That* was none of *my* business.

Incidentally, I was messing around on my phone because I

needed to look some things up. At the very least I supposed I needed to figure out a universal name for the girl. Though she had said "universal," to put it simply, there were a lot of names for girls out there, weren't there? That was what I was investigating. That said, the lists of most popular names changed every year, and I got the sense there wasn't really any one name that could be considered 'universal.'

A surname would be easy—something like Takahashi or Satou. Names like Tanaka were already taken. Still, it felt kind of awkward for me to offer up a given name for a girl. She'd said I could call her whatever I wanted, and instinctively, I already half felt that Satou was the best option.

While I investigated and pondered things I was not even sure that I needed to, the day of our reunion came. It was two days after the last time she had appeared at the bus shelter.

"Been waiting for you, Kaya."

I heard her voice from the faint lights the moment I entered.

"It's been a bit. I don't visit the safe houses very often these ××."

"What's this about a safe house?"

"Right, we should continue our conversation. Where should I start?"

I was glad to hear her get right down to business. I closed the door and sat down in my usual spot. Her nails were in a tidy line, as though she had her hands atop her knees, her eyes pointed fixedly at me.

"So, I actually came here with a lot of questions about you, Kaya. Mind if I go ahead?"

"Sure."

I had no reason to refuse.

"Um, so while we were apart, I checked some ×××××."

"Sorry, couldn't hear that. You checked some what?"

"Right." Her eyes moved up and down as though acknowledging something. "Books?"

"That I understand."

"I looked through some books, and sure enough, there's no country called Jappan anywhere in our world. Not currently or formerly."

Given her phrasing, she was not speaking metaphorically—Japan as a country truly never existed. If I believed what she was saying, the possibility of her being a ghost was shrinking.

"You live in a country that shouldn't exist, and know nothing about the sirens, and can't understand the words I say, but... there's something that's been bugging me even more than that, even since before we could talk to each other." Five of her nails drew nearer to me, only one of them extending further. It was obvious she was pointing. "Your eyes and nails don't glow."

She seemed to be suggesting that it was normal for her to find this mysterious. As I stared deeply into the lights, I remembered that those were her eyes and awkwardly averted mine.

"Because of that, at first I assumed you were a figment of my imagination, that my mind was just making up all the right things for you to say."

Honestly, I had sort of thought the same thing.

"Still, I have no way of confirming that. Even if I asked you whether you were just a product of my imagination, you could say no, but that might just be my imagination as well."

"Yeah, same on my end really."

"I'm glad you get it. Even though that might just be my imagination too."

It was difficult to determine just from the shape of her eyes, and there was a strong chance that I was just seeing what I wanted to, but even if it was just my guess, it seemed that she was smiling. Though I couldn't actually see it, this smile made me feel for the first time that she might actually be a person.

"The next thing that occurred to me, which I mentioned before, was that you might be a dead person. You said you were alive, but you might actually be dead, and your ×××× is just lingering in my safe house for some reason."

I assumed the word I couldn't hear was 'spirit' or something. I figured I would ask later, so as not to interrupt her.

"But if *that* were true, it wouldn't explain why you would mention a country called Jappan. So, based on what you've told me so far, I've landed on a more accurate theory than you being dead."

Of course. And that would be...

"Is that what you were saying last time? About us not being in the same world?"

"Yep. That's the most ×××× answer."

"So...are you saying that you've come from a different world into the one that I'm in, where Japan exists?"

I was thinking she was perhaps some kind of traveler from another world who had made her way to this shelter, but she looked like she was shaking her head.

"I don't think that's right. Right now, I'm in my safe house. I need to ask: Kaya, where are *you* right now?"

Right here, I was almost tempted to answer, though I knew she was not asking such a straightforward question.

"I'm at a bus stop."

"Bus stop...? The bus stop is for...some kind of vehicle?"

"Yeah, a bus."

"...Gotcha."

What was that about?

"Kaya, there's one more thing I'd like to confirm. Can you give me your right hand?"

Again, I had no reason to refuse, so I did as I was asked, gently stretching out my right hand, which definitely fully existed beyond just my fingernails. I was honestly shocked at myself for how readily, how casually I did this. Then, before I had time to prepare myself, something cold touched my hand.

"Whoa!"

I reflexively withdrew it. What the heck *was* that?

I looked at her to see her eyes fixed on me, the nails of what were probably her left hand floating exactly where my right had just been.

"Again, if you don't mind?"

Nervously, I held my hand out again as asked. Though I had reflexively curled my hand into a fist, this time I felt the cold thing from before gently stroke my palm and the back of my hand instead of gripping it, as though trying to confirm the sensation.

"I can touch you. Do you feel me touching you, Kaya?"

"Y-yeah."

I could tangibly feel the sensation of something cold and thin, probably a finger, tracing along the surface of my hand. A little calmer this time, I looked to confirm it visually. The sensation of being touched moved in sync with the light. My back was damp with sweat.

This experiment continued for some time. Even after the lights finally moved away, I could still feel the sensation lingering on my skin.

"Thank you. It's seeming like my second assumption was closer to the truth."

I looked at my own hand. I realized that I had only been listening dimly to what she was saying.

"Y-yeah."

"If my assumptions were wrong, then maybe only one of our ×××× was making it across to the other side, and it only looked and sounded like the other was right there. But I don't think that's it."

I focused all my attention on her words, not wishing to lose a single one while she was explaining her logic. I got the sense that once more the word hidden in the noise meant something like "soul," so it was easy enough to guess what she was trying to say. She'd thought that perhaps I might have been something like an image on a projector screen. However, that didn't seem to be it.

"After all, I can touch you."

"Yeah, I could feel you touching me too."

The ghost of the sensation still remained.

"So, here's what I think is going on: For some reason, the safe house I'm in and the place you're in are connected. Despite this, both of our perceptions of this place differ. To you, it looks like we're both at a bus station, right?"

"That's right."

Only her eyes and nails, though.

"To me, it looks like you and I are both in an underground safe house."

"We're what...?"

I wasn't particularly rattled by this—merely surprised. But if what she said was true, then what she'd mentioned before about something being finished up above us was referring to a world other than my own.

"This is my most ×××× assumption at this point. What do you think, Kaya?"

What *did* I think? Honestly, I thought this was all incredibly inventive. Her theory was like listening to a fairy tale. However, what I had just experienced—something invisible touching my right hand—proved to me that she was very real. Even though, as she said, the feeling of being touched might have been nothing more than my imagination.

"Well, what I've been thinking is..."

I had no idea if what she'd said was right or wrong, so I decided to just explain to her what I had been thinking over the past few days. She herself had already thought of the possibility of one of us being a ghost, or merely a product of the other's imagination, so I floated one of the other various theories that had occurred to me: that she might simply have lived in a time before the name "Japan" was in use.

"I see. So you're saying that I was assuming that we live in different worlds, but you think there's a chance we live in the same world but separated by a vast period of time. On the contrary, the world *you* live in might be the one in the past, and maybe later on there was some huge disaster and the country known as Jappan vanished."

It was a disturbing thought. It would explain her talk of a war, though.

"The fact that there were no mentions of Jappan in the past when I looked into it could just mean that that information was inconvenient for whichever country won the war, and so they struck Jappan from the ××××."

"Sorry, struck Japan from the *what*? Couldn't hear what you said."

"Records. Does that work?"

"Yeah."

"I also had some thoughts about these words that you can't hear, if you don't mind. Thinking about it, it's actually weird that we can talk at all."

It was true. If we were in different countries, or even just different time periods—let alone if we were in different worlds entirely—incomprehensible words aside, it was bizarre that we could more or less carry on a conversation in the same language to begin with. Even the slightest amount of distance would usually cause a cultural or linguistic clash.

"Now this is just my theory, but consider that maybe of the countless different worlds there are, including differences in time and place, it just so happens that the linguistic structures of your world and mine align. Where I come from, there's a saying: 'Words gave birth to the world.'"

"But humans made words..."

"Words must be pretty powerful though, to be able to connect to another world."

Her voice sounded more optimistic than anything else. *She's a lot more of a dreamer than that laid-back voice of hers would imply*, I started to think, then winced at how very basic it was of me to think for even a moment that a person's personality could be determined by the sound and tone of their voice.

"But then why are there words that only I can't understand?"

"Because they're words that don't exist in your world. The fact that I can understand everything you say either means that you just haven't said any words I'd be unable to hear or that your influence on this space is stronger than mine. Earlier, you mentioned a vehicle called a bus, which I've never heard of, but I could still hear it. I could hear your name too."

"Oh right, about that universal name."

"Did you think of one? I'd like something as short as yours, something simple."

Well, that immediately cut out Satou, the surname. I felt my enthusiasm dying already.

"I looked into it, but I couldn't really come up with anything like you mentioned."

"Anything's fine, really."

Anything? All that I knew about her was that her eyes and nails glowed, that she had a husky voice, that she lived in a country that was currently at war, that she was in an underground bunker, and that her hands were cold.

"How about...Chika?" I offered. *Underground.*

"What does that mean?"

"Well, like, 'underground,' since you're in an underground shelter."

It was a completely silly reason, but most people's names were given for fairly silly, vapid reasons. She narrowed her eyes slightly and nodded with a simple, "Okay."

"All right, then. From now on, in your world, my name is Chika. A nice, ×××× name."

"I didn't catch that last bit. The word after 'nice.'"

"Concise?"

"Got it. That's good, I'm glad."

I was glad to know that the word caught in the noise was an affirmative. I'd been worried it was something sarcastic. With that, her name was decided. I don't know that it was even necessary, considering I didn't plan on referring to her in the third person. Still, the fact that she liked it was a bonus. Nothing good could come of putting a person you wished to talk to in a foul mood.

"So, did you come here to ride on one of those bus things?"

The question came suddenly out of nowhere. Typically, you could tell a person was talking to you by looking at their mouth. If I didn't focus, I felt like some of the sounds were going to slip right by me.

"No, this bus stop is no longer in use. I just come in here to rest. I come here every night, actually."

"Oh, let me guess."

"Hm?"

"I think our time zones are different. The sun is still up here—even though I can't see it from underground."

"What, it's still daytime there?"

"It is. I mean, I wouldn't exactly call it daytime, but I get what you mean."

For the record, as a follow up, I did ask her what word she *would* use, but her reply once more vanished into the static. The word "daytime" was not used colloquially in her world. I tried to figure out how many hours we were apart by, but while Chika's world also used "days" as a unit of time, their seconds, minutes, and hours where slightly different from ours. Since a full understanding would require comprehending a lot of words that were getting lost to the static, I swiftly gave up. At any rate, what was important was that it was nighttime here but daytime there.

"I wonder if time moves at the same rate for us," she said. I had a similar curiosity. She seemed to have thought of a lot of different possibilities under the assumption that we were in different worlds. "Like, for all I know, the sun rises and sets dozens of times in your world in just one cycle of ours. I've read stories like that before."

As have I, I thought.

"Well, the sun's only risen and set twice since I last saw you."

"Okay, then the cycles are the same. It's only been twice for me too. There have only been two wars as well."

Wars.

"You've mentioned that before. So, about that war…" I started, only realizing after I had already steered the conversation in that direction that I had not prepared any follow-up questions. I might have finally gone too far. There was a war going on in her home. Chika might die tomorrow; her family might die today. "War" carried a certain imagery. The shadow of death that hung over it brought my words to an unnatural halt.

"There's a war going on right now," she said plainly, as though she was irritated but had no other choice. "Is there a war in your world right now too?"

"There isn't, but I think there'll be one soon."

There had been a lot of talk about it in the paper and on the radio lately.

"I see. It's rough no matter where you go, huh?"

"I guess. I mean, unlike where you are, there's no one killing each other in the streets here, so we don't have any safe houses or anything."

"Really? Guess we have different ××××× then."

"Different what?"

Any concept of what had just occurred to her was as hazy in my mind as her expression, but I could see the placement of her nails. Both her hands looked to be placed atop her thighs, sliding back and forth. Maybe that was a habit of hers when she was thinking.

"Rules. Do you understand me when I say that word?"

"Yeah."

"We must have different rules. What are wars like in your world?"

"I don't really know the details, but..."

I explained to Chika all that I knew about wars in our world, based on what I had learned in school, seen on the news, and read in books. All of it was hearsay—secondhand knowledge. It was unrealistic of course, as I had never seen any of it with my own eyes, but Chika listened dutifully to my explanation, letting out a pained sigh partway through.

"So a lot of people die in wars in your world?"

"Yeah. I don't know how it'll be the next time, but a long time ago my town was completely wiped out."

"That's so...terrible."

"Oh, wars aren't like that in your world?"

"Well, in my world..."

I straightened up my mental posture to listen.

"...there's a thing called ×××××, and like I said before, there's a stipulated set of rules, but it's very different from how wars are fought in your world." Unlike mine, the tone of Chika's voice suggested that war was an everyday reality for her and felt far more concrete than the vague concept I had. "Or rather, from what I hear, a long time ago in our world we did have wars that resulted in a lot of casualties, like in yours. But since the rules were established, people who are just going about their lives like we do no longer die in wars. This was apparently decided ages ago by an agreement between some larger nations. That's just what they teach us though, so for all I know, history has been rewritten. Anyway, with the current rules of warfare, it rarely results in our deaths."

"Well, that's good."

The fact that there was currently a war going on still made me fear for Chika's safety, but I was relieved to at least know it was unlikely she would die.

"You were worried about me, huh?"

Again, I could only imagine Chika's expression from the shape of her eyes, but she looked like she was smiling. Of course, as much as I was worried for her safety, I was also afraid I would have to give up the chance to see her again, so I awkwardly asked, "What are the rules?"

"There are a lot of them. It'll be hard to explain it in a way that you can hear. The simplest one is about my eyes and nails, which you can see. I did mention before that it's weird that yours don't glow."

She pointed to various places.

"This is completely normal in our world."

If that was supposed to be a basic rule, then wouldn't it mean that she was simply born that way? I waited for her explanation, offering up a suitable verbal acknowledgment.

"To put it in simple terms, our eyes and nails are colored for the sake of ××××."

"Um, for the sake of what?"

"Identification? Distinction?"

"Oh, okay."

So, it was like a mark.

"Each country has its own color. When you're born, everyone gets their own country's color, so that you can tell friend from foe. This is just a vestige from when countries were still next to one another and people mixed together, though. Now, it's only used to tell when enemy soldiers are trying to blend in in another country. And no one fights after the sun goes down."

Of course. I tried to imagine a map of where Chika was. Perhaps the various nations were divided by some sort of wilderness or oceans. Or maybe something that did not exist here.

"Since you have soldiers, is there a military?"

"Yeah. There are people whose job it is to fight. They decide on dates and times to ××××."

"Dates and times for what?"

"Um...days for attacking and days for defending, and which country they're going to fight in. On some days they go on the offense, some days on defense. It's fine on the days when they're on offense because the soldiers aren't here, but on defense days we have to go into the safe houses, like now."

"I see, so that's why you're here some days and not others," I suggested. Her toenails moved to the surface of the bench. She had probably pulled her knees up to her chest. "Or rather, today your country is on defense?"

"Yeah. I think it'll be over soon though."

I could tell from her tone that she was filled with regret at the fact that she would have to leave soon. She obviously had a different sense of values regarding wars.

"Oh, in case you were worried though, the people who do the fighting rarely die either. I don't really know the details, but apparently they've been researching ××××, so there haven't been any incidents of mass casualties lately."

"Oh, I see." I assumed that the word I could not hear was something like "tactics," so I did not press further. "But if they try to fight without killing people, how do they determine the victors?"

"××××××. Er, um, they have certain set *objectives*. There's, like, this big round thing, and if the attackers can get it outside of the country, they win. If they don't carry it out within the time limit, then the defenders win."

What the hell? I was stunned. That was way more... It was like a video game—one which people might actually die in.

"Sorry, but that's just like... It sounds like the adults made some kind of messed up game."

"That's because they did. Fewer people die, but more get *hurt*. Houses and all sorts of other structures get destroyed, and it interferes with our lives. They should have just stopped this whole thing when they were putting the rules together."

It was the first time I heard her get this emotional. Normally, this sort of voice would be accompanied with a facial expression, so it was rather novel for me. This was probably what she sounded like when she was feeling resentful. Her voice carried a tang of anger, like dark ink forcibly seeping into one's heart.

"I've thought of something, though," she said. The hint of anger had seemingly vanished, but without seeing her face I could not tell when the switch had occurred or by what degree. "Now that you've heard about the rules of war in my world, maybe you could use them to guide your own world, to stop so many people from dying. Maybe you came to be able to speak to me so that you could transform your own world. If that's true, then maybe we really could think of my world as the future of yours."

Putting aside the timeline, the idea that *I* could ever become a leader was just way too creative. I doubted I would ever have the power within me to put an end to the senseless killing that was born of human stupidity. However, if there was the slightest grain of truth to this, there was still one issue.

"If that's the case, since that goal has already been achieved, we might not see each other again."

I had meant this as nothing more than a statement of fact.

"I wouldn't like that much either," said Chika. I suddenly grew embarrassed, realizing that my own sadness at the prospect of parting had made it into my expression and my voice. Of course, I had reacted that way because I had still nowhere near achieved my own personal goals, but it would be a little vexing to cheapen her evaluation of me now, assuming she thought of me as someone likable. I was glad to know that she was just as bummed as I was at the idea of us never meeting again.

"Ah, there's the siren."

She swiftly covered her ears. It seemed she was afraid of the sound. Shouldn't the end of the war be a positive thing, though? I couldn't hear it, of course.

"What does it sound like?"

"...Oh, you can't hear it. That's good, it sounds terrible. The sound makes your ×××× vibrate."

"Makes what vibrate?"

"Um, the inside of your stomach?"

Your internal organs, she probably meant. Or maybe it was something a little different, something internal to a human that I didn't know about.

Chika stood up without the slightest bit of hesitation at the possibility that our mission might have been fulfilled and we might never see each other again. She turned toward the wall and took one step forward. I could tell by the movement of her toenails.

"See ya, Chika. Don't get caught."

Chika had her own life in that other world, one which I could not keep her from. So it was all I could do to at least persuade her to come see me again. To my surprise, she looked back at me. Our eyes met, and the lights seemed to shift into a smile.

"Next time, I want to learn more about you, Kaya."

Leaving only her voice behind, the girl who had always been in darkness vanished. Left all alone, I looked at my watch. We had talked a lot longer today than we ever had before. It had been a largely disturbing conversation with all the talk of war, but to be able to hear about the world she knew was *huge*—even if I still couldn't abandon the possibility that she was lying or that this was all simply in my head.

Still, she had touched me.

The feeling of her cold finger tracing my hand was real. I could almost still feel the trail of it lingering on my skin. I stood up slowly, trying not to let that feeling go.

I exited the shelter. The air was so much thicker outside; it was hard to breathe. I was back in my own world again.

If we did live in completely different worlds as Chika said, I tried to imagine what sort of place she would go home to. She'd said it was daytime there. The war might still be winding down where she was. Or perhaps things would just be carrying on as always. Did it rain in her world? Was it cold there right now, or hot?

For now, I just needed to get home and put in order all that I had heard about this world of hers. Regardless of whether or not I could actually change the face of warfare in my world, this might have been the first step in making my own life into something special.

As I walked the path home, I grew self-conscious. Once again, I had done something utterly basic.

It was the first time in a while that I had actually gotten excited about a conversation. Nothing had come of it yet, but the thought still occurred to me—I was just that sort of person.

We were ten days into March, and spring was just around the corner. I held no special feelings towards the changing of the seasons, but this being a sign of the sure passage of time, I was once again growing anxious.

I had not seen Chika again since that night. It might have just been a problem of timing, but I began to worry that perhaps our goal really had already been fulfilled. I knew there was no point in worrying over it, so for the time being I decided to focus on the things that did matter to me.

It was still too early to be certain, but at the very least, the things that she told me did not seem to align with the world I knew. There was still the possibility that every word out of her mouth was a lie, but I had no way of confirming that. Even if she was ultimately deceiving me, right now I had no choice but to believe her. If nothing else, the resentment in her voice when she spoke about the war could not have been a lie.

Chika probably really did live in a different sort of environment from me.

It occurred to me that perhaps she had not appeared at that bunker because the war was over. By that token, however, wanting to see her meant wishing war upon her world. If I could sincerely wish for and rejoice in another person's misfortune, I would have, but I knew myself to be a boring, vaguely sympathetic person, so I gave up on that train of thought.

I started visiting the bus stop in the early evening in addition to later at night, but Chika still did not appear. She had said there were no wars after the sun went down, which meant that she would not be in the bunker at night, and thus chances were slim that she would appear when it was still midday at the bus stop.

Still, I had no idea what our time difference was, so I couldn't say this definitively.

I went running every day, as I always did. The only thing that changed about my runs is that I started focusing on maintaining an optimal heart rate, and that I had altered my route on the way to the bus stop—the heart rate was primarily because I had been given that watch. As for changing my route, there was no real reason to do so. If I were the sort to keep a diary, and someone pilfered it, they would quickly grow weary of reading about my life.

I started running as usual, gradually increasing my speed. The watch on my wrist was designed to keep track of both exercise intensity and heart rate so I could improve my cardio-pulmonary capacity over time. There were various presets installed which would sound a warning alarm if I started going too fast or my heart rate got too high.

I wondered if there was a sort of scenery I could only see if I kept training in a way that put too much strain on my heart. Would a life-threatening workout erase the boredom that lay behind the exhilaration?

Should I try it? I wondered, beginning to increase my speed, when suddenly I saw a familiar face up ahead, vapidly raising a hand to wave at them though at the same time praying they wouldn't notice me. Given that ignoring them was utterly out of the question, I slowed my pace and gave a "Yo!"

I'd intended to keep running right by, but of course my classroom neighbor, Tanaka, decided it was fully acceptable to strike up a conversation with someone who was running with a "Whatcha doin'?"

Reflexively, I stopped.

"I mean, isn't it obvious?" I asked. "I'm running."

I spoke a bit faster than normal, probably thanks to my elevated heart rate.

"Yeah, I can see that. I'm asking *why*."

"Does that really need an answer?" Enough of these frivolities. "I'm running just to run."

"I don't get you. I mean, if that's why you're doin' it you could at least look like you're havin' a little more fun. By the way, I'm walking my dog."

First of all, I hadn't asked. Second of all, I could clearly see that. Even so, I glanced down at the dog at Tanaka's feet. When we locked eyes, the dog sidled up to me. She should have been using the leash to keep the animal in place at her side, but instead her arm stretched out towards me in tandem with the dog's movement.

After the dog did not leave, even after several moments of just staring at me, I realized that it was after something. I gave it a single pat on the head, but this did not satisfy it enough to return to Tanaka.

"This dog has no loyalty," she said. "Gets attached to everyone."

Just like the owner... I doubted the dog truly was attached to me, and nothing good would come of it if so—either for Tanaka or the dog.

"Anyway, didn't realize you went running this way."

I'd had no idea that my recent route change would run me straight into Tanaka's walking route.

"This is the first time I've run this way."

I didn't ask, but I supposed that meant she didn't have any set route herself.

"Seems like lightning struck here recently and a tree fell down. I was gonna go see if it's burnt."

To what end? I wondered, but I knew that if I asked her what the point of her doing so was, she'd just give me some meaningless reply. I didn't bother.

"You wanna come? Seems like you've got some time."

"No thanks. I'm running."

"But aren't you just running 'cause you don't have anything else to do?"

Why would you go around saying things that shatter people to the core without even thinking about it?

"Oh, right."

I waited to see what else she had to say, though I was indifferent to it. I hated this.

"I saw Izumi."

I *really* hated this kind of thing. I couldn't stand people who just said whatever they wanted without any rhyme or reason. I had no idea what sort of reaction she expected out of me, but I decided not to take it seriously.

"Did you now."

"Have you been in touch?"

"Nope. Guess it's good to know she's alive, though."

"Anyway, I'm just lettin' you know I saw her."

Having said what she wanted to, Tanaka and her dog were on their way. Pretty sure that dog didn't care about going to see some burnt-up tree. Being forced to go look at something by someone who just assumed you'd want to see it only created ill will. I wouldn't blame the dog for feeling that way about Tanaka.

The word "distracted" now came to mind, but that wasn't right; there was nothing all that enthralling about running in the first place. It was just that talking to Tanaka had sapped my willpower, so I gave up on my self-imposed heart rate challenge. I resumed my usual running, stopped by the bus stop, and ran back home as I always did.

Izumi.

Thanks to Tanaka, a name I could usually put out of my mind entirely now clouded my whole vision, dragging at my feet. Not that I really found it much of an obstacle.

Once more, all I wanted today was for Chika to be there. With that in my heart, I headed to the bus stop that night, but all that awaited me within the shelter was a darkness and silence beyond compare.

It was five days after that when Chika appeared again.

On an unrelated note, exams had started up at school. As I did every night, I set out for the bus stop, my mother calling behind me, "Try not to get caught." Chika was not present when

I opened the door to the shelter. But as soon as the weight of my disappointment pressed me down onto the bench, something flickered in the corner of my eye. I turned my head to see the lights I had been waiting for.

"We meet again, Kaya."

I was glad that Chika spoke first in her placid tone. If I had gone first, all the anticipation that had built up within me might have squeezed my voice into a squeak.

Chika sat down on the bench in her usual position to my right, as though she thought nothing of the fact that I was here with her.

"Chika, what are you sitting on right now?" I asked a casual question so as to disguise my panic and overwhelming joy, though I was also genuinely curious. I was sitting on a long wooden bench myself, but I wondered what she was sitting on.

"A ××××."

"Sorry, that was a bit too fast for me to catch."

"Um, a long chair?"

"Got it. Same as me, then."

Maybe the fact that the bunker Chika was in resembled this shelter had something to do with the fact that our two worlds were able to align.

"It's been a while. I'm guessing there wasn't any war?"

This time I asked a question I had already prepared. If Chika said yes, it would mean that I had been hoping for a war to happen somewhere, but I needed to at least find out what rules governed her visits.

"No, that's not it."

I was relieved. I could get by without praying for Chika to live amongst some vague misfortune. Knowing this freed me from acknowledging how lost and petty I truly was.

"A family member who lives far away died suddenly, so we had to go help with some things. I was with everyone else in a bigger safe house over there."

"Did they die because of a war?"

"No, they were ill. She was just my ×××× though, so I hadn't really spoken to her before."

"Your...what?"

"My grandfather's younger sister. My older brother is the only one in our family who's in the war business, so he's the only one with any chance of dying from it."

It would be easy to say something trite to Chika like, 'I'm surprised you can stay so calm,' given how matter-of-fact she could be about the shadow of looming death that hung over one of her family members, but it would also be insensitive. Whether you're in the same world or a different one, there are few times when people can truly relate to one another.

"Anyway, I mentioned this last time, but I've thought of some things I want to ask about you, Kaya."

"Okay," I acknowledged casually, but in fact I had been ready for this. It was not as though I *wanted* to talk about myself, but I figured that if I told Chika anything she wanted to know, I could learn more about her in return. You get as much as you give.

Short of that, I would never have any interest in volunteering information about myself.

"First off..."

She probably would want to know about my family or my life up until then. The sort of information that would tell you who you were dealing with.

"What sort of things do you like?" she asked instead.

I had been fully prepared to respond, but the words caught in my throat. Things I liked... The question was far too abstract, and furthermore, what was the point in knowing someone's interests before anything else?

"Things I like...um, do you mean like my favorite foods?" I tried to narrow down the question a bit.

"Is eating your favorite thing to do?"

I didn't dislike it, but that wasn't enough for me to declare that eating delicious food was a passion of mine, or that meals were my favorite part of the day, so I shook my head.

"That's not what I meant. If we're talking about hobbies, I guess my favorite thing would be my daily runs."

"Running is your favorite time of the day?"

"Well..."

I certainly couldn't call it my *favorite*. I had assumed she just wanted to know my hobbies, which were nothing more than the things that kept me going every day outside the basic necessities. I didn't agree with her assumption because I wanted to tell her what I *actually* considered my favorite part of the day, but I couldn't think of anything. If I was honest with myself, I didn't have a favorite part of my day, or even one that I cherished at all. Rather, I doubted such a special time existed in this boring life of mine.

It was true, in some regards, that the time I spent here was special to me, but I didn't say that. I didn't want her to think I was the sort of basic person who cherished talking to others.

"I can't really think of anything, but do you have any better idea of that, Chika? What time of the day is most important to you?"

It would be a lie to say that I didn't have the slightest bit of hope that our goals would overlap, that she would say that it was the time she spent here. It was just as true that I hoped she wasn't the sort of person who would give such a basic response.

"For me..." I got the sense that she was about to say something I couldn't hear, but that didn't happen. "Probably the time just before I go to bed, when I'm all alone in my room."

It was a stereotypically girlish response, incredibly so. A selfish feeling of disappointment started peeking out from within me, but I shooed it away. I still hadn't heard the details.

"Can I ask why that time is so important to you?"

"It's because everything is all mine."

She sounded like some sort of world conqueror in a storybook.

"I like all the things I have in my room and in my head. In my room, I have my important ××××, my books and my music, and all the journals I've ever written in. Inside my head, I have thoughts that no one else will ever hear, and my feelings. Even if someone comes barging into my room, they can never see what's inside my head. No one can even see my expressions. I love that time, when I can exist just for myself. That's the real world, at least for me."

Concerned, she asked whether there was anything I had not heard out of all the words she said. I asked her what else she had in her room besides the books and music and journals.

"How do I put this... It's a way to experience a story through smell."

"Like a perfume?"

"Not quite. It's something that conjures up people and places. A bunch of scents come together to make up the sensation of a story. I'm guessing that doesn't exist in your world."

Not that I knew of. Or maybe it did, but I had never heard of it. I had no idea how well what I was imagining lined up with it, but I decided to file that away for later.

That aside, depending how you looked at it, what Chika was saying was far too much like a shut-in's way of thinking, rather insular. However, I soon realized something.

"Do you like being in your room because there's a war going on in your hometown, so you don't get to go out much?"

I wondered if it was because she had been born into such an unusual society, but it seemed I was off the mark. She hummed as though she was searching for the right words, then gave an *um* and began, "I don't think it really has to do with the war. I like being in my room because there are none of the things that I was forced into liking, and I'm permitted to keep it that way. There might be songs that imprinted themselves on me, or things like the ××××, that scent thing I mentioned earlier, but no matter how I encountered them, none of those things are something that I came to like because of anyone else. That's why my room's important to me."

I sort of got what she was trying to say, but we had far different intrinsic values regarding our rooms. For me, my room was nothing more than a simple box. It protected me from the rain, I could sleep there, and at least no one else could see me. In exchange, though, trapped in that space, my own, boring self still lorded over me.

It was stifling.

"If you can't think of anything important, does that mean you have everything? Or that you have nothing?" she asked.

As usual, I was briefly thrown by the voice suddenly issued from a mouth I could not see, with no movement to match it. This time, though, as much as I ruminated on the meaning of those sounds in my head, I could not understand the intent of the question. Still, if I could answer such a question while fully ignoring the intent, then it was obvious what was there or not.

"Nothing...I guess. Why?"

"I thought that maybe you couldn't think of anything you cherish because you're all filled up by some color or other. Are you full? Or are you empty? You said there's nothing. Can I ask what you mean by that?"

I wondered if she had gotten the wrong idea. I figured I should explain to avoid any unnecessary pity.

"I don't mean that I don't have a family or a house or anything. And I don't mean that I'm sad because I don't have any friends or lovers. It's just that there's nothing in my life that I really consider important."

I didn't want to be careless here.

"You don't pretend much, do you?"

I couldn't quite grasp the meaning of her words.

"Pretend?"

"Yeah, pretend. More importantly though, how do you feel about the fact that there's nothing special in your life?"

I had to answer honestly.

"It's boring. Utterly boring. But I'm kind of at a loss, because it's not the sort of void that can be filled with books or music, like you mentioned."

"You really *don't* pretend."

Those glowing eyes stared fixedly at me, as though she was forgetting to blink. Slowly, the meaning of her words began to seep into my skull.

"Fundamentally, I think people—though I'm not sure if 'people' means exactly the same thing in your world—but all the people in my world live their whole lives pretending. The biggest lie of all are when we pretend to understand or like each other."

"Ah yeah," I said. "I get it."

"I don't think the pretending is good or bad so much as a

necessary part of life, but I'm surprised to learn you don't do that. Is everyone like that in your world?"

"No, everyone here lives their lives pretending too. It's not as if I don't do it as well."

I had pretended plenty of times in my life. I hadn't thought of those moments as pretending at the time, but looking back, they probably were. It was because it was all pretend that I had begun to think, *Is this all there is?* To borrow Chika's words, even if I didn't pretend, I might live my entire life just waiting to feel something special.

"I'm sure I spend less time pretending than other people do, but I do it too. Yet I don't feel like I'm doing it just to live."

If I were doing it to live, I would have never caught the attention of those scum at the bottom of the human race who make up reasons just to torment others, like I had in elementary school.

"I think I'm pretending because I want to find something I don't have to pretend about." Rather perplexing, if I do say so myself. "So, are you saying that your feelings towards your books and music are pretend too?"

"No, I really do like them, but when I'm outside of my room, I pretend to like a lot of other things. I just like being inside my room because it's only filled with things that I don't have to pretend about."

That made sense. I got then what she meant about liking her room. Still, I didn't think she realized that even those feelings of liking the things in her room were just another form of pretending.

She was filling up the voids in her life with things that other people created.

"By the way..."

It still sounded like a strange turn of phrase for a being made up of only eyes and nails to use. I supposed the thoughts and feelings people hold are governed far more by our sense of sight than we imagine.

"Yeah?"

"I know about friends and family," Chika said curiously, "but what's a luhver?"

"Er, wait, you don't know? Um, how do I put this... Two people who share a romance, I guess."

"Hmm. I've never heard of rohmanse either."

This was the first time in all of our conversations that there was something I knew about that Chika did not. Would I need to phrase this a different way? How else do you say the word "romance"?

"It's um... Huh. I'm really not sure how to put this. It's when two people like each other and start going out."

"And that's different from being friends?"

"It is, or rather, I'm not really sure where the boundary lies, but it means something different."

Words like marriage and family came to mind, but those weren't necessarily connected. I also thought of explaining it as "the opposite sex," but surely there were cases where that didn't apply.

"The difference between romance and friendship is that

romance is usually with someone of the opposite sex, and the relationship usually involves sexual attraction."

"I feel like friendships sometimes involve that too though, and sometimes not."

"Er, well, yeah, I guess."

How was I meant to explain this? In using Japanese to explain Japanese words, it felt more like I was revealing my own general perception of the concept and that my worth as a person would be judged in the process. It made me self-conscious.

She seemed to understand the concept of friendship. I had already given her the keywords of "like" and "attraction," so perhaps if there was a concept similar to romance that she was aware of, there was a good chance she might realize it. There was also as good a chance that she'd just say another word I couldn't hear.

Or did no such word exist in her language at all?

"Chika, do you know about marriage?"

"That I understand. It's one of the steps in making a family."

"Romance is usually part of the process of achieving a marriage in my world."

"Huh, guess we differ there then. We usually just marry someone we're friends with who we don't hate, as long as it's convenient for both parties."

"Convenient?"

"Like in terms of work or the distance between your houses. I guess you all just add romance to that list in this world. What is it like? How does the process go?"

"Are you asking what we do?"

"Do you do things you don't do with your friends?"

I remembered when I had once tried immersing myself in romance—for the experience—but I swiftly realized that I was just pretending yet again. At the same time, a name flickered to mind, but it was all right for now. Since I had once had people I called friends, I did know what sort of things you didn't do with them. A number of things popped to mind, of which I chose the ones that as far as I was aware were all right to talk about in mixed company.

"Like, touching each other, for example."

"Oh wait, when I touched your hand, was that inappropriate for our relationship in your world? I'm very sorry."

She blinked for longer than she usually did, the lights slowly fading in and out—probably a habit of hers when she was apologizing. There seemed to have been a strange misunderstanding, which I quickly corrected.

"No, that's not what I meant. Even friends sometimes hold hands, I think. I meant more like...kissing."

"What is that?"

It was embarrassing enough just saying the word, but now she wanted me to describe the act?

"Is that like making babies?"

If she knew about *that*, did it mean that they produced off-spring the same way in her world? I had no idea how I'd react if she told me they just grew right out of the ground.

"No, that's not it. You touch each other. With your lips."

Why did I phrase that so awkwardly?

"With your lips...?"

"Yeah, you put your lips together."

"But why? Is it like some kind of marking?"

"No, it's not about leaving a mark or anything."

Why indeed, though? I didn't know anything about biology, and I couldn't explain it in terms of feelings as I didn't really understand romance itself.

"Apparently some countries besides ours also use it as a greeting, but in my country, it's an expression of love. I'm guessing you all don't do that?"

"We don't. We don't do that when expressing love for family or friends either."

All right, so she did have *some* concept of love. She had said that friendship sometimes included sexual attraction, so perhaps the scope of what she considered friendship was broader than ours. Perhaps we were only causing trouble for ourselves by dividing human relationships into so many distinct words and categories.

"Kaya, do you have anyone you consider a luhver?"

Chika's voice sounded suddenly, interrupting my thoughts. However, the "Huh?" that slipped out of my mouth was not because I had not registered her question but because I was shaken. And I was further shaken by the mere fact that I was shaken, distracted by both my own memories of the past and Tanaka's words from the other day.

"I...I don't."

As far as I could discern from her eyes and nails, Chika wasn't bothered by my clipped answer. On the contrary, after that came a bevy of other questions, so I explained to her that lovers were usually pairs, that having multiple partners were frowned upon, that most people were friends before they were lovers, and that it was not unheard of to have more than one partner in a lifetime.

"I did have someone before, but we broke up."

I had offered this information up myself so as not to be caught off guard by another question.

"When you stop being luhvers, do you become friends?"

"That happens in some cases, in other cases not."

Definitely not, in my case.

There was no point in discussing my love life more than I already had. To my chagrin, Chika still seemed curious about this concept of romance, something which she did not have.

"It's weird that you'd have to share such a vague type of relationship with only one other person."

"I don't know. I mean, I guess we all just want to be special, probably."

People spoke about affairs with such passion that you'd think they were the most important person in the world.

"So being someone's only luhver makes you special."

"A lot of people feel that way. Not just when it comes to romance, but sometimes with friendships too."

"I see. I don't know if you could call what you and I have friendship, but when we're here, you're the only one I see."

It was half a joke, but I think she was trying to cheer me up. I appreciated the sentiment, but unfortunately I was not the sort of person who would think himself special just because someone said he was.

"Thanks."

Even if she lacked any concept of romance, I couldn't tell Chika that lately I thought of nothing but her, day or night.

Today, we were given far longer than usual before the siren sounded. I asked Chika about her daily routine, which was something I had been curious about. She told me how she went about her day with occasional explanations of the words I couldn't hear.

In the morning, she awoke, then went shopping at a place we would refer to as a market before returning home to eat with her family, something I couldn't understand even with an explanation. After that, if it was a "Defense Day," she would enter a bunker at the designated time. The war might start either before or after lunch. The place where we met seemed to be Chika's closest personally preferred safe house to her home. After the war, if the area around her house had been ransacked, she would clean up. But thankfully, her home was far from any crucial locations so there was rarely any damage. When the war was over, or on days without a war, she would help her father, who was a custodian of the national library. Then she would head back home, eat dinner, and go to bed. In the past she had attended what I would refer to as school, but she had apparently graduated at sixteen.

I wondered how Chika felt about that life.

"I guess it's whatever."

"What do you mean?"

I assumed "whatever" meant the same as "boring."

"Life is just something I live so that I can keep thinking and feeling. It takes a body and a life to have the thoughts that exist only in my head, to experience books and music and all sorts of other things. That's what I'm living for. My body is a vessel that keeps my heart beating, and I just go throughout my days trying to keep that body alive. So, it's whatever."

It was different from saying that every day was boring. Every day was worthless from the beginning, no point in treating days like they were important *or* being pessimistic about it. That was how it sounded to me.

"Do you mean that life, of itself, is meaningless?"

"If I could still keep thinking and feeling after death, then yes, it would be. But if I died, I have no idea if I'd ever be able to open a book again, or if my whole existence would just fade away, so for now I have to keep on living. I doubt my room would be there either. War and illness are detestable simply because they might snatch away my ability to think and feel."

I was sort of moved by Chika's words. It was the first time I had ever heard a perspective like that. The only reason I was not truly, *deeply* moved was that I had no idea whether such thinking was commonplace where she came from. It was wholly possible that this was just a statement of common sense for her.

"Would my way of thinking be strange in your world?" she asked.

"It's the first time I've ever heard anything like it, but it does make sense, so I don't think it's all that strange."

I hated people who thought of themselves as strange.

"That's good. People have gotten mad at me in the past when I ×××× things like this. In my world, there's nothing more precious than life itself. Even if it changes nothing in my world, it's nice to be able to talk to someone like you, who understands me."

Her eye lights narrowed.

"Are there any things you talk about that a normal person wouldn't? I'd like to hear them, if you don't mind."

There was nothing to gain from letting someone else see what was inside your heart. Even knowing this, I faltered at her suggestion. I wasn't looking for any sympathy—I didn't want someone to tell me how interesting I was. If was only because I was here in the bus shelter that I even considered letting someone else hear about the sorts of things I would normally never think of sharing with others.

"I can't really think of anything."

"Gotcha. Well, there's not much else I can offer you, but let's just keep in mind that if there's ever anything we'd like to talk about, we'll always have someone to say it to—that goes for both of us."

I did not agree to this—after all, I had no interest in lying to her. But I couldn't just do nothing. I had to give her something so I would get something from her in return. At the same time, I realized that this denial was also something of a relief. Why was that? Perhaps the absence of any responsibility made me feel more carefree.

"In exchange, though, would you tell me about all the things that have been happening in your life lately?" she asked. "Even the little things, it doesn't matter."

"Sure, but I mean, there's really nothing. Best I could tell you about is the weather. And I guess a tree somewhere nearby was struck by lightning the other day."

"Whoa, a tree within walking distance of my home was struck by lightning too! It'd been growing there since I was little, so I went to ××××."

"You went to do what?"

"Um, I pulled it apart and took the pieces and burned them in the ×××× in my house. We do the same when nearby trees get burned down in the wars. I don't really get why, but it's an old custom."

I didn't ask about the mysterious thing in her house, not wanting to bring the conversation to a halt there. I was sure it had to be a fireplace or some similar thing. I guessed every place had weird old traditions no one understood.

"It wasn't raining when the lightning struck, but I heard it's supposed to rain tomorrow."

"I think it's going to be clear here."

"Oh, I see. Sorry, I just suddenly started feeling like we were somehow in the same place."

I didn't want to ruin the terribly cozy atmosphere that Chika's reserved laughter had created, but I was curious about something.

"Are there wars on rainy days?"

"A lot of times they cancel them when it rains, since we can't hide in our bunkers."

I understood her resentment about the wars—if they were so concerned for the citizens, they shouldn't have had the wars in the first place. Every day on our media, they talked about preparedness for war, but it was absurd. They just shouldn't start any wars to begin with.

I wasn't sure how much time we had left until the siren. I asked Chika, but she said that it varied. Given that there was no telling how long we had, nor if there would even be a next time, I had to absorb as much useful information from Chika as possible, but it was hard to determine what would be most useful.

For the last several minutes we had, I listened to Chika talk about her interests and the toys that let you experience stories through smell. If it was something that did not exist in our own world, perhaps I could put the knowledge to practical use or even devote myself to creating them. However, it was difficult to imagine and comprehend a form of entertainment that differed based on the perceptions of each recipient by a verbal explanation alone.

"Should I bring one next time?"

"Is that against the rules?"

"I think it'll be fine. It doesn't release that strong of a...scent."

Mid-sentence, Chika's nails moved up to her face. The siren was sounding.

"See you later," she stated simply before vanishing the way she always did.

With those four short syllables, we promised that we would meet again. We had no idea if there would be a next time, and we knew we might just live out the rest of our lives in separate places. Perhaps it was better to say we had stumbled into a promise of sorts. A promise was a troublesome burden. I had placed that burden upon her, just as she had upon me.

Still, I could worry all I wanted, but there was nothing I could do about it now but look forward to our reunion and the possibility of experiencing another world's culture in the future.

I stood up and went outside, when suddenly I realized something.

I was starting to truly believe that Chika was not a ghost or a figment of my imagination but a real, living, breathing being.

Even now, I don't know whether that was a good thing.

Soon, a war broke out in my world as well.

Despite a clear forecast, it was raining. In this world, however, this was no impediment to a war.

War or no, the lives of our citizens were not dramatically affected. Thus, the sudden rain occupied my thoughts more than the notion of fighting ever did.

My basic brain was churning. The rain, the lightning, my grandfather's sister. Could it be...

Perhaps there were other things besides the bus stop that connected Chika's world and mine.

I had some ideas I would need to confirm the next time we met, though there was no telling when that would be. As a rule, I didn't go running on rainy days, instead staying at home to work on some solo strength training. Still, I couldn't afford to miss out on an opportunity to meet up with Chika, so I would have to at least go out later that evening to check.

Because the downpour had come on so suddenly on a day that had started out fully dry, a number of students were frantically contacting their parents, holed up in the school building until the rain stopped. I had a folding umbrella stashed in my locker, so I instead grabbed that and headed straight home. Perhaps it had finally paid off that this item had been born as an umbrella, getting to demonstrate the worth of its own existence for the first time in so long. Just as the rain gave umbrellas meaning, it also put a stop to the wars in Chika's world.

You know, Izumi had always hated the terms "rainy girls" and "sunny boys"—terms predicated on the belief that someone's very disposition could alter the weather. It made sense that she would reject the human folly of thinking that we could have any effect on the weather in the same way that we could predict it, that we could try to interpret the will of the heavens. Humans are such dreadfully basic creatures after all.

Saitou left the classroom before me that day. It was always either one of us, so today I followed behind her, arriving at the shoe lockers without incident.

I waited for her to change her shoes and move out of the way, then changed mine as well—the same pattern as ever. However, as I placed my indoor shoes into the locker and turned toward the exit, something out of the ordinary occurred.

For some reason, Saitou was still standing there. She had paused in the entryway, looking up at the sky. Before I even had time to consider why that might be, she rushed out into the rain, as though she was embarrassed at having faltered.

"Hey!"

My outburst was harried, as I'd called out on reflex. Ignoring someone who was about to get soaked right before my eyes was practically akin to violence. It was fine if she didn't stop—I had no obligation to chase after her. I thought it would be nice if she realized that I might be talking to her and turn around, but I was startled when she actually did.

"Here, take this. I've got another one."

I walked up to her and handed her my umbrella. She looked at me, her eyes wide, clearly equally startled by what I was doing. To my further surprise, she accepted the umbrella with an unexpectedly clear and crisp "Thank you," opened it, and walked out into the rain. I had imagined there would be some back-and-forth about whether she could accept the umbrella or not, or else that she might just ignore me entirely. I was shocked that she would bother to engage with me at all, though I was also concerned that the engagement itself felt like she was only speaking to me because it would be a pain not to.

Such were the governing principles of my own life.

Incidentally, I was lying about the spare umbrella.

Exactly one week from that rainy day, the sun finally showed itself again, and spring break began. After the break, I would be a second-year student.

I cared little about my matriculation, but the fact that it had been a month since I had last seen Chika weighed heavily on my mind. At first, I assumed we would only get to see each other once, maybe even twice, but lately I was starting to feel like it meant something that we had been able to meet so many times. Though we still had no idea when our connection would come to an end, I found myself waiting for whatever it was that connected us to give birth to something special. How terribly inventive of me.

It was two days after the sky cleared that Chika appeared again.

"Sorry to rush, but I brought it. The ××××—ah, um, the thing that makes smells."

I heard a sighed laugh from the invisible mouth, as though she had not quite found the exact words she was looking for. My impression of her had changed somewhat from the first time we met.

"Oh, thanks."

"Normally you put it on a cloth or something, but you probably wouldn't be able to see that, so are you okay with just smelling my fingertips?"

"Sure, if you don't mind."

I watched her movements as she picked up the item that probably sat beside her. I pictured it as something like a little bottle, but obviously it was difficult to grasp the shape from just the movement of her fingers. Though I watched her carefully, I could only make out her rubbing her fingertips together until she suddenly appeared to be finished applying the scent.

I stood up and sat back down, shifting slightly to the right so that Chika could put her fingertips to my nose. As I approached her, the sensation of being near someone grew vividly stronger.

"I tried setting it to a rainy scene. Here."

Her glowing nails grouped up and were offered to me. I moved my face in slowly so as not to get poked in the eye and reservedly breathed in.

There was an odor. It was difficult to describe—a scent I had never experienced before. As she had mentioned, it was not a strong scent, nor was it unpleasant. If you asked me whether I liked the smell, though, I couldn't tell you. It was neither sweet nor acrid, and though she had called it "rain," it was nothing like I had imagined.

What *was* this smell?

"So?" she asked, drawing her nails away.

"I've never smelled anything like this."

"So, what was the rain scene like for you?"

"Nothing."

Her arms retracted. The change in the shape of her eyes was probably her head tilting.

"I didn't imagine anything," I clarified. "There wasn't any scene in my head like you described."

"Wonder if I should've put a bit more on."

She repeated her previous action and then extended her fingertips again. Considering how this would go—but hoping my imagination was wrong—I once more brought my face to her fingers.

"Yeah, it's an interesting smell, but I can't quite put my finger on what it is. It's like having an itch somewhere that I can't scratch. It's like my brain doesn't know how to react to it."

"I wonder if there's just nothing in your world that corresponds to this."

"That's a possibility."

I was disappointed that I hadn't picked up on anything. This had proved to be a pastime of Chika's that I simply couldn't enjoy in the same way, without my even getting the chance to determine if it jived with me or not. Still, the sensation of not being able to comprehend had itself been a valuable experience. It was yet another piece of solid proof that Chika was likely not a being of this world.

"Well, what kind of scene do you get from this scent, Chika?"

Chika silently brought her own fingers up below her eyes. I now knew for certain where her nose was. The structure of her face truly seemed humanoid in nature.

"The forest."

"Yeah?"

"There's a girl walking through a dense forest while a light rain falls, light enough that most of the droplets are absorbed into the canopy before they ever reach the girl. After a short time, there's a loud sound from somewhere. The vibrations from that sound shake the canopy, and the rain that was caught on all the leaves and branches falls down at once, drenching the girl. That's what I picture."

I tried to picture this myself. I could imagine my own version of the scene, but I doubted that the details—the color of the leaves, the girl's expression, the amount of rain in Chika's imagination—were the same. Of course, perhaps that was the nature of this form of amusement. A creative work always leaves some amount of space open for interpretation, so perhaps this form of entertainment, one which produced stories from scents, was meant to offer a much higher degree of freedom of interpretation than a novel would. Or perhaps there was simply some extra dimension that the residents of Chika's world took from scent that I wasn't privy to.

"Would everyone in your world get rain from this scent?"

"The rough idea might be the same, but whenever I try to describe in words what I imagine, it always takes me a lot longer than other people, maybe because I always try to feel out the little details. I think I tend to take my time with enjoying it more than other people do."

This was in line with all I knew of Chika's personality so far, so I could see that.

"How is it made?"

"There are people called ××××××× who make scents, with which they craft stories over time. It's an incredibly specialized profession."

I ignored the part that I could not hear, assuming that it was the name of the profession and likewise assuming that I still would not catch it on repetition. I asked her if it was a profession that she herself aspired too, but she seemed to just cock her head.

"I wonder. I mean, if there was no one who could make something that would be utterly perfect for my room, I would want to make it myself. But when you do it as a career, you have to think about how other people are going to receive what you make, so I don't think I'd be suited to it. I only live for the things that I personally think and feel."

"I see."

I appreciated this thought process of hers, or at least, I found it interesting. I realized that there were a few ways in which both our philosophies aligned. For some reason, this reminded me of something else.

"Oh, right. Chika, there was something I wanted to ask you about."

"Sure, what's up?"

"About the weather and your relatives."

I told her what had occurred to me on that rainy day, which I had been thinking about ever since. Put simply, I wondered if there were things besides this bus stop that overlapped in the places we were both in. I had started to even consider that the two overlapping worlds might be mirroring one another, based on the phenomena that had been occurring. This was such a wild leap that I was almost embarrassed at myself when I first thought of it, but it was worth bringing up the possibility to Chika. As predicted, she showed not the slightest hint of ridiculing or shooting me down—not so far as I could see, anyway.

"It was cloudy for seven turns of the sun in my town too. So it might be possible. The same with the lightning. Would be nice if we had a little more proof, though. Has anything else happened around you lately?"

"My school's gone on break."

"I haven't really had any kind of break in a while."

Right. Chika had told me before that she already graduated school, so that was unlikely another parallel. It would probably be difficult for her to understand something she wasn't experiencing firsthand. Was there anything else that had happened in my copy-paste of a daily life?

"Is there anything you've done that you wouldn't normally do?"

I was exasperated at myself—the first thing that came to my mind at her question was something that Chika would probably find utterly inconsequential.

"No, well...huh, probably not?"

"I see. Hmm..."

Chika scrunched up her eyes, moving her hands back and forth on her thighs. I'd initially assumed this to be a habitual motion, but perhaps she was just cold. Either way, the conversation was at a standstill. I thought for a moment and decided it would be best just to bring up the thing I had thought of previously. Better to grasp at any possibility, rather than just wasting time.

"Um, do you know what an umbrella is?"

"Yeah, you pull them out when it rains."

"This probably isn't much of a story, but—"

"I love hearing whatever you have to say."

For a moment, I was lost for words.

"It really isn't much of a story. The day after the last time we met, there was a huge downpour, and a person I don't normally talk to didn't have an umbrella. So I struck up a conversation and lent her mine."

So what? I thought. Most of the time, the world around me did little to defy my boring expectations. Still, maybe it was because I was here at the bus shelter, or because it was Chika I was speaking to, but words I never would have expected came to me out of the dark.

"You see? That wasn't *nothing.*" It sounded to me like she was smiling, tinted with vague surprise. "That very same day, I happened to pass close by a career military fighter. Normally, I wouldn't talk to them at all, but it had started raining, so I lent them my umbrella."

"Seriously…?"

It was still too soon to confirm that the two worlds were experiencing things in parallel. Chances were still high that these happenings were just coincidence. However, I could no longer readily dismiss it, either.

"Why don't you usually talk to them?" I asked, realizing that it was a fundamentally pointless question. It only concerned me because I was hoping that her reason wasn't discriminatory. If I'd wanted to keep the peace, I should have just avoided asking—but if I was going to associate with someone, just as I should give them the benefit of the doubt when possible, I also shouldn't overlook their faults.

"I'm afraid...afraid that we might pick up the scent of each other's consciousnesses."

"The scent of your...consciousness?"

"Yeah, the scent. I'm afraid that some trace of my own philosophy of living for my own impulses will attach itself to them, and it'd interfere with their will to live for others, particularly when their lives are truly in danger. Likewise, I'm afraid that their own personal philosophies of fighting and living for others will contaminate my room, my brain. I know it's selfish of me though, so I don't usually talk about this."

"So then, why?"

Why did you talk to them? I didn't need to clarify what I meant.

"Because that day, there was only the smell of the rain."

For the first time, I thought how cruel it was that I could not see her face—for a reason besides a simple desire for easier comprehension. Her voice conveyed far more than I could ever understand.

I wanted to know what was going on around her narrowed eyes. I wanted to know how her excuses, and penitence, and kindness, and mirth all factored into her expression. Or was it perhaps because I could *not* see her face that I perceived so much emotion within her words?

I had no idea, but regardless...I truly wished to see her face.

"What kind of person did you lend your umbrella to, Kaya?"

"Hmm, how should I describe her... We run into each other at the same place every day, but I've never spoken to her, nor had I ever planned to. She keeps her head down, and she's always quiet, never saying more than necessary, so I don't really know what sort of person she is."

As I spoke, I felt I was describing the exact same sort of person as me. I started to walk it back but was interrupted by Chika.

"So, someone who's completely different from you. Just like the person I lent my umbrella to."

"Oh yeah, for sure."

I was suddenly worried about what sort of person Chika thought I was if she saw Saitou and me as clear opposites. Just as my seat neighbor Tanaka had said, I was fairly convinced that she and I were two peas in a pod.

"Whatever the connections between both our worlds though, could they really affect one another in that intricate of a way?" I wondered.

"Well, if you and I are the starting point, then what starts off as these smaller coincidences might grow into larger ones as you move farther away."

If that were true, we needed to figure out how big of a deal these smaller coincidences were, and what they could grow into. Were they pure chance? Or would we be able to intentionally influence each other in some way? For example, was it nothing more than coincidence that we had both lent out our umbrella, or had one of us lent their umbrella because the other had already done so first? If it was the latter, then both of our actions started to take on a deeper meaning.

However, I couldn't bring myself to share Chika's opinion that the thing connecting both of our worlds might be the two of us. There was no way the catalyst that could send ripples through our entire world could be a boring person like *me*. Even if this connection *was* real, the origin was not us but this bus stop and Chika's bunker. The worlds themselves had to be connected somehow—that seemed far more likely. These places were far less boring, so it made much more sense for them to be the connection.

"Before the next time we meet, let's each try doing something that we wouldn't usually do."

"Good plan. I'll try to think of things to do that are easy to understand."

And with that, I realized I had once again made a promise that would bind us to this tenuous relationship that could end before we even knew it. Human relationships were built on the knowledge that one day, whether it's tomorrow or decades from now, one of you was always destined to betray the other. Thus, I wanted to see her as many times as I possibly could, though my intentions had nothing to do with the separation that would inevitably occur.

After all, there was no telling when someone or something entirely unrelated might spell our doom.

There was no way I could possibly prepare myself for such a moment, and yet it came.

I picked up on a rattling sound. At first, I had no idea what the sound was. I had, foolishly, completely ruled out the source as a possibility. The next sound reached my brain through my ears before I even realized the danger I was in.

"What're you doing out here?"

The psychological shock was so great my butt almost flew right off the seat. I reflexively looked to the source of the voice, not considering hiding Chika. Curiously, though I had permitted someone to invade in this space so easily while I was not paying attention, now that my focus was drawn, my nerves were so sharp it was like everything was moving in slow motion. Before I even saw who had opened the door and spoken to me, I ran through all the possibilities of who it might be.

As I saw the intruder's face, lost for words, they peevishly started speaking, half to themself, with a muttered "Are you serious...?"

"It felt wrong, but Mom was getting worried about how late you've been coming home lately, so I followed you. When I saw you go in here and not come out for a while, I thought you were doing some kinda weird drugs or something. Guess that's not it. That's good."

My brother—resident mama's boy—looked a bit bashful, perhaps caught between apology and relief that his younger brother wasn't doing something strange in a place like this.

I started off with an "I swear" as well, proof that we really were brothers. Not that I would ever admit that, even with my dying breath. This was not a rejection of my brother so much an objection to the idea that DNA could really influence that many parts of our lives.

"I was just resting."

That was the best I could come up with after cycling all the way through my brain. I tried to act normal, not letting a fraction of how I was really feeling slip to my brother. All the while, I desperately pleaded for him not to notice Chika's eyes and nails. And for Chika not to say a word.

My brother was nothing like me. If he saw Chika, he would immediately peg her presence as something occult and run away, warning me never to come here again. Then, he'd probably start spreading the word around town, which would be a nuisance more than anything. All I could do was wait and hope that he would leave without anything happening.

"I usually take a break here or in the park a little farther down."

"Still, what are you even doing running in a place as dark as this? I thought you might've been meeting up with someone dangerous or something."

I *was* meeting up with someone. He just hadn't noticed.

"I come out here to think, so I prefer places without other folks around. Plus, I've apparently got my family following me around, so if I was doing something bad, I'd be caught right away."

"I see. That's true."

I did not let my eyes so much as flicker in Chika's direction—I didn't want to do anything that would lead him to notice her, no matter how unlikely that was. Thankfully, she caught on to my not addressing her and remained silent. The sudden visitor had probably put her on guard. I was sure she was capable of that kind of deduction.

"Anyway, it's getting late. Let's go home."

I pretended to think for a few moments and then shook my head.

"No, I'll head back in a little bit. If we come home together, it'll look like I just tricked you or something, won't it? Just head back and tell Mom I'm all right."

There was no actual logic behind that reasoning, but my brother just nodded with a "Right, gotcha," followed by "Don't stay out too late. Try not to get caught," before he left the bus shelter. I was thankful that he was not as prudent a person as Chika.

I didn't say anything right away in case my brother came back, instead closing my eyes and steeling myself. For a moment I nearly disparaged him, but it was my fault for not being prepared for something like this. I should have kept my guard up.

When, after some time, my brother showed no signs of returning, I stood up and shut the open door. Then, I finally turned back to face Chika.

However.

I saw not a single mote of light before me.

"Chika."

No reply.

"Chika, are you there?"

There were no lights anywhere.

In an instant, I considered three possibilities. The best was that she had, in a moment of quick thinking, shut her eyes and hid her nails with the other parts of her body. However, she wasn't responding. The next best possibility that occurred to me was that the siren had gone off while I was talking to my brother. If she had managed to slip out of her seat without me even noticing, then surely my brother would not have noticed either—and while it was unfortunate that we would not get to talk any more that day, I would just have to wait for our next opportunity.

The worst possibility, however, stuck in my brain.

Could someone else invading this space have severed the connection between this shelter and Chika's bunker? If the conditions that governed the connection between this world and hers involved this shelter, Chika's safe house, and the two of us, could an intruder—a stranger to this situation—have disrupted that overlap?

"Chika...?"

I knew that she was probably already gone. Still, I called that name.

Obviously, there was no reply.

It was impossible to know which of those possibilities was correct. It might not have even been any of them. Regardless of the reason, if it turned out we were never able to meet again because of something like this...

Just the thought of it made my vision start to darken.

I still had no idea what connected us. Maybe there was nothing to begin with.

Useless as I was, before I left, I offered a prayer. That was all that I could do.

Even though I had accomplished nothing.

— ✳ —

"Kaya."

Would there ever again come a day when I was so relieved just to hear someone call my name? It had never happened before that moment.

Two weeks had passed since my brother had intruded on the bus shelter, and I was now a second-year student.

I had been worried sick that Chika and I might never meet again. It was bad enough that I was about ready to start ranting about it to the people around me. And so, the moment she next appeared, I had planned to tell her in certain terms just how happy I was and how worried I'd been. I would explain what had happened on my side that night and ask why she had vanished so suddenly, but more than anything, I would celebrate our reunion. I'd even started dreaming about it.

And yet, I never could have imagined the words that would come out of my mouth when I heard my name.

"Chika...what is that?" I asked before I sat down. Chika did not look at what I was pointing to. Instead, she drew her hands to the spot, a set of bright lights just a bit above her toenails that I had never seen until that day.

"Ah, so you can see it."

Bright and clear.

The lights, which were not as uniform a shape as her eyes

or nails, were somewhere around what would probably be her shin—assuming she was human. They were a series of overlapping lines of all shapes and sizes, like earthworm trails crossing one another. They shone more brightly than her eyes and nails, as though asserting their vitality.

"I got hurt. I was bitten by a loose ××××."

I had to assume she was referring to some kind of domestic creature, like a stray dog. Certainly.

"Will you be all right?"

"Yeah, this is nothing. It'll heal quickly."

"That's good. But, um..." The worry I felt upon hearing she was hurt was genuine. Still, I had to ask, "Why is it *glowing*?"

I thought of a number of possible answers—maybe the dog-like creature had some kind of venomous fangs or the medicine they used was that color, but I was totally wrong.

"Kaya, does your blood *not* glow...?"

I shook my head, breathing in deeply as I did. For the first time, I was certain about something: Chika and I were not the same type of life-form. It was not something as trivial as time or space that separated us—we lived in totally different worlds. All of the information and theories Chika had provided me with up until now were settling into a clear outline.

Of course, I'd never once considered discriminating against Chika simply because she was a strange life-form from another world. Her blood glowed. I had to accept that fact and move forward on the assumption that my common sense would not apply to her.

I then turned my attention to one more surprise, one which I was bursting at the seams to make Chika aware of. I felt like a kid. Unfortunate as it was, that was the best way to describe my behavior.

"No, our blood doesn't glow."

"I see. We really are in different—"

"But look," I said, interrupting her, lifting the hem of my sweatpants to show Chika my own leg. It was my right leg, the opposite of Chika's injured leg.

"Did you get hurt?"

I'd wondered if it might be too dark for her to see, but apparently my injury was clear to her.

"This is what *our* blood looks like."

Plain, dried up human blood—completely unlike Chika's.

"What happened? Were you attacked by a ××××?"

"No, I just tripped and fell while running."

It was a lie. The embarrassing truth was that I, for no particular reason, had kicked a piece of lumber that was lying on the side of the road in a sullen fit and knocked my shin into it. As it turned out, there was a nail protruding from it.

"Never mind how it happened, though. I'm just surprised. I didn't think you would've gotten hurt too."

"Even stuff like that seems to be having a mutual effect."

"I should probably take care not to let this get infected then. Wouldn't want you to end up in pain too."

Our two worlds, and our separate lives in those different worlds, were affecting one another. The peculiar circumstances were getting me so worked up that I had ended up telling what might almost pass for a joke. To cover up my sudden awkwardness, I tugged my pant leg back down. Even the fact that I was still standing there made me feel like I was getting carried away, and it embarrassed me. I sat down in my usual spot and put myself in order, looking at Chika. She looked silently back at me. I suddenly worried I had said something rude.

"I mean, uh, not that I'm not upset that we've both gotten hurt. Sorry if I gave you the wrong impression there," I reflexively apologized before Chika could say anything.

"It's okay, I wasn't thinking that."

The narrowing of her eyes was the only tell that I had that she was (probably) smiling.

"What were you thinking, then?"

Her eyeline lowered slightly from my face. I had more than enough time to consider what kind of reaction this was. Whenever I lowered my eyes like that, it was because I was searching for the right words. Finally, her eyeline raised again.

"I was thinking how happy I am to see you, Kaya."

"Oh, yeah, I'm glad we could meet again. I was...thinking the same thing."

While bearing the embarrassment of hearing such a blunt declaration, I embarrassed myself doubly with my own reply. Thankfully, I was able to hide some of my shame in the natural flow of the conversation. I continued, "That reminds me," before launching into the topic that had been on my mind since earlier in the day.

"Sorry about last time. Someone showed up suddenly."

"I figured that was what happened."

"Yeah...it was my brother."

I'd tried to act normal around my brother after that evening. If I seemed displeased with him, he might suspect that I had been somehow inconvenienced by being spotted at the bus shelter, which might bring about another intrusion just when I had gotten to see Chika again. To prevent that, I was currently acting the same way around my brother that I always did, neither getting close nor pulling away.

"Aw, I was hoping I could see what kind of person he was."

That meant she had left before she had the chance to get a proper look at him.

"I figured you had already slipped away before I could talk to you again so that you wouldn't be seen, but what actually happened with you?"

"The siren went off. I saw that you were talking to someone, so I left without saying anything so as not to interrupt. Sorry about that."

"No, no need to apologize."

I had been worried sick, but that didn't matter now. We would certainly need a countermeasure in case anything like that happened again, but I also wanted to avoid doing anything unusual that would alert anyone else to Chika's presence.

"The siren is practically sacred to us. We have to obey it. So if the siren ever goes off again when someone shows up over there, I'll probably have to do the same thing."

"Honestly, that worked out well since it kept my brother from spotting you. That won't be a problem in the future though if we can come up with a plan."

As I was speaking, I realized something: Chika regretted that she had left me without hesitation or reluctance, and she'd just told me as much. That she even felt that way made me happy. Sharing a genuine friendship was a boon in achieving all sorts of goals.

A sound like we humans would make when we're thinking came out of the darkness—a "hmm" from Chika. I wondered if she had already come up with a countermeasure.

"That said, I sort of wonder whether your brother could see me at all."

"What do you mean?"

"Well, because I couldn't see him."

"Huh?"

As I pondered what she meant, Chika, ever the intellectual, offered, "Let me explain: I only knew that someone else had arrived over there because you turned away from me and started talking. I couldn't see who you were talking to, though."

"Wha..."

"You very rarely talk to yourself."

Her voice was tinged with friendship, shared secrets, and the slightest bit of teasing. I wondered how she could know such a thing, but I soon remembered: She had seen me alone in the twilight in this shelter before. This time, however, that fact did not embarrass me.

"So you think that he wouldn't be able to see you, since you couldn't see him?"

"Yeah, and I figure that if anyone else showed up in this safe house, you wouldn't be able to see them either. Just like I couldn't see your brother when he showed up there with you."

"So, I can only see you."

"And the only one I can see here is you. I'd mentioned that before when we were talking about feelings, but the incident with your brother is proof that that might actually be true, I think."

It was not the places that were connected. It was both of us.

Just the two of us.

Though the very proposal sent nervous shivers down my spine, I wondered if this was a bad thing. The fact that Chika, who had shown me friendship, was saying this gave me some pause, but I had to tell her.

"In that case, that just increases the possibility that you only exist in my imagination."

"Yep, that's true."

This was not a surprising response, given Chika's nature. Still, her somewhat vapid nod in response was a bit of a letdown.

"I feel the same about you," she said. "But we have no way of proving that. Still, even if you are just a figment of my imagination, I'm all right with that. I would still cherish the version of you that exists solely inside of me."

Putting that together with the feelings she'd shared about her room and life choices, things were starting to line up. This made sense.

Still, for me, that was not good enough. If Chika was a being of my imagination, then she would extend no farther than what already existed inside of me. That just couldn't be. That would mean there was no point to our meeting—that we had never actually "met" at all. Just, no.

"I wonder if there really is no way to prove it."

"I don't think there is. There's no way to tell how much of this is our own imaginations, how much of it is just happening inside of our heads. Like, even if I stabbed you with a knife or something."

It was a disturbing thought, but I had admittedly been thinking along the same lines. Still, I wouldn't consider doing anything that might have us harm each other.

"But even that wouldn't be proof of my existence to you, would it? Even if you felt yourself get stabbed, it might just mean that you forgot you had actually stabbed yourself. From that perspective, it wouldn't get us anywhere. Even my whole world might just be a product of my imagination. It might not exist at all."

I couldn't claim that idea was too far-fetched at this point. I couldn't even fully deny that even someone as basic and generic as me could spin from my own imagination a nonsensical world of peace and death. Everyone's dreams feel like reality to them. My entire life, from my first breath up until this moment, could all have been a dream. But that said...

"If you were stuck in a dream that you didn't wake from until you died, would there be any point in recognizing it as a dream?"

"No, I don't think so. Hey, give me your hand, Kaya."

I dutifully extended my hand out to Chika, as I had once before, like I was waiting for a typical handshake. Her cold hand gripped my fingertips. Every last bit of this might just be a dream. Even if I realized that, and even someday accepted it, this was all far too cruel.

"Even if it means nothing, I'd like to say it once more."

What could she need to affirm? That there was no way to prove whether this was a dream?

"Even if this is all just a dream, I'm still glad that I met you. That's enough for me."

Her voice was husky and warm. I could almost picture it wafting through the air to my ears, from where it soaked down into my whole body. As that voice gradually reached each part of me, I felt the skin of that portion rising up, gentle waves of numbness coursing throughout my entire form. When that sensation finally reached my fingertips, where Chika was touching me, I pulled my own hand back.

"I-Is that a goodbye?"

Why had those words come out of my mouth when it was the *last* thing I wanted to say in that moment? Chika laughed softly, breathily.

"It's not. Though that did sound like it would have been a goodbye in a story, didn't it?"

Yes, yes it had, it had sounded exactly that way to me—yet that was not what I wished to say. But then, what *did* I want to say? I racked my brain, but the words had seeped out of me with that strange pulsing sensation in my body.

"If this were a story, this is the point when one of us would wake up from the dream," I agreed, saying something that was probably in line with what I'd meant to. I must have wanted to say something to cheer Chika up.

"That's true. But the fact that no one woke up makes it a little more possible that this isn't a dream, ever so slightly. Which means that we can only strengthen the density of our own realities."

The density of our realities—the viscosity of the proof that we were here. Our own realities, according to us, nothing to do with wars or strangers or common sense or anyone else. A way to take this world from dream into reality. The real Chika, who only I knew.

Right. Now I remembered.

"That reminds me. I did something—like what you said before. I did a few things that I wouldn't normally do to see if they would have an effect on your world. I have no idea if any of them would leave more of an impression than that wound, though."

"I did the same. Could you tell me about yours?"

"Of course."

In the week since the new term had started, I had been doing everything I was supposed to, despite my worries about Chika. I was fully aware that I was merely pushing away the anxiety that came with not having a set course of action, but regardless, I'd still done the things I needed to.

"Um, well, for starters..."

I'd done three things that, as far as I was aware, I would not normally do. The first was how I conducted myself towards others.

This was a simple one: greeting people. I considered Chika's recent anecdote about her and the soldier and decided to target a specific person with this action, imagining that each entity that existed around us might have some counterpart in the other's world.

"Good morning."

The first time I had been ignored, so I tried again, louder.

"Good morning."

"Huh?"

In our school, we did not change classes. Tanaka, who had previously sat in front of me during our first year, stared back from beside me with a quizzical expression. I could understand that reaction; here I was disrupting our routine relationship, which usually consisted of nothing more than Tanaka bugging me once every three days. For the first few days, Tanaka seemed to find this creepy, but starting on the fourth day, that greeting would actually develop into a conversation, and on the fifth day, she started showing me some pictures of her dog she had taken that morning. I hadn't wanted it to go that far, but I supposed it was all right.

The second action involved things. I carefully polished all the shoes in our house. I had chosen to do this after thinking about the way I could always see Chika's toenails. I was curious what sort of effect this might have on Chika's world, depending on whether or not they wore shoes there.

Obviously, after trying to affect people and things, my final action should have to do with a place, but I was a little lost on how to handle that. The easiest place to experiment in would be at home, but I wanted to avoid anything that would affect the room that Chika cherished so much. In the end I decided on school for the location, though I knew it might just end up overlapping with my first test. I decided to remain at school for an hour after the final bell.

On the heels of my greeting from before, my seat neighbor Tanaka looked at my unnatural behavior with some suspicion, but we talked more and more during my extra hour, finally wrapping up with a proper, "Don't get caught," before we parted. Saitou left the classroom in a hurry, as always.

Putting the matter of Saitou aside, when I told Chika of all the things I had done, she muttered an "I see," then seemed to be thinking—as far as I could tell from her eyes and nails.

"We do wear shoes too. I don't do so in here, but of course we do outside, where you might step on something dangerous after things get destroyed in the wars. I've never shined my shoes, though. I have had the chance to go some places I normally don't, but they have nothing to do with school."

"Such as where?"

"××××××××, which you probably can't understand."

"Yeah, why?"

"Because it's a place that has to do with the wars. It's where the siren comes from, where they tally the number of the injuries and the rare occurrence of deaths. I was there on duty to report the damages. I have no idea if there's any connection between the fact that you've been greeting someone who you don't normally and all of the people I don't know that I was on duty with who I've been greeting."

"Gotcha."

So she had greeted an unspecified large number of people.

"I was thinking that maybe only things like illness or injury have an effect."

"What about the umbrella, then?"

"Maybe it wasn't lending the umbrella that had an effect but the fact that we both got soaked in the rain, which could lead to either of us falling ill. But that can't be it, since there was the lightning too."

It was true—that was different. But, well, I guess there was another way of thinking about it.

I hadn't had the perspective to look beyond the actions themselves to the circumstances surrounding them. It was reassuring to know that the person before me had ideas that I didn't, but frustrating that I had not thought of them myself. I wanted to be able to provide her with some useful new perspective, whatever it might have been. That was the simplest way for us to have a positive effect on each other without actually crossing the border of our worlds. It was mortifying that I couldn't come up with anything that easily. I unconsciously let out a sigh.

"We could do so much good for one another if we could figure out the rules that govern the connection between your world and mine," I said.

For example, if there was something blocking your partner's path in the other world and stopping them from reaching something important, you could move the corresponding object in your own world and allow them to pass—even that sort of thing would be useful. I had used a gimmick like that to beat a game I played once. If you moved a wall in the other world, you'd clear an obstacle in this one and could get to the treasure.

"That's true. Like if my being happy could make you happy too, that would be really nice."

Right. The best possible scenario would be helping each other to live satisfying lives. Though I obviously wasn't going to expect Chika to single-handedly grant my wish alone on that front. I decided to put aside pondering the rules for now. Instead, I wanted to hear about the special things that Chika had done that week so I could gather more fuel for my thought process.

"First off was food."

"Food?"

"Yeah. I thought it would be pretty big if our actions could affect each other's daily necessities, so I wanted to test that. Specifically, I went a day without drinking any water."

"Er, did you drink anything *besides* water?"

"Nope. I decided to forgo all liquids. Did you have any days like that?"

"Uh, no, I didn't."

"I see. That's good. At least that means we can still eat as we like," she said, as though that wasn't significant at all. Though her diligence in investigating this was reassuring, it was also a bit worrying.

"You don't need to try anything that's going to jeopardize your health."

"Are you worried about me? It was fine. Listen, they say that a person can see thirty sunrises without water."

"Seriously?"

My reaction wasn't surprise at learning that people can live a month without water—as far as I knew, humans definitely *couldn't* go that long without it. My surprise was more because I was struck once again with certainty that Chika and I were fundamentally different organisms.

"Is it not the same for you?" she asked.

"No, we couldn't survive that long."

"Between that and the blood I guess we really are different from each other, huh?"

There was a marked tranquility to both her tone and her words. Perhaps she lacked the emotion of surprise itself, just as she couldn't comprehend the concept of romance.

"I don't think the other thing will worry you like that."

I grew nervous about how upset I must look for Chika to give that preface. Everyone fears others reading them wrong.

I suddenly remembered something rather intrusive, given the moment—something that had happened the day before last. But that had nothing to do with what was going on right now.

"I went to see a friend, someone I hadn't seen in a very long time because of a fight."

She looked briefly up to the ceiling and then back to me.

"You recently told me that thing about luhvers, yeah? It made me think of someone who was special to me, but we'd grown estranged, and I wasn't sure what kind of relationship we might still be capable of. I was hoping we could be friends again. In the end, though, no matter how much time had passed, it didn't change the way we both think. I was the one who rejected the idea of being friends again. I don't regret the decision. Still, I got a little scared of that path being closed to me, that our relationship might truly be over."

Chika had shown me her own fear, over and over. Perhaps that was because she was so brave.

"Um, Chika," I started. She narrowed her eyes and waited. "I...think that did have an effect."

Her eyes widened slightly. My eyes were open wide—in shock. Something that I had thought was unrelated had in an instant been upgraded to monumental.

"I...actually did the same thing."

"You went to see someone who you used to be friends with?"

I would have already mentioned it if it had been an active choice. However, it wasn't.

"I didn't go to see her. She called me. Actually, do you all have telephones? You use them to talk to people far away."

"That's like a ×××××."

I couldn't make out the word, but she caught my meaning. Good.

"Anyway, I got a call."

I was sure that this word would be enough for her to understand that I hadn't heard her.

I'd meant to continue right away, but I found myself hesitating. Chika took this opportunity to ask, "From who?"

I started to say the name, but I stopped myself. What she was asking about was the relationship.

"A girl who used to be my lover."

There was nothing to be embarrassed about. It was just that talking about her here felt wrong. Still, it was just as wrong to be racked by guilt while talking about her. That was nothing more than a flare-up of my half-hearted ego.

"I did the same thing as you. I closed myself off from a future where I could be the one to repair the relationship."

"Really?"

"Yeah."

"Were you afraid?" I could feel in her question only a hair's breadth between her heart and her words.

"I wasn't afraid of disrupting our future. There's no reason for her to associate with me, just as there is no reason for me to associate with her." No, that wasn't it. "If I was afraid of anything…"

If I said any more, I would be stepping into extremely basic territory. I didn't want to show my real self and run the risk of disappointing Chika. Still, this was Chika, whom I apparently shared mutual influence with even in matters of the heart. She would figure it out sooner or later. Chika had shown me her fear; there was nothing strange about letting her see mine in equal measure.

"If there was anything that I was afraid of, it was that if she was unhappy, or even died, because of something I left behind inside her...if I ever found out about something like that, I would never stop blaming myself. Even if I didn't do anything to her."

This was not a hypothetical fear. It was something I could actively predict based on past experiences.

Allow me to talk about the past for a moment.

The relationship that she and I shared lasted just three months, during our third year of junior high. Only three months, she had said, but both at the time and even now I felt that I spent those three months "pretending," as Chika put it. Thinking back on it now, I should have been honest. By half-assing things and pretending to have some real consideration for her, I had created an air of disaster between us. I put up a front as a sympathetic person and drew words of parting from her, muddying the path with a superficial shared understanding.

And then, she tried to take her own life.

One of our classmates, knowledgeable on the subject, said that her method would have never resulted in her death. I looked into it myself and confirmed it was true. I wondered which it had been: Did she know that she wouldn't die, or was she determined nonetheless? Even if her method wasn't truly fatal, if she hadn't known that, didn't that still mean she was fully intent on dying?

I couldn't permit myself reckless apologies or worries. Eventually I realized that I didn't need to waste time on human relationships. And soon, the number of people who casually approached me at school drastically decreased.

"I don't think we have a direct effect on each other's emotions, but the action I took is pretty similar to yours."

"What did you say to her?" Chika asked. I had no idea if she wanted to test the extent of the shared influence or if she was merely curious to know more about me.

What had I said to close off our future?

"Nothing particularly special," I replied.

It really hadn't been anything special. I had said something very generic, something I would say to just about anyone. It was...

Y'know, Izumi, we really are boring.

"That...does seem special to me, though."

"...Not really."

It really wasn't special. Every last one of us is a really god-damn boring individual. That was all I was saying. Boring. Basic. Every single person in the entire world mistakes themselves for someone special and uses that feeling to make excuses for their behavior, whether it's in clinging to dead romances, dragging others into their messes, hurting people, worrying about things, or whatever. Not that Chika, with no concept of romance, could ever understand that.

"It's really not special."

"I don't get this rohmanse thing, but if I treat it like an extension of friendship, I think she must still be pretty special to you if you would say something to her that's so obvious that you normally wouldn't say to anyone else."

Obvious.

I stared at Chika as I took in the meaning of that. Her voice came again before it had fully finished sinking in.

"I don't know if she'd see it as a good thing or a bad thing, but most of us live and die without ever being special. It's such an obvious truth, but most people don't seem to realize it—at least the people around me. But if you say something like that aloud, people get upset with you and act like it's an insult."

"That's...that's true."

"But it's not like that."

I had inadvertently interrupted, despite my intention to listen to what she had to say all the way through. Regretful, I shut my mouth. Perhaps because she could see what I had done, Chika's eyes narrowed.

"Only the people who realize that fact can truly live. They dismiss the idea of ever making themselves into someone special."

"...I see."

That was how I'd always lived my life.

"That's why I think that girl must be special to you—that's the place you're starting from since you're willing to admit that you *aren't* special yourself."

"The place I'm starting from...?"

Izumi and I had never made that kind of progress.

"You were hoping something would change, weren't you?"

"...I was."

I really, truly was.

As I nodded, a light bulb popped on inside my head. There was a moment where my words and thoughts aligned. Chika had suddenly put a name to a notion within me that I had struggled to put into words.

I wanted something to change. That was it. That was how I really felt about Izumi. I finally saw it. Even if I was just pretending, I wanted her, the person who I thought I loved, to change. I couldn't deny my own arrogant wish for her to change herself into a person who suited my needs. I wanted her to escape from the place where she was subject to the whims of my own boring self and of the boring love that we once shared.

Even if it was just a case of overlapping coincidences, we had tried to acknowledge each other as individuals. Izumi, at the very least, had truly seemed to hope she could be someone special. In that alone we were alike. I couldn't overlook the fact that she aspired to the same thing as me.

And yet, in failing to make her wish a reality, I had only hurt her again.

"Still, if it's a sin for you to be afraid of that, then I'm a sinner too."

"You did the same thing? To that estranged friend of yours?"

She neither affirmed nor denied this. Instead, her eyes turned away from me for several seconds, and she breathed in.

"Finding someone who's committed the same sin as you is a lot like holding hands with someone."

Her voice was husky and gentle. I didn't think that such a thing could ever happen within a living body, but I felt it—just once, my heart beat hard, probably the single most powerful heartbeat I had felt in my entire life. The next moment, its rhythm returned to normal.

On one hand, I was uneasy about what that strange sensation might have been, on the other, a far too novel notion floated through my head: The telltale beating of my heart told me that my spirit and Chika's were holding hands.

Though it may have all been in my imagination, that single heartbeat had made what I felt inside me all the more tangible.

Ugh, what the hell? I was gonna make myself *puke*. "Our spirits were holding hands?" *Seriously?* And I was just starting to get along better with her. It was nice to have a friend who could bring me closer to my goals, but that wasn't it: We were just becoming *friends*. We hadn't actually done anything, nothing at all. There was no reason yet for me to feel any sort of satisfaction, even in the back of my mind.

I knew that well.

From that point until the siren sounded, we discussed a number of possible ways for us to spend our upcoming days. The discussion was prefaced with a warning to not let ourselves get gravely injured. Chika had said this jokingly, but we could not discount the possibility that any injury could put both our lives at risk. It was reasonable to guess that if the same level of damage carried over from one side to the other, what might leave one of us on the verge of death might take the other less resilient party out entirely.

Aside from the injury awareness, we set out some other clear guidelines. Last time, we had both tried doing things that we would not normally do. This time, only Chika would proactively do something unusual, while I would do everything within my power to live as normally as possible. This had been Chika's proposal, as she hypothesized that there was a possibility that, just like the shared events in our worlds, each of our actions might affect the other to varying degrees.

In the case with Izumi, I had done nothing more than pick up the phone, while Chika had gone out of her way to actually see her former friend. Putting aside lightning, rain, and death, if our own proactiveness choices had any effect on the actions and outcomes, then me venting my anger on that piece of wood had directly led to Chika getting hurt. Realizing this, I had no choice but to apologize for what I had done. Still, the fact that we could proactively have some effect on one another's lives was a happy thing. If we could intentionally affect one another, there were a lot of potential benefits.

What I needed to do was devote myself to keeping up in real time with domestic weather reports and news of other incidents, as well as any other events of global import. If Chika did this as well, then we could confirm whether there was any interference between our worlds. So now, any time I had a free moment at work or school, I was always on my phone, skimming the news.

As a result of this, or rather, because I no longer had a rea-son to make conversation with her, my seat neighbor Tanaka looked puzzled about my return to my former behavior. I did still reply when she greeted me, and I responded to any attempts to start chatting about her dog, but I was no longer the one to initiate these exchanges. "What's with you?" she'd ask, but I had simply gone back to my normal self. The only new information I obtained from Tanaka in those few weeks was that her dog's name was Allumi.

Once more, I was back to my normal life: my life in a world without Chika. My normal, boring life with my normal, boring self and the trivial people around me. Ever since I met Chika, my whole life had begun to revolve around those dozens of minutes I spent with her. I began to wonder if it was unusual for me to live like my time at the bus stop was my reality, my life outside of it like a dream, but that wasn't true.

I *had* to look out for the special things in my own world.

In and of itself, my meeting Chika meant nothing after all. Even my heart skipping a beat when I was lucky enough to see her again only came from my attaining one more chance to find something special—nothing more, nothing less.

Based on the information that we shared with one another and my own investigations, it did not seem that Chika's actions had had any effect on my world. It was unfortunate, but there was nothing we could do about that. There was still a lot I didn't know. So, putting that aside, I decided to ask Chika what the average life was like for people of her world, when she suddenly said, "Obviously we have no way of knowing this, but I wonder, if we had been born into each other's worlds, would the way that we each think and live have turned out different?"

I doubted that I would have turned out exactly the same regardless of where I was born, just because of who I am. There was no way someone as boring as me wouldn't be shaped by his birthplace and surroundings and the people he knew. If I'd been born in a different place, I would simply be a different type of boring individual. If I had been born on enemy soil, I'm sure I would see Japan as an enemy by now.

"I do think I would be different, but I wonder how much you believe in your own soul, in the firmness of your character."

"I feel that there are things inside you that never change, no matter where you are," she replied. "But it's different for your philosophies, lifestyle, and preferences. If I was in your world right now, my voice and appearance would be different in a way I might not even realize at first. That's about where I'm at. The same would go for if you were in my world."

Given that I knew her only by the shape of her eyes and nails, even if I were to see her in the flesh in my world, I doubted I would recognize her.

"If you were that different, you'd be basically a different being," I replied.

"On the surface, that might be true, but don't you think there are things deeper down, immovable things that we can't choose?"

By my reckoning, if your personality and appearance and voice were different, then you were already 100 percent not yourself. Perhaps even Chika's philosophy that there were things within us that we could not oppose was something that she had been born into her world with, that would be different in ours.

"Things that we can't choose? Like what?"

It was a difficult question, I must say. Thus, I prepared myself to have to wait for her answer, but that turned out to be unnecessary.

"I'm pretty sure that, even if I had been born in *your* world, I still would have met you."

"...You mean like fate?"

Fate—a word that carried the same meaning as *resignation*.

"I don't think it's like fate. I guess I'm saying that the part of me that wouldn't change is good at meeting people."

Once again, the novelty of her thought process was on full display. That said, in a way it seemed to touch on the meaningless delusions I'd been having as of late. Naturally, I never thought about this during my daily life—only at night on the evenings when Chika appeared at the bus stop. My thought was this: What it would be like if Chika were a resident of my world and we met? I had already put even more thought into that than Chika. There was no use talking about things that could have been, but still, I was curious. If she were the same sort of life-form as me and lived a normal life in my world, would we have even noticed each other? If we had ever chanced to meet, to recognize each other's existence for even the shortest while, might we have formed some connection? Was there even the slightest chance that I would have enjoyed talking with Chika in this way if she weren't a resident of another world?

It was pointless to imagine.

As I said before, if Chika had been born into this world, she would probably have a completely different set of values. The Chika who lived in that world met the me of this world. That was what made this meaningful, and if we could derive nothing from it, then it would *mean* nothing.

This was reality, though, so there was no point in thinking about things that were entirely impossible. To even speculate about impossible things like this wasn't like me at all. I *knew* this.

But despite knowing it, I still kept thinking it was because, deep down, I had begun to feel a sort of jealousy for those who had been given the chance to simply live near Chika. But that simple opportunity didn't mean anything in and of itself. I knew that as well.

However, as the days rolled by and my thirst grew, these were the thoughts that came to me. I hoped that the special one known as Chika would always be there. I wished I didn't have to wait out these empty, boring days.

"There's the siren. See you later then, Kaya."

"Yeah, see ya."

The moment we parted and I was returned to my normal life, I was consumed by a singular thought: *I want to see her again.*

Somehow, the scent of the rainy scene that Chika had painted on her fingertips still lingered in my mind.

— ✳ —

My time at the bus shelter passed by in the blink of an eye.

"Hey, Suzuki."

Was it lunch break? Yeah, it was during my lunch break. My seat neighbor Tanaka, ever incorrigible, had struck up a conversation. Ever since those few days where I had been the one to speak to her first, she'd grown much more familiar with me. In retrospect, I should have thought of an approach with fewer drawbacks.

"You think she's on some kinda drugs or somethin'?"

I turned my face to see her pointing to Saitou, who was sitting some distance away from us. Honestly, just how easy did she think it was for someone to get their hands on drugs of all things?

"How should I know?"

"So a cult, then?"

"I *definitely* wouldn't know."

"Why would a cult be less obvious than drugs?"

"Well, drugs are a real thing. Beliefs are a state of mind, so you can't see them."

"Oh..."

I looked at Tanaka, who gave an impressed nod. I suddenly felt a bit foolish for answering so seriously. I didn't care if Saitou used drugs or was some kind of religious fanatic. If she was, she could just keep living her life in those deluded dreams.

Something I had discussed previously with Chika crossed my mind. If there was a dream you could never wake from, then there was no point in recognizing that it was a dream. Drugs and religion at least held meaning for whoever took part in them.

...*Not*. Even thinking that for an instant was ridiculous. Chika was encroaching on my boring, everyday life. I was growing twisted.

"But like, I mean..." Though I'd asked for no follow-up, Tanaka continued the conversation. I decided to let her keep talking because it would be more trouble to stop her. "Hasn't she been kinda weird lately?"

I answered her question with a noncommittal reply, using as little of my facial muscles as possible. The response was meant to convey my utter lack of interest in Saitou, but deep down, I reluctantly agreed with Tanaka.

I wasn't interested in her at all, but if I *did* had it in me to reply, I would have had to agree: Saitou *was* acting strange lately.

It had been two months since the incident with Izumi. We were in the rainy season now and had switched to our summer uniforms. The newspapers and radio reported to the citizens that the situation with the war was changing by the minute, while online foulmouthed pundits bashed each other over it, as they always did. As an experiment to test the theory that I could have any effect on the way that wars were conducted in this world, I tried spreading information about the way wars were fought in Chika's world on various social networks, but I was either ignored or chewed out by people with even more free time than me. It was only a week before, in the midst of these horribly uneventful days, that I noticed a change in Saitou.

"S-see you tomor..."

I couldn't quite make out the end of those trailing words, but she was clearly saying, "See you tomorrow." The "Wha?"

that came out of my mouth wasn't because I didn't understand, but because I had never in a million years imagined that Saitou, who had left the classroom at the end of the day and headed promptly to the shoe lockers as she always did, would ever turn back to talk to me before she departed. My reply to this greeting was a rude one, but it came so suddenly that I had no chance to react. Well, I supposed now I sort of got what Tanaka felt when I greeted *her* out of the blue. For better or worse, Saitou left immediately after she spoke, so she probably didn't catch my confusion.

Before I could even make sense of this suspicious behavior, the next day, the same thing happened again.

"S-see you...tomorrow."

This time I was prepared and heard her all the way to the end, so I replied with a simple, "Yeah, try not to get caught." I knew that my words had gotten across from the rare smile that quirked Saitou's lips, the first I'd ever seen, one corner of her mouth tipping upward.

I passed the next week overly on edge, hoping that she didn't have something to tell me or anything annoying like that, but now it seemed that I was not the only one who had noticed the change in her. I doubted she had started taking drugs or joined a cult, but I wondered if someone had maybe advised her to start being more friendly. The next day, she greeted me yet again.

Tanaka continued, as though my response had been utterly irrelevant to begin with. "Like, she's started talkin' to me about all sorts of random stuff. She never did that before. And, like, since this was all brand new, I asked her if something happened. And you know what she said?"

I hated people who thought it was funny to ask questions you couldn't possibly know the answer to, like blood types or star signs. Even more so when they then answered those questions themselves.

"She said she had 'an encounter.'"

The hell? I mean, that *was* the sort of answer you might expect from a new religious convert. It was far more likely that she had started dating someone and was learning to socialize, but that was an awkward way to put it. And it was all the more irritating that Tanaka hadn't asked the most basic of follow-ups: "An encounter with *what*?"

Fundamentally though, it didn't matter what she had encountered. I was a little concerned that *any* encounter could alter her behavior in that way, but I didn't need to get emotionally invested in that. There were things far more deserving of my attention than Saitou.

It had been over two months now—I'd met with Chika five more times since I talked about Izumi—but through all our discussions, we had yet to draw any further conclusions about the connections between our worlds. The most we had been able to determine was that the weather in my neighborhood was the same as in Chika's home area. When it was clear here, it was clear there too, and when it rained here, it rained there as well. I wondered if the climates in the corresponding regions in each of our worlds were the same, but Chika's world map seemed to be completely different from ours, and we did not have the time to be making any fastidious investigations into which countries corresponded to which.

As such, it seemed unlikely that Chika's theory about the two of us being able to personally affect each other's worlds was correct. We continued trying out things that we normally didn't do, but very few of them seemed to be reflected across worlds. For the most part, our lives were so incredibly different that we were unable to detect any real pattern to these mutual effects. The theory that we had previously considered about proactive actions having an effect on the other party also seemed to be incorrect. Attending school while wearing my shoes on the wrong feet, stocking up on a ton of snacks that I didn't normally buy, and going out of my way to pet Tanaka's dog all seemed to have no effect. Though when I met up with Chika two days afterward, I got a rip in my sock, there did seem to be the subtle crossover effect of her buying a pair of replacement shoes on that same day.

The heck was that supposed to be?

In other words, we still basically knew *nothing*. We had wasted the past two months.

A waste—a true waste. Indeed, I could think of this time as nothing but absolutely, positively wasted. I couldn't even appreciate all the things we'd done for the sake of fun, not when we'd made absolutely no progress whatsoever. Having fun wasn't what mattered here. An impertinent feeling like "fun" didn't mean anything. It had to be rejected.

I was beginning to feel like it was time to tell Chika my true purpose and how I really felt. In meeting her, I'd hoped to obtain something that would give my life some real meaning, something that I didn't think of as dull. So I didn't want to use our time just getting to know each other, but to find that something as quickly as possible before we could no longer see one another again. If I told Chika that, she would probably do all that was in her power to help me. If she were, say, to start introducing me to one element of her world's culture after another, I might even find that something straight away, optimistically speaking.

Lately, that idea had been floating persistently at the front of my mind. What I hadn't been able to do... What I hadn't been able to do was...

I didn't want to believe that this was weakness, pure and simple.

I wanted to believe that it was not just that I was afraid that Chika would let me down.

I wanted to believe that, but at present I could not deny the fact that I simply was afraid of letting her know the calculating way I thought about our meetings, and that she'd hate me if she found out. I couldn't ignore that I was just another basic person, scared of losing the friendship I had found with an intelligent, imaginative resident of another world. Thus, I could only keep fumbling for some sort of meaning in the fact that we had met, that we were getting to know one another in itself, as we slaved away the days with these experiments.

It wasn't until Chika asked, "What's up? Is there something in my eyes?" that I realized I had been staring dully into them. Thinking it would be rude to hastily avert my gaze—and perhaps to protect my own fragile sense of pride—I let my eyes slowly drift to the dust-caked floor.

"Sorry, no, I was just thinking."

"Is it rude to stare into people's eyes in your world?"

She was merely asking me a question of values. Sweat ran down my spine as if I was being accused of some wrongdoing.

"It's not necessarily rude, but just like you asked, if you stare at someone for too long they might think that there's something on them, so you shouldn't do that. That's why I apologized. Is that not the case in your world, though?"

"Sometimes in my world, you stare at someone for a while when you have something you want to say to them but can't manage to get the words out. What were you thinking about?"

"I was just wondering whether there really isn't any way for us to actually taste these."

"True. I guess if I somehow got pulled into your world and had to live there, I'd be stuck eating tasteless food *forever*."

I knew by the narrowing of her eyes that this was a joke. I could imagine by the gradation of her eyes, so much more vivid than her usual expression, but it was nothing but my imagination. No matter how I strained my eyes, I still couldn't see her nose and mouth.

Tonight, we both sat in chairs in our respective spaces, two body widths closer than usual. The reason for this was that we were experimenting with tasting foods from each other's worlds. If that was all there was to it, we could have just sat in our usual positions and handed each other the food, but a problem arose when I tried to hand Chika a CalorieMate bar. The bar passed right through her hand, falling onto the bench. Likewise, I couldn't interact with the invisible solid food object that Chika had prepared either. Mysteriously, however, we learned that if we got close and Chika brought the food directly to my mouth, I could eat the food from her world. I didn't understand the rules behind this, but I ate it anyway.

As I tried to process the taste, a sensation I had felt before returned in stark recollection. No matter how I chewed or swallowed, I could taste only the absence of nothing. Just as with the odor-producing device from before, my brain could make no sense of the actual flavor. The texture that I could sense reminded me of something—macadamia nuts, maybe? I conveyed this, and then it was time for Chika to try the CalorieMate from my hand. I didn't want to collide with her invisible face, so I held my hand out and waited for her mouth. By degrees, her eyes came closer to my hand. I felt her cold breath on my fingers, and finally the CalorieMate grew shorter. She had already informed me previously that she did indeed have teeth.

"So...what's it taste like?"

I had no idea if she was chewing, but it at least seemed that her mouth was in the same place as a human's.

"No idea. But it's not like what you described. There really is no flavor at all. No smell either!"

She had gotten something different out of it, but either way, if neither of us could taste anything then there was no point in sharing food. Smell was out, as was taste and flavor. That was when I wondered, if it was going to be this difficult to share our cultures, what could the two of us possibly accomplish—and I started absently staring into Chika's eyes.

"I know what you said about coming to my world was a joke, but what if there really *was* a possibility, however small, of us actually traveling to each other's worlds?"

I had already half abandoned the notion, since seeing nothing but her eyes and nails meant that the probability of us *actually* being able to exist in the same place was quite low.

"We can't completely throw out the possibility. We may not know how to do it, but just as you and I are connected, there might be some way to make it work."

If that was true, then there would be nothing better. If I could have the special experience of spending time in another world, nothing could possibly compare to the discoveries I might make there, nor the things that Chika could tell me. All I could think about was how much I would want to go if I could. Not *I'd like to go*, but *I want to go*. The desire burned within me, even without any guarantee that I'd be able to return home.

And Chika would be there.

"Which would you prefer?" she asked me.

"Huh?"

"For me to come to Jappan or for you to come here?"

"I..."

It was obvious, wasn't it? The clear choice was...

"I'd want to go there. Obviously, this world is already boring to me."

It was only for a moment, really—nothing more than a distant, fleeting thought. However, I could now allow such a thought to cross my mind for even a second. For that moment, I thought, was there really that much difference between me going there and her coming here?

Chika giggled. I figured she had seen right through my foolishness.

"It's probably not very interesting here either."

For some reason, I had neglected to consider something so obvious. I supposed it was hard to imagine without much information.

"I'd be fine either way, whether I went there or you came here. I do have my room here." Her eyes narrowed. From this distance, I could actually see the pupils clearly in her eyes.

"I'd be fine either way as well, as long as you were there," she said.

She might have been addressing those mistaken feelings within me directly. If not, there would have been no way for her to reach that shut-off part of me.

"Still, it would be a problem if I couldn't taste the food in your world."

"Would be nice if maybe you comprehended the flavor a bit over time."

"I guess it'd be like just being born; we'd probably come to understand the tastes as we adapted to the other's world. Wonder if that day will ever come...?"

"I wonder."

"The possibilities are boundless. If it's impossible in either of our worlds, maybe there's a *different* world where our senses of taste might adapt."

Here we went again, wasting our time discussing a future that was unlikely to ever happen. I should have realized that while we were in the midst of the conversation, but it was unfortunately only later that this occurred to me.

Finally, without having accomplished anything productive besides comparing notes on taste, I parted from Chika again and returned to my uneventful days.

"Working sucks."

"Well, it is *work*."

Today, as always, I shared a pointless exchange with my seat neighbor Tanaka, got my characteristically awkward farewell from Saitou, and then headed home. Naturally, I went running after.

Same as it ever was.

Same as it ever was.

Same as it ever was.

Same as it ever was.

As every single day passed by identically in my everyday life, the sense of anxiety inside me only deepened.

The food of the other world had done nothing to evolve my palate. At this rate, the fact that I had met Chika was never going to mean a *damn* thing. This monumental opportunity had fallen into my lap, and here I was, basic as always, sitting idle. That was more terrifying than anything.

Well, no, there was *one* thing that was different from before. I didn't care in the slightest about how dull Tanaka thought her part-time job was, but when she started that job about a month ago, I changed my running route. The convenience store that I normally used as my turnaround point was the very store that she now worked at. I changed my route to avoid running into her.

However, while I'd die before I called it anything like *fate*, as I was running my new course the other day, I ran into a familiar face—not a human face but a canine one. As I ran past the backyard of an aging, traditional-style house, I saw a dog—one that would follow just about anyone around. I paused in my run, and the dog trotted to the end of its leash. It didn't bark but simply hopped around my feet to beg me to pat its head. When I turned onto the main road and checked the name on the doorplate, the home sure enough belonged to Tanaka, though she would have been at work at the time.

Now that I knew the place, as an experiment for Chika, I started bringing the dog treats. It helped that I had heard that Tanaka's parents both worked away from home. I did worry that someone might snatch the overfriendly dog if it was left alone like that, but it seemed that had yet to cross anyone's mind. I knew this because I ran the same route almost every day.

Today, I laced my sneakers up tight and set off in my usual direction.

Lately, as I ran, I started thinking more concretely about what I could get out of Chika to make my life something special. You could even say I was posing this question to myself as a challenge.

It was difficult for me to experience any of her culture via taste or smell, and sight was out of the question from the beginning. That left only sound and touch—but simply touching something wasn't enough to stir my heart. Thus, I had no choice but to use my ears, words, and thoughts. Using those, perhaps Chika could tell me the teachings of the religions of her world. I couldn't imagine myself as some sort of religious fanatic, but I couldn't rule out the possibility that learning some new religious philosophy might give me the power to change my own worldview or perhaps even the entire world around me.

Of course, as was evidenced by my attempts to change the ways of warfare, there were limits to what a high school student could do. It would require a tremendous amount of time and ability to actualize such a thing. It was too dangerous to stake it all on a single idea.

It would be far more effective if I could simply bombard Chika with questions and receive the answers, but I obviously couldn't do that. Still, I didn't want to ruin a good time.

What an inconvenient feeling it is to see someone else as something valuable.

Before I met Chika, if I had a goal in mind, I could ignore any worries I had about being disliked. Perhaps I did once feel it more acutely, but when I broke up with Izumi, I was perfectly able to ignore that feeling once I realized I was faking it and decided what to do, just as I was perfectly fine with the fact that everyone at my junior high stopped wanting to talk to me. My objectives came above all other things. My relationships with others changed once I started high school, but everyone else was just as basic a person as I was. I kept living only for my own goals, no matter what anyone else thought.

But I couldn't live like that any longer.

How stupid of me to start thinking of a relationship *itself* as my objective. However, the fear that I felt at the thought of being cut off from Chika was real. Whether or not she was a resident of another world, this was stupid. Knowing that, I should have been able to cleanse myself of those fears. Yet I still couldn't force myself to twist this away with the strength of my resolve.

"Heyo."

As I ran, deep in thought, I arrived at Tanaka's house. I called out to the dog, Allumi, who trotted up to my feet as always. I took a single step into the backyard, reaching out my hand to pet it. I had stopped feeding the dog out of concern for its health, but I had instead started calling to the animal.

I stooped down and offered my hand. I didn't dislike dogs. I thought the fools who thought pet ownership gave their life significant meaning idiotic, but that wasn't at odds with my finding dogs cute.

I wished I could separate these thoughts from my thoughts of Chika, but I apparently couldn't manage to think that way.

That way...

...

"Hm?"

That way?

What way?

I held Allumi's front paws as the dog stood up to greet me, frozen to the spot.

Just then, something terrifying passed right by my heart. I inhaled, and exhaled, and watched the retreating form of that something.

Regardless of my opinions or intentions, I thought that Allumi was cute. Even when I had no interest in food, I still thought doughnuts were delicious. Even if I didn't enjoy running in and of itself, it still gave me a rush. It had nothing to do with my objectives, or being special, or the things I wanted to achieve, or what I wanted to accomplish with my life. It didn't matter why we had met, nor whether we could manipulate anything with our intent.

I thought of Chika.

I thought.

"Ah," I unconsciously gasped. For the first time ever, Allumi let out a little bark in front of me, perhaps startled—I realized I was gripping the dog's paws too tightly. "Sorry..."

The words were directed toward Allumi, and yet all of my self—my entire being—was contained within that apology. Sweat poured from my whole body, yet it had nothing to do with the exercise. My temperature was rising. I wanted to scream at these emotions, but I held back. I dug up, dragged out, and turned all the memories in my head upside down.

How? Where the hell did these come from? When?

In the process of checking and discarding every recollection in turn, I remembered.

When I spoke to Chika about Izumi, I had felt something. The way my heart beat. That floating sensation.

That thing—that was—that's a...this is...this *feeling*...

An emotion that couldn't be twisted by opinions or intention had started to bud.

"...No way."

There was no one here to contradict me. As though to aid in giving birth to this great new feeling, something other than the tedium that always lingered in my heart, I let out a groan that pierced my whole body. I steeled myself against being overtaken by these emotions. It felt like they were draining the blood from my brain.

This emotion.

No, that wasn't it.

This was something else.

This couldn't be something directed at Chika herself. I should have felt nothing more than a trivial interest in a being from another world, a special being. That was how it should have been...

And yet.

If...if that were the case, if that should be, if that was how it was, this was bad.

I would be the one getting in my own way.

Of course...if I was honest, I could see one lucky thing in all of this, if a small one. This would be my salvation: Even if these feelings were truly for Chika, they would never go anywhere. After all, Chika could not understand them. No matter what words I used, I would never be able to properly convey it.

Chika would never see the true shape of the feelings that were likely growing inside of me.

For that, I was truly grateful.

— ✳ —

Let's try to be objective about this.

A person with dangerous thoughts would still experience the gratitude of others if they saved someone, as long as those thoughts were never revealed. So, no matter what feelings lingered inside me, as long as they didn't come across in my actions, it would be fine. Or at least, it should have been.

Still, it was strange.

I could feel a distinct nervousness running down my spine, clearly different from before. It stung down to my eardrums.

More times than I could count now, I'd cursed my own indecisiveness. Or maybe not cursing, just being disappointed in myself. Though by this point I could truthfully do neither.

"What's the matter, Kaya?"

Chika was breathing. Chika was sitting beside me. Chika's eyes were turned my way.

I forgot to even reply. I couldn't play it off. I was shaken by her very arrival.

"Sorry, I was just thinking."

"About what?"

About Chika, of course. And about my own foolish thoughts regarding her.

"About you."

Both as an experiment and as a means of measuring myself, I answered truthfully.

"What about me?"

At that point, I could have just spilled exactly what I was thinking. It wasn't like she would get the message anyway. The reason I chose not to was for fear that if I did, it would dominate the day's conversation and waste our time together. There was no point in subjecting her to something that she couldn't possibly understand, anyway. That said, I had no intention of lying, either. Instead, I put a spin on it.

"I was wondering if the time that I spend with you means anything more significant than us just having fun. Like, whether it's something that could change both of our lives or not."

"Yeah, that's what you've been after, right?"

"Been after...?"

"Yeah. Personally, I haven't really been trying to get anything more out of these meetings than spending time with you. Testing out whether we can have any effect on each other's worlds is fun in and of itself. You've been trying to get something more meaningful out of it, though."

"Has that...been a burden on you?"

"Nah. It doesn't bother me or anything. The world runs on people who are looking for things. You might just be setting both our worlds in motion."

"I mean, it doesn't have to be anything that grandiose, but

yeah. Anyway, I have to reiterate, I do cherish the fact that you and I met at all."

I really did feel that way.

The fact that I had met her was special. The time I spent with her was special. It was an encounter that might change my whole life. However, my odd uncertainty about what form I hoped this change would take clouded my vision.

One could think it was enough that Chika's existence itself shielded me from the blandness of my everyday life. That *might* have been enough—*if* I was assured that this could go on forever. But maybe it wouldn't. You could never know when the ties that bind people might unravel.

I wanted something special that could never be undone.

I wanted an eternal high.

Thus, even if the budding feelings I recognized that day might one day grow into a more intense feeling for Chika herself, I couldn't call that happy. I needed to find something more than our meetings, something that could persist even if she wasn't there.

The feelings we have for others are nothing more than a momentary consolation. Worse, they impede our clear judgment. I couldn't accept them so easily.

"Have you figured it out yet? What this time we share means?"

"We still have no idea how much effect we have on each other's worlds, so at the moment I think all we can do is share information directly. And given that we can't convey smells or tastes, I was wondering if there's something that we should be telling each other with our words. Like you said, the world is made of words, of things that we share with our voices."

The words that we should share. Not something ineffable like kindness or passion, but something tangible that we could both comprehend under our own value systems and carry into the rest of our lives. At the time, I still didn't know what those words could be, but if we kept exchanging information, perhaps we might stumble upon some shortcut to that.

As I waited for her response, I watched one of her fingernails, presumably her index finger based on the alignment, move to what was most likely her cheek.

"Something we can share with our voices... We could share stories, but that would take up a lot of time."

"That's true. Stuff like folk tales would be much shorter, though."

"What kind of folk tales?"

Thinking on the classics, I decided to introduce Chika to the tale of Momotaro. When I finished, Chika began pondering the meaning of the story.

"I guess it's a story about helping those who are willing to help you," I finished.

"So it's better to have someone there than not, even if those in question are animals?"

Well, *that* sure was one way to look at it.

Next, I listened to a folk tale from Chika's world. I asked her for something very orthodox and was presented with a story about a man who tried to get rich by selling water to a town that was built by the shore. It was probably a much more worthwhile story than Momotaro, with its lesson that it takes ingenuity to accomplish things, but otherwise I really didn't get anything novel out of it. There were an absurd number of similar stories in my own world.

"Okay, well, putting aside stories for now, I wonder if there's something else we can tell each other."

Perhaps history or religion. As I pondered this, Chika let out an "Oh!" from beside me as though she had thought of something.

"Maybe songs," she said.

"Songs?"

"Yeah. We can't share our cultures with smells or flavors, but maybe we can share them with songs."

"Hmm..."

I had, in fact, listened to a lot of songs before, wondering if there was any music out there that could change your whole life. It was around the time when I was really into reading, back when I still had some faith in the creations of others. Naturally, the only conclusion I had come to was *Is that all there is?*

"Do you not like music?"

Still, there was a chance that songs themselves meant something different in our worlds, so it would be silly to reject the idea outright.

"I used to listen to music, but I lost interest pretty quick. I would like to hear a song from your world, though." As I spoke, I suddenly grew embarrassed, realizing I was pressing her to sing.

"All right, I'll sing one then."

Getting to hear a song from another world was exciting, pure and simple.

"I know it's a bit sudden, but could you move a little closer? We aren't allowed to sing loudly."

She meant that she needed me to move closer so I could hear her even if she sang softly. As though the thing budding in my mind had started to take root, my body felt twice as heavy as it had every other time I'd made the same movement. Still, to avoid any pitiful-looking hesitation, I dutifully followed her orders and moved over to the right.

Chika moved the same distance toward me, and I could feel the sensation of someone moving beside me on my right arm. Normally, I would not have been so sensitive to such a sensation, but now it was as though I could feel the very ripples in the air that her movements set in motion.

Oversensitive to her presence, I faced forward instead of looking at her. I *couldn't* look at her.

"I'll sing now."

Her voice was so close it was like the vibrations of her vocal cords were transferred directly to my eardrums.

I swallowed back something like a scream, pulling back from where she would have been sitting and turning to look at her. Her eyes were right at the spot where my ear would have been moments before.

"What's wrong?" she asked, tilting her head curiously. I slackened my pursed lips and took a deep breath so she wouldn't catch on. I could tell by the placement of her nails that she was sitting much closer to me than she ever had before.

"I was just surprised at how close you were."

"I see, sorry. I was trying to stay close and sing quietly because I was worried I might get too loud while I was singing. Don't worry though, I won't bite. Now get back over here."

I averted my gaze from her two narrowed eyes, slowly moving back to the spot I was in before. I turned just my eyes toward her and saw Chika right there beside me. The only part of her expression that I could actually know was floating there in the air. I wondered what sort of emotion the rest of her body would have expressed.

"All right, I'm going to sing now."

I could hear her breathing in, then felt her breath graze my cheek.

Her voice, more a whisper than an aria, seeped into my body. I had been nervous that some part of the lyrics might have used some specialized expression from her world and disappeared into static, but it turned out fine. However, I'm not quite sure how to put this, but the melody possessed a roughness that neither my ears nor my brain had expected. I was absolutely certain that even if she had immediately asked me to hum it back to her, I wouldn't have been able to, despite the sound ringing in my head.

Still, it was a pleasant song. I felt as though I had heard a new facet of her voice.

As she finished, I could feel the very membrane of her existence that clung to her surface, something that couldn't even be called body heat, moving away from me. I turned my face cautiously to the side, but her eyes were still right there.

"I'm not sure if I sung it well, though," she said humbly, at which I explained the sensation I had just felt. "I see. So that's how it felt to you."

"Yeah. What kind of song is that in your world, anyway? Like, something that children would sing? Or a song from a popular artist?"

"It's a song I've been hearing a lot lately when I go for walks outside. I've heard it so many times now that I've memorized it."

I had somehow expected her to pick some nursery rhyme or an old standard, but apparently it was nothing more than a song she had happened to hear. Still, if I thought really hard about it, it wasn't all that strange that Chika, who had little interest in the place she was born or even in her own life, would not have chosen something simply because she knew it from childhood.

"Could I hear a song from your world too?"

"Yeah, sure."

I accepted this request readily, having already suspected it might come. There was no reason for me not to honor our equal exchange.

"Guess I should do something in the same vein?"

"Sure, just as long as you don't sing too loud. Though I guess you'll probably be fine."

True enough, I rarely spoke very loudly in the first place.

"Okay. Could you point to your ear, though?"

"Right here."

The light of her eyes disappeared, replaced with a single light that was probably her index finger hovering at a place just below my seated eyeline. She had likely closed her eyes so that I could see the placement of her nails more distinctly.

I realized that hesitating would do me no favors, so I decided to get it over with before my heart could consume my whole body and halt me in my tracks. Previously, I had been startled by how close she was to me, but I would have to get just as close to her if she was going to hear me at the same volume. I brought my face closer to where her ear was.

I turned toward my only landmark in the darkness and cautiously drew nearer. I kept my breaths shallow so that she wouldn't sense my discomfort.

This should be the right place, I thought, just a moment too late, as the tip of my nose collided with something soft.

"Oops."

I quickly drew back, only to see her looking at me, slightly wide-eyed.

"What's up?"

"Er, I'm really sorry. I couldn't tell how close I was, so I guess I ran into your ear or something."

"Is it that rude to touch someone's ear in your world?"

"It is—or at least, I figured you wouldn't like it?"

"I was a little surprised at you touching me, but I knew you were getting closer so I wasn't surprised it happened. Plus, it's not like you're a stranger, or someone I hate."

With that, she got back into position.

"If it's hard for you to judge the distance, then maybe we should just have you confirm where my ear is with your finger."

I hesitated for two full seconds at the suggestion, then timidly reached my hand out to the place she indicated. Careful not to poke her with my fingernail, I moved cautiously forward until I felt something come into contact with my fingertip. I wasn't certain which part was her ear, so, despite it feeling a bit inappropriate, I traced my finger along the spot. As I moved it down, I felt something cold and soft—her earlobe, probably. That meant that what I felt before was probably the cartilage of her upper ear. Her ears were the same shape as a human's.

I gripped her ear with as little force as I possibly could, in the spot where I figured it would be most difficult to cause her any pain. Though I couldn't see it, her body was very evidently there. The fact that I couldn't feel her hair meant that it was probably cropped short or perhaps tied back in a ponytail. It was even possible that she didn't have any hair at all. Given that suddenly groping her head to confirm this would be a huge faux pas—at least in my world—I decided to just wait until there was an appropriate time to ask her.

Chika lowered her hand from her ear. Using my own hand as a guide, I brought my mouth close to her ear, careful not to collide with it this time.

"Okay, I'm gonna sing now."

It was obvious that I should whisper, but my own bashfulness plugged up my throat. I turned away and coughed once, then released her earlobe.

I had only ever sung in front of others in music class, or when I was dragged along to karaoke back in junior high while I was actively trying to make new friends. I never thought the day would come when I would be singing for just one person.

Ideally, I should have sung Chika a similar current popular song, but music for me was nothing more than background noise that came through the radio. Still, it would feel wrong in this exchange for me to offer up a nursery rhyme or similar, so instead I chose something I recalled from back when I was pretending to actually enjoy music. She would get bored if I went too long though, so just the chorus.

Once I was finished, I pulled immediately away from her ear. She slowly opened her eyes. Asking her for her impressions would be like requesting an evaluation of my singing voice, so I simply waited to hear what she would say. Deep down, I did wonder how my voice felt to her.

"Your voice is clear and quite powerful," she said finally. "I can really feel your heart in it."

I highly doubted that my heart had actually closed the gap between our bodies and spoken to Chika, but I was still stunned.

"As for how it sounded, it's like you said before. I could understand all the words perfectly, but this music itself sounded pretty strange to me. I'm glad that I could understand it pretty well from the tone of your voice."

"Ah, yeah, me too."

I was a coward. Earlier, I had not conveyed exactly what I'd felt in her voice. It felt like, if I spoke about the same things that Chika had, it would only make the fact that I saw her as herself that much more intense. In a fit of cowardice, I had kept it to myself. How could I possibly tell her that in the wake of what she had said to me? I had no idea what my voice actually sounded like, but it certainly wasn't clear or powerful.

"The way people in your world arrange the words in your songs is really pretty, but it's like nothing that exists in my world. I guess what's significant is the music," she continued. "Like you said though, it's a weird sensation, but if I tried to sing it back right now, I don't think I'd be able to vocalize it easily."

"I see. So I guess that means there's not much point in songs, either."

"Guess not. It was fun though, so it meant something to me at least."

If I had been able to tell her "Me too," then perhaps I could have smiled along with her, but that was the one sentiment I couldn't voice.

"Well, guess there's no sense in us trying it over and over."

It was true. Just as there was no point to music that we had tried to hear but knew we couldn't comprehend. If there were songs with lyrics incredibly important to our worlds, we could simply tell each other those lyrics. There was no need to hear each other sing anymore. Still, it felt unfortunate to me that this might be the last time I got to hear Chika sing.

"Do you ever wish that things around you were different?"

The question came suddenly from right beside me, still at singing distance. I swiftly banished the thought that we might never sit this close again either.

"I don't really think much about what's around me. People should do whatever they want." It was a bit dull of me, but honestly, as long as they didn't interfere with me, I didn't care how other people wanted to live their lives. As long as they didn't bother me, it was none of my business if they lived or died. "Why do you ask?"

"Because like I said before, it seems like you have some sort of objective. I have no idea what effect we can have on each other's worlds, but I was thinking that I wish there was something I could do in this world for you."

"...Wh—uh, thanks."

Chika was kind, though I knew that kindness didn't make someone less boring.

"Do you have something like that? Something around you that you wish was different?"

"Hmm..."

From this distance, I could feel the air of her hesitation down to my core.

"Like you, I just want everyone to live their own lives. As long as we don't bother each other too much. So, if there's anything at all, I guess it's the ××××?"

I'd noticed that lately there were fewer words from Chika that I couldn't hear. Perhaps she had purposely been avoiding words that might be hard to comprehend.

"Sorry, I didn't catch that last word there."

"It's an animal, the kind that bit my leg. There's a pack of them in the neighborhood, and sometimes they howl at me or chase me. I sort of wish they would just go away."

It was the fault of my slow imagination that I thought for even an instant that it seemed like a rather precious worry. The size or ferocity of these animals was not something I could possibly surmise. Chika didn't sound particularly emotional about it, but there was a chance that was merely out of fear.

I wished that there was something I could do for sweet, gentle Chika. That was a completely normal human emotion to feel.

"But that's all. Beyond that, I have my room, and the time I spend with you and my other friends, and I would never want that to change."

Of course, this was Chika, who lived with ever-present war. I was sure that she would have hoped for the wars to end, but of course there was nothing that I could personally do about something as large-scale as that, so I guess I was a little relieved that she hadn't said it. I didn't like to be reminded of how powerless I truly was. I was a coward. I had been this entire time.

"I'll try to think whether there's anything I can do about that animal. I want to make things around you better," I said, though I had absolutely no idea what to do.

"Thank you. Still, even if you don't do anything, the fact that you're there for me means something. I want you to know that."

When she said that to me, I knew for certain: I had no idea how much longer I could hide my feelings.

— ✳ —

I thought about it all night and decided to do something for Chika immediately the next day. The only animal I had any connection with—who might have some effect on the animal that had been bothering Chika—was Allumi. Simply giving the dog food had not had any effect on Chika's world. Even so, we had absolutely no idea what laws governed the connection between our worlds, so it didn't hurt to try.

Knowing that Tanaka, the dog's owner, had work that day after school, I decided to head over straight away. My intention today was not to give Allumi head pats. It was to take a look at the dog's collar and leash and to find out what made Allumi bark.

All in preparation for a kidnapping.

That was the word that popped into my mind, but it really wasn't all that dramatic. It was simply an experiment, one which I was uncertain would even have any effect, in which I would keep Allumi chained up somewhere for a night or two to see if it could drive that animal away from Chika. If Allumi got away once, they might even put up a fence at the entrance to Tanaka's house. If my plan could affect Chika's world and lead to better animal control all around, I'd call that a win-win.

Upon hearing my usual footsteps, Allumi bounded over from the shade of a well, snout pointed out and awaiting my arrival. I stopped in front of Allumi and gave the dog the usual pets as I observed the chain that ran between the doghouse and Allumi's collar. If possible, I wanted make them think that Allumi had run away.

I looked at the collar. It was fashioned exactly like a human belt but smaller, with a buckle. If I unfastened and redid it, it would seem like Allumi had slipped out all on its own.

Thinking through how I was going to do this deed, I put my hands around Allumi's stomach and tried picking the dog up. I was lucky that this was a smaller breed. I figured there was a chance Allumi might make a big fuss, but it didn't happen—the dog stayed perfectly quiet. Thankfully, none of my worries had come to pass, but was this *really* the right choice for a guard dog?

I tried loosening the collar, but even then, Allumi made little move to struggle. While it was rather anticlimactic, this meant it would be a simple feat to borrow Allumi for a bit and then return the dog back home. Even as I refastened the collar, Allumi just brought its nose to my arm—sniffing, not even nipping. I almost wanted to chide the dog for this utter lack of vigilance.

Later, I planned to return here at night and check what time the lights went out at Tanaka's house. Depending on the usual household patterns, I thought I might even been able to snatch Allumi away that night. But first, I had to think practically about where I was going to chain the dog up.

And thus my plan was put in motion.

But though I stopped by Tanaka's house that night and the next night and the next, one hour later each time I made my way back from the bus stop, I never once saw all the lights out at once. During the latest hour I visited, the only lights were on the second floor. I had no idea if that was *her* room, but I mentally scolded Tanaka that if she was going to be sleeping in class all the time, she should go to bed earlier.

I would probably have to go home and slip out of the house again in the middle of the night. It would be a pain to avoid waking my own family.

On the fourth day of not seeing Chika, I arrived at school at the usual time to see Saitou laughing along with Tanaka and her pals in the corner of the classroom. I was not particularly interested in this, but my eyes were still drawn to the unusual sight.

I took my seat and stared at my desk. Normally, I would be fully absorbed in my own thoughts, but today, I lent an ear to Tanaka's conversation beside me. It would help to catch anything that might aid me in spiriting Allumi away. Of course, naturally, Tanaka would never do anything I wanted her to, and so all my concentration that morning was wasted.

"Ah ha ha ha ha ha! Allumi is so cute!"

That day at lunch, as I waited out the period in silence as usual, there was a commotion beside me. It seemed my neighbor Tanaka was sharing around a video of Allumi. *Go do that somewhere else,* I thought. But she hadn't been to work for the past three days, leaving me unable to check in on Allumi, so I decided to sneak a peek. Just then, our eyes met.

"What, you wanna see too?"

"...I was about to lodge a complaint. You're too loud. Go do that somewhere else."

"Wha? It's lunchtime. If you want quiet, go to the library or somethin."

I was irritated at how she said it, but she did have a point. I started to shift my weight to my feet to stand up and leave when she turned her phone screen my way.

"C'mon, look at this cutie."

I reflexively looked and saw Allumi on the screen wrapped up in an old bath towel and rolling around. Tanaka's laughter rang in the background like a soundtrack. I was glad to see Allumi doing well.

"Cute, right?"

I managed a nod but was still annoyed, so I stood from my seat. I heard a "What's with you?" behind me, followed by a "Suzuki's like that no matter who tries to talk to him," from someone else.

Life went on as usual for some time after, with neither the chance to abscond with Allumi arising nor any appearances from Chika. The rainy season would be ending soon. Incidentally, I had heard a report that the war would end before the rainy season did, but more recently there had been concerning reports that the flames of war were spreading—even to Japan.

It was two weeks after I made that grand statement to Chika that I obtained some useful information. I overheard that Tanaka would be staying the night at a friend's place that coming Saturday. If she wasn't home, a full lights out at their home might come earlier. It was helpful, furthermore, that this information had not come from the owner in question herself. I heard about it from her posse, so it was doubtful that any suspicion would fall on *me* after the fact.

On the night I set the plan into motion, the wind was blowing in its usual direction. I set out on my bike. A collar, a leash, and dishes for Allumi's food, as well as water that I had purchased ahead of time, had been set aside in the bus shelter. My plan was to wait a bit at the bus stop, talk to Chika if I was lucky (though the odds of that were low), and then head to Tanaka's place around midnight.

I was glad that it wasn't raining. I didn't want Allumi to get soaked, and if it was raining, there was a chance they might have brought Allumi inside for the night anyway. I reached the bus stop in the dark, parked my bike, and slid the door open as always. Chika wasn't there. If she had been present, I intended to tell her about my plan and then ask her to check on the status of the violent animal in her neighborhood the next day, but I would just have to leave that for later.

I sat down on the bench. Thinking about it, you could say that my plan would be the first instance of Chika's presence having a negative effect on my world. Of course, my concern was not for Tanaka; I was only worried about Allumi. Though it would just be for a couple of days, being removed from its familiar home when it had done nothing wrong might prove stressful. Maybe I should have bought some more treats or something. I'd consider it if the abduction went well.

I'd come to learn recently that if Chika did not appear by 11:30 p.m., it was unlikely she'd show up any time after that. When I sat there alone in the quiet, checked my watch and found that it was past 11:30, I would be sad. Yet, if I had to admit it, lately I was also somewhat relieved. I wasn't interested in seeing who else I might become at the mercy of such bizarre emotions.

Once again, 11:30 p.m. rolled around. I picked up my things and set out.

For the first time ever, I was glad that our town was in the middle of nowhere. If you tried to snatch a dog in a more populated area, you'd be reported on the spot. Previously, Chika had told me that she lived in a town with a lot of people. Apparently, the local flavor had nothing to do with the link we shared.

I urged my bike forward along a hilly road with a nice incline for training. The wind felt pleasant as I cruised downhill.

I purchased a water bottle from a vending machine I passed along the way, running mental simulations of what was about to occur in my head as I rode. Finally I arrived at my destination. There was no one around. I parked my bike a short distance away, careful to walk as quietly as possible as I approached the traditionally built home. At a quick glance, it didn't look like there were lights on either the first or second floor. I made a quick lap around the house, stealing a glance through the front, but it was pitch-black inside. Still, that didn't put me at ease. There were two cars present, likely belonging to Tanaka's parents, which had not been there during the day. If Allumi raised any commotion, I would have to run immediately.

I slipped in through the back gate to find Allumi lying there prettily, gazing up at the sky. There was a full moon tonight. Before I could even call out, Allumi picked up on my scent, noticed me, and trotted over. There were no lights, but the bright moonlight was enough for Allumi to confirm who I was. I was glad the pup seemed well.

Now, the real trouble began. I had practiced this many times during the day, but it wouldn't be surprising if my loosening the collar at night put Allumi on guard. Honestly, I could not even complain if I was barked at, being an intruder. Despite my worries, though, Allumi just sat there quietly and waited for me to loosen the collar. Even as I was refastening it to give the illusion that Allumi had run away on its own, it merely sat there, patient. This worried me for a different reason.

Honestly, in terms of executing my plan, I could not ask for a more favorable outcome. I picked Allumi up and slipped away from the house, placing the dog gently in my bike basket. It looked a bit cramped, but Allumi neatly folded up its legs and tucked right in. To keep the dog from fussing, I offered it a treat it would have to chew on for a while. Once it was occupied, I fastened the new collar and leashed it to the basket, straddled my bike, and started riding.

It was almost a letdown how smoothly the abduction had gone. I rode down a road with even fewer people than the one I had taken to get there, headed for my destination. I'd thought about taking Allumi somewhere far away, but I needed to know how much of an effect this would have on Chika's world, so I decided to keep the operation close by. That said, sticking close to my home would raise too many suspicions, so I instead chose a place that I could stop by while I was out on my runs.

We entered a mountainous area that would have been a ver-
dant green during the daytime but was now pitch dark. Going
down a road it'd never seen before made Allumi understandably
anxious, and it looked up at me and let out a small bark. Still, a
creative part of my mind imagined this bark was more of a criticism—more of a "What do you think you're doing?"—as though
the two of us were partners in crime on the run.

I reached a steep slope and stood up in the saddle to put my
weight into peddling up it. At the top of the hill was a bus stop. It
was in shambles, darkness all around it, with an adjoining shelter
that looked like it might crumble at any moment. I had found
it recently when I was riding around looking for a place to stash
the dog. Like my usual haunt, this stop was no longer in use. I'd
run this way numerous times in the evening, but not once did I
see any cars or people along the road. It was the perfect place to
hide Allumi.

I opened the door of this new bus shelter and carried Allumi
inside. The dog waited, patient as ever, for me to attach its collar
to the bench inside.

"Sorry, this'll just be for a little while."

I put some treats into a deep plastic bowl I'd purchased at
a convenience store, filled another with water from the plastic
bottle, and placed them both before Allumi.

Now my goal had been achieved, and it was time for me to
leave the shelter. I closed the door and started to climb back on
my bike when I heard Allumi bark once more. I took off as quick
as I could toward home. My initial plan had been to leave Allumi

there for two days, but I recalled hearing that dogs experienced time differently from humans. It was probably best I return it home the next day. I considered altering my plans.

I went home and went right to sleep, and when dawn broke, it was Sunday.

I wondered if Tanaka was back yet. There would've probably been a big commotion when she got home and found Allumi gone. I didn't intend to cause a classmate any needless suffering, but I was doing this to keep Chika safe.

Some sacrifices had to be made.

On the weekends, I always went running in the morning. Thus, I was able to go check in on Allumi without ruining my daily routine. I ran for about twenty minutes, food and water in hand. When I opened the door to the shelter where Allumi had been since the night before, I was relieved to feel comfortable air cling to my face, not much different from outside. One of the reasons I had chosen this lodging for Allumi was the thick canopy overhead, which shaded the roof from the sun.

Upon seeing me, Allumi stood up. I stooped down and scratched the dog on the head. I could see some dust clinging to the fur of its belly. I put some food in the dish and replenished the water supply, which Allumi happily began lapping up without a single complaint.

It occurred to me that Allumi would probably need a bit of exercise. It was a Sunday morning. Few people passed through here, and if anyone saw me from a car, it would just look like I was walking my dog. I detached the leash from the bench and set out with Allumi. I figured it might start immediately running for home, but that didn't happen. We just walked around the surrounding area for a little bit before I returned the dog to the shelter.

I decided I would check in on Allumi again that evening and decide whether I should keep the dog for one more night. That settled, I left the bus stop behind.

That night, I set off on my bike toward the first bus stop.

"Evening, Kaya."

While I had no way to determine any pattern to the situation and thus no way to predict her appearances, I was nonetheless kind of surprised to actually see Chika at the bus shelter that evening. When I mentioned this first thing upon seeing her, Chika began to seriously consider the implications.

"To be honest, I had planned on going to a different safe house today, but something came up—I had to go back near my house and ended up here. I wonder if it's got anything to do with that."

"Are you asking if my intentions have any effect on *your* plans? I wonder if it could really be that subtle."

Even if it was, that didn't seem very useful. The fact that I had even predicted this could've easily been a fabrication of my own mind after it happened.

"Even if that's true, I'm not sure we can make anything useful of it, but if we really are connected down to the depths of your consciousness, that's kind of heartening—if also a bit frightening."

I understood her sentiment exactly. It would be terrifying to be linked to someone else's consciousness. It was scary to think that I might not be my own person, regardless of what I felt about Chika or anything like that. At the same time, if she wasn't her own solid individual, it made all of this much less meaningful.

At any rate, talk of will and predictions aside, chances were high that this was all just a coincidence. It was prudent to consider the most logical possibility.

"Oh, right. So I tried relocating a local animal to see if it would do anything to that scary animal you mentioned. I wonder if it's had any effect yet."

"Oh!"

The lights of Chika's eyes widened, and she made a reserved sound of understanding and surprise.

"I noticed that I hadn't seen it around lately, so maybe you *did* have some effect."

"When you say lately though, do you mean in the past few days? I only did it yesterday."

Which led me to wonder, had some phenomenon in Chika's world prompted my decision to act and kidnap Allumi? The thought made me shudder. Once again, I had to question my sense of self.

"Was I the one affected, then?"

"I mean, we still can't assume that the party who acted later is the one who was affected. Even if our weather is the same, we don't know for certain how the time aligns in your world and mine, nor do we have any way of finding that out."

The thought of the event that happened later being the cause rather than the effect was sounding very sci-fi.

"Plus, I'd like to believe that we both still have free will. So I'd like to think it's thanks to you that I don't have to be afraid anymore. Thank you."

"That's...well...that's good."

I really didn't require any thanks, but if Chika could rest even a little bit easier, that was good enough for me.

"Well then," I continued, "just to confirm whether I really affected things, I'll try taking the animal on this side back home. It might put you in danger again, though..."

"No, I'm all right. That would just mean going back to normal, so it's not so bad."

"Right."

Really?

I thought that through, though I really didn't have to.

I *hated* the idea of things going back to normal. When I thought of this time that I shared with Chika, when I thought of losing my something special, it felt like all the blood drained from my heart. I needed to find something I could use to satisfy my desires, something with which I could make my own heart beat. If I could not do that, fear was inevitable.

Chika seemed to imply that, should that day come, it wouldn't bother her.

"Has anything nice happened around you lately?" she asked.

"No, not especially. Did you do something?"

I figured she wanted to know the results of some experiment, but her eyes drifted side to side.

"No, I wasn't asking to confirm any effects. I was just hoping that at least one nice thing had happened in your world, since you did something so nice for me."

She wasn't talking about her world affecting mine but rather my world affecting itself. It wasn't about my actions having a positive effect on Chika but on me. My happiness, wrought by my own hands and no one else's. That was what she'd asked about. Honestly, I should have been happy that she thought that way about me and accepted things as they were.

But I couldn't.

Though it was contradictory to say, Chika's words pulled me right back down to my own world. It was like she was telling me I couldn't let myself get addicted to my meetings with her.

"Thanks."

There was something that had occurred to me some time ago floating there, right above my palm. I reached out and grasped it.

Perhaps.

Perhaps my search for some meaning in Chika's existence, my being overwhelmed by all these special feelings...perhaps it was all just me running from myself.

In all this time, I had never figured out *why* Chika and I met. Perhaps this was because there was nothing to understand in the first place.

Maybe Chika was simply there. Maybe she didn't exist just to make me happy. I'd just been averting my eyes from that possibility, hadn't I?

If we kept spending all our time just investigating these cross effects, when we someday parted for good, all I'd feel would be the loss of all this wasted time, and I still wouldn't be rescued from my boredom. So then, what would be the *point* of it all?

I needed to tell her something important—something incredibly important—that would show her the will that I myself possessed. And yet, from then until the moment Chika noticed the siren and departed, I couldn't bring myself to say it: that perhaps there was no point to our spending time together at all.

I was alone in the shelter.

My head swirled with the thought that our time together was utterly pointless. At the same time, I chided myself not to let my own thoughts stray too much. My own voice rang loudly in my ears, unyielding. I could no longer ignore the clear warnings from my heart.

I heaved a sigh.

For now, I just needed to go check in on Allumi and return the dog back home. I had something to do. Thankfully, Chika had never appeared two nights in a row, so I had some time until our next meeting. This meant that I'd have time to think about what to do in the future. For now, I just needed to get out of here.

I stood up, opened the door, shut it, mounted my bike, and headed for the second bus stop. The wind felt cool against my skin. I'd heard it was going to rain tomorrow. That was part of why I was considering returning Allumi home tonight.

Even if we stop seeing each other because I never fully opened up about my feelings, at least I can see this matter—dealing with the animal that's been harassing Chika—through to the end, I thought as I rode my bike. My heart and mind were both rejoicing that I

wouldn't have to think about parting from Chika until then—
a joy that came prematurely.

As long as you don't trouble yourself with difficult things, life is
easy. If I just let my emotions wash over me and breathed, I didn't
have to worry about a thing. No need to waste energy on worrying.

But that isn't really *living*.

When you have doubts, you have doubts. There was no certainty to my feelings or thoughts.

I climbed the final hill to the bus stop where Allumi was
stashed, muttering silently to myself all the way. Perhaps because
I had shocked my body with the sudden exercise, or because the
oxygen supply to my heart where Chika dwelled—so close to my
lungs—was choked off, my wristwatch let out a single electronic
beep.

I parked my bike and quietly let air into my lungs. In the
absence of any noise but the trees rustling in the wind, the sound
of me dismounting my bike and putting out the kickstand rang
impossibly loud. I couldn't hear Allumi from the shelter. I was glad
the dog had figured out how to while away the time quietly.

I had no idea how much intelligence or emotion your typical
dog, or any animal for that matter, possessed. I didn't know who
decided that their minds were inferior to humans'—for all we
knew, they only *acted* stupid in front of humans. It's probably
because humans considered things less intelligent than them *cute*.
I started hating myself all the more as I opened the sliding door,
realizing that the only reason I didn't find other humans cute in
the same way was that I recognized that we were the same breed.

Allumi was not there.

My heart leapt to my throat. I felt dizzy in a way that I had once before.

For several seconds I stood there frozen, unmoving. Then I returned to my senses, realizing there was no point to standing there in shock.

Allumi was gone. All that was left in the shelter were the collar and leash I had put on it, along with the half-consumed food and water.

Clearly, the dog had escaped. Thinking that perhaps Allumi might be crouching somewhere in the darkness in the corner of the shelter, I went inside, but it was nowhere to be seen.

Had I left too much slack in the collar? Or had I underestimated Allumi's strength? It didn't matter which, I just needed to look for it.

"Allumi!"

I figured there was a fair chance that a dog as overly friendly as Allumi would come when I called, even if I wasn't its owner. The dog might not come back, but as long as I got a reply, I could run to wherever it was. No matter how long I waited, though, I neither heard nor saw any sign of the dog.

I entered the tree line and began to search. I looked hard for anything—if not Allumi, then at least some sign it had left behind. I switched on my phone flashlight, but the beam only went so far.

"Allumi!" My voice echoed out once more, but there was no reply.

What could I do? What the hell should I do?

As my head spun, a singular thought occurred to me: Had Allumi gone back? Back home?

Dogs were supposed to have a homing instinct. Maybe being dragged here by me, a stranger, had awakened the strength in Allumi to escape its collar and get back home.

That would be ideal. Whether human or dog, I never intended to hurt anyone. I would truly never wish for such a thing.

Go back home, I prayed. *Go and sleep in your doghouse with that peaceful look on your face.* I mounted my bicycle and headed for Tanaka's house, praying all the way.

How absurd it was for *me* of all people, someone who lived for no one and nothing but myself, to pray for someone else.

I reached my destination. Allumi was nowhere to be seen.

On the second floor, the lights were on. Though it was wildly, horribly optimistic of me, I thought that perhaps Tanaka had gone out searching for Allumi, found the bus stop, and taken her dog back home. It wasn't impossible. There was nothing impossible about it.

Or maybe, since Allumi had gone missing, the dog had now been brought inside the house. Perhaps it was up on the second floor right now, playing happily with its owner.

It was equally possible that Allumi had escaped the collar and gone somewhere far, far away. Even if it hadn't, perhaps it was taking a lengthy detour on the way home. It could be sneaking around some abandoned house right now. Someone else could have snatched it, even...

None of these were impossible scenarios, but they couldn't all be true.

I rode my bike around the area surrounding Tanaka's home, but Allumi was neither walking nor sitting anywhere. I was getting nowhere fast, but just thinking about it would get me nowhere even faster. My stomach roiled with nerves. I knew that there was little I could achieve at this hour. It would be better to search in the morning when it was light out. Still, I couldn't go home yet, so I instead made countless, pointless loops between Tanaka's house and the bus stop. And by pointless, I of course meant that I accomplished absolutely *nothing* at all.

Though I should have done so much sooner, I finally returned home, trudged up to my room, and tried my best to sleep as I always did.

On Monday morning, I set out before breakfast, telling my family it was for training. It still hadn't rained yet. I biked to Tanaka's house, but Allumi wasn't there. I thought about ringing the doorbell to inquire about the dog's well-being, but that would just make me look suspicious. I could ask later at school.

With little else I could do about the situation, I just rode around the area as I had the day before. I saw plenty of dogs walking with their owners, but of course none of them were Allumi. I went to the bus stop where I had confined them again, but they weren't there either. I'd brought the collar and leash with me in a plastic bag, just in case.

Where did Allumi go, and what was the dog doing now?

Where might it go from there? I couldn't recall thinking about anyone else this much lately besides Chika.

Defeated, I returned home, ate breakfast, and headed for school. At the very least, Tanaka would be there, and I could confirm the situation from her in person. I figured I could just casually ask about Allumi before class started without raising any suspicion. However, when I arrived at school, there was no one sitting to my right—even after the bell rang, the teacher arrived, and first period began.

I found myself irritated that she had the nerve to skip school on a day like this. I put aside the not-impossible possibility that she had skipped school because of something awful happening in her life, but soon, I had nowhere to run.

I ate lunch in the cafeteria that day. As usual, the food wasn't something I was particularly interested in eating. I returned to the classroom to stare at my desk when I heard a voice. I was able to pick up on this only thanks to someone who didn't realize that a whisper was sometimes easier to hear than a normal, quiet tone.

"Did you hear?"

"Hear what?"

"I heard that Allumi *died*."

My right knee jerked suddenly up and into my desk, robbing the rest of the classroom of sound. I didn't mean anything by it.

There were probably some who looked at me, wondering what the noise was about, but I didn't meet their eyes. I just stared at the wooden top of my desk.

...Wait.

What?

What?!

Of course...

Allumi. Dead?

That was all I could think.

That was all.

I couldn't remember.

I couldn't remember a thing.

I couldn't remember Allumi approaching me, unguarded, the first time we met.

I couldn't remember the times I patted Allumi on the head.

I couldn't remember Allumi gobbling up the treats that I snuck it.

I couldn't remember Allumi popping up to greet me the moment it heard my footsteps.

I couldn't remember Allumi sniffing my arm.

I couldn't remember Allumi cradled in my arms, trusting me.

I couldn't remember any of that, so from then until it was time to leave, I just sat there quietly in school. I didn't bother to cover my ears, so I heard rumors that it was a traffic accident.

After school, in my usual copy-paste routine, I headed to the shoe lockers. Today, Saitou, who had been assaulting me with awkward greetings every day lately, just looked at me curiously and headed silently home, as she used to.

I headed quietly home as well, then set out once again. I was still in my uniform—there was no point in changing.

It was raining.

That meant it was probably raining in Chika's world too. I had no idea what effect I might have on her side, so I walked carefully up the stairs, umbrella out.

I thought at first of ringing the bell, but I realized that doing so might summon another family member for me to have to talk to. Still, I had to call her out somehow. Just in case, I headed to the backyard first. There I found Allumi's owner standing there with an umbrella, staring at the empty doghouse.

I walked up to the back gate. I was sure my steps were audible, but Tanaka didn't turn around, just stared at some spot below her knees. Her back was turned to me, so I couldn't make out her expression. I called her surname clearly, but she didn't react. I called out to her one more time. Her head and waist turned slowly back, but her voice was as disconnected from her expression as Chika's was.

"What?"

Why? Why are you here? Why are you talking to me?

Why are you still alive when Allumi's dead?

I heard all those questions in her voice. Time to do what I had come here to do.

"I came here to talk to you."

Tanaka gave no reaction. Even her face didn't budge an inch.

I decided to continue.

"I killed Allumi."

Still, no reaction. She just stared at me.

"I came here in the middle of the night and took Allumi away.

I had it tied up somewhere else, but I was too lax and it slipped the collar and escaped. That's why Allumi died."

"Wha...?"

It was a gasp of a sound that nearly disappeared into the rain.

"You can report me if you like."

"The *hell* are you saying?"

Nothing moved besides her lips.

"You don't have to forgive me."

"You..." Her voice crackled from deep within her throat. She stared at my face. Her half-parted lips began to tremble, which finally erupted across her whole face as she stared at me. "What the hell..."

She just stared.

"What the hell is wrong with you?!"

She flung her open umbrella at me, but it got caught on its own air resistance and fell to the ground at my feet.

Tanaka crumpled to her knees on the spot, sobbing. Large raindrops fell onto her yellow T-shirt, covering it in splotches.

Leaving someone to get soaked in the rain was equal to a crime in my mind, but I had nothing more to say to the devastated girl, nor would it be helpful for me to try, so I left the large traditional house behind.

I went home and did some resistance training and ate the dinner that my mother had prepared. I looked out my window as I returned to my room and saw that the rain had stopped. I knew that the chances were next to none, but just in case, I decided to head to the bus stop—not the one where I had kept Allumi, obviously.

Coming here was basically habit at this point, so it wasn't like I had a particularly strong desire to see Chika today or anything like that. Naturally, I did want to know whether anything had happened in her world with Allumi's passing, but by the time I opened the shelter door I had already half written today off, figuring we could talk about it whenever next time came. Given that, I'd expect to be shocked to see those shining eyes and fingernails there, but as it turned out, that wasn't how I felt at all.

This was the first time we met two nights in a row.

"Hey, Chika."

"Hey, um..." I figured that her response had been short to match my clipped greeting, but her next words told me that I was mistaken. "Has anyone around you died?"

There was worry in the voice that came to me from between those eyes. Trying my best to hide how shaken I was, I sat down. "No *person* has died," I replied. "Why do you ask?"

Chika breathed out, perhaps more loudly than she needed to.

"Someone died near my home. I don't know the details, but apparently a battle came to my neighborhood. Several people who fight for a living died, and we had to bury them. I came here because I was worried that might have had some effect on your world." She paused there, blinking slowly. "You had a really sad expression just now."

She didn't say I looked sad—just "a sad expression."

I wondered if that meant I'd only been slightly unsuccessful in hiding my expression, not enough that Chika could read it for certain—or if I looked so terribly sad that it was making her sad too. Either was unforgivable.

"Did...something happen?"

Do we really have to talk about this? I thought. Still, the conversation would be meaningful if it helped us learn more about our connection.

"A dog died."

"A dawg. That's an animal that lives with people, right?"

"Guess I did explain that before. Yeah. I killed it."

"I see." She showed neither sorrow nor reproach. Instead, she simply asked, "Did it do something to you?" Right. She probably assumed that I would never kill an animal unless it was too dangerous to let live.

"No, it was pretty nice," I clarified. "We do have some stray dogs, but for the most part where I'm from, like you said, they live with people. They're treated like friends or family. I killed a dog that lived with someone I know. It was innocent. It was never violent and was friendly to everyone. It was happy to even eat right out of my hand."

"Then how could you do such a thing?"

"Well, I abducted it, and when I was away, it got into an accident."

"No, sorry, what I was asking was—"

"I abducted it because I wanted to see what effect it had on our worlds, and it got away because I was careless."

I explained the situation as best I could, not in a way that would make Chika think it was her fault, but I didn't want to contradict anything I had told her so far.

"Right, so that's what you were talking about yesterday." She nodded once and then shook her head. "But anyway, what I was asking wasn't *what* you did to that dawg or why."

"Then...?"

What? I looked at Chika, silent and questioning. Her voice reached my senses without her eyes budging a millimeter.

"Why did you tell me this in a way that would make me feel sorry for this dawg?"

There was no sound. It was quiet, no weight or sensation. And yet it felt as though Chika's silence in the wake of that question had grabbed me by the hair. I felt like my heart was being wrenched from my body. It wasn't. That was a delusion. A creative one.

"I wasn't looking for any sympathy. I was just stating the facts," I said, looking her straight in the eye. I wasn't lying. She gave one long blink and then looked down.

"That must have been hard for you."

"...Huh?" No. "It wasn't."

"But you look like it was."

"I'm telling you it wasn't. It was hard for *Allumi*, not me. And for the ones who lost a family member. I was the one who took their dog away."

Of course, Chika had no idea who "Allumi" was.

"I'm sure it was hard on them too."

"They're the *only* ones it was hard on."

I wasn't the one suffering.

"I can't even begin to imagine that pain." That was true. She knew nothing about this. "But I realized just now, while the weight of it isn't the same as what that family or dawg went through, you're in pain too."

"You're wrong. I'm not."

"But you look like you are."

"I'm telling you, I'm *not*!" That wasn't true. "I'm the one who *killed* it!"

I was the one at fault. I had no right to feel pain. I had no right to suffer in the slightest, not when I could never know even a fraction of Allumi's pain or the family's sadness. Of course I couldn't stomach hearing words that even suggested kindness toward me, any favor, not when I knew everything that I had done.

"You don't know *anything*, Chika."

Indeed. She didn't know a single thing. Chika knew nothing about Allumi. I didn't need empty consolations from someone like her.

"Stop it."

My request was sincere.

"I feel like you're going down a bad path, Kaya," she said.

"You're right, I suck, so—"

"I just don't want you to take yourself somewhere even more tragic."

"*Stop* it."

I didn't want to hear that from her.

She was wrong. What I wanted to hear, what she should have done, was to criticize me. I couldn't bear for any other words to reach my heart. I could not possibly accept this kindness.

"You can just be here."

"But *I killed Allumi!*"

I was a bad person—a dreadful person. I wasn't the sort of person you should speak kind words to, who you should extend a helping hand to. I knew that better than anyone. *So please, Chika, stop it.*

"No matter how twisted of a thing you've become in your own world, when you're here, you're still you."

"Why...?"

I was fully aware of my own sin and that I ought to be judged. And yet, I also knew that I was a disgustingly weak, basic person.

I couldn't help myself. Weak people, even knowing with all their hearts that they ought to be punished, will still look to those who offer their hand in the hopes that it might make things just a little bit better. *Pitiful.*

So I begged her silently to stop this before I turned my weak, greedy eyes to the grace that was being offered to me and began yearning to cling to it, to those invisible hands that were reaching out from Chika's heart.

I wanted to take her hand, but I knew that if I did, so many precious things would end. The alarm bells in my heart keened. I couldn't look at her. I couldn't take her hand.

I covered my ears and heard sirens ringing.

And yet. Even so. And still.

I...

I felt like I was suffocating.

I never hesitated to act when it came to the motions of daily life, detached from like, dislike, interest, dispassion, whether or not something benefitted me, and any similar concepts. Such was my guiding philosophy, whether eating, or sleeping, or running, or breathing.

I was weak—weak, weak, so incredibly weak.

I saw her hand.

"Allumi was..."

And suddenly, I took it.

I knew exactly how pitiful I was, but I could not stop myself from speaking.

"Allumi was a good dog!"

"Are you sad that it's gone?"

I shook my head.

"Not as sad as its owner."

"Still, if you're sad, then you should admit those feelings."

My words continued spilling from my mouth aimlessly.

"I am sad. Yeah, I'm really sad. Allumi let its guard down around me. It should have barked and called for help. But it didn't, and that's why I killed it."

"You can't forgive yourself, can you?"

"I can't."

"Well then, I forgive you."

This girl made of only eyes and nails, two years my senior, offered those simple words to me. Chika was made only of eyes and nails, but somehow the words she had set down between us were soft and sweet.

"It might not mean anything to you, but I forgive you. Truly."

"I don't need to be forgiven. I don't deserve that kindness."

"Kaya." She blinked long and slow, as she did whenever she apologized. "This isn't kindness." The two lights pierced through my soul. "I *want* to forgive you. I stood by and watched as the people who work to ensure our way of life were killed. The more seriously I consider it, the less I understand what I should think of the being I know as *myself*. And so, I want to do whatever I can. I *want* to forgive you."

Her voice was filled with melancholy, as though she was holding something beautiful and delicate. Unable to ignore that ephemeral voice, I immediately popped those soft, sweet words between us into my mouth and devoured them.

"In that case..." I swallowed. "I forgive you, Chika."

I had no idea that those words would linger there inside me and never leave. Or rather, maybe I *did* know. Perhaps for a moment I even thought that I was fine with that.

"I want to forgive you too."

"Guess we'll be sharing the same sin."

"...That's fine." Though I could only see her eyes, it seemed she was neither happy nor sad. "I want to share the burden together."

We could only share things with our voices. We only had the faintest picture of each other's worlds and values. Here we were, deigning to pardon one another from totally different worlds. It was only forgiveness, and yet, it was odd.

Somehow, ever so slightly, it felt easier to breathe.

"If you're fine with it, then let's do that," she said. As she spoke, I suddenly realized something. I finally realized it.

Perhaps she—Chika—could *not* change my life.

Perhaps she only existed for this weak, pitiful version of me. There was someone who would forgive me so I could accomplish my goals in this world just as I was *right here*. And if she wasn't here, I would have stopped being myself. I would be crushed, suffocated, and terrified by the idea of being a normal, boring human. Looking back, Chika never guided, nor persuaded, nor criticized me. She was simply there, sharing her thoughts for her own sake. And she permitted me to be just as I was too.

Perhaps that was the only meaning there was. Perhaps her entire presence in my life was simply meant to support me. That had to be it. Thinking about it, it was simple.

I looked straight into her eyes, as I had when we first met. In that moment, I was sure it was fine to simply stare, no meaning behind it. Deep in my heart, I felt saved by the fact that her eyes and nails were there, looking only at me.

I had thought that people could never save each other. It felt like a fragment of those soft, sweet words had caught in my throat, but I swallowed it back down, ignoring it.

"Thank you." I had not intended to speak, but again the words spilled from my mouth. "Thank you for being here for me. You brought me back."

There is surely a mass to one's true heart, something that your lips cannot bear the weight of that comes rolling out in front of others. That weight increases all the more when it's an emotion you've never once felt before.

I had never been so happy just to have someone there for me. Never before had such a trivial thing brought me such joy.

"Just having you around has brought me closer to my goals. Sorry for being so loud earlier."

I lowered my head, penitent.

If I wanted to accomplish anything, I couldn't wallow in regret and sorrow. I could repent for what I had done, but it would never be enough. No number of apologies to Allumi would ever make up for what I'd done. Thus...there was no point in dwelling on it.

Allumi was dead. Rather than sit around mourning, I had to fulfill my purpose. That was the most just thing I could do.

Thinking about it, what happened with Allumi might have just been a symbolic event. Grieving Allumi's death was nothing but egoism, as was fretting over Izumi's suicide attempt. Feigning some heroic mourning over only your visible sins was nothing but a lie if you averted your eyes from the sins that others could not see.

I had taken away something special from so many other people in my quest to make myself special. I had stolen food from the mouths of so many others to live. That's how humans live, ignoring what they cannot see. That's why wars exist, no matter what world you live in. I could spend my entire life wanting to be forgiven by everyone I'd ever hurt, and it would never be enough. I was fully aware of this.

But there was nothing that I, a single, weak individual, could do about it.

If Chika was there, though, it was different. With Chika there, willing to forgive me, I could still fight. I could resist my own boring life being stolen away.

Chika could *save* me.

I could no longer deny that Chika was more to me than just a resident of another world. Yet I couldn't figure out what you would call what I was feeling. Still, that had nothing to do with my purpose, nor with Chika. Nothing could replace the fact that Chika was here with me. But the moment I recognized that fact, worries bubbled up to the front of my mind. Just having Chika here helped me breathe, but I couldn't think of a single way in which *my* being here helped Chika.

I had to repay her somehow. I looked deeply into her eyes. After several more blinks, she spoke.

"Pain probably has a big influence."

"Pain?"

"Yeah. We can't know whose actions came first, but lives have been impacted around us both. Lightning struck and a tree was hurt. Injuries are the same."

"So being hurt, being broken, has an effect."

"I can't remember, did my accessory breaking have any effect on you?"

"This is the first I'm hearing about it."

"Oh." She chuckled at her own mistake. "Should we find out if that kind of thing will help you fulfill your purpose?"

"...No, let's leave it aside for now," I said, refusing a proposal that I would have leapt at immediately before now. All I wanted to do today was prove to myself that the conclusions I'd just come to about myself were true. And so, my next words were not directed toward Chika.

"Meeting you was my purpose."

I stared silently into her eyes. She looked back at me, unblinking.

"I can't say that I won't one day try out what you suggested, but for now I just want to hear about you, Chika."

She gave several short blinks, then her eyes slowly narrowed.

"Sure thing. Next time we meet, let's not talk about the world or anything. Let's just talk about me and you. That sounds good to me."

Promises were nothing but a curse, but just this once I could, with genuine joy, nod my head and say "Yeah, let's."

From the way she was speaking I assumed the siren would be ringing soon, so I had replied with similar finality. But that wasn't the case.

"Okay," she said. "I better get going. My family's gonna be worried."

She stood up, oddly not making the sour face she usually did toward the siren. My confusion must have been obvious on my face.

"There wasn't any war today," she explained. "All those people died though, so I got worried about you."

I was shocked.

"I don't know if my coming here changed anything, but I'm glad I got to see some of those clouds hovering over your head blow away."

I was surprised that Chika would do something purely for my sake, with no benefit to herself. I was happy of course, but I also felt that something dreadful might happen if I took this fact at pure face value. So the next words that rolled out of my mouth were rather absurd.

"Do you..."

"Yeah?"

"Do you...know everything I'm feeling?"

I wondered if she knew my feelings, all the emotions that I felt toward her that I couldn't place. I immediately regretted asking, although I truly did have some suspicions. But Chika just shook her head.

"Obviously I can't know what's in someone else's heart. So please, tell me."

If I had to mush my heart up and summarize it in a single phrase:

"I think...I *like* you, Chika."

By the time I realized what I was saying, it was already too late.

"Thanks. I like you too, Kaya. All right, see you."

"Oh, sure. See ya. Try not to get caught."

I could tell by her response that she hadn't understood the gist of what I was saying at all—which was a huge relief. The lights of her eyes and nails disappeared into the darkness.

I had no idea how much effect both our willpower had on our connection. In that same ignorance, I no longer simply wanted to see her again—I was *determined* to see her again. That was why I had made that promise. Even so, how could I possibly say something like that out of nowhere? I knew that thinking about it would only make me want to claw my own chest open, so I swiftly put it out of my mind and left.

When I opened the shelter door, a light rain was falling. If Chika's hypothesis that getting hurt had a mutual effect was correct, if I caught a cold then Chika might catch one too.

I hurried home.

Our promise to tell one another about ourselves the next time we met would never come true.

There are things that we, as humans, cannot accomplish by our wills alone. The greatest, most irresistible force in the world is death. There are many different reasons why we cannot escape the inevitability of our own deaths.

What else could there be besides death, then? Illness, perhaps. Maybe, since we cannot escape it, we say illness is born of the mind. What of old age, then? It is perhaps because it is unavoidable that we fear it so direly.

There are other things as well...such as accidents born of human stupidity.

It was early morning. I was shaken awake by a loud noise.

I couldn't react immediately upon waking. I leapt up, looking around the dark room, but the moment the obvious notion of turning on a light occurred to me, I felt something sharp in the soles of my feet.

"Ow."

I flinched at the stabbing sensation. Finally, I realized that the sound I'd heard was glass breaking. I sat up in bed, pulling out the fragments that had lodged themselves in my feet. I set my pillows down on the floor as stepping stones to protect myself from further damage and managed to make it across the room to the light switch.

As I expected, when I turned on the light, I was greeted by a room covered in glass. I cursed the fact that I rarely slept with my curtains closed. The floor was now littered with not only glass but also some of my CDs. Near the glass there was some sort of metal plate. I didn't have anything like that in my room, so it must have been what came in through the window. Just as I was wondering what the hell it was, someone knocked on my door.

"Kaya, everything all right?"

Hearing my brother, I vacantly opened the door.

"Something just came in through my window."

I showed him the palm-sized metal plate, which he looked at curiously. Neither of us had any clue what it was, so we set about cleaning the place up. My brother went around with a broom and dustpan, then helped me tape some cardboard up over the shattered window.

As I picked up my CDs, I found that two of their cases had broken like they'd fallen in some awkward way. They were ones I'd listened to at some point and just randomly put down. It was fine, though.

The collar I'd bought for Allumi was still in its place on the shelf.

I tried my best not to think about it, but that was similarly impossible for a human to do, so a single worry floated into my mind: *How will this affect Chika?*

Of course, my worry for her safety was first and foremost. But even if she herself was safe, she and I held our rooms in a very different regard. I was gripped by her hypothesis that pain could affect the other reality.

That said, even if it did have some effect on her room, as long as it was nothing more consequential than what had happened in mine—like some old CDs getting broken or something—that was fine. I didn't care if my room got a little messed up. As long as there were no life-threatening injuries, things would be okay.

Still, I didn't want to see her sad. I truly felt that for her, this girl who was nothing more than eyes and nails.

I was worried, but for the moment I could do nothing but pray for the safety of her and her room. I straightened up the books and CDs I had left in careless stacks, thinking it might even have some positive effect on her surroundings.

I slept a little longer in the now well-ventilated room and then told my parents about the window in the morning. When I showed my father the metal plate, he said, almost half-doubting himself, "Is that a piece of an *airplane*?"

Whether or not that was true, it was not an unreasonable thought. No matter how peaceful our daily lives were, we were still in a country that was racked by war. It wouldn't be too surprising if some random airplane had been less than properly maintained.

When I arrived at school, my neighbor, Tanaka, was already in her seat and talking to some other students. She spared me not so much as a glance. I half suspected she might actually throw something at me, but that didn't happen. I had already prepared myself to try and accept anything that came my way, but there was nothing.

First and second periods passed as though nothing had happened to anyone.

I had a single hypothesis.

Perhaps Tanaka had decided that I had never been anything more than a random face in the crowd, someone unworthy of recognition, just one of the many you pass on the street. In doing so, the person who killed Allumi no longer existed. Perhaps that was a way of managing her hatred. In fact, when it came time to pass a stack of handouts my way, Tanaka did so without hesitation.

If my hypothesis was correct, then it had finally happened, I realized. The girl who sat beside me had finally ceased to acknowledge me as an individual. Finally, we were equals.

Even if it was meaningless, it was for the best. This way, we could both just live our own separate lives.

I went home, went running as I always did, and when night fell, I headed for the bus stop. Chika was not there.

I was worried about Chika's room, but the timing of our meetings wasn't something I could control. Or even if I could somehow, we still didn't understand the rules.

All I could do was wait patiently, as always. I was prepared for that. But three days passed, and then five, then a week, two weeks, and by the time my window had been fully repaired and school moved into summer vacation, my patience was more than running out.

What if she had gotten hurt?

What if she had lost something important to her?

No, what if, completely unrelated to the room incident, Chika had merely given up on me?

Had I said something I should not have last time? No, my words couldn't have been unwanted when she didn't even understand them.

The flames of anxiety took a million fiery forms in my heart. I couldn't let myself even imagine that we might never meet again. I think I was successful, to some extent.

I knew it would do nothing but wear me down, but every night as I opened the door, I prayed with every fiber of my being and my whole heart that I would see her there. Thus, when I finally saw the lights of her eyes one night, I practically collapsed onto the bench, slamming my hands when I sat down with unnatural force.

"Oh, sorry," I quickly apologized, not wanting her to worry for my physical health. If anything, I was filled with relief right now. I was sure there was a bit of joy somewhere in my tone.

"It's fine," Chika said, but nothing more. I wish I'd had the subtlety to sense something from her tone, and perhaps I normally would have, but that day I was overwhelmed with a sense of relief and joy.

"I've been worried about you," I said. "Glad you're safe though. Something came in through the window of my room, so I was worried that you'd been hurt."

"I'm fine."

She wasn't facing me. I thought nothing of it.

"I'm super glad."

She ignored my words. There are limits to a person's stupidity, but it wasn't until I noticed how little she was speaking today and leaned forward, peeking at her invisible face, that I was finally stricken with a sense of unease. I could not immediately place where that unease came from, but when Chika noticed what I was doing and turned toward me, I finally knew.

"Chika, what's wrong with your eyes...?"

"Huh?"

"The lights in your eyes are *dim*."

It was as I said. Looking closely, the light of her eyes appeared fainter than usual. It was the sort of color shift you'd expect from someone quickly wiping up some fluorescent paint.

She reacted oddly to this, turning away from me almost immediately. Then, as though she realized there was no point in hiding what I had already noticed, Chika looked back at me. I could sense her emotions just from the movement of her eyes.

"It's fine. They'll be back to normal soon."

"Wait, so did you get hurt?"

Though somewhere deep down I was hesitant to ask, when I thought of how she had averted her eyes, worry won out.

"Hurt...? Well..."

Her words came slowly, a second between each of them, and I suddenly deeply regretted that I had asked at all. At a certain point, I almost said, "Never mind, it's fine," but I was beaten to the chase.

"Kaya, when people cry in your world, do their eyes swell up?"

"Ah, yeah."

"That's...that's what this is."

She had been crying. However, tears weren't always caused by grief. As I listened to her, before I could feel sympathy or worry, I imagined the sight of tears rolling down her cheeks, reflecting the light from her eyes. It was beautiful. But I soon regretted those thoughts when I realized that these might be tears of deep sadness.

"Was anything broken in your room?" I asked.

She did not immediately reply. The amount of time between a question and an answer was a good indicator of the answerer's intentions. I could only wait. The unusually fragile lights of her eyes seemed to quiver silently.

"Your room..." she said.

"Hm?"

"Your room was fine besides the window?"

"Ah, yeah. It just shattered, so it was fine."

"I see. Well then, I have no idea how these effects work. It's gone."

What was gone? Someone? Something? As I searched for a reply, before I could even ask, she clarified.

"My room...is gone."

"...What?"

"There was...nothing left."

"When you say 'nothing'..."

She wasn't exaggerating, was she? If so, I was stunned to hear that the damage had been so extreme—especially when so little had happened to my room.

I thought of a house I had once seen on TV that had burned to the ground in a fire, but I was sure that wasn't the right way to picture this. What could have happened? Was it raining airplane debris, like in my room? Was it the war? Had it burned down? Been destroyed? Ransacked?

I was staring at the side of Chika's face as I considered how to reply, so all of my shallow thoughts were washed away with the next surprise.

I knew now that Chika's cheeks and chin were the same as a human's were.

I had been picturing it all wrong: The lights were flowing. Her tears weren't reflecting the lights of her eyes. Rather, the light was falling with the tears. With every drop, the lights in her eyes grew ever-so-slightly dimmer.

"Chika," I said, though I had prepared no words of comfort or courage. I merely feared the silence. She turned her face to me. I had been the one to say something, so I had to take the initiative to speak. "Can I ask what happened?"

"...Sure."

She had more than enough reason to refuse this, but she nodded and explained.

As expected, it was the war.

Lately, the wars had been spreading to the region Chika lived in, which was not normally used for skirmishes. This was why those career soldiers had died nearby around the same time that Allumi died, as she had mentioned. The fighting had suddenly made it to her house. Chika hadn't been given any details and hadn't been able to find much out. It was only a rumor, but from what she'd heard, the soldiers of her country had been using weapons that prioritized killing the enemy over protecting the livelihoods of their citizens, so they'd done extensive damages to the residences. When she exited the safe house she'd been in at the time, Chika returned home to find her room with the wall blown in, the interior destroyed.

"I wonder if someone might have used it as their hiding place during the fighting."

I meant to say that perhaps it wasn't on purpose, perhaps it had helped save someone's life, that maybe she was just lucky that the fighting hadn't made it to her home before, but still...

"Whatever."

Her whisper sounded like a scream, like if she didn't stifle it, she might rip herself apart in her grief.

"My whole world is gone."

Another droplet of light spilled down from the weak light of her eyes and dripped from her chin.

I couldn't say anything at first. I simply didn't know what to say. I had never lost anything that important, never lost my whole world. Losing Allumi might have come close, but at least I had come back from that.

It broke my heart. I felt horrible pain in the face of such immeasurable grief. Still, there was no point in telling her that I was hurting along with her when there was no way I could possibly empathize, so I repressed it as best I could. Hopefully she wouldn't be able to tell from my expression or tone.

What could I say to her? What could I do?

I thought about it, but no matter what I did, I couldn't give Chika her room back, nor could I give her back the world that had existed inside it. I wished I knew even just one thing that Chika might want, but no matter what I gave her, it would do nothing to cover the stain of her grief.

I was utterly powerless.

"Still, I'm glad you're safe."

I thought I could be forgiven for saying that much, but I soon realized I was fundamentally mistaken. A war was not a natural disaster. It wasn't the sort of thing that was unavoidable no matter what humans did. It was born of human stupidity. There was no reason for it to happen in the first place. It wasn't the sort of thing where you could be happy as long as you were safe.

Moreover, for Chika, the only thing that truly counted as living was getting to enjoy the things she loved. Simply making it out alive meant nothing.

"Please don't die, Chika."

My fears burst through my chest, spilling out as words. Before I had a chance to regret them, Chika shook her head.

"I won't die," she said. Even without seeing her expression, I knew there was little resolve to that denial. "But now, I don't know where I'm supposed to *live*."

Neither did I. How could I, when I still didn't even know where I could live or even what the point was?

"I'm sure you aren't in the mood to think about it right now, but can your room be rebuilt?"

"I...I don't really know the details, but it seems like repairs are going to be a problem for a while because of the war. I'm staying at the house of a nearby ×××× right now, but when you have somewhere to stay, the government tends to put off doing repairs. It's stupid, right? This isn't *living*."

"What about your room at the place you're staying now?"

"I don't have one. They said we don't need our own rooms just to live."

The sadness of losing her world, the despair of seeing that world swept up in circumstances she could do nothing about... those emotions stained her words, deep and heavy.

I thought, and the thoughts struck my heart so hard I felt it might shatter.

How wonderful it would be if we were in the same world right now, if I could actually reach my hand out and save her. If only I were in her world and could stand beside her in the face of the destruction—even if I couldn't rebuild her room, even if I couldn't stop the wars.

Delusions, fantasies, and daydreams were worthless.

Delusions, fantasies, and daydreams could never bring Chika's room back to life.

All we had was reality.

Right now, she and I were here, and living in our separate worlds. We couldn't travel to each other's worlds. Even if it were somehow possible, we still didn't know how. All we did know right now was that there were two worlds and that they somehow affected each other.

That was all...

"Hey."

A sound I'd never heard before started ringing in my head.

"If the war ended, could your house be fixed?"

"I mean...if there was an obvious victory, the next war probably wouldn't start right away. Even if the war didn't end, maybe it could happen if it kept raining. But I'll be waiting a while for either the war to end or a monsoon to come."

It was just a question that had popped into my mind, but it gave me strength.

"Are there no other times when they stop the war?"

I worried that I might make her mad. I figured she might tell me not to insult her, or not to make light of someone else's problems, or not to try to sympathize when it had nothing to do with me.

"I guess when there's some illness running rampant amongst the fighters. Or..."

Still, the thought that I would do anything for Chika was real. There wasn't the slightest lie in my desire to repay Chika, the one who had saved me just by being there.

"Or when the siren hasn't rung."

"Right, you said it was basically sacred."

"It is. It rarely happens, but there've been a few times when the siren hasn't rung on time. Like you said, it's sacred, so there's no replacement for it, and when it's in bad condition, it takes some time to restore it. They don't have a war on those days."

"And what if the siren was broken?"

"It's protected, so breaking it would be impossible. But I read that it's super old and mechanically complicated, so it'd be fairly impossible to make a new one now."

"...I see."

A thought suddenly occurred. That thought grew into an intention. That's how people chose their actions.

"This might be it."

"Huh?"

This might just be it. Perhaps it all boiled down to this singular purpose.

"Something I can do."

"What are you...?"

"The reason our worlds are connected."

"Uh...*huh*?"

I ignored her bewilderment, blinded by the brilliant light that was shining from within me.

I immediately apologized and tried to play it off. I don't know if she was convinced, but she at least pretended to be. That was fine for now. I didn't want to get her hopes up pointlessly. I'd tell her next time. If what I was thinking was correct, we could rejoice then. And if I was wrong, we could just try to figure out a different tactic.

I thought that was how I felt, but I was only fooling myself. In truth, I *knew* that I wasn't wrong. I knew that this wasn't a delusion, or fantasy, or even a mere daydream.

If only. If only I could stop the wars in her world.

That would give meaning to all of this.

That was how strong my will was at that moment.

An impact—Chika had saved me from my despair, so I believed I could rescue her from hers.

Though maybe that was just my *hope*.

Breaking the siren.

If I could break the equivalent of the siren in this world, then I was sure there was a good chance the untouchable siren in Chika's world would break too.

I thought about the question of whether our shared influence was between Chika and myself or between the places we were in. That had become a hot topic of debate between us. I'd been a proponent of the place theory. But now that I considered the leg injury, the hole in the sock, and the most recent room incident,

I began to, rather haughtily, agree that it might in fact be the two of us that connected our worlds. If that were the case, then just as with Allumi, it should be simple for me to find this world's version of the siren.

There was only one thing that I heard, day after day, that governed my actions: The bell. The school bell.

I was afraid that I would be committing another sin by going through with this plan. Still, breaking the bell wouldn't kill anyone. On the contrary, doing it might save lives.

It would take me a day to get the tools together, then two more days to attempt to sneak into the school and observe the guards and the teachers who stayed late to do overtime. I was fully aware that I would be found, apprehended, and rebuked for this, so I should have just gone into action immediately, but the operation would be fruitless if I were interrupted before achieving my goal—I couldn't skimp on preparations.

I didn't see Chika again before the day of the mission. My days were cookie-cutter copies of one another. In the meantime, I investigated how to break broadcast devices, but I also looked into the punishments that had been given to idiots who had attempted similar things in the past.

Essentially, Chika was always on my mind, and that was all I could have hoped for. I hadn't the slightest illusion that what I was about to do was wrong. Still, I felt rather sorry for my family. My boring but well-meaning family had no idea that their weak-hearted son was about to cause a commotion at school. There would be, if nothing else, calls from the school, and harsh warnings, and the inquisitive gazes and distrust of this son would soon turn my family's way.

This was no cause for happiness.

Thinking about it, though, it was no different from what had happened with Allumi. Only in this case, the family being disrupted was my *own*. Humans lived by causing trouble for others, by hurting others. I had to accept that, move past it, and achieve what I set out to do.

All for the sake of something much more important.

"Thanks for the food," I said as I finished my dinner that night and stood up from my seat.

My mother replied with the standard response for when her children thanked her: "You're welcome."

I naturally returned an "mm-hmm," my brother's voice lagging slightly after. It was a perfectly routine day. I thought it strange that everyone was fine with carrying on every single day like this when no one truly found it entertaining.

"Oh, right, Kaya," my mother called just as I headed to my room. I looked back to see her gazing at me, mackerel nanbanzuke pinched between her chopsticks. The TV was switched off. Music flowed from the radio in the background. "I talked to your grandma on the phone today. She really wants to see you. She's worried about the war, but she still wants us to come out for Obon or something."

"I'll think about it."

"That's not really something you should have to think about," she said with a weary laugh, biting her mackerel. "It's good to show a little respect for your grandmother now and then."

Respecting my elders was not one of my top priorities, but I got the feeling that if my grandmother knew what I was about to do, she wouldn't want to see me anyway. I said "I'll think about it" once more, then started up to my room. I heard a "You must get that from me!" called out from behind me. While I was thankful to her for raising me, I had my doubts about how much heredity and DNA really defined a person.

After resting for an hour in my room, I went out, as always—empty-handed this time. I would be sneaking back out in the middle of the night when it was time for the mission to properly begin. I walked to the bus stop as I always did and confirmed that Chika wasn't there. Instead, I just sat silently alone in the shelter.

Well, not *just*: I was thinking about Chika. I wasn't thinking about who she was or about the reason I had met her. I was just thinking about *her*.

The time passed quickly, and I returned home without anything notable occurring. At the stroke of midnight, once silence had fallen in my home, I once more stepped out of my room, a bag full of tools on my back. The hallway was quiet. I wondered if my brother might still be awake, but there were no lights on in his room.

I made my way down the stairs and headed straight for the front door. I'd intended to set right out from there, but as I reached my foot out for my sneaker, something suddenly popped into my head.

I was lost. I hadn't accounted for this. However, just in case there was even the slightest possibility, I turned toward the living room. There, by my family's usual gathering spot, was my radio from elementary school. I picked it up and headed back to the front door. This time, I put my sneakers on and slipped out the door, careful not to wake my family.

I had a feeling someone was going to call out from behind me, but this turned out to be a groundless fear. I stepped outside and locked the door.

The night air slowly filled my lungs. My body felt light. That feeling raised my spirits even more.

I put the backpack and radio into my bike basket and set off. Along the way, I stopped by a dumping ground behind one of the abandoned houses. I smashed the old radio on the concrete, certain by how the parts flew out of it that it was broken. It made a loud sound, but I hadn't seen anyone else passing by. I once again mounted my bike.

It really was lucky for me that our high school was an older public school, its security systems not at all up to date. Obviously, breaking a window or something would instantly set off an alarm, but my work would be over in a flash. Specifically, I would climb over the back fence behind the first-floor broadcast room, smash a window, and break the broadcast equipment.

That was all there was to it.

I was fully prepared to face the alarms and the security cameras; I didn't intend to run from my crime. I was doing this for someone important to me. There was nothing to be ashamed of. It was fine if what I was doing was considered a crime in this world.

I hadn't even the slightest inkling that stopping the war in her world would stop the war in mine. That much didn't even matter to me. Instead, I moved my body, thinking only of Chika.

I followed the fence around the school and reached my intended destination. I parked my bike, took a small hatchet out of my pack, and flung it onto the school grounds, then hopped over the fence. I picked up the hatchet and checked my watch.

I had no idea if this would all go according to plan. I might even make some grievous error. Still, I was going to follow through. I couldn't help but feel elated.

I faced the window and readied my hatchet. I was not at all nervous about sneaking into the school at night, breaking a window, and doing something worse from there. There was one thing, only one thing in my heart right now. Something that excited me.

Something I desperately hoped and wished for.

I might just get to be Chika's hero.

Reflected in the window, under the moonlight, I saw my own bright smile.

And then, I brought the hatchet down.

You should never run when you're desperate to see someone, I felt. The delusion that my feelings would be dispersed through the vibrations of my body, my ragged breath, and my flowing sweat felt all too tangible. I breathed as shallowly as possible so as not to let my feelings escape with the carbon dioxide flowing past my lips.

Now I walked quietly to the bus stop where I always met with Chika. The only sounds I heard were my own footsteps and the branches rustling in the wind. I had abandoned my bike at the bus stop where I'd detained Allumi.

The plan had gone smoothly. I enacted it swiftly and ran. Of course, the school was probably in an uproar by now, and perhaps they already knew who the culprit was. Still, at that moment, that commotion was of no concern to me, nor this place.

By my reckoning, if the bell and the siren did in fact have some influence on one another, I didn't need to destroy it entirely.

The sock and the shoe.

The window and the whole room.

Allumi and the dozens of people.

There was clearly a difference between the destruction in this world and that in Chika's. A small bit of damage here became much larger there, destroying people and things. As for injuries, Chika's might've simply been more severe due to her physical strength and the surface area of her body.

This was naturally an optimistic assumption, but I believed it, baseless as it was.

My plan safely concluded, all I wanted now was to see Chika. While it was another optimistic assumption, I got the feeling I would be seeing her again very soon.

A tinge of ultramarine was spreading across the sky. I had never headed for the bus stop at this hour.

What would I say to Chika if she was there? I hoped she'd laugh. I hoped she'd be happy. Such were the thoughts that crossed my mind as I reached the bus stop. Wearier than I realized, I wrapped my fingers around the handle of the sliding door, then let go. I grabbed it once more and pulled the door straight open.

Chika was there.

"How...?"

Though I'd fully expected to see her, the question still slipped out of my mouth. How, at a time like this? How were my wishes already coming true? How?

"I really wanted to see you."

"Me too."

This was not a lie.

"I didn't think you'd really come, though," she said.

Neither did I.

I sat down on the bench. My thigh muscles were stiff, probably from pedaling at full tilt earlier. I looked at Chika. There was a different emotion in her eyes than usual. I couldn't read it clearly, but she seemed almost shaken.

"Kaya..." she started. Her voice was trembling. I wondered if something had happened to make her cry. As I worried over this, she blinked a few times and then uttered, "The siren...it broke."

All the strength flooded out of my body. The stiffness of my muscles, the nerves that I realized I'd been feeling, my anxieties and worries all fled from me at once, and I nearly collapsed on the spot, nothing left in my body to support me. However, something else soon filled my heart, propping me up like a backup power source, and my mouth moved.

"Good. It worked."

Chika's eyes went wide.

"Kaya, *you* did this...? Well, I mean...actually, I came here because I wondered if you *had*."

"Yeah, I did. My hypothesis was right. I broke something that corresponded to the siren before I came here."

"I hope...it wasn't anything too important?"

"No, it was something pretty trivial in this world, though I might get in a bit of trouble for it. There's a chance I might not get to come here for a couple of weeks. Still, I'm glad it worked."

Chika didn't blink.

"Will this stop the war?" I asked.

I saw her nod. That split second was the happiest of my life.

"There won't be any wars for a while, starting tomorrow. That's what we were told."

"What about your house?"

"They said that the damaged homes will be repaired while the fighting's off."

"I'm really glad to hear that."

My heart was filled with joy. Chika's room would be restored. Chika's *world* would be restored. Chika's reason to live would be restored. Chika wouldn't have to be sad. I was truly thrilled.

And yet...why did I hear neither relief nor joy in Chika's voice?

"Kaya."

Her voice was hoarse as she spoke my name. Why?

A worst-case scenario suddenly flashed into my head.

What if I had been overeager in my actions? I had broken the bell, aiming for the siren, without consulting Chika. But what if that siren—regarded as sacred in her world—was important to Chika? I had been assuming that Chika, who was interested in little outside of herself, wouldn't care about the sacredness of this bell, but what if I was mistaken?

Suddenly, I was overcome with worry.

"Wh-wha...what..." She seemed to have difficulty getting the words out, her lips perhaps trembling. I gulped audibly and waited for her to articulate. "Kaya."

"...Yeah?"

"What can I possibly do for you?"

What came from her were meaningless words, fully beyond anything I had predicted.

"Huh?"

"You did something to protect my world. What can I *possibly* do for you?"

She gave a long blink. A droplet of light fell from where her eyes were.

"No, uh, what? No, Chika, I'm sorry if I made you sad."

"I'm not sad."

Those words were the most powerful I had ever heard out of her mouth. But that didn't matter, as long as she wasn't sad.

"I'm glad, then."

"...Why? Why would you do that for me? Someone in a completely different world?"

For Chika, whose experiences I would never truly share, whose body I couldn't even fully see. As I thought about it, only one reason came to mind.

"Because I wanted you to be happy."

I heard her sharply inhale.

"Kaya."

"Yeah?"

"I'll do whatever you want."

I tilted my head.

"If there's anything at all you want to know about my world, I'll tell you. I want to pay back what you did for me in any way I can. Your precious kindness deserves some reward."

"Oh, I see."

I finally realized—she was *happy*. Moreover, she had said that I was precious to her. Could there be anything better than that? Her happiness had been my goal. Could there really be anything more?

There couldn't be.

Still, something was bothering me. There was one thing that Chika had gotten wrong. My actions were not kindness. They were nothing so forthright. I needed to make that clear. My strange elation couldn't be contained. It was bleeding into intoxication. My actions, and Chika's joy. Thinking about myself in that moment, later with a sober mind, still made me blush.

"Chika."

"Yeah?"

"I do have one request."

"Okay."

"I'd like to touch you, just a little."

"Huh? But that's nothing."

"That's all I want."

Chika, accepting but not fully understanding this request, nodded and stared at me. I rose off the seat and moved closer to her. We were two body widths apart, then one, and then we sat closer than we ever had before. We sat angled toward one another, and for the first time, our knees touched.

"If this gets uncomfortable, just say so."

I waited for her to nod, then gingerly stretched my right hand out toward her invisible body. Obviously, I was not so consumed by my own lusts that I would reach for where her chest or whatever would be, assuming her body had the same structure as a human woman's.

I merely wanted to confirm that she was there. And I wanted to make her certain of me.

I wasn't thinking that I wanted to make Chika happy with my kindness. I wasn't operating by a drive as vague as that.

I wouldn't fool myself anymore. I had done it because Chika was special to me. I treasured the things she said and the things she thought with every fiber of my being, and not simply because she lived in another world. In the end, this was nothing more than my own intentions, my own ego. I wanted to make that clear to myself as well. I wanted to drill into my own skull that any sense of justice and mercy I thought I possessed were all lies.

I brushed one of her small, shining nails with my fingertip.

I felt her hands, cold as ever. On what would be the backs of her hands if she were human, I felt humanlike tendons.

I traced up her hand with my finger, finding what must be her wrist. A little farther up, I felt a soft material. I thought at first it might be a long-sleeved garment, but the fabric was spread out, not encircling her arm.

"What kind of clothes are you wearing?"

"It's something that covers your whole body from the top down. It's called a ×××××. You might not have them in your world."

Perhaps it was like a robe or a cloak. Judging by the feel, it was light and soft.

"Seriously, if you don't like this, just say so."

"Okay. But I mean, I don't mind being touched by you."

I was both thrilled and terrified that she trusted me so much.

I tenderly gripped what was probably her arm through the clothes and moved slowly up. There was a bonelike protrusion midway, probably an elbow joint. From there, her arm got a bit thicker, and even farther up I found another bony protrusion, like a shoulder.

"So your bodies are the same as ours."

"Yeah. I can tell that from looking at you."

Her eyes narrowed in amusement. As far as I could tell, that meant she was smiling. Seeing this at such close range made my heart throb.

I had already achieved my goal. I could stop this now. But she didn't tell me to.

My fingers trailed toward her neck. When I reached where

her neck must be, I saw her eyes quiver slightly. I frantically pulled my hand away.

"What's wrong?" she asked.

"I thought you were upset."

"...You're so sweet, Kaya."

Her eyes narrowed again as she softly gripped the hand that had just been touching her. Then, she guided me to her neck, to the spot I had just reached, placing my hand there with hers, like she was taming some sort of adorable creature.

Her neck had a pulse, just like a human's. Even if her heart flowed with glowing blood, it was a sign of life.

She brought my fingers up to her chin. I felt the contour of her face. As I traced the edges, Chika laughed like she was being tickled. I felt the air of her exhalation on my fingers. I pressed one of them to her cheek, confirming it was there but careful not to stab her with my nail, before following it with my palm. Her cheek took the warmth of my palm. Though we were in different worlds, we could share heat.

Chika *was* there.

"Hey, Chika."

I couldn't think of a single excuse for my actions—not that there was something in the air, or that I was drunk, or that my lips were speaking all on their own.

"What is it?"

Even if I didn't say a thing, I was sure that my body temperature would convey my feelings. I steeled myself, wanting to make my intentions known.

"I doubt you'll understand this, and I don't intend to make you understand it. There's something I'd like to say though. Sorry in advance."

She probably wondered at first what I was talking about. Still, Chika saw me as a treasured friend, so she put her own hand atop mine on her cheek and said, "Tell me."

How much courage could I possibly muster here?

"Chika, I like you."

"Yeah, I like you too, Kaya."

"That's not what I mean."

Rather that tilt her head, she moved her palm just slightly.

"I think we talked about this before. In my world, there's a concept called romance. It's different from friendship, different from family. To be honest, I don't think I could even fully define it for you. It's not the extension of some other feeling. I don't even know if it even has a clear connection with sexual attraction. But whatever it is, I feel it in my heart, right now." I swallowed here because I was afraid to even breathe. "I like you in a way that qualifies as romantic. That's why I wanted to touch you. But that's something you can't understand, just like how sometimes I can't hear the words you say. I'm sorry. That's why I wanted you to hear me out."

I have no idea how pitiful my face looked then.

"Sorry for being so selfish."

Chika stared at me from up close. I didn't have the awareness to fully tell what this girl was thinking when I could only see her eyes. Was she shaken? Was she afraid in the face of this unknown emotion? Or was she consumed by some other negative feeling that didn't even exist in my world?

I could ponder it all I wanted, but I would never know the truth. All I could do was wait.

I stared into Chika's eyes.

"Kaya."

Never before had I been so nervous to hear someone speak my name. Our eyes remained locked.

"Teach me how to kiss."

As I'd felt just once before, my heart gave a single, echoing throb.

"Wha...?"

"I'm sorry. Like you said, I can't understand this rohmanse thing."

"Uh-huh."

"No matter how strong of an emotion it is, there's no way for me to comprehend it. But I want to cherish that feeling, the way you do. So teach me. People kiss each other when they're having rohmanse, right?"

I was suddenly shamefully lost.

"Well, I mean, um, kissing is..."

"When you put your lips together, right?"

"I mean it is, but..."

She didn't take her eyes off me.

"So how do I do it?"

"Um, I mean, you don't mind doing that?" I needed to get that much out of the way. "If you're forcing yourself to do this to pay me back because I broke the siren, then please don't bother."

"I'm not," she insisted. "We don't have a practice of putting our lips together, so I don't have any feelings toward it to force myself through. I'm doing this because I value you and your feelings. But we don't have to do this if *you* don't want to."

Saying this, she moved her hand off mine and down to her knee, entrusting herself to me.

This was a concept that didn't exist in her world, a practice fully unknown to her, so I could have come up with any reason I wanted to get out of it. But I could no longer run from my feelings for her, and I didn't want her to think even the slightest bit that I'd lied by refusing her now.

No, even that was an excuse.

I wanted to touch her. I wanted to get as close as I possibly could.

I wanted to know how her lips felt. I was intent on doing this. My warning that I was about to start caught in my throat, and I could not speak.

First, with the position of her eyes as a guide, I moved my fingers from her cheek, looking for her nose. I noticed my fingers shaking.

"Is it scary?"

She could feel me shivering.

"Nah, um, no, but...I guess I am scared. I don't think I can come back from this feeling."

"Is not coming back from it a bad thing?"

"Not as long as you're here."

"Well, I *am* here."

I could tell her face was moving as her eyes narrowed. My fingers slipped down from her nose and alighted on something soft. I felt that something soft flex as her eyes returned to their usual roundness. It was probably the corners of her mouth rising and returning to normal. At first, I was simply glad to know that Chika's expression was in fact a smile, desperately holding back the feeling of something strange welling up in the corners of my eyes.

"Is here, on your lips, okay?"

"Yeah."

"Okay then, close your eyes."

The two lights immediately disappeared. The only thing before my eyes now was darkness. Still, I felt her. She was *definitely* there.

From the outside, this would have been a ridiculous scene, but that didn't matter. All we needed was what was true and real to us.

"What should I do with my mouth?" she asked.

"Just keep it closed. You don't have to close it tightly though, just relax."

"This feels like when I'm sleeping."

All sense of intention disappeared from my fingertips. By tracing the softness, I could tell that her lips were the same shape as a human's. There was a slight gap between the top and bottom, not closing entirely.

"Should I stay still?"

"Yeah, just wait. Just like that."

If I said something as ridiculous as "Just wait for my lips," I would have laughed in my own face. It would've been a forced laughter to ease my own nerves, of course...and I couldn't actually laugh in that moment.

I felt my heartbeat grow louder with every pounding pulse. I worried that this tension might even spread to my lips. Nervous as I was, though, I didn't intend to stop at this point. I cast aside the logical version of myself that was certain that if I stepped onto the slippery slope of intent, desire, love, and then lust, I might be dragged all the way down it.

"Okay then. Um, if you do hate it..."

"I'm fine," she said, cutting me off, and I said not another needless word. I was afraid I would lose my resolve if I spoke again.

I moved the middle and ring finger of my right hand, which had been on her lips, to her cheek. Of course, I couldn't find her lips without a landmark, so I kept my palm on her chin, touching my thumb to the corner of her mouth.

"Teach me how to kiss," she had said. There was no point in trying to explain it. I just had to do it.

How to kiss.

Wait, how *did* you do it?

It wasn't as though I had no experience, but thinking about it, I had never once actively thought about the methodology of kissing. Should I aim for her top lip or bottom? Which of my own lips should make contact first? How forcefully and for how long?

I honestly had no idea how to kiss.

It probably didn't help that I had never proactively done it. I thought hard, but I really had no idea. I couldn't stand around keeping her waiting forever though. Simply having knowledge and experience of something was hardly any different from flat-out not knowing about it at all. Still, it was a bit late for dwelling on what I did and did not know.

I lowered my head and took a deep breath. I looked once more to the place where Chika's face would be and brought my own face closer. What shape was I supposed to make with my mouth, again? Chika had said it was like being asleep. I'd go along with that.

I swallowed my spit and relaxed my lips. A small gap formed between them. Keeping position with my thumb, I moved in slowly. I tilted my head slightly so as not to run into her nose.

Both of us were already perfectly silent, wordless.

I wondered what she was thinking. Maybe she found this interesting as an artifact of a foreign culture. I hoped she felt something more than that, even if it was just nerves. I hoped that she felt the same way as me. My own nerves and my raging heartbeat were threatening the still darkness around us. I ignored the sound of the watch on my left wrist.

And then...we touched. Our upper lips collided.

Chika's lips moved slightly on reflex. I held back a moment, but she didn't seem to reject it, so I chose to believe that—as she had said before—she was all right with this.

We took a breath together.

We moved from just touching our upper lips to fitting a bit closer together until our lower lips touched as well.

My whole body went numb. For several seconds, I was frozen in that position. I could feel her heat close by. At the tips of my lips, I felt a distinct warmth and moisture.

With all my strength, I slid my bottom lip from Chika's, poking at her top lip. Chika gave not the slightest reaction. All I could feel were her lips, distinct from the rest of her face. The slick sensation sent electricity through my body again.

I could give only the tritest of impressions.

Her lips...were sweet.

There was nothing on the tip of my tongue, but I knew I was picking up on some sweetness.

Her lips parted slightly. I wondered if this was the right time.

To be honest, I hated to think that it was already over. This was our last time together in this place after all, now that the siren was broken. Still, I didn't want to annoy her. Softly, I pulled my lips, which were pinched gently around her upper lip, away. In this midst of this, I had already taken my hand from her face to remove the insistent watch from my wrist and place it atop the bench.

I looked at where her face should be, subtly took a deep breath, and waited until the two lights appeared as though surfacing from underwater. Nothing I wanted to say felt like it would come out right, so I just waited for her response. My heart still raced.

How did she feel about this new experience? Not as a member of a species that practiced kissing but as someone who had feelings for Chika, I just hoped that she didn't find it uncomfortable.

"There was a bit of suction, huh?"

Those were the first words from the lips I had just been touching. I felt my heart racing overtime, pumping blood up to my face. Including her comment that it was like when you're sleeping, Chika had ended up teaching *me* how to kiss. How utterly pitiful.

"How was that, Kaya?" she asked.

How was it?

"Um, well, I doubt it would make sense to you, but I'm happy." I answered as earnestly as I possibly could, knowing that she wouldn't fully understand me. Even so, I was glad we still had time before dawn. "As long as it wasn't unpleasant for you, I'm glad."

"It wasn't. It just felt strange. It was like when you get too excited hugging a friend and your faces collide, but you were doing it carefully, lovingly."

Of course I'd never embraced anyone I'd call a friend, so that was beyond my experience.

"Are there any rules to it? Or routines?"

"No, I don't think so. But what we did just now is what they call a 'kiss' in my world."

"There's no set time or force?"

"No, not really."

"Even I could probably do it, then."

"Hm? No, uh..."

I realized that my explanation had been lacking. She seemed to have misunderstood me somewhere.

Getting close and pushing your lips against someone else's was called kissing. But she must've thought that the person on the receiving end wasn't kissing just because those actions were performed upon them. Just as hurting someone and being hurt were different, there was a clear distinction between kissing and being kissed. That was very likely her train of thought. In other words, she probably assumed that she still hadn't kissed anyone yet.

"Kaya, would you bring your face closer?"

And now, knowing that there were no strict rules, she seemed to believe that she too could perform this kissing that she had just been taught. I had even told her that it made me happy.

"Does it mean anything to cup someone's cheek?"

"No, I was just using it as a landmark since I can't see your lips."

"I wonder if I've got the right impression of it, then. Could you lean in this way a little bit?"

It was sneaky of me, but I did exactly as she said. I hesitated to tell her that the one who receives the kiss was an equal part of the action.

Her body, and her lips, drew nearer. I knew what was about to happen. I pretended to be surprised.

"Okay, Kaya."

"Okay."

"Close your eyes."

She had probably mistaken this for a rule as well. Not bothering to correct her, I shut my eyes.

All my attention was focused on my lips, so I was genuinely surprised by the first sensation that came to my body. A soft, familiar material grazed my neck, then something thin came down in the space between my neck and shoulders. I realized it was her arms.

I didn't open my eyes, but not because of any rule—because I hated the thought of Chika stopping. Just as a child might try not to wake from a dream, my eyes stayed firmly shut.

I felt her hands clasp behind my neck. She strengthened her grip, and I relinquished myself to the gentle pull toward her. Slowly, second by second, she overlapped her lips with mine, gently, as though to seek confirmation that she wasn't doing something wrong.

Soft and sweet.

After we were firmly pressed together, she slid her bottom lip up to touch my upper. I swiftly realized that she was imitating me. This meant that it would be over soon, I thought to my dismay. The first time, I had resigned myself to it.

Why couldn't I do so a second time?

Before her lips left from mine, I pecked gently back at her bottom lip. Then, as if imitating me, she moved her lips and nudged back. I did the same again and got the same response. As we repeated this again and again and again, something like saliva got mixed in. Realizing this, I pulled away slightly.

"Chika...!" I said, still close enough that my trembling voice made her lips quiver. My eyes were still shut.

"Yeah? What?" Her voice, which seemed to course through the arms still wrapped around my neck, made my heart and brain shudder.

"I realize that no matter how many times I say it, you won't understand what it means when I say I like you."

I lowered my voice, even though there was no one around to hear us.

"Uh-huh?"

"I know there's nothing we can do about that, but it still makes me sad. So it's selfish of me, but I'm never going to forget the way that I feel about you right now. Even if the feeling fades, or blurs, or we one day stop seeing one another, or even if I die and become nothing but a ghost, I will never, ever forget what I feel in my heart in this moment. Please forgive me."

All I had ever dreamed of was having something special, immutable. For my dreary days never to return. Now I had that here inside of me, and so I let her know.

"I forgive you," she said. "And I'll never forget you sharing a special feeling from your world with me. I don't understand rohmanse like you do, but I'm glad that you feel such a significant way toward me, and that's the truth."

"Why aren't we in the same world, Chika?"

"I don't know. But...I hope we can cross that border one day."

We could not live together.

"Chika."

"My dear, dear Kaya."

We could not be together forever.

"I like you, Chika."

"I know."

I didn't know if she even fully understood me.

I didn't even know her real name.

All we could do was affirm one another's existences here in this intersection between our worlds.

There were people in that world who were closer to Chika than me.

There were people in that world who saw her more than I did.

There were people in that world who *understood* her better than I did.

I knew that all too well.

And yet, in this moment that we now shared, just being here, alive, I was more connected to her than anyone else. This I believed. It wasn't an over-assumption.

My eyes still shut, I wrapped my arms around where her back should be. She didn't resist as I hugged tighter, pulling her close. She held me tighter as well.

For the first time in my life, there was someone who I yearned to be so close to that our very beings would meld into one. And so I remained, until numbness overtook my whole body.

The war in my world showed no sign of stopping.

Perhaps because it had been summer vacation, or because they had mistaken me for someone who was usually very well behaved, the punishment I received after security camera footage identi-fied me as the culprit wasn't extreme: crafting a lengthy written apology, a week of house arrest, meeting with a school guidance counselor and an outside counselor as well. My father chewed me out thoroughly, and even my normally mild-mannered mother gave me a good slap. I worried that the slap might have some ill effect on Chika, but my mother's hand hadn't left a mark on me, so I figured it should be all right.

What I most regretted was that I could no longer go out shopping or running without being followed by the watchful eye of my family. My brother once caught me trying to sneak out in the middle of the night and stopped me, saying "You'll make mom sad again." As someone who had already brought shame upon my family, I was in no position to push my way through that.

Of course, it wasn't going out for runs that I was concerned about. What I wanted was to see Chika.

In the aftermath of that night, we decided some things about the future. Or rather, we were at least able to establish that while the war was off, Chika would have limited opportunities to visit the safe house. Realistically speaking, we did not know when the siren would be restored, and when the war would come thundering back into her life. As such, it was probably best that she spend her days getting her fill of a life free of any need to visit the safe house. Even so, I was glad to hear her say that she would still come here, wanting to see me, even if it was out of nothing more than consideration for my feelings.

I intended to simply bide my time quietly at home as though nothing had happened, but at one point when I was alone with my mother, four days after she had first raged at me, her anger over what I had done suddenly boiled up once more. I had been in the kitchen at the time, drinking some milk.

"Kaya."

The radio in the corner of the room, dramatically better-sounding than its predecessor, was crooning.

"Maybe I'm off the mark here, but it doesn't seem like you've reflected on your actions at all."

For supposedly being off the mark, that was a surprisingly straight pitch.

"I have been. I feel bad for causing you trouble."

"But you haven't reflected on breaking something of the *school's*, have you?"

I really hadn't. I did know that I'd done something bad, but if I had to do it all over again, I would do the same thing without fail. I didn't suppose that really counted as reflection. Still, immediately shaking my head at this would worry my mother all the more. As I thought about how to answer, she let out a sigh.

"If you haven't been reflecting on your actions, does that mean there's something you were trying to protect by doing that?"

"Yeah...there is," I answered honestly.

"I don't know what it is, but you're obviously certain of whatever you were doing."

"I am."

It seemed my mother understood me much better than I'd expected. Still, even genetics or blood did not connect us all the way down to our souls.

"You can't let yourself have such strong convictions that you convince yourself it's all right to hurt others over them."

As I sat there, not replying, the DJ on the radio began playing a new song—as if to fill the silence that stretched between my mother and me.

"It might be impossible to avoid hurting others when you've really put your heart behind something, but if you go around intentionally causing people harm, someday you're going to end up hurting the things that you treasure, the beliefs that you're trying to protect. Those who can easily hurt strangers to help their family will one day hurt that same family to help themselves. And in the end, even they get hurt. I'm just worried you're going to end up that way."

"I see." So, that was what she was getting at. "But that's why I feel bad about causing trouble for you."

"Listen..."

As she stood there, heaving a great sigh, I stood up to put the milk back in the refrigerator. I truly did feel bad about making trouble for her, but my mother knew nothing about Chika or her world. There was no way she could possibly understand why I had done what I'd done. Even if I told her that it was something worth even hurting people over, she wouldn't understand me.

Plus, I had already hurt something important for my own goals, and I was learning from it, even without her trying to explain it to me. This lecture was dull and pointless.

"You realize, Kaya, I'm not going to live forever."

Her words caught me from behind just as I moved to return to my room. *That's obvious,* I thought. Everyone dies someday. That's just natural.

That was the last time my mother and I spoke face-to-face.

The morning my week-long grounding ended, I flew out of the house like a racehorse out of the starting gate. It took me some time to get back into my jogging rhythm, but I thankfully hadn't fallen out of shape at all. My body craved running as strongly as it did food.

Chika wouldn't be around in the daytime, so it felt pointless to go to the bus stop. But I wasn't interested in seeing anyone I knew and getting weird looks, so I headed off into the mountains. Hydrating myself as I ran, I soon reached my usual spot. I was relieved to see that the bus stop was there as always. It obviously wouldn't up and vanish, but just seeing with my own eyes the place that put my heart at ease gave me the strength to pick up running once more.

By the time I got home, I was drenched with sweat, so I took a shower, changed my clothes, and ate some somen that my mother had made. The afternoon went roughly the same way, and before I knew it, it was nighttime. My family gave me dirty looks about going running after dinner, but they permitted me to leave under the conditions that I come home early, keep away from the school, and take my phone with me. At the very least, I didn't *intend* to outright violate any of these.

It being August, even the evening breeze was not particularly comfortable. I felt my back prickling with sweat as I made my way down the road to the bus stop. I sipped from the water bottle my mother had made me take to avoid dehydration.

I had no idea if Chika would be there, but just the possibility of a reunion made my heart leap. An expectant, bashful nervousness coursed through me. If she wasn't there, there was nothing I could do about that. While I was aware of this, somewhere deep down I was convinced that I would see her. The ridicule I lobbed at myself for acting like a basic, garden variety high school boy gave me a little more room to breathe. I wrapped my fingers around the door handle and opened it to see a set of lights that existed nowhere else in the world.

"Oh, Kaya! You're *here*."

The relief in her voice mirrored all the joy and reassurance in my own heart. I closed the door, vibrating with shameful anticipation at the thought that she was actually happy to see me.

"Sorry I haven't been coming here," I replied, then I looked at the bench. I wondered how close I ought to sit, but eventually my reason won out and I sat down at the normal distance from her. "I was stuck in my house. The school punished me, like I said would probably happen. Sorry if you came here while I was gone."

"I came a few times, but it's fine. I was worried it might be a long time before I saw you again, so I'm just so happy you're here."

I wanted to tell her that it made me happiest of all just to hear her say that, but my shyness stole my words. I had not yet lost enough reason that I could just do whatever my id told me, as I had last time. Yes, *that* time. My cheeks grew hot in the darkness.

"Sorry to make you worry. Any news about the war?"

I noticed then that all the light was back in her eyes.

"They still haven't given an estimate for when the siren will be fixed. It's slow going, but my house is being rebuilt. It's all thanks to *you*."

"I mean, I wouldn't say that, but I'm glad nonetheless."

I'd felt guilty the entire past week. Though she didn't see it that way, the last time we met I had more or less used breaking the siren as a pretense for touching her, so it felt bad to receive too much gratitude for it. Still, I was happy that she was happy.

"So what did you do while you were stuck at home?"

"Nothing in particular. I wrote an apology and did some strength training. Oh, right, my mother hit me—did anything happen to you?"

"She *hit* you? Like, she was violent toward you? Nothing happened to me, but are *you* okay?"

"Oh, yeah, it didn't really bother me, and it was my fault anyway."

"Glad you're all right, then."

It was clear from her tone that she was worried, which I felt bad about. I needed to change the subject.

"So what have you been up to?"

"I've been helping with the house repairs and collecting things to put in my new room when it's done, like some books and that scent thing I brought here before."

"Oh, nice. I know I won't get to see your room, but it's still exciting."

I was glad to hear her have some optimism about her world again. Like I said, I would never get to see it, but I was excited to know that her world was being rebuilt.

"Did anything else happen?" I took a swig from my water bottle while I waited for her reply.

"Let's see... I was thinking about that kiss."

I sputtered, wasting water and choking as some of it flowed into a part of my body where water should not go.

"Kaya, you all right?"

"Guh, sorry, sorry. I'm fine."

It should have been obvious, but of course I was the only one who was embarrassed. It could be easy to forget which of our practices and contexts weren't shared.

"Wait, is it weird to go around thinking about kissing during normal life in your world?" she asked.

Was it?

"I mean, I don't think it's really all that weird. My water just went down the wrong way."

What a lame recovery, I thought.

"Please try to drink a little more slowly."

"Already done."

"Anyway, I was thinking about the kissing and, well, you said that it's something that people do as a means of expressing the emotion called rohmanse, right?"

"Yeah. Usually, anyway."

"Well, I was kind of worried that for me to kiss you when I have no idea about rohmanse might be considered rude in your world." She blinked once, slowly. "What I said before, that I want to cherish your feelings as much as you do, is true. That's why I asked you about kissing—because I wanted to understand more about rohmanse, even just a little. But I started wondering if I was being rude and you only went along with it because you're so nice. I'm really sorry if that's true."

"It wasn't rude," I immediately, firmly declared. There was a surprising strength to my tone. I had no idea that *she* had been worried about what we did.

I thought it over again and realized that *this* was what it meant to be part of two such utterly incompatible cultures. When you want to show off your own culture, sometimes you might end up ignoring the other person's viewpoint, and when you try to respect their culture, you might worry that they find everything you're doing incredibly strange. It was quite the delicate situation.

It was why wars persisted. But that much was lucky for me. It gave Chika and I a perspective we could share.

"It wasn't rude at all. In fact, I was worried that I took advantage of your gratitude to ask for something that doesn't exist in your culture and made it weird."

"I didn't dislike it at all. My gratitude then, and now, was completely genuine. Even if I can't understand it, I'm glad that I got to share something with you thanks to this rohmanse thing."

"I...I see. I'm glad too."

All I could do was blush.

"I'm really glad I wasn't being rude," she said.

"Sorry to make you worry. I really don't think there's anything you could do that would bother me."

All that said, it did make me happy that Chika had been worried about the same sort of thing I was. I knew there were differences in the ways we felt, but because we understood so little about each other's alien cultures, we were both trying our best to make sense of them.

"That's good. Um, well then, if you don't mind it, there are some more things I'd like to know about rohmanse."

"Sure, I can tell you anything I know," I said, then immediately wondered how much I *did* know.

"Rohmanse is like a feeling of wanting to get closer to someone, right? So I was thinking the practice of kissing must be a way to get as close to the other person's body as possible?"

"Something like that, I guess. I don't know the origins of kissing, but that sounds plausible. I feel like that's a big difference between romance and friendship, that it makes you happy to be both emotionally and physically close."

"Do you feel that way?"

"I do."

"Then let's get close."

As she said this, Chika's lights moved up high. Before I could react, she got close to me, sitting at my side so close our shoulders touched. As she sat down, our knees touched, whatever garment she was wearing sandwiched in between them.

"Is this bad?"

"N-no, not at all!"

Of *course* it wasn't bad. I was too shy to look her in the eye from this distance, though, so I turned to the front. What I assumed to be one of her arms was adjusting to the heat of mine.

"Since you first touched me, I've been thinking about how warm you are," she said.

"I did think you were a bit colder than people from my world."

"My body temperature isn't especially low, so I guess we're just colder overall."

Though we couldn't convey taste or smell, heat got through just fine. I tried to keep my heart in check as I wondered what that difference might mean.

"My body heat might be a bit higher than usual."

"Is it? I'd love to be able to confirm that, but since you're the only one I can see here there's no one else I'd be able to touch at the same time."

Even if there was someone else who could see Chika, would I really be able to go along with that? I supposed I might have considered it in the past, but only before I realized my romantic feelings.

"Right," she continued, "if you wanted, I could try bringing someone else here with me next time, so we can find out whether you can see them? We might be able to tell if I'm the only one you can see."

This proposal was the next logical step of our conversations, and by all rights it was something that we probably should've tested out, but I shook my head.

"No," I said. "Seeing you is enough."

What I said was true, but behind those words was the sinking feeling that Chika still didn't see me as her one and only. I suppressed the feeling lest it show on my face.

"If you ever do want to try, just let me know. I offer this only because I'm so grateful for all that you've done. But the part of me that treasures you feels the same way. As long as I can be with you, that's enough for me."

Any petty thoughts within me were painted over by her words. What simple creatures we were, those of us who knew of romance. Chika didn't know the first thing about romantic love, and yet every single word she chose seemed to perfectly reflect my feelings. Or perhaps it was *because* she knew nothing that she was able to speak words that would delight a person in love without shame. There were so many words that I couldn't say to her because I knew of the love I felt inside my heart.

Putting all that aside, though, I didn't want to deny Chika's feelings of gratitude, so I offered a counterproposal. I'd been thinking about it while we were apart.

"Well then, let me ask something of you instead."

"Sure."

"I want you to draw me a picture."

"Huh? But that didn't work when we tried it before."

I had in fact brought a pen and notebook with me once, thinking I could get Chika to write down her language and the words that I couldn't hear. As Chika said, it had failed. She couldn't hold my notebook or pen.

"Well, when I tried to hand you that pen, it just fell on the ground. But remember how we were able to eat the food when we gave it to each other directly? I figure if you hold the pen while I'm also holding it, it should work."

"I see. That might be good to try. But you don't want to try words like last time but a picture."

"Yeah. There's something I want you to draw."

"What?"

It was impossible to know whether asking for this would be rude or not, so I was prepared to say I was sorry if she found it offensive. "A self-portrait."

"Hmm..."

"Ah, never mind," I apologized, almost on reflex. As I turned to her, the first time I had ever done so from this distance, she tilted her eyes curiously. I already knew we were close, but the distance still stunned me.

"Why are you apologizing?"

"Well, I..."

I wasn't sure I could explain this, even if I was in my right mind. If I thought too hard about it, I certainly wouldn't be able to, so I gave her the first answer that came to my lips.

"I just thought it might be rude of me. I've developed feelings for you without even knowing what you look like, so it seems weird to ask for a self-portrait just so I can try to form a mental image of your appearance."

"I see. But I mean, that's not why I didn't agree immediately. You really don't need to apologize to me, for multiple reasons."

"Multiple?"

She lowered her gaze, hesitant. I wondered if there was some major reason why she couldn't draw a picture. Had I asked something rude of her without even realizing it? I waited for her reply, worried, when she finally moved her invisible lips, still looking away.

"Well...I'm actually *really* bad at drawing, so I don't think a self-portrait would even start to capture any of my actual appearance. I don't think I could manage a picture that would give you any real impression."

"Not at all?"

"I really don't think so."

"Heh."

I know it was rude of me, but I couldn't help but let out a compounding laugh, both at how cute it was that the worldly Chika was so bad at drawing that she'd been worried about even admitting to it, and at my own mental picture of how bad she might actually be. Naturally, I did apologize, not wanting her to hate me.

"Sorry, I don't mean to laugh at your shortcomings. It's just that you were so *serious* about it."

I had apologized, but she continued to stare at me, silent, as though wounded. Crap, was she actually angry at me this time?

Still, her eyes seemed completely different from when I had heard her raise her voice in anger before. Certain that my intuition must be lacking again—as someone who'd never had a talent for reading people—I apologized once more.

"I really am sorry if I made you feel bad."

"It's fine, I don't. You'd probably just laugh more if you saw my drawings. That's not why I was quiet. I was happy."

"Happy?"

It would have been even more shocking to learn that Chika was the sort of person who enjoyed her own shortcomings being laughed at, but that wasn't it.

"That was the first time I've ever seen you smile. It made me happy."

"...Was it really?"

I was aware that I rarely smiled, but still, in all the time we had spent together, with the sense of fulfillment I had cultivated here, had I truly never *once* smiled?

"Yeah. As far as I can remember, anyway. I don't know how it is in your world, but here, seeing the smile of someone you treasure is a joyful thing. I was so happy at seeing it for the first time that I couldn't speak."

"I...I see. I'm not sure it's something so amazing in our world that it'd leave you speechless, but, yeah, seeing your smile makes me happy too."

I remembered how much joy coursed through my body when I'd been able to confirm that narrowing her eyes meant she was smiling. And now, though it wasn't enough to render me silent or reduce me to tears, I was happy to hear her say how much I meant to her as though it was natural.

"Well then, I'll make an effort to smile a bit more in the future."

"Don't force yourself, of course, but it does make me happy to see."

"I'll just try to keep it in mind."

For the first time in my life, I was aware of my own smile. What else might this lead to?

I wouldn't have any idea how bad Chika's drawings were until I saw them, and we had no idea if the experiment would even work in the first place, but we decided that I would bring a notebook and pen with me the next time I came.

Just then, my pocket vibrated.

There was no one outside of my family who had my contact info and would bother to use it. I knew without looking that it was my mother texting me "Time to come home" or something. I would normally just ignore this, but I already owed them a debt for all the trouble I had caused.

"Sorry, Chika, I have to get going."

"Rare to see you leave first."

That was true. I never wanted to be the first to go.

"Yeah, my family's calling me."

"I see. Hey, Kaya..."

Knowing that my time with Chika was ending, my tension melted away in proportion to my heightened sense of regret. This was the first time I realized how much emotional and physical strength it took to be with the person you liked. My regret was real, but there was also a moment of relief.

"What kind of times are you supposed to kiss someone?"

And yet, I found myself dragging that strength back at breakneck speed. I had started to look away, but she sucked my gaze right back in.

"What kind of times...? I guess...when the atmosphere and timing are just right."

"I don't get it."

We were struggling enough just to understand each other's cultures without trying to understand things like "the mood" too.

"Okay," she continued. "Are there any kinds of *feelings* that prompt it?"

"Well, whenever you want to do it, I guess."

Why do you eat? Because you're hungry. That was how stupid my answer sounded, but I had no idea how else to put it.

"Obviously I can't feel it, but do you mean, like, when your rohmantick feelings grow really strong? Like when you feel an especially strong love for your family and really want to hug them."

I had no idea. I'd never felt anything like that with my own family.

"I guess so. It's like when you love someone so much you can't help yourself."

"Kaya..."

I had never expected the flow of the conversation to go this way, but no part of me was capable of refusing her.

"How do you feel right now?"

My desire to be faithful to Chika's principles and my own selfish desire to be faithful to the love I felt were at odds with one another, so I continued to fret, unable to separate them. But in the end, I could only give an honest answer.

"Like I love you so much I can't help myself."

"Is there a limit to how many times you can kiss?"

"No."

She'd said that she didn't get it, but there they were, the timing and the atmosphere. If we both closed our eyes, it didn't matter if I couldn't see her or she couldn't see me. We found one another in that quiet darkness.

"Sorry for being so selfish," she said when we moved back to our original distance, echoing words I was sure I had once said myself. "I just wanted to increase the number. I thought that I might get more used to it, get better at it. But it feels like I'm just using your feelings."

It would be foolish and overblown to say that she had shot right through me.

"As long as you didn't dislike it, I don't mind."

In the end, I kept my foolish words to myself. Over and over again our lips intertwined as I stayed in her embrace, once more unable to divorce my consideration from my feelings, before I headed back home.

A honeymoon.

I knew the word, but never did I ever think it would actually come to mind. However, embarrassing though it might be, I doubted there was any word I could give that better described my time with Chika.

As summer turned to autumn, I obtained no new information of note. The two of us simply spent time together. Our time together tasted of honey, condensed from nectar gathered from so many different places and times, brought here to this secret hideaway.

The picture-drawing experiment had been a success. First, we had her hold the pen and notebook with her hands on top of mine, moving our hands together without pulling away from the items, and we managed to draw a picture. But even just thinking about the picture we drew makes me laugh, so I won't try to describe it.

I had her write some words too, but of course I couldn't read her language. Strangely, whenever she pulled the pen away from the notebook and I took my eyes off the page, all the lines that she had written down disappeared. Capturing it with my phone camera was equally fruitless. To be honest, I had already tried secretly recording her speaking, but all that was left on the recording was my own voice talking stupidly to long gaps of nothing. Unfortunately, it seemed that capturing any phenomena between worlds was impossible. I tried memorizing the shapes of the letters she had drawn and looking them up when I got home, but all I could determine was that it was no language that existed anywhere in our world.

In the end, all I had been able to ascertain via the notebook was that Chika did indeed look somewhat like a human woman and that the buildings in her world were also rectangular in structure.

Even though I had been the one to request this drawing and who wanted to see it, I was somehow relieved not to actually get any more details about her appearance. It gave me full confidence that such information was extraneous to the way I cherished Chika, girl of only eyes and nails.

Our days were joyful ones.

The usual eventual dearth of conversational topics that might usually occur between normal friends or lovers never happened with us. We never had to "make" conversation; being from different worlds, our whole lives were entirely foreign to one another, and our interest never waned. There was always some new tradition, some fascinating new philosophy, in every bit of information she told me. All these things and more I learned just from the sounds that came out of her mouth. It was a special time.

Chika always seemed to be picturing various things from my world when we spoke. It would be a bit grandiose to say that the proof was in the pudding, but time and again she demonstrated that she had realized things that I hadn't even told her, based solely on things I'd talked about and my appearance.

"I'm guessing there are times in your world when there are big shifts in the temperature?"

"The temperature? I guess it does change with the seasons."

"*Seezins* refers to a time period, right?"

"Yeah. Oh, do you not have seasons in your world? In this world, or at least in this country, we have four types of seasons. The season we're in right now is called autumn, and the one when I met you was called winter. It's cooling down a little bit from the hot season now, and when I met you it was cold."

"I see. That explains it."

"Explains what?"

"I'd noticed the number of clothing layers you wear and the thickness of them changing. We change our clothing based on whether we're in a place with a high or low temperature, whether it's raining or clear, whether the sun is up or down, and based on our jobs, but not with the passage of time. So I figured your world did have some big fluctuation of temperatures, like these seezins."

"Oh, we change our clothes for different locations too, but fundamentally that follows the seasons. Obviously I can't see it, but are you usually wearing the same sort of thing when you come here?"

"The colors and patterns are different, but we don't have as many different varieties as you all have."

"I don't really own that many styles, personally. When I come here, I'm always wearing clothes that are easy to move in. During the day, I'm usually in my school uniform."

I suddenly realized that my explanation here might be lacking, wondering if they had the concept of school uniforms in Chika's world, until she said, "That's something that you wear to school, right?"

"Yeah, do you have anything like that in your world?"

"No. We just wear our normal clothes."

Frankly, I was surprised. She seemed to have instantly extrapolated the function of a uniform based only on the fact that I went to school during the day and that I wore those clothes during that time. It made me happy to realize just how much of a force to be reckoned with she was, and that it seemed she thought of me even when we were apart.

"Are girls colder than boys in your world?"

"Hmm. I think it depends on the person. Is that how it is in your world?"

"I once read that women have lower body temperatures than men. I wonder how close they are, though."

"I know that women here usually do get colder."

"So it is true..."

"I'm guessing you assumed that my temperature is higher than yours because I'm a man, but I think I run hotter than even other guys because I get a lot of exercise."

"I see."

"Chika, are you cold?"

"No, I'm fine. I'm never cold when you're here."

Yes, we were close enough for her to feel that. Obviously, she hadn't planned to turn my bones to jelly, but sometimes intention and result are two wholly separate things. In that, we were the same.

There's a reason I say in *that*.

Though it was trivial at this point, we had established that on the organism level, we were two totally different things. One day, I had gotten a really good feel of her hair. This happened for no reason other than we had incidentally moved close to each other. Anyway, when I placed my hand on what seemed to be the back of her head, I was surprised to realize that I was touching her hair.

"What's the matter?"

"Is this all your real hair? Even from the part where it's tied back?"

"Yeah, it's real. Is it weird? Is it different from your hair?"

It was different.

Probing with my hand, I found that her hair was tied into what would probably be referred to as a ponytail in our world, but there was a clear difference between the texture at the top and where it was tied. Not only did no single hair of mine possess such a huge difference in texture along its span, but I was shocked at how peculiar the tips of her hair felt compared to the roots, which were already a bit stiffer than I'd expected.

If I were to compare the last ten-odd centimeters of her hair to the closest material that I knew of at the time, I would say that it was like soft, supple *wire*. I say wire, but it wasn't the sort of thing that would stay in any one defined shape. Like our hair, it bunched and curved and swayed. I had perhaps accidentally touched her hair before but not even realized it from its texture. However, I got the impression that if she wanted to stab someone with it, it might even pierce skin. Perhaps that was why she kept it pulled back.

Was there, in fact, anything in my world that resembled that texture?

"You don't have to touch it if it feels weird to you."

I suddenly deeply regretted taking the time to figure out how it felt to me, as I seemed to have caused her some undue concern.

"It's not like anything I've ever touched, but it's not unpleasant. I'm happy, actually. There are still parts of you that I don't know about."

I knew, of course, that there was still *plenty* of Chika that I didn't know about, but I was honest when I said that getting to know those parts little by little made me happier than anything. But although I hadn't conveyed it to her, there was more than that to my words. I was happy that I had found yet another new part of her to love.

"Could I touch your hair too?" she asked.

"Oh, of course."

Chika touched my hair, which I had put off cutting lately because of the cool weather. It was refreshing; it was the first time that being touched by someone actually put me at ease.

"It's soft all the way through. It feels nice. It really is *completely* different."

Yes, it was. Regardless of whether she was a completely different life-form, here we were, able to touch one another and try to understand each other.

It really didn't matter if she was a person or not.

That day we experienced the closest proximity of our two worlds.

A honeymoon.

It truly was one.

The word in Japanese, *mitsugetsu*, was originally a literal translation of the English word "honeymoon," referring to the first month of a marriage, a time like the sweetest honey.

I was happy.

I could live now, knowing that sweet honey truly existed.

My...

Who could ever say something as universal as that?

—— ✳ ——

"When is your birthday, Chika?"
"You mean the day I was born? It's ×××××××××××××××."
"Sorry, I couldn't hear that at all."
"Hmm. How should I put it then...hmm. It's soon."
When I tried to drill it down, it seemed that her birthday was probably about two weeks away. Though that was based on her perception, so no matter how desperately we tried to confirm it, the day might not line up exactly.
"Why?" she asked.
"My father's birthday was not long ago, so I was wondering if you celebrate birthdays in your world too."
"I see. We do. When you wake up, you get ××××× from your family. It's like a special celebration."
"Oh. Here we eat cake and give people presents."
"What's this *cahke* thing?"
I described the shape and ingredients to her and learned that there was a similar food in her world that went by a different name.
"I'm guessing the day you were born is a really important day in your world."
"I guess so. Honestly, I think it's more just ceremonial, using that day as an excuse to do something exciting."
"Well, if you have fun with it, I think that's a good thing."

When I saw her smile, of all the choices I could make, simply nodding and saying "That's true," immediately rose to the top of the list.

"I wonder what I could do for you," I said. "If I got you a cake, you wouldn't be able to taste it, and I can't give you a present either."

"Thank you for that. But the time I get to spend with you is already more than enough."

No matter how many times I heard that, it still warmed my heart. I could never get tired of it.

"Well, if you do think of anything that I could give you, please just let me know."

"Let me think. Oh, then could I make one request?"

"Of course!"

A request from Chika—that was rare. My voice brightened immediately. Though, of course, I was nervous about whether her request would be something I could actually fulfill. She'd be disappointed if she bothered to ask me and I told her I couldn't grant her wish. I'd be disappointed in myself as well, even if it was likely to go that way.

Thus, it was a true relief that my worries proved groundless.

"You remember when we shared songs from our worlds before?"

"Yeah." It had been several months prior, but I recalled it vividly.

"I'd like to hear you sing again."

"Uh...wha?"

"You don't have to if you don't want to, though."

"No, I mean, it's not that I don't want to...I hate to be all, 'Oh, it's not like I hate it,' but anyway it isn't like I *hate* singing."

It was a little embarrassing, but not enough for me to refuse her request. What was more pitiful was that odd display of panic just now, if anything here was less than desirable.

"Still, are you all right with something that meaningless?" I asked.

"It's not meaningless to me. I get to hear a song from another world, and I get to hear your voice sounding different from usual, so I think it's something really special."

When she put it that way, of course she'd be happy.

"Well, that's fine then. Even now if you want."

"No. I want it to be special, so let's wait a little longer—until the day I was born is closer. I'm happy that I not only get congratulations from my family but from you too."

As I told her how happy I was to get to congratulate her as well, the thought of her family crossed my mind. I'd been imagining a world of people of only shining eyes and nails living in darkness, but of course everyone over there, Chika included, would be fully visible to one another.

To be honest, I was jealous of her family getting to see what she looked like. However, it was because I couldn't see her that I could boast about this unique, one-of-a-kind bond that we shared—a relationship unlike any other that existed expressly because we could not reach one another.

We talked about birthdays for a little while longer, until it came about time for Chika to return to her family. I saw her off and then left the bus shelter as well.

I looked at my watch. I had stayed a bit late tonight. At this point, a long while after the end of summer break, my family's lingering resentment toward me seemed to have abated, and I no longer took any heat or fussing when I stayed out late. Thanks to this blessing, I'd been able to enjoy my time with Chika all the more.

On the way home, I thought about the song that Chika had requested. I realized that I had forgotten to ask her if it was okay if it was the same song as before. Either way, I needed to drill as many songs into my head as possible, including that one.

Two weeks wouldn't be long. My life when Chika was not by my side was a bland parade of the same old high school days, easily digestible no matter how much you consumed of it. Now that I had Chika, all the color seemed to have drained from every other part of my life. My family, classmates, and everything else, already little more than the scenery at the periphery of my vision as I ran through life, were now so desaturated they were nearly pure white.

I wondered if the world looked the same way to other people, even those who had found something special themselves. No, probably not. I couldn't ignore how often people said that once they found something special, the whole world seemed to shine before them. Having found my singular precious thing in this world, I knew that what shined was not something as vague as the world itself. It was my own heart and nothing else.

When I opened the door of the bus shelter as always, I prayed that this would not be the day that I finally stopped seeing her. I knew deep down that time would come someday, but I still wasn't prepared to steel myself for that possibility.

Coldness, hardness, softness, sweetness. I lived my life dreaming of those things.

Ever since the war had disappeared from Chika's life, I usually saw her once or twice a week. It all depended on whether she could slip out from under her family's watchful eye to visit the safe house—it seemed it wasn't an endorsed course of action to spend much time in safe houses when there wasn't a war going on in her world. Still, it was a trivial issue on my end; I never knew ahead of time when she would appear, so I just had to come here every day. It made me happy that she made as much time as she could to see me, despite the obstacles.

Though I didn't know it for certain, I managed to predict the date of the visit that would be the closest to Chika's birthday. On the second time we met again, counting from the night when I had promised to give her my birthday wishes, I spoke to Chika about it and we agreed that I would present her the song the next time we met. If it happened to be after her birthday had already passed, we would deal with that then.

Like I had initially predicted, that day soon came.

As always, I opened the door with an inappropriate level of nerves, as though each time were the first time we were to meet. Whenever I saw that girl of glowing eyes and nails there, my heart, and perhaps the whole world, nearly burst with joy. There were no words with which I could describe this feeling.

"Kaya!"

Her voice sounded more frantic than usual. I called out to her as well, sitting one body's width away from her. As I did so, she sidled up next to me.

"You seem like you're in a good mood, Chika."

"Yeah, I've been looking forward to today."

I had expected this response, but I still had to ask, "Your birthday hasn't passed, has it?"

"Not yet. After the sun sets and rises again, it'll be the day I was born."

"Oh, so tomorrow then. That's perfect timing, but you didn't force yourself to come here today, did you?"

Until meeting Chika, I had never thought to consider that questioning the motives behind someone's every action might be harmful to them. Of course, Chika was still the only one I felt this way about. If I was a good person, I could have directed this newfound empathy toward everyone around me, but that was not who I was.

"No, not really. It was the same as always."

"That's good, then. Oh, right, so I don't know if they say this the same way in your world, but..."

Never once in my life had I said this stock phrase with so much actual sincerity behind it.

"...Happy Birthday, Chika. Even if it's a day early."

"Thank you. We don't really use the word 'birthday' here, so I'm happy that I get to hear something special, just from you."

By now, I should have been able to look Chika in the eye without any shyness, but for some reason her smile alone always made my heart flutter.

"When the day you're born comes, I want to say Happy Birthday to you too."

"It's not for a while, but when it does come, I'd like to hear how you say it in your world."

"Okay, I'll do that. Is it really far away?"

"Yeah, some months still."

The end of February—actually, the day I had first met Chika. She was glad to learn this, saying it would be easy to remember. I couldn't recall anyone other than my own family ever being happy about my birthday before.

"Anyway, sorry to rush you, but how about that song?"

"Sure, okay."

I was surprised at my own enthusiasm.

"What's up?"

"Nothing, it's just a little nerve-racking being put on the spot, huh?"

As with the last time, neither having much experience with singing for someone important nor being at all suited to the task, it was difficult for me to perform it naturally. That said, this was what Chika wanted. I doubted that my own singing voice was worth anything at all, but this was a celebration. Even if it was meaningless, I had to put my heart into that song.

The last time we met, Chika had requested two songs of me— the one I had sung before and a new one. This was so that she could see whether there would be any discrepancies in how the first song sounded between performances. The last time, neither of us had managed to get the melodies across quite right. I got the feeling that the same thing would happen today, but I was sure that Chika suspected the same, so there was no point in discussing my concern.

"I'm facing forward now."

I doubted the volume of my voice would have any effect on Chika's world, but still I brought my mouth close to her ear, singing softly as I had before. I don't even know why.

If my nose was to collide with her ear on that night, I would hardly be flustered about it. We had already confirmed one another's existences and then some.

I was both ashamed and happy to be nervous thinking about such things. Inside my heart, I would not let myself be swayed by anything but my feelings for Chika.

How truly happy this made me.

"Okay," I said. "Let me know if I'm too close, or my voice is too loud."

I brought my hand to her ear and drew my face closer.

"Okay."

Once at an appropriate distance, not so close that my nose would hit her, I positioned my lips and softly inhaled. Truthfully, the oxygen from that breath should have been used to sing Chika her song, but before I did so, I suddenly thought of all the things that had been lingering in my mind until now which I was finally able to put into words.

"Thank you, Chika. I'm so glad that I met you."

That low whisper used up all my breath, and I frantically took another. I could tell by my fingers cupped beside her ear that she was nodding, even with her eyes closed.

"Me too."

There was a pause. I waited to hear her voice, floating out of the darkness as ever, say more.

"I'm glad I met you *first*."

I probably should have just let that slide, should have thought nothing of it.

I pulled my fingers away from her ear and moved my face back from hers, sitting up straight once again.

"...Kaya?"

I feel like I would have been able to process this more readily if it were a normal conversation, but for some reason, there was a lump in my throat.

"Kaya, what's the matter?"

"Chika."

As I spoke her name, whatever was lodged in my throat forced its way up onto my tongue. I chewed it, tasted it, and rolled it around, trying to determine what it was. Several seconds later I finally identified it, but I was lost for several seconds more, wondering whether it would be right to confirm this with Chika—or no, perhaps that's too rational a way to put it, whether I should finish chewing this thing and spit it out.

Eventually, the unpleasant sensation in my mouth won out.

"What do you mean?"

"What do I mean about what?"

She looked at me, her head tilted.

I grew afraid.

"About meeting me." It was obviously a groundless fear, but a *fear*, nonetheless. "You said 'first.'"

No.

I had so, so much time to think about things. Truly. I honestly had more than enough time while I awaited her reply to put my feelings in order, collect my thoughts, and prepare myself to accept what might come.

It was Chika and I who rendered that time unusable.

We had gotten too close. Here, in this shelter. In the months since we had met.

Chika's eyes quivered, and being who I was, I spotted agitation among all the emotions conveyed by just those two lights. Or perhaps it was something that even others could have seen.

"Are there others besides me?"

"What...do you mean?"

"Who you meet here."

If we had never touched, we could have both stayed in our own delusions.

"You're the only one here."

Here.

"Are there other places? That connect to this world?"

"...I still haven't been able to determine if it's the same world as yours."

Which meant...

"But based on a number of ××××, I think it's possible it might be the same world."

"Where?"

"As I mentioned before, there are a number of safe houses. This is just one of many."

"Wait, so you..."

"Kaya, what's wrong?"

What did she mean, *"What's wrong?"*

I felt my fingertips going numb. I opened my mouth, realizing I needed to raise my body temperature.

"How could you hide this from me, Chika...?"

"I didn't mean to hide it from you."

"Then why were you so disturbed when I asked you about it?"

"I don't even really know, but I mean, if I *was* disturbed—"

"You *were*."

"*If* I was, it was because you were making such a scary face at me."

The shape of her eyes changed. It was obvious she was troubled. Though I knew this, the things I wanted to say had their own mass, and they spilled out from my mouth.

"Through all of the conversations we had, why would you never once mention that?"

I should have immediately checked myself at the mention of my frightening expression. You could even say that would have been the best course of action, but I only understood that in hindsight.

Chika thought long and hard, then started in a tone that anyone would peg as making an excuse, "Well...in part because it just didn't come up. Also, *she* told me early on that she didn't want me to tell people that she was in that place. As we talked it over, we confirmed that there was no way for me to tell anyone exactly *where* she was, and I didn't think there was any reason to tell you anyway, so I didn't bring it up."

Learning that it was a woman did not bring me any measure of relief. Chika was talking to a human other than me. There was another human looking at those eyes and nails. Another person who had proof that Chika's world existed.

"Of *course* there was a reason to tell me. What about all the connections between this world and yours?"

"But didn't you say you wanted to talk about us, instead of about our worlds?"

"That's not the same thing!" I said, raising my voice. Never had I imagined Chika would argue something so pedantic.

"Kaya, what's going on? You're acting strange."

"I..."

Something occurred to me. Chika had shown me a glimpse of this new truth before, perhaps.

Body temperature.

Uniforms.

Of course. Come to think of it, I had never given her any details about what a dog was, and yet she had known that it was an animal that lived with humans.

Once, she had talked about an accessory that I had no recollection of. Could she have been telling me to keep my voice down because this other person spoke loudly?

This whole time...

Chika said that my expression scared her, but I knew that what was inside me right now was not anger or hatred but sadness and loss. There were doubtless other emotions wrapped up in there as well—anger, and hatred, and love, and jealousy—and perhaps she could see all of them, but it was no trifling thing.

I was sad.

"You really are special to me, my one and only," I croaked.

"And I think of you as my one and only, as well."

"And what about that other person, whoever she is?"

"You don't stop being special just because there's someone else."

I knew that what she was saying was right, but that was only the meaning of her words, seen through a framework of ethics and morals. The senseless thoughts, feelings, emotions of the human mind did not fit into that framework. There was no way she could possibly understand.

Perhaps romance was not the only thing that was beyond her comprehension. Maybe she could not understand attachment to others at all.

"That's not something people can accept that easily."

Her eyes quivered again. Putting my own disturbed feelings aside in favor of hers didn't feel the least bit justifiable.

"Would you really stop being special just because I met someone else?"

I could not immediately deny this.

"You're the only one I've tried out rohmanse with, though."

As I tried to put the feelings squirming deep inside me into words, waiting for them to come together properly, the two lights narrowed.

"I see. Kaya, you..."

I looked at her and could not breathe.

"...were just *pretending*."

Her smile was not one of happiness, of joy. I felt that so starkly that my heart and body ached.

I wasn't.

I absolutely wasn't.

That wasn't true.

I was glad that this was something that I could immediately, distinctly deny, but the sound I should have been making didn't reach my ears. My lips quivered, and my teeth didn't seem to fit together right. I couldn't breathe or speak. I should have at least just shaken my head in response, but somewhere between the light that blinded my eyes and the voice that deafened my ears, I had forgotten even how to render a denial.

Chika spoke in my stead.

However.

"You met ××, and just lov ××××× yourself, ××××n't you?"

I couldn't hear her.

"××××× sad××××, even if ×××××××× kis×× and the song ××××× still special but you ×××××××××."

I couldn't hear her at all.

"How could ××××××××××××× belie××××× liked ××××××××××××××××."

"I can't hear you."

Why? I thought that the only things I couldn't hear were words I didn't know, concepts that didn't exist in my world, but I couldn't make her out at all. I had no idea what she was trying to say, not in the slightest.

As I sat there, dumbfounded, her eyes pulled away from mine. They moved up high and then looked at me.

There was a deep sadness in them.

"I need to ××××."

Of course I couldn't hear her, but in all the months I'd known her, with the connection that we had forged, I knew that her standing up meant that it was time for her to leave. So, I wrung out the last little bit of air left in my lungs to at least tell her, "Try... not to get caught."

Though she was still troubled, she seemed to respond to my words, but it was caught up in the noise and I had no idea what she actually said.

Soon it was dark, and as usual, I was alone. Unlike usual, however, I could not bring myself to stand from the bench. Instead, now that I sat there alone, I was able to unpack my feelings, one my one.

Then I realized the true impact of what I had done.

I wanted to explain myself, to apologize immediately, but Chika was already gone.

All I had to do was wait a few more days.

I should have done so at any point before then, but I had been at the mercy of a passion so strong I thought my whole body might burn to ash.

Naturally, feelings of regret or remorse aren't enough to actually kill you, but from then on I was plagued by the feeling that I truly might die.

No one can die from just an emotion. It would not be until much later that I realized this.

Realizing it did not settle my feelings, though.

That time never came.

I never saw Chika again.

The person who had cherished me as her one and only vanished into the darkness, and the color never returned to my world.

An Encore No One Called For

AS IT TURNS OUT, our lives aren't long enough to judge things in such emphatic terms as "fun" or "boring." You can allow yourself to be taken by emotions that are little more than a passing breeze, but that gust of wind will soon blow away, leaving you wasting the rest of your life in want of the memory of that gale.

The phrase "the rest of your life" might conjure up images of some elderly person in physical decline, but that's not what I mean. Age is only one factor—the aging of a person's soul is measured in how much time has passed since that wind blew into their life. Once you're old, everyone laps at the stagnant breezes of their own winds and says "Those were the days" or "That was the best time of my life."

You could claim that the only meaningful times in our lives is when we're touched by that wind. It would be easier if the end of our lives came sooner, but most people—myself included—lack the courage to actually take our own lives, so we're left with no

other way to chew through the days than to either sit there para-
lyzed or to idly while our lives away.

Sometimes, we find something to pretend to devote ourselves
to. Sometimes, we get ourselves addicted to things. Sometimes,
we get our hands on luxuries. And sometimes, we get our hands
on *people*.

Then we die in vain.

I realize how foolish we are as creatures to cling to our own
individuality so fiercely, but from the moment we're born, we're
made to realize that we're nothing more than another fragment
of that human stupidity. Though it's unfortunate, it's pointless
to allow our days to be consumed by such an inevitable disappointment, so we have no choice but to accept it. This world isn't
something that warrants such strong emotions.

Even when I received news of my mother's death from my
brother, as I expected, I didn't feel particularly strongly about it.
I wondered at what point my mother had been blown by that wind
and pitied her, thinking that she must have spent the rest of her life
chewing on that memory like gum, just like everyone else.

It had been roughly eight years since I'd last visited my birthplace. I'd set foot there again only once to collect some things
left in my room when my parents decided to move, shortly after
I graduated from university. I threw away most of it, taking only
a few things back with me. The new house, which had been built
in the same neighborhood as our original home, carried no trace
of me, and I left any reason to return to my birthplace behind.

I only bothered to return, eight years later, because I thought it might be nice to at least offer a prayer for the mother who had fed, clothed, and sheltered me for the first eighteen years of my life. In my meaningless, trifling days, surely I could at least spare the time to clap my hands together for her.

I received word on Friday and attended the wake on Saturday. My father and my brother, who had remained behind—ever the dutiful son—had taken care of the arrangements and everything else, so all I had to do was show up, look like I was in mourning, and pray for my mother's happiness in the next life. I made the necessary greetings as my father brought me around to all the relatives and neighbors for introductions.

Once the repast had ended, most of the people went home, leaving the venue quiet, with only close family lingering behind. As I stood outside during our vigil afterwards, smoking a cigarette, my brother drifted over and lit one as well.

"Sorry 'bout all this," he said. "I know you're pretty busy right now."

Weird to be worrying over your little brother when your parent just died.

"I mean, it's fine."

I knew that wasn't what he had followed me out there to say.

"Y'know, Mom was always worrying about you."

"Huh."

I hadn't seen my mother or brother in years.

"It was always, 'Oh, I do hope Kaya's happy. He was such a brooding child. I hope he's not in a funk or something.' From her, that is, not me."

My brother laughed at his own joke. I put on a smile as well.

"That's our mom, huh."

"I think she'd be relieved to see you actually able to share a smile with folks around you. You used to be so prickly all the time."

He laughed again. I laughed back and said, "Guess you're right," playing the part of the cheerful younger brother as I exhaled smoke.

Listening to him talk, I supposed it was good that I had come here one last time to say a prayer for my mother like this. At the same time, I realized I would probably never come back to this place without her ever again.

When morning came, the service proper finally began. I was not particularly moved by any of the proceedings, and when I saw my mother's body go up in smoke, reduced to nothing but ash and bones, I was only struck again with how cold and empty human existence truly was—but that was only the slightest of chills.

Once all the proceedings were over, I informed my father and brother that I would be leaving right away, as previously discussed. I couldn't imagine what they thought of me, the second son who was abandoning all familial duty. I left the funeral home behind, the pair of them smiling at me as I went. From my mother's perspective, it would probably be a relief just to know that the cleanup was not being left to me of all people.

I called a taxi to the parlor and told the driver to take me to the station. Typically, I was of the mind that a taxi driver shouldn't make conversation with their passengers; today I felt much the same.

"Are you from around here, mister?"

"Yes, I am. I came back to see my family due to some unfortunate circumstances."

I'd fully intended to ignore him, but I'd gotten out of the habit.

"My condolences."

"Thanks."

And that was the end of the conversation. I wondered just what in the hell the point of that conversation had been, who it was for, but then nothing we do in life is every really *for* anyone, or for any purpose, so I couldn't fault the driver. Anger just leads to exhaustion.

I gazed out the car window. In the past, I would have expected to see little else outside but the abandoned houses that had been left to nature and the like, but it was different now. Progress marches on, and now the only vestiges of that era were the fields that sat empty smack dab in the middle of clumps of condos, like pitfalls.

"This place has really changed, huh? You're probably too young to remember, but it used to be nothing but mountains around here."

I could have told him, *I do remember,* but I realized that the driver was not actually expecting a reply and left it at a soft sigh. I'd half expected to feel more emotional about passing through this area, but no matter how close nor far I was from it, my emotions remained equally flat. As I traced my way through my memories, as I always did, the taxi arrived at the station.

It was still a rural station, but it was markedly cleaner than it had been eight years prior. I took a look at the timetable and then purchased a coffee at a little takeout stand that had not been there the last time I was here. A shelter sat prettily beside the ticket gate. Perhaps a train had just come, as there was no one inside it. I took a seat on the bench that sat against the wall. The cold season was well on its way out, but there was no point in me standing around freezing on the platform.

Inside the shelter was a space heater and a clock—or rather, a large LCD display. I took a sip of my coffee as the news played at an unintrusive volume. The coffee was weak, but that wasn't the shop's fault. Everything that entered my mouth was weak, tasteless, meaningless on my tongue—coffee, tobacco smoke, or other people's spit. The fact that I was not yet accustomed to this, that I would still even acknowledge a flavor as weak, was perhaps proof that even my senses were still tethered to my memories. In memory lay expectations, which were only betrayed by reality.

It had already been fifteen years. Was that a long time? Or was it actually a short one? You could just as easily say that it was much too long as you could that it was far too short.

Again, I wandered through my memories—the special something that existed only inside of me. I traced through the things that I would not, *dared not* forget. Remembering was the only thing that kept me alive.

I hadn't realized I would grow old so quickly.

I stared at the clock as I sipped my weak coffee. At some point, someone else entered the shelter. Out of my peripheral I glanced at the person, who had sat down on the bench at a gap, and saw a woman in a gray coat. It was a small-town train station, so I stole a glance at her face thinking she might be someone I knew, but her brilliant, willful gaze and thinly pressed lips rung no bells. I could only assume by the hope for the future that her expression betrayed that her own powerful wind had not yet blown away.

To be frank, I was jealous of her.

By the time the train was scheduled to arrive, a few more people had entered the shelter. The woman sitting beside me stood up almost in sync with me, moving through the manned ticket gate to the platform. The train soon arrived, and we boarded, finding the car fairly empty despite it being a weekend, and the woman and I sat side by side, again with some distance between us. It would be a bit over an hour before we reached my transfer station. Now and then the train stopped, taking on more passengers, and by the time we arrived at my destination there was a decent crowd, most of whom stood from their seats at the same station where I was exiting. That woman got off at the same stop as well. A headphone cord ran from her ears to her pocket. It was clear to me as I watched her walk in front of me, back straight, heels clacking, that she had not yet come face-to-face with that gale, or perhaps she was right now in the midst of a maelstrom. Jealousy bubbled up once more. On the flip side, I also felt a sort of grief as I thought of the dull, muffled world that lay ahead of her.

That said, the same fate awaits everyone in this world, so this was not a sentiment I felt toward her specifically. I rarely held an attachment to any individual person. I no longer had strong feelings about anyone.

I was never going to see this woman again. Or so I thought.

We walked in the same direction, and before I knew it, we were on the same train again, though this car was a bit more crowded and we were no longer sitting next to each other. After another hour of swaying on the train, I finally disembarked, but she remained on it. I hadn't imagined we'd ride together even that far from such a rural origin point, but that didn't really mean much to me either.

By the time I exited the ticket gate at the station, I had already forgotten about her.

A week after my mother died, on the day I celebrated my thirty-first birthday, I saw her again. This time, it wasn't in a station shelter or on a train but at a radio station I visited for my job. Apparently, she worked there. I'm not sure how unlikely of a coincidence it is to run into someone from your hometown in the finite number of business transactions one does in one's life, but human lives are so long that I suppose it isn't totally impossible.

The fact that I had no recollection of this woman, even though I had visited this station several times before, meant that

I either simply hadn't encountered her or that it was because I never looked at anyone's faces unless it was necessary. It only occurred to me that she was the person I had seen at the station back home because she stared at me for an unnaturally long time as we passed each other. I thought this suspicious until I realized I had seen her recently. She was probably wondering if she'd seen me somewhere before as well.

Once a human identifies a target, it's impossible for them to ignore it, so the next time I visited the station, I noticed her again. I caught her staring at me as she recognized my face, and I greeted her, thinking she must have some business with me. But she simply returned a polite nod and left. I had no business with her myself, so I made no move to stop her.

This situation didn't change until circumstance brought us together for a fourth time. Well, honestly speaking, it wasn't the *fourth* time.

"I *knew* it..."

It happened when I was introduced to her as a representative of the program I was getting an ad placed in, as the pair of us blithely exchanged business cards. She received my card first, looked at it, and then looked at me again curiously, muttering something vague.

Ignoring her boss—who stood beside her giving a concerned, "What's wrong?"—she looked at me and said my name.

"I thought that was you, Suzuki-kun."

I made a baffled expression at this address.

"Um, here," she continued.

If we were acquainted, she should have just given her name, but instead she offered me her card. What a weirdo. I took it and looked at the name. *That* name.

"Remember me?"

To be frank, I didn't. For her to call me Suzuki-kun... Was she someone I had met in college or one of the various acquaintances I had made since becoming an adult? Or, given the station we'd rode from, was she someone from as far back as my high school days?

However, as a member of society, I was aware that telling someone upfront that you didn't remember them tended to upset them. I knew that could cause further trouble, so I started to try to save face, but thankfully she took the initiative and revealed herself.

"We were in the same class in high school. Though, um, I guess we didn't talk all that much."

I didn't talk much to anyone, so that didn't narrow it down any.

"We used to always end up at the shoe lockers together on the way home."

Now I remembered.

"Oh."

This was Saitou, from high school.

I looked at her card again. I supposed that *had* been her name. I looked at her in half feigned shock and told her that I did remember her.

"I'm so glad you do! I'd been wondering since I saw you at the station. I wasn't sure though; you've changed a lot from back then.

You always have such a big smile when you're here. Ah, sorry for getting so worked up. This is Suzuki Kaya-san, an old classmate."

She explained the situation to her boss, who looked at her, then me, giving a loud, "Well, that's wonderful! Please be kind to this old buddy of yours."

What was so wonderful about that? I had no idea, but I made a similar expression as him and said, "What a shock, huh?"

These words were mainly meant to smooth things over, but they were at least 2 percent sincere.

Saitou had noted that I was different now, but really I was the one who should be saying that. Putting aside the fact that she was wearing makeup, I could sense no trace of the Saitou I had once known, as far as I remembered her. Between her face, the air with which she carried herself, and even her height, she was like a completely different person. The Saitou I knew never had such hope in her eyes and would have never been so overjoyed by a reunion with an old classmate. Obviously, I had never known her outside of the school building, and it had been more than ten years since then, but still.

Regardless, this reunion, and the fact that it was a reunion with Saitou, held little significance to me. I now had a work acquaintance who was also from my hometown. That was all.

Naturally, even after we had already exchanged business cards, I saw Saitou every time I visited the radio station. That said, she was never the one I was scheduled to meet with. We'd see each other, nod, and go our separate ways. We sometimes stopped to make chitchat, and once the timing had even worked out for us to get coffee with a few folks, but that was the extent of it. The fact that she always had such boundless energy concerned me, but that was really none of my business. The only thought I had about it was that someday, once that wind left her sails, she would probably return to her old self.

Until one day, I heard, "You wanna grab dinner sometime, Suzuki-kun?"

It was when I received this sudden invitation from Saitou, who was nothing more than a former classmate who I had just happened to cross paths with while working, that I began to wonder if she truly *wasn't* the Saitou I once knew. I wasn't inclined to turn her down, though. It didn't matter to me either way.

"Sure, let's do that. We can coordinate our schedules. I'll give you my LINE."

We had never really had much in the way of one-on-one exchanges before, so this was our first time trading personal contact information.

Our tiny reunion took place during the May holidays, after the frantic days at the start of the school year had ended. Saitou was dressed in dark business casual and I in a suit, having had a single work function to attend that day. On that topic, I of course never attended any high school reunions, but I wondered whether she had. With the way she was right now, there was no way she hadn't gone. I asked her as we waited for our food at a tidy little restaurant.

"I haven't," she said. "They've mostly been on the weekends, and weekends mean nothing to radio station employees. I had a few fairly good friends by our third year, but I'm happy enough with just contacting them individually."

"Though of course we've fallen out of touch by now," she added when the drinks arrived. She shared a pointless perfunctory toast.

"Is there anyone from back home you still keep in touch with?" she asked.

"Nah, not really."

"That's how it gets once you're a busy professional. Plus, I mean, well...don't take this the wrong way, but you weren't especially approachable back then."

Her tone, both wry and considerate, made me chuckle as I replied, "Yeah, I think I get what you mean." I didn't deny the accusation because I realized she was probably referring to the incident I'd caused. Stubbornly denying the facts was a surefire way to make someone uncomfortable. Acknowledging your faults and telling the other you had grown beyond them was necessary to maintaining stress-free relations.

"Honestly though, I was surprised to see how much...gentler you've gotten. Sorry to bring this up again, I just didn't think it'd be appropriate to mention at work."

Considering how the conversation was going, it would be just as strange if the topic hadn't been broached. I chose my words carefully, trying not to make her feel awkward.

"I mean, I guess I have changed, but I was just as surprised. Remembering how you were in high school, I'd have never imagined you inviting me out somewhere."

She looked a bit bashful, perhaps aware that she might become the subject of the conversation. I wondered if it was a forced expression.

"Well, when you put it that way, I guess I've grown up too, and I've gotten a lot more friendly. I think I got less standoffish starting the middle of our second year, though."

Now that she mentioned it, there had been a point at which her demeanor had shifted pretty drastically, though I hadn't remembered exactly when that was.

"Thinking about who I was back then, and remembering what you were like at the time, I would have never imagined us becoming work acquaintances. I invited you out because I thought that was a bond worth cultivating, but to be honest, I half expected you to turn me down."

"I figured it couldn't hurt to be nice to someone from a company I'm doing business with," I said sarcastically with a feigned smile, realizing she was still looking for some proof of my inner change.

She gave a toothy grin and replied, "Wow, you even have a sense of humor now."

I carried bite after bite of tasteless food to my mouth, downing drink after drink in the hopes of dulling my senses. The conversation with Saitou did little to hold my interest, but I rarely got much enjoyment out of conversing with anyone these days, so at least it wasn't especially painful. I made the right faces at the right times and spoke at an appropriate volume. That was the essence of conversation. It was necessary to avoid making trouble at work by upsetting Saitou, former classmate now turned business associate.

"Oh, right, so what did you go back home for?"

"Ah, my mom passed away."

"Oh, I'm so sorry... You have my condolences."

"No, you don't have to apologize, we'd known it was coming."

Why did people always apologize for bringing up a relative's death?

"I don't really go back there anymore," I continued. "Do you?"

"Oh yeah, when I have time anyway. I don't really have any reason to go back, but it sometimes helps to recharge my batteries."

So it wasn't so much a miracle of fate that had brought us together on that platform as it was my intruding on Saitou's routine.

"Is it work that usually keeps you away? Or do you have a family here now?"

"Work. As you can see, I'm not married."

"Right. Same here, as you can see."

She held up her left hand to show me the ring finger, as I had just done. She let out an alcohol-laced sigh, then gave a vague apology for throwing out information that I hadn't even asked about. If she was going to apologize for every single little thing, we would get nowhere.

Once we were through with most of our meal, we topped it off with some coffee and dessert. Saitou seemed to be the sort who favored luxuries like booze and sweets and coffee, making sure to treat herself to dessert and drinks every day. Afterward, she invited me to join her for more drinks. It didn't matter to me either way, so I went along with her. The restaurant bill came out to an even number, so it was easily split.

We shared another toast at a bar near the restaurant. We raised our glasses casually to one another as we sat at the counter, I with a gin rickey cocktail and Saitou with a Caol Ila. As the alcohol seeped through our insides, Saitou brought up a topic more personal than she had ventured back at the restaurant.

"So, what did you usually do with your time back then?"

"Nothing, really. If anything, I guess I did a lot of running."

"Guess you were pretty athletic."

"I mean, it's not like I was into any actual sports. I just ran because I didn't have anything else to do."

Though I truly had no interest in the answer, I returned the question.

"I guess I listened to a lot of music," she said.

"Oh, is that why you got the radio job?"

"I guess so. I do have a lot of fun now when they invite me to help choose the music they're putting on. It's fun, or rather, fulfilling. Guess that sounds a little self-important."

"I think it's cool that you can say stuff like that."

"It really isn't all that cool though. There's a lot that goes into it."

Well, of course there was a lot that went into it. There was a lot that went into everything in life, but I responded with the appropriate, "Well, even if it's tough sometimes, it's nice that you have fun with it."

So that was it. In a way, Saitou had managed to reach a future that she had painted with her own hands. I wondered if the reason it seemed that her own wind had not yet passed her by was because of her own eclectic desires as a person or simply because she was right in the middle of the storm.

"Do you enjoy your work, Suzuki-kun?"

I had never once assigned a value to how enjoyable my work was.

"I guess I get a sense of accomplishment from how weirdly busy it gets. There's a lot that could be improved, though."

"Guess it's like that everywhere."

"It's true, but you still gotta keep on living."

Obviously, this was painful, but it was also inevitable.

"You're right, that's true."

She nodded deeply, smiling at me, as though my half-hearted responses actually meant something to her. People sometimes feel that they understand others better when they realize that they share a circumstance with someone else. I supposed she must have started to feel some affinity for me, noting some similarities between my transformation and her own journey from high school to her current self. This was clearly a misconception, but given that everyone in this world looks the same in some ways from the outside, it was inevitable that someone might draw this sort of comparison.

What was inside of me couldn't be empathized with. But of course, there was no real harm in having a work colleague who felt positively toward me, so I perked up the corners of my mouth and nodded, saying, "Guess so."

Using this conversation as a launching point, we continued to volley quips back and forth, as though we actually shared common ground as rather prickly people in high school who had learned and softened over time—as Saitou seemed to assume. Suddenly, she said, "I really was bored a lot back then."

"Back then? You mean, when we were younger?"

"Yeah. Still, I don't really hate my old self when I think about her."

That was when I realized it. When we were first reunited, I had been a bit stunned at her transformation, but there was nothing that shocking about it. She'd undergone an infectiously commonplace transformation. She had changed, yes. Saitou had become an adult who looked back fondly on the past. Her transformation had only stood out to me because the outward changes had been so marked.

Of course, that made it even more mysterious to me that she still looked like her wind hadn't passed her by. Though she was intoxicated, the light in her eyes was one that people like me, simply whiling the rest of their lives away, did not possess.

Still, that was none of my business. I had no interest in knowing how her life would progress.

These days, I no longer hesitated to slurp down the time that I would have cherished so much back then, consuming it bit by bit as though separating out a braid of hair strand by strand.

We continued nodding back and forth at our routine conversation, until we realized we had already blown past midnight and it was now approaching 1 a.m. I watched Saitou take a wobbling step as she stood to use the restroom, having drank quite a bit, and took the opportunity to settle the bill. Saitou, lover of luxury, was probably not quite ready to go back home, but I figured it was about time to call it a night.

I told her this when she returned, bleary-eyed. She didn't seem to disapprove but started to ask about paying me back. I told her that it would be a hassle to try and take money from her, instead suggesting that she treat me next time, if we happened to do this again. She agreed.

I left the restaurant and stepped out onto the main road, hailing a cab. I let Saitou ride with me, figuring that we probably lived in the same direction, given that we had been on the same train line before. However, when I heard the neighborhood that Saitou mentioned to the driver, it wasn't one I recognized as on the same train line as mine.

"God, I'm really drunk, sorry."

Saitou put her hands to her cheeks as though embarrassed by herself. My head was swimming plenty too, so I threw my left hand down onto my seat to avoid touching Saitou where she sat beside me, and responded with an appropriate, "That's what happens when you drink." It wasn't really a problem, honestly, but there was no point in dwelling on it either way, so I just told her, "You can sleep until we get there, if you want."

However, she shook her head, brushing off my offer with a "Thanks, I'm all right."

"I'm sorry," she continued, "You can just write this off as the alcohol talking if you want to, but I'm really happy right now."

"About what?"

"I just think it's amazing that two people who were both so bored back then could actually have fun drinking together like this."

Bored. Fun.

There she went again, deciding my feelings for herself. Though...she was right about the former.

She lowered her hands from her face, resting them on her bag that sat on her lap.

"Y'know..."

She started to say something, then was silent for a bit, staring at the back of the seat in front of her. She let out a sigh, the sort you'd expect before a once-in-a-lifetime confession or someone admitting to an old crush they'd given up on.

"I used to really *hate* you."

She glanced at me, giving a self-deprecating smirk.

"I feel like it's been long enough, so will you hear me out? At first, back then, I thought that I couldn't *stand* you. You seemed like the sort of person who thought that you were special but got annoyed when other people did the same things and acted the same way as you. That was the sort of misguided self-aggrandizing I understood, but there was a specific moment when I decided that I didn't like you at all."

I had no interest in knowing when, but she seemed like she wanted to tell me, so I had to let her.

"Can I ask when?"

"Yeah. Remember when you lent me your umbrella?"

I thought back, replaying my memories and stopping on the

scenes that I normally skipped right over. I guessed something like that might have happened.

"Not clearly, but..."

"You did once, on a rainy day when I forgot my own umbrella. Normally I'd be happy about it, but it felt like, you know... I was like, what a half-assed good Samaritan this guy is. Like, why bother even being considerate for other people if you're gonna look so unhappy about it?" She added, half to herself, "I guess I hated how similar we were," before looking out the window.

Even being told that someone had hated me didn't stir my emotions. I had no interest in any evaluations of me that didn't have a bearing on my livelihood, and I certainly wasn't going to take the opinions of some person from the past to heart.

Still, I knew what I was supposed to say to her here. I knew exactly why she would have brought up that topic. She had only announced her former hatred of me to show how her own evaluation of me had changed since then. I could have just ignored this, but again, none of this mattered to me, so I provided the response that I was sure she was hoping to hear.

"You know, I hated you too."

I purposely let out a smile with the words, and when she turned her eyes back from the window to me, she looked like I had practically saved her.

"Really?"

"Yeah. I guess I hate folks who are like me too."

That wasn't true at all, but I didn't see any point in revealing my true feelings.

She turned forward, tittering, "So you did, huh..." as she let her hands slide from her bag down onto her seat.

The movement was unreserved, and her pinky brushed the ring finger of my left hand. It would be as much a pain to avoid this, so I just waited for her to pull her hand away herself, but she at no point showed any signs of doing so.

Her pinky rested atop my ring finger. Then it curled around it like a crochet hook.

I gave her a sideways glance. She was not looking at me. I saw the serious expression on her face as she continued looking forward and made a choice.

None of this mattered either way, so I untangled my ring finger from her pinky and rested my hand on the back of hers. I softly intertwined my fingers in the gaps between her own slender ones. After a moment of hesitation, she closed her hand around mine.

Soon after, the taxi arrived in her neighborhood, whereupon she directed the driver to an apartment building. I pulled my hand from hers, and we thanked each other.

"See you later. Oh yeah, try not to get caught. Heh, haven't said *that* in a while."

Her cheeks lifted as we exchanged our farewells, then the cab door closed. Alone now, I directed the driver to my home, watching as Saitou opened the auto-lock door of her building.

Not that it mattered either way.

— ✳ —

When you grow into a boring adult, there's little wonder or mystery that you don't understand the workings of. Even the weird legends back in our hometown were just vestiges of those who fled from the war and used those abandoned homes to hide so they wouldn't be attacked by the people who already lived in the area. Eventually, those bloodlines began to mix and the refugees became indistinguishable from the rest, leaving nothing behind but words and old habits. They weren't fairy tales, or creepy myths, or anything like that.

Many of the pointless actions that men and women take eventually turn into rituals.

Today, for the first time in a while, both of our days off had aligned, so there was no reason for either of us to force ourselves awake. But she leapt out of the bed anyway, immediately making a racket.

I looked at the alarm clock, which seemed to have made its way over to my pillow somehow at some point in the night. It was five minutes to ten. First to rise, Saitou was now sitting in a desk chair, apparently waiting for her computer to boot.

I sat up, pulling on a T-shirt that was on the floor nearby, and scooted to the edge of the bed.

"Sorry, did I wake you?" she asked.

"Nah, it's whatever. Got some work e-mails?"

"No, I just forgot something's going on sale today."

"What is?"

"Tickets to a show."

The word "show" was one that I rarely used in my daily life, so it took my brain a few moments to register what it meant. She meant a concert, presumably.

"It's a performance by a band I like, Her Nerine. They've been on the program I direct a few times too. I completely forgot about the pre-sale lottery, so I figured I'd aim for the general sales, which open at ten o'clock. Two minutes left... *God*, this is always so nerve-racking."

She sat there, looking a bit sloppy in her underwear and T-shirt, hand on the mouse waiting for the clock to turn. Of course, this was *her* home, so I was probably the one who could stand to look a bit more put together.

"If they've been on your show, couldn't you just get some tickets from them, Sanae?"

"Just a sec."

Apparently, the clock had ticked over. She stared at her screen, voracious and so silent that I didn't even think she was breathing. She clicked once at some specific moment, then started clicking over and over again at regular intervals. Did it really take that much work just to get some tickets? Not being an active music listener, I had certainly never purchased concert tickets, so I had no idea.

To clarify, Sanae was the name Saitou had been given by her parents—her first name.

Finally, she thrust both her fists up into the air.

"*Yes! Got 'em!* Sorry for making all this noise so early. Anyway, what were you saying?"

"Glad you got them. But I was saying, since you already have a connection with the band, couldn't you just get tickets from them?"

"Mm, now that you mention it, I probably could've."

Saitou spun her chair around, facing toward me. She had a habit of overacting all her casual everyday words and actions. Even now, she pretended to be embarrassed of her private self, but her words and smile suggested she was actually quite proud.

"I don't want to corrupt our business relationship with my own love of what they do, though."

Approaching the things you like with an immaculate internal self-satisfaction... I didn't understand the point when the end result—going to a concert—was the same. That said, it was totally unnecessary to be exasperated by or disparage someone else's self-satisfaction.

"I do have my place in the business though, so I do what I can."

I chose some words that I figured she would want to hear—if we were a couple in a TV drama.

"Gotcha. Well, maybe I'll go make us some breakfast. Something you'll like."

"Oh, thanks! But you know, we could just sleep a little longer."

Counter to what she had just said, Saitou stood from her chair and walked toward me with eyes fiery, sitting down beside me. Her slender fingers traced my own sinuous hand.

"I mean, that's fine with me, but if we go back to sleep now, we'll never make it out in time."

We had an errand to run together that afternoon. Honestly, I didn't really care about it either way, but the way things were going, it seemed like we'd be using up too much physical energy first thing in the morning, which was a bit of a pain. I pressed my lips to hers briefly and stood up.

"You can grab whatever you like from the fridge," came her voice from behind me, heavy with afterglow. I moved to the kitchen and opened the fridge.

I had at least enough cooking skill not to disappoint myself with the dishes I made. And in the past four months that we had been together like this, I had come to grasp some idea of the things she liked.

In the kitchen, whose layout I was now familiar with, I made an omelet with milk in it, a little more than half-done, and slid it onto a plate with two slices of fried ham and some lettuce folded in the middle. I toasted one slice of bread and cut it in half, which would be enough for us to share. I set it down in front of Saitou, who was sitting at the table waiting and sipping some instant coffee.

"Sorry it's so basic."

"That's fine. I'm usually eating by myself in a hurry, so it's nice to share a meal. Thank you."

I accepted her praise with an appropriate smile.

After we finished our leisurely meal, we quickly cleaned ourselves up to go out. There was no point in wondering what use we might make of our leftover time, as Saitou had already started working on her computer.

"You should really try taking a day off sometimes."

Though of course, I didn't actually think that at all. People were free to use their own time however they wanted. I'd only said it because I figured it was what Saitou would want to hear.

"It's fine. I do this because I enjoy it."

"You know, I'm always impressed you can be so enthusiastic about your work."

"I am pretty proud of it, though you could also say that I kind of use it as an escape."

She smiled as she looked between her computer screen and her phone. What she said was true; her heart and soul were completely governed by her work. Like many others, she'd made the mistake of believing that this was her *raison d'être*.

Finally taking a break from her work, she came up behind me as I sat on the couch and wrapped her arms around my neck. After lingering like this for what seemed the appropriate length of time, I got up and put my phone and wallet into my pocket. When we made it to the front door, it was warmer outside than I'd expected. I stepped outside, waiting for her to lock up.

Saitou and me walked to the station wearing clothes that were suitable for the season, our age, and our income levels. We had plans to go to the theater today. It was not something that either of us had much interest in, but Saitou had gotten it in her head that we should go see a performance by some little acting troupe she'd heard of from somewhere, reasoning that we could only do this on a day off. It wasn't anything that was worth my turning down.

As we walked, Saitou rattled off what she had learned from looking up this troupe, when I realized that she was staring at my face. *This again?*

"Is there something on my face...?"

I knew that there was something she wanted to say to me, but that question was traditionally how we started these exchanges.

"No, I was just thinking how handsome you look today," she'd say, taking a good, hard look at me.

In response, I'd say, "I know," or some other similarly affirmative words.

At this, Saitou's face would scrunch up, and she'd chide me with a "You could at least *try* being humble," after which we'd look at one another and laugh.

I had no idea what was so funny about this, but Saitou was always orchestrating such exchanges, sometimes several times a day. It did me no harm to go along with it, so I did. I had plenty of time in my life to waste on these things.

I had some idea of how this had started—it was during a conversation several days after that day in May when we'd affirmed through our actions that we would grow into the sort of relationship we had now. Saitou had explained to me why she would want to keep me bound to her as a lover.

"I just look at you and think, I'd like to see a bit more of this person, both emotionally and physically."

"Physically...?"

"I like the face you've grown into."

I realized that, to some degree, there was a bit of deception and bashfulness mixed in to hide the true nature of her thoughts. I also knew that I had an appearance that the opposite sex found somewhat attractive, and that my expressions usually weren't the kind to make others uncomfortable, so I just said, "Well, guess I'm glad to hear that." Saitou had latched on to that immediately, leading into these private exchanges of ours that persisted to this day.

Incidentally, when Saitou had asked me why I decided to go out with her at that same time, I gave her the answer I figured she wanted to hear:

"From what you've said, it sounds like you've had a tough path up until now. I just want to know more about that." Then, I doubled down. "And because I guess I'm just more of a sucker for a pretty face than I thought."

Perhaps because of her makeup and her expressions, Saitou's face gave a very different impression from the gloomy one it once did—that was the sort of thing that men would probably like, so I supposed my answer wasn't entirely a lie. That seemed to lighten her mood, so it didn't matter what I really felt.

Just as the taste of food had somehow deadened for me, at some point so had my hunger and fatigue and lust. They were not *entirely* gone, but while I could satisfy my hunger and fatigue on my own, there were a limited number of ways to satisfy that third desire. It was advantageous to have a member of the opposite sex of a certain level of attractiveness by my side to make it past the physical and mental hurdles. That was as much as I ever thought about the appearance of the opposite sex.

There was no real kindness born of that.

Though Saitou took as many opportunities as possible to touch me while we were in private, she was not the type to demand physical contact when we went out. We kept a fair amount of distance between us as we rode the train to whatever station for whatever theater.

The crowd was sparse, perhaps because this was an amateur performance.

I had never once been moved by witnessing someone else's creation, but I had forced myself to experience many different things when I was a teenager, so I did at least have some basis for judgment. Even if I wasn't especially moved, I could still typically understand the structure of the story that was being told. That said, what I witnessed this time with Saitou surpassed even my own lack of knowledge, veering into the incomprehensible. It didn't help that I had no idea what the men on stage were even referencing.

In other words, I couldn't even find the plot.

Perhaps, back in the day, I would have been fascinated by the fact that such a work even existed. Now, though, I felt like I might as well have spent ninety minutes staring at a blank wall.

There were a few words from the performers and the director after the show, but I didn't get the point of that either. The curtain fell and the house lights came up, and the pair of us looked at each other. I could tell by her expression what she thought of it. We stood up at once and exited the theater, then we decided to wander around the area.

After a little while, as though she had finally surfaced from underwater, she let out a sigh.

"Phew!"

It almost sounded scripted.

"I didn't get that at all. Oh, I mean, sorry if you liked it, Kaya-kun. Did you get it?"

"No, honestly, I'm relieved to hear you say that. I had no idea what was going on either."

That seemed to relieve some tension in her. I had realized over the past few months that she seemed to derive some special sort of joy from sharing opinions with the people close to her.

We stopped at an independent café nearby for a late lunch. The weather was nice, so we took a seat on the terrace and opened our menus. Neither of us were particularly indecisive when it came to these things, so by the time a waiter came over with our water and hot towels, we were ready to place our orders.

"I really didn't get that show, but..." As Saitou sipped her iced tea, which had come out first, something possessed her to bring up the performance again. "They were *super* passionate. Like, they seemed really genuine, like they were honestly excited about what they were doing. I did enjoy that about it."

"Yeah, it did seem like they were pretty into it."

"Right?"

That meant nothing to me. I doubted that she had gotten any special meaning out of it either, but she seemed to be trying to eke some sort of symbolism out of the performance. I supposed it was scary to think that you'd wasted your time on something utterly pointless. It was only after that gust of wind had left you that you could learn to recognize and admit that all time was a waste.

What was the point in wringing sentiment out of things? If values and emotions didn't bubble up from within you naturally, then it was all just a lie, wasn't it?

"What's the matter?"

"Oh, nothing. I was just thinking those guys were probably just college students."

"At least half of them are, apparently. They said so online."

We started eating at once when our food arrived. "What a sophisticated flavor...!" she opined, confirming for me that this was a dish that even other people would find bland.

"I wonder sometimes," she said haughtily.

"About what?"

"When I see young people like those performers, or the ones in bands, I wonder if I could have ever chosen that sort of life. You ever think about that?"

"Mm, not really, I guess."

Not in the slightest. If I thought about what I could have done differently every time I had regrets, I'd be dwelling on those things forever.

"I think you have a lot more confidence than I do. I feel like I worked pretty hard to get to where I am today, but I have no idea if I can maintain such a good life in the future. So I end up fantasizing about the other lives I could have lived."

Her evaluation of me was *completely* off the mark.

I didn't think her evaluation of herself was correct, either. I could tell by the way she talked about herself that she genuinely believed her life was a battle that she had fought and won. Even if she did lack confidence in herself, uncertain if she could continue living what she thought was a pretty good life, now and then Saitou still seemed to mistake her own life for something *special*.

"No matter what path you chose, I'm pretty sure you'd thrive, Sanae."

"I guess. If you think so, then it must be true."

She must've really had a lot of faith in me.

"I suppose there's no point in talking hypotheticals anyway. You can wish all you want, but it won't change your life overnight, and you can't take back the past. You said that you studied military and foreign policy in school, right? Did you ever consider finding a career in those fields?"

"I was interested in them as school subjects, but I don't think I'd like to work in them."

That was a lie. I wasn't interested in them, but I'd had a goal in mind. However, I wasn't lucky enough to possess the intellect of someone who could change the world as a scholar.

"What about you?" I asked. "You were in legal studies, weren't you?"

"Being a lawyer never really crossed my mind either. Though when I was in school, I guess I did think that it would be pretty fun at least once."

"When was that?"

"Mmm, don't remember. Guess I'm going senile already!"

She laughed. I laughed along with her.

"But then, we're the same age, aren't we? I'm sure you've already forgotten all about back then too."

Then, suddenly...

"No."

Once this surprise, unplanned denial had spilled from my mouth, I had no choice but to continue the thought. But when I thought about it, this was something I needed to assert, but at least it wasn't an inconvenience.

"There are some things that I'll never forget."

I meant to say this calmly, with a smile, but the tone came out all wrong. My brain had given the right commands, but my mouth had not received the message. Saitou's right eyelid twitched slightly. It was something of a habit of hers when she felt that the atmosphere had shifted.

"Like that time I lent you my umbrella," I went on to explain.

"Oh, c'mon, you only remember that because I *reminded* you! I thought you actually had something *serious* to say." She seemed to be waving this off to give me a last chance at an out.

I thought about it. Some genuine part of my heart had suddenly made itself known. Still, it was hopeless. Anything else was fine—I'd share whatever other opinions I had with Saitou, or anyone.

There was only one thing that I would never, ever forget, and that was the only thing that I could share with no one else.

I smoothed things over with Saitou, and we ate up the rest of our flavorless meal.

Through these bland, endless days, how could I possibly forget—ever even *think* of forgetting—that incomparable gale? Those glittering memories?

— ✶ —

Typically, it was Saitou who selected our date spots. It would probably be unnatural if she did it every single time, so I'd at least offer some semblance of an opinion, but she never took it into account. Of course, to maintain a stress-free relationship, it was important not to blithely accept everything, so I sometimes intentionally picked little squabbles during our conversations. Other than that, there was no reason for us to have any particularly noteworthy fights, and even now, it didn't seem that there were any big conflicts brewing on the horizon. In that respect, the sort of distance Saitou had when it came to romance probably helped. She wasn't after the sort of persistently passionate romance where she had to see me constantly or affirm our feelings for each other every single day. What she wanted was a relationship that was little different from friendship, with occasional dramatic, fiery moments. As far as I was concerned, this was exceedingly easy to deal with.

It took me far longer to comprehend Saitou's relationship with her work than her relationship with romance. Previously, we'd had a conversation along these lines:

"When you talk about radio, people imagine a lot of late nights, but actually, most of the work gets done during the day. I'm currently in charge of an afternoon program, so my schedule is pretty standard, but there's always the possibility of reorganization. Do you listen to the radio, Kaya-kun?"

"I always have it on when I'm at home. And I listen to your show on demand."

I listened to it so I could keep up with the conversation when the topic came up. Her eyes widened as though this surprised her.

"Really? Sorry, I'm just so surprised!"

"That I listen to the radio?"

"No, that you're actually interested in my work. You never talk about you own job, so I figured you didn't care about other people's either."

She was right. I didn't care about any of it. Until that conversation, it hadn't occurred to me that Saitou was arrogant enough to believe that people who take interest in their own careers must also be interested in others' work. Still, Saitou's arrogance wouldn't cause me any inconvenience, and I was thankful to get the chance to reaffirm that her work was her pride and joy, knowledge which helped our relationship run more smoothly.

Given how much value she placed on her work, she was probably in the blustering prime of her life right now. I envied her life, if that wind of hers didn't leave her until she was so old that she could no longer work the way she did now.

Before I knew it, it had been about half a year since Saitou and I had started dating. Like most working adults, both of our work hours were usually from morning until night, so we were only able to see each other in the evenings when our professional and personal affairs didn't take priority, or on the rare occasion that both our days off aligned.

Saitou had seemingly been pretty swamped at work lately, but today, she appeared almost performatively free of fatigue, the light in her eyes threatening to scald me with its intensity.

"Hey there! I'm starving!"

"Hey. What do you wanna eat?"

"I'll let you decide today."

Saitou was wearing casual autumn wear while I was in a suit, though she hadn't had the day off. She seemed to have finished up her work by early evening and had headed home to wait for me to get off. On days like this, if we hadn't already decided on somewhere to go, we would meet up at a drugstore near her place.

Today was no different.

"This isn't really my wheelhouse, but I'm fine with anything but curry. I already had curry for lunch."

"Gotcha. How about the usual, then?"

By now, I had spent enough time with her to understand where she was referring to. "The usual" was an izakaya that was popular with area locals. It was independently owned, and there were only a few employees on staff. We had been there frequently enough that I now recognized most of them, and Saitou, who often went there on her own, was treated as a regular.

"Oh, you brought the boyfriend with you today!"

I gave the appropriate smile and nod as a female employee who always seemed to be there greeted us in a gratingly chipper voice. We parted the noren curtains and stepped inside. Saitou seemed to enjoy talking with the staff here, much preferring a place where everybody knew her name to some strange place where she'd just be treated as part of the scenery. That said, she was fully aware that not everyone shared her preferences, so if I

YORU SUMINO

had been opposed to this the first time she brought me here, we would have never come here together again.

We were seated side by side at the counter. Saitou asked the waiter about today's special and ordered that, along with drinks and some menu items we'd ordered before. I was about to ask her if anything noteworthy had happened today as a conversation starter, as I usually did, when Saitou spoke up first.

"I know this is kind of out of the blue, but I wanted to talk to you about something!"

"Hm, what's that?"

I knew without looking at her that Saitou's eyes were shining. It was rare for her to get this fired up at the start of a conversation. Usually, she'd start off by talking about the news or something that had happened that day, something like that to feel out the vibe. She must have had some particularly good news to share.

We clinked our beer steins together, then Saitou quickly turned to the topic that she wanted to address.

"A while back, we were talking about whether we were still in touch with people from high school, right?"

"Yeah, I told you that I hadn't been in touch with anyone for a while, and you said that you really weren't either."

"Right, right, but there are still one or two people who I hear from now and then, and today I got a text from one of them for the first time in ages and gave them a call. We decided to go get lunch together soon!"

"Huh."

Just as I was starting to note how unlike her this was, wondering if this was something that she absolutely needed to talk to me about, the waiter approached and placed our appetizers on the counter.

"Oh, thank you! Right, so, there was a girl in our class named Aizawa Shihori. Do you remember her?"

"Aizawa...?"

As I thought about what to say, the waiter started elaborating on all the appetizers.

"I have some recollection of her, but I don't think I ever talked to her much. Oh, this one's *really* good."

"Oh, it is! Anyway, you say that, but were there any of our classmates that you really *did* talk to?"

"Well, when you put it *that* way..."

"Shiori-chan did remember you, though."

I stopped moving my chopsticks and took a sip of my highball.

"You talked about me?"

"Oh, sorry, should I not have...?"

"No, that's not it. I'm just surprised that I was even worth bringing up."

I had plenty of guesses about what people thought about me back then.

"She was surprised to hear that I'd gotten back in touch with you and that we were dating now. She asked me what you were like these days. I told her you were a good guy."

I was sure she wanted me to be embarrassed by this.

"Little embarrassing for a former classmate to have to hear that."

"Aw, c'mon, don't be like that. Anyway, Shihori-chan got married. Her surname is Imai now. But yeah, we're gonna get lunch!"

"Mm."

"You wanna come too?"

It was an innocent question, or, rather, an arrogantly ignorant one—Saitou was assuming that just because she had overcome the barriers between her and our classmates, there was no reason that others couldn't do the same.

"I'm sure my being there would just make things awkward for her. You go ahead."

"I mean, I figured it'd be fine since we're all adults now, but I see what you mean. She did say that you could come if you wanted, though."

I swallowed down the awkwardness of my next breath with my highball. Why on earth would Aizawa Shihori say a thing like that?

The chumminess of the waitstaff came in handy here. Every time the waitress stopped by, she had a few words to say, allowing me to sidestep the invitation. As such, the meeting between Saitou and Aizawa Shihori remained an event for just the two ladies. There was a chance that Saitou might learn something less-than-positive about me, but facts were facts.

It was possible that this might even be the impetus for the two of us to break off our relationship. If that did happen, it'd be just as well to me. Saitou seemed to be thinking the exact opposite, though, and brought up a further topic as she snacked on some kabocha.

"Well, never mind meeting up with Shihori-chan, anyway. But there *is* something else I was hoping you'd attend with me."

From how formal she was being, I had some idea.

"Sure, when?"

"Next month is my birthday, remember?"

"November 23rd, right?"

"Yeah, on Labor Thanksgiving Day!"

She had sighed enough times that people usually didn't thank her for her work that it was easy enough to remember.

"My parents said they wanted to come here to have dinner with me, and...well, I was thinking you could come too."

"...Huh?"

"Oh! I mean it's fine if you don't want to! S-sorry!"

"It's not that I don't want to, but are you sure I should be intruding on your family time? Since it was your parents' idea, I'm sure they'd rather spend their time with their lovely daughter."

To be honest, the idea really didn't bother me. I had met the parents of other significant others before, and I was fairly practiced at meeting new people for work and interviews. I had only voiced what sounded like hesitation in the hopes of gauging exactly how seriously—and with what intention—she had proposed this meeting.

"Jeez, you know I see them all the time."

My playing dumb was purposely overt, as I certainly did know that. I wasn't trying to offend her and make my own life harder for no reason.

"Are you asking me to formally meet your parents?"

She opened her lips once, gulping both air and her resolve into an "Mm-hmm," as she nodded. "That's correct. But if you don't want to, it's fine."

It was clear from the number of pieces of nankotsu karaage she was popping into her mouth that Saitou was waiting for my reply. I understood now—her excitement when talking about Aizawa was just a trojan horse for the true seriousness of her real motive. I assumed she didn't want me to think of her as a burden. I had probably wounded former partners that way. I didn't have to think twice about what choice to make.

"I just hope they think that I'm right for you."

There was a certain face Saitou made when she wasn't sure just how much joy or excitement she was allowed to show. I knew exactly how to handle this.

"Just gotta make sure they don't think that someone just as gloomy as their daughter has come along."

"Kaya-kun, I *swear*...! You *are* right, though."

That was enough to finally get a smile out of her. She seemed to live in fear of premature joy more than most people. She couldn't cope without that happiness being handed to her wrapped up in a neat little bow. As far as her life was concerned, her wariness toward feeling joy probably wasn't such a bad idea— though it occurred to me that the joy she was feeling *was* still premature.

Perhaps relieved that one important preliminary step was now out of the way, Saitou began drinking. It seemed to me she had been drinking more heavily as of late. As I listened to her grumble about work, I wondered on what measure Saitou based introducing me to her parents as a prospective partner.

If I had to put into words what she valued most in life, it would probably be a sense of accomplishment. Getting that sense of accomplishment from her work gave her the greatest joy. This was obvious from the things she spoke about on a daily basis; her work definitely gave her a sort of hope. Thus, I had to assume that for Saitou, romance was only a means of satisfying her own lustful desires and her desire for approval as a woman. That said, it was starting to seem that her relationship with me wasn't so frivolous but something that she imagined could progress to marriage. Was it simply because she felt like a prisoner to social norms?

Well, whatever the reason, that was fine.

It didn't matter to me if we got married; I would just keep existing until I died. You can detour all you like on your road back into the ground, but the destination remains the same no matter which path you take.

"Thanks for another great meal! We'll be back!"

We left the izakaya with plenty of time for me to catch the last train after seeing Saitou home. I watched her chattering with the waitstaff and gave a bow. As the sliding door clacked closed behind us, she wrapped her hand around my elbow.

"Sorry about asking you to meet my parents out of nowhere."

I looked down to her after she spoke—she was making a face like she had just bitten into some acrid fruit.

"It's fine. I did figure this day might come eventually."

I spat exactly the words she was hoping to hear.

"Thank you. I'm glad...really glad." She tittered at herself, then let go of my elbow. "I've actually been nervous about this all day."

"Hard to imagine you getting nervous about anything."

That was just a facade she kept up, I realized.

"I guess it must look that way, but I'm actually a pretty anxious person. I was seriously nervous today though. Probably the most since *that* time!"

"Which time?"

"When we held hands in that taxi, on the first night we went out for drinks together."

I guess that had happened. The memory had sunk down to the bottom of my muddy heart, no more or less valuable than any other.

"My folks are going to be so surprised I've found a good man like you!"

All part of the usual conversational routine. I laughed back, "I certainly hope so."

As always, I couldn't help but notice that there was some vanity behind the trigger Saitou had pulled, something which could be mistaken for shyness. I wasn't sure to what degree, but I knew there was a side of her that saw me as some kind of ornament. It didn't bother me—I was fine with it. It was fine if our relationship was somewhat muddied. It's fine for your feelings for others to stagnate. Outside of the singular gust of brilliance, when it came to the meaningless rest of your life, that was all fine.

We arrived in front of Saitou's building. I asked her vaguely about her plans for her day off tomorrow and said goodnight before leaving. Or at least, that was the plan.

"About that night," she suddenly said, staring at her own reddened palm. "When the taxi stopped here, I wondered if you might come up with me. I got excited thinking about what might happen if you did. But you were ever so much the gentleman." She laughed, teasingly. I knew what she was trying to say. "I guess you've got work tomorrow, huh?"

It meant so little to me. Not just work—everything. Thus, I responded as she was hoping.

"I mean, I'm not so much of a gentleman that I can't leave a spare tie at a girl's place so I can head right out for work again in the morning."

As long as Saitou was happy, that was all that mattered. As long as I didn't cause trouble, that was all that mattered. If she still had some hope for the future, some delusion that she could be happy, that was all that mattered.

I couldn't help but envy how ignorant and foolish she was that something so simple could still make her smile.

"As long as you don't smoke at my place, I don't care if you do so when we're out or whatever."

"Nah, I'm gonna quit. I hate leaving the smell of cigarettes on your clothes and hair."

"What a considerate fellow you are."

"It just seems obvious to me. It's not like I smoke all that much anyway."

"Ah, that's true."

"If you want me to give up smoking, I will."

"I mean, it's fine. I don't want you to change on my account."

"It's really not that big a deal."

"But I think it is. Giving up something you like just for someone else, that is."

"I really wouldn't call it 'giving up' or anything."

"Listen, it's *fine*! I think people should change for themselves, not others."

"For themselves, huh?"

"Yeah. So, when the time comes for you to give up smoking, I want it to be for yourself first. Like out of concern for your own health or because you think it'll make you more attractive if you quit."

"I mean my health is fine right now, but if it'll make me more attractive, maybe I will quit."

"It's hard for a guy as handsome as you to be all alone."

"But I've got you, don't I?"

"Hee, suppose so, guess I can be there for you."

In the darkness, my fingers, which once seemed to grasp life itself, limply grasped Saitou's arm atop the three-quarter bed.

As planned, the meeting with Saitou's parents went off without a hitch.

I'm sure that I gave off the impression that I was a competent adult and implied well enough that things were going smoothly between Saitou and me. I'm also sure it was clear that my income would not be an issue. Saitou was the most nervous out of anyone present. It occurred to me to ask if this was the first time she had brought a partner to meet her parents; as it turned out, it was. I was curious why I was the first, but I supposed it was a matter of age.

I, naturally, was not nervous in the slightest. Throughout the meeting, I gauged her parents' reactions to meeting this romantic partner of their daughter's. They seemed relieved, though at the same time looked like someone had taken some toy of theirs away.

I gave them a proper trivial greeting as we saw them off at the hotel nearest to the station.

Once we were alone, Saitou invited me to stop in somewhere else. I was sure that this was a form of self-care for Saitou, so that was fine. We stopped in at a bar we had been to before, about ten minutes' walk from the station, and sat down at a table. Thinking about it, more than half of the time I shared with Saitou was spent either sleeping or eating. There was nothing else for two boring adults like us to do.

She ordered a strong-smelling beer, the one she always drank when she had gotten past some tough spot at work or in her private life. She took a sip of the Laphroaig she had ordered from the bartender and heaved a heavy sigh.

"Thanks for everything," she said. "I really have to thank you."

"I was a little nervous, but it was fun."

"Really? I got so worn out just freaking out about whether one of my parents might say something weird."

She let out another sigh and clinked her glass to mine almost as an afterthought.

"They really liked you."

"I sure hope so."

"They were absolutely *gushing* when you left to go to the restroom."

Just because someone said something about someone else when they weren't present didn't mean that evaluation was true. Saitou's position in that moment was half a family member, half my dating partner. Obviously they weren't going to be entirely frank in front of their daughter. Not that there was really any need for me to be certain of their true feelings.

I sipped my drink in time with her. Every few times you took a sip while drinking with someone else, you were bound to lift your glasses at the same time. Doing so kept the rhythm of the conversation steady and your partner in good spirits. As we continued discussing the night's events, Saitou changed her glass out for a second drink, and a third.

"I'm glad that they liked this too."

She lifted up the necklace that hung from her neck, eyes moist. I had given it to her at midnight the night before as a birthday gift.

"Yeah, they said it was cute, didn't they?"

"Mm, that's not what I'm happy about, though. It's cute because a professional made it to be cute. *Obviously* it'd be cute." Through her intoxication she seemed awfully proud of the conclusion she had come to. "I'm happy because they thought I suited the necklace I was wearing."

"Not that the jewelry suited you?"

"Well, *yeah*, because it's something that you chose, based on our memories and what you thought I would like. I'm happy that other people can see it too."

I wondered exactly what was so great about that, and the moment's pause born of that thought apparently conveyed my doubts to Saitou. Or perhaps she had merely intended to explain herself from the start.

"I don't think there's anything that could make someone happier than knowing they're in their beloved's thoughts."

"I see." I understood what she was saying, but I couldn't empathize. "That's a very *you* way to put it."

"C'mon, stop makin' fun of me!"

Grinning in a way that was not at all unhappy, Saitou ordered another drink from the bartender.

"I don't know about having anybody in my thoughts, but I chose it because I thought it would make you happy."

That wasn't a lie. It was simply the best choice for putting her in a good mood. No matter how you tried to put it into words, you could never truly know someone else's heart, so that was enough. There was no need for empathy. We both just had to play the appropriate parts.

I had even chosen that statement because I thought it would make her happy. However, she didn't react with a smile and a blush, as I'd expected.

"Say, Kaya-kun," she started but did not continue. It was that typical cowardice of hers, leaving Saitou unable to speak if the other party wasn't interested. I looked at her curiously.

"What?"

"Am I enough for you?"

It was an abstract question, one to which I did not have an immediate answer. It wasn't that I *couldn't* answer, but I could sense that the appropriate response was silence.

"Sorry, I dunno what I'm saying. I even had you meet my parents. Everything's just moved so fast from that first night up until now, so I guess, to put it nicely, it...it almost seems like fate."

Wasn't she the one who liked to insist that there was no such thing as fate in this world?

"I guess I've just been kind of worried."

"About what?"

"That I'm hogging your future."

She took a gulp of the amber-colored liquid.

"I dunno about marriage or anything like that, but if we keep on like this, I might be stealing precious years away from you. Though I sure hope that won't be the case."

She left off at another awkward spot. She mistakenly thought that not spelling everything out meant that she was letting the other party have their say—or else she was just pretending to have that misconception. But leaving words that should be said unspoken was only a way to try to get the other person to complete your thought. It was as good as trying to bring someone under your control.

Of course, knowing all that, I finished her words for her.

"We might take different paths one day, and we might grow apart."

"That's true."

"But even so, I'll never think of the time I've spent with you as a loss."

None of my time was even valuable enough to be wasted.

We might have years or decades ahead of us. There might be marriage, children, and more in our future, but none of that was a problem for me. There was nothing that I could hope to gain by using my time any other way. It was probably for the best that Saitou used me to her heart's content: She could use me to experience that gale of excitement in her free time. And then, if the two of us lived together like zombies once the gale left her, it was just as fine. That was the sort of pair we were.

On the off chance she was able to read my mind, I wondered if she would be mad at me for belittling her.

She smiled bashfully and said, "Look at you, acting all cool!" with an elbow jab that didn't connect.

"When you put it that way, though, there's actually something I'm curious about."

"Yeah?"

"Uh-huh."

She set her glass down for a moment, the liquid inside sloshing, and tilted her head slightly.

"Have you ever had a love that you'll never forget?" she asked, with that same light in her eyes that had long since left mine.

I was confident, certain even, that Saitou knew nothing about me, but I could still feel the hackles rising on some part of me that I could never show her. But through all the endless hours I had learned to hide that part of myself, so I doubted she could read the bristling that coursed through my marrow.

"One or two, maybe. They do say that men tend to keep an old flame or two around in the back of their minds."

She couldn't possibly have read me. And yet, she muttered something inconceivable.

"...*Liar.*"

The word that fell from her lips in that hushed tone slunk around my feet. I could almost picture it tightening around my legs.

She took another sip of her drink after giving me a smile, one that suggested the muscles of her face had formed it regardless of her emotions.

Liar, she said. What could that mean?

Had I made her think that something about me was a lie?

Could she read some part of me?

Had she sensed something about me?

Saitou, of all people.

"What am I lying about?" I asked. Her smile widened.

"Mm, well, I mean, I bet you've always been popular. I'm sure it's not just one or two."

That was a lie too, and I was sure that she had said it knowing that I would realize. If she had wanted me to think that she was being serious, her words would have matched her tone.

So then, why...?

If what had nestled itself within me was something common to this world, if it was something that everyone experienced, then it wouldn't be shocking for her to guess what was going on in my head—but it was nothing like that. Saitou could not *possibly* imagine. It was beyond imagining.

I pushed no further. If I did, I realized it would have destroyed our relationship, which had been progressing with corpse-like placidity thus far, in an instant.

Perhaps whatever was hidden within her could deal a fatal blow to our relationship. A few days later, though, I got a call that might eliminate any need to worry about such things.

My company was recommending that I be transferred somewhere far away.

A surprise transfer had always been on the table. There was no point in hiding it. I decided to ask Saitou out the next day and tell her. It was the night before her day off. I knew that telling her I had something important to talk about would only frighten her, so I invited her over for dinner as casually as possible.

I told her I had gotten a nice bottle of wine from my boss. I did not want to leave this tale with an anticlimactic ending no matter how Saitou reacted to my news, so I thought it wise to have her over to my place, somewhere where neither of us could leave without fully making our intentions known. There was nothing peculiar about this; I had invited her over plenty of times before for the sake of an alibi. Incidentally, I had lied about the wine.

Once both our workdays were said and done, I met up with her at the station and we headed for my place. We passed through the generic condo entrance, exchanging a friendly greeting with a parent and child we passed by. When I unlocked the door and stepped inside, I could smell the lifelessness of my own home.

"Stark a place as ever," she remarked. "It's the same size as my place, but it feels so much bigger."

"I'll take your coat."

I hung both our jackets on hangers. As she had noted, there was nothing in my home beyond the bare essentials for living. I had only a minimal amount of furniture and appliances plus a computer; no television or bookshelf in sight, much less any decorative items.

After she finished gargling in the bathroom, I called her over to the L-shaped sofa that sat framing the coffee table.

"You wanna start with the wine? I do have beer and stuff too."

"Well, it's a special occasion! Let's wait until the food gets here. Waiter! A beer, if you would."

"Gladly, Miss."

I poured one of her favorite canned beers into a glass and placed it on the table. "Pour the rest how you like," I told her and then returned to the kitchen. At Saitou's request, I'd ordered Italian food for delivery. I'd bought some cheese to tide us over until the food arrived, and I piled it on a plate and placed it before her. I opened a beer myself in response to her thanks and sat down kitty-corner to her.

I could have just launched immediately into the topic at hand, not bothering to wait for the food, but given that the conversation might result in a loss of appetite, I thought it best to fill our stomachs first. As we waited for the food to arrive, I filled Saitou in on this fictitious boss of mine. I set him up as a good-natured single guy who enjoyed trying out different restaurants. I also explained that the wine had been a gift for finishing up some last-minute work for him.

After a little while, the doorbell rang, and a young man— probably college-aged—handed us a number of dishes. Saitou and I placed them on the table with plates and chopsticks, and then I set some glasses on the table alongside the red wine. Saitou had already drained her second beer.

After we poured the wine and said our thanks, Saitou, who had just taken a bit of salad, put her hand to her mouth happily.

"Is delivery food getting good these days or what?"

"It really is!"

We sampled all the dishes as we carried on a vapid conversation. The wine seemed to suit her palate. Every item tasted as bland to me as ever.

As always, here I was, eating with her. We shared an active connection only in the things that had a direct link to living. The only other things for us to do were the necessary tasks to lead a hassle-free life. That was why I needed to have a talk with Saitou, my girlfriend, about the future.

With a sip of wine in my mouth, I waited for the right moment. I opened up the chicken fritters and tried to catch a gap in Saitou's chatter, thinking it was about the right time. However, Saitou, who had really picked up the pace in her imbibing, chose that moment of all times to knock over a glass full of wine. Casting a sidelong glance at her as she panicked, I grabbed some dish towels from the kitchen and sopped up the spill. I tasked her with separating the food that was still edible from what had been soaked in wine.

"God, I'm so sorry! I think I'm drunk."

"That's unusual for you."

"Mm, I haven't been getting much sleep lately. That might be why it's getting to me."

As I noted concern for her health, the conversation shifted to the usual kvetching about Saitou's work. We had completely blown past the moment for the subject I wanted to bring up, but we still had plenty of time.

"It's like, there's this misogynistic side to my boss, and every time it crops up in casual conversation I have to wonder, like, what is going on in this office?"

"I see... I think it'd be one thing if you were really happy there, but have you thought about moving to a different station?"

"I can't say I haven't, but it's not realistic, considering I don't have a whole lot to show for myself right now."

Despite having already noted how drunk she was, Saitou took another swig of her drink. So she had been backed into a corner by her job, the thing that was supposed to be her raison d'être.

I wondered how she really felt about that. If she felt betrayed, then perhaps that gust of hers already had one foot out the door. Or perhaps it meant that her once-in-a-lifetime gust had nothing to do with her work in the first place.

After a while, Saitou had finally aired out enough complaints to satisfy herself—or maybe she was simply tired—she clapped her hands together and said, "Sorry for griping so much in the middle of such a good meal."

"It's fine, food that tastes good always tastes good," I said, when suddenly, the perfect pass came hurtling my way.

"On the previous note, have you ever thought about changing careers or anything?" she asked.

I glanced upward, then tilted my head as though I was thinking hard.

"Mm, well..."

There really was no need for me to contemplate it, since I had just been given the perfect setup for the talk I already wanted to have. Thus, my reaction was only what I felt constituted the appropriate hesitation to a sudden question from a lover.

"What's up?"

"Well, actually, there was something that I wanted to talk to you about today on that subject."

Her right eyebrow twitched at my tone.

"What? You're..."

Her mouth clamped shut as though she was trying to force back the words, *"...scaring me,"* that probably would have followed. That was how it looked to me, anyway.

Choosing my words carefully, I explained to her that I might be transferred. I told her everything, not concealing any detail—the timing, how long, and that the proposed location would be quite far away. There was no point in hiding anything. The most important part was what would come after I had clearly outlined the facts.

"Anyway, nothing's been decided yet, we're still just in talks. But, um, I wanted to get your opinion on it. What would you do if I got transferred?"

"Hm…"

Unlike mine, her sigh probably actually came from the heart.

"I realize that neither of us could easily quit our jobs," I continued. "But to be honest, I don't want to have to end things with you, either. Still, it's like you said before. I'm worried that if we couldn't see each other as much anymore, I'd just be wasting your time."

This was largely a lie, but it *was* true that I wasn't actively hoping to end things with Saitou. I was ultimately leaving the decision up to her. I had no problem with carrying on a long-distance relationship, and if she decided to break up with me on the spot, I would accept that just as well. As long as there wasn't any lingering animosity, I didn't care either way.

I waited as she took one pensive sip, then another. I figured that just staring at her while she thought would put unnecessary pressure on her, so I took a bite of some of the food that was still left on the table. It was important to determine whether a partner's silence was merely a step toward a statement of intent or whether that silence itself was the statement. In this case, I knew that Saitou was trying to think of something to say, so it was best for me to simply wait.

After a gap, I felt her aim her sights on me.

"Like you said before, Kaya-kun, I don't think that any time spent with you could possibly be a waste."

"Uh-huh."

"So, if you're all right with it, I don't think the distance is enough to break us up immediately, but I do think we should decide which way this is going to go."

She had a showy way of putting it, as usual.

"You mean whether we're going to break up now or later?" I asked, tilting my head. She smiled thinly, shaking her head like a tree branch swaying in the wind.

"No, that's not what I mean."

Then, what *did* she mean? "Which way," she'd said.

She took another sip of her drink in place of taking a breath. Then...

"Maybe I'll just quit."

"...Huh?"

Despite my confusion, the thin smile on her lips rippled across her whole face.

"Maybe I'll just quit my job and go with you."

For the first time in ages, someone had actually managed to surprise me, but even the shock of that soon faded.

"I think we should discuss this when you aren't drunk."

"Delusional" was the apt term for her current state of mind. Saitou would never throw her career away for some man. Even if she wouldn't have used the word "gust," she herself should have realized that her youth and her raison d'être were likely based in her work.

"I am drunk, but that's not why I'm saying this."

"Then...?"

"I've thought a bit about this before."

"About what...?"

"I'd wondered what I might do if something happened with you and I couldn't continue my current work."

That wasn't even worth considering. That kind of absurd thinking didn't suit her in the slightest.

"Obviously, my work is important to me, and it's given me a lot of irreplaceable experiences. But if I had to quit my job to live with you, I do think that option is on the table. I still feel that way."

She was talking about a slight misunderstanding as though it were something quite grave. I was willing to spend the effort to correct this.

"Even if you came with me, there's no guarantee you'd be able to find a job like the one you have now."

I said this in a sincere, non-judgmental tone.

"That's true. I've always wanted to try working at a record shop or something, though. Wonder if any would be hiring."

It didn't seem like she'd gotten what I was trying to say in the slightest. I immediately gave a "Listen," as she talked about this, as though she was thrilled about this future full of possibilities, pressing my lips in a way that I normally wouldn't. Drunk or no, she was talking nonsense, and my irritation was starting to show.

"You *really* need to think this over," I said.

"Do you not want me to come with you? Is this your subtle way of breaking up with me...?"

"That's not it, but weren't *you* the one who just said that your work is irreplaceable?"

She agreed without any hesitation. "Yeah."

"I can't let my circumstances take that job away from you."

That job, or her gust of wind.

"Bold of you to think you could take *anything* from me. I'd never let anyone take that from me. No one's circumstances matter but my own. If I need to quit, then I'll quit of my own volition. I said it before, didn't I? People should change for their *own* sakes."

I supposed she had said that. I had no idea when though; it felt like it had happened both recently and a long time ago.

"So, I'm saying that if I quit my job, it's because I *want* to go with you. And, I mean, there's still a chance you won't be transferred, and I still have some work I'd need to wrap up, so it's not like I could just up and leave either."

I listened closely to what she was saying. Chills ran down my spine. Why hadn't I realized it sooner? It felt like I had just rounded a corner and suddenly come face-to-face with something terrifying.

"So I don't need you to feel responsible for this. I'm just saying that, if the time comes, I'll be prepared. Though if this isn't what you want, then never mind. Of course, you've dated me long enough to know that I won't back down without a fight, even if you tell me no."

She gave a clownish grin and took another drink.

Bit by bit, I was realizing what those chills meant.

No way.

It was dawning on me what it was Saitou had been hiding from me all this time. If what I was thinking was true, then what a monumental *fool* I had been. But that was understandable, perhaps. How could I have known that the person here beside me would have such a ridiculous thought, even for a moment? I instinctively took another sip of my own drink. I didn't want to believe this.

"Now that I think about it, we have been dating a while."

As she said, the two of us had spent quite a lot of time together. I thought about our relationship up until now. Then I looked again at the face of the woman in front of me. Our eyes met, the expectancy in her gaze confirming for me the identity of the terror I felt rising inside of me.

The signs had been everywhere. I hoped desperately that she was lying.

"Kaya-kun? What's the matter?"

"I..."

I was thinking. Had I misread her? Was I wrong about what I should have felt toward her? I stared into her eyes. All this time, I had envied that light that lingered in her eyes. I had dated her thinking that she was someone still being blown by her own wind, that she was someone who would enjoy that wind for a long while yet thanks to her work, and that she was someone who might hold the secret of living an enviable life.

But I realized now that I might have been fully mistaken.

"Were you actually planning on breaking up with me today?"

She said this jokingly, but there was a sincere fear in her eyes, and I tried to gauge what was going through her mind. Why was she looking at me like that? What was so scary about the idea of being without me? For Saitou, I was nothing more than one of the many men she might meet in her life. It just so happened that we were former classmates, and that, through a number of coincidences aligning, we had reunited. So why would she be so afraid that I, just one of the various men she had dated, might disappear from her life? Couldn't she just find someone else? Wasn't she just keeping me around so that she could have someone to satisfy her lust and her need for approval close at hand?

Was that...not it?

I hallucinated cracks forming in her eyeballs.

I cursed my own foolishness.

"Sanae."

"Mm?"

This was out of hand.

"I have to do this. We need to talk."

"Wait, what *now*?!"

Her fear redoubled, and I could see that she realized this, trying to twist herself away from it with the power of will and alcohol. The smile she faced me with looked to me like nothing but sorrow.

"There's something important I have to tell you."

"What? You're scaring me...!" She voiced her own terror.

"Sorry for scaring you."

I meant that sincerely. If I were my normal self, the person I had been until now, I might have chosen my words with a bit more consideration for how her heart worked.

"But I have to do this."

I had to tell her the truth.

"Please don't look at me like that."

She had to know the sort of person I truly was. It would be far too cruel for her to have to live not knowing that.

"I'm sorry."

If I did this now, there might still be time. Without that gale—that briefest time in a person's life—you could not be saved. We had to be allowed to live our lives dwelling on that time alone. Naturally, even Saitou deserved that chance.

She couldn't live her life thinking that *I* was her gale.

"Sounds like a fire truck. Wonder if there's a fire nearby," Saitou said as though to try and disperse the tension that filled the room. She took a sip of water.

"Sanae, you need to listen to me."

"Ah, here we go then." One corner of her mouth quirked up. It looked a bit cruel, but I nodded.

"There's really nothing else left for us to do."

"Kaya-kun, have you done something?"

"Nothing."

She was acting as though I had utterly lost my mind, but that wasn't true. This was the sort of person I had always been—she just hadn't been aware of that fact. To be frank, it hadn't been necessary for her to know, but now that time had passed.

"I'm guessing you think this is about to be some kind of break-up talk, but it's not."

Saitou had to know the truth. She took another sip of water, readying herself. I heard her swallow.

"That might end up being the conclusion we come to, but I just want you to know that there isn't anything that's led me to believe we should split."

"I don't get what you're saying, but I have no intention of breaking up with you."

"I'm just thinking that after this, you might want some space."

"Have you been cheating on me?" she joked. She had a very commonsense way of thinking when it came to romance.

"I suppose that I have been lying to you, but not about an affair or anything like that."

She waited for me to continue.

"Or rather..." Same as Saitou often did, I paused for a breath before getting to the crux of the matter. This felt like the first time I was telling her the truth.

"...I can't love anyone," I said decisively, then continued before she had a chance to respond or interject, "which also means that I would never betray a girlfriend or spouse for the love of another."

She stared at me silently, taking in my words, deciphering them, and processing them.

"I mean, that's fine, isn't it? If it's difficult for you to love people."

"It's not that it's difficult, it's impossible. At least now, anyway."

"When you say you can't love anyone..." she repeated. It seemed she finally understood what I was trying to say. "Does that include me...?"

I was glad that she did have some faculties of reasoning. After far too long, I nodded.

"Yeah. I don't think that I could call what I feel for you love of any variety. It isn't even friendship, or a sentimental attachment from us growing up in the same town."

I kept my eyes firmly locked on hers, so that she could be certain I was being sincere.

"As far as I'm concerned, you're..."

Never once had I addressed her so bluntly. That was probably because it would have hurt her pride, which was proportional to her severe lack of confidence.

"...a former classmate who I happened to run into, and when we formed an acquaintanceship I thought that I might as well date you. That's all you are to me. Just an opportunity."

Her hands, which had been folded atop her knees, unclasped.

"But isn't that what most dating is like?"

"That's not what I'm saying." I looked her square in the eye, shaking my head to distance myself from her assumptions. "Even now, I still don't really like you, Sanae." There was no point in waiting for her to question this, so I continued. "My feelings for you right now are no different than that day we met at the station, when you were just some stranger sitting next to me."

"I..."

She fell silent, but it wasn't a strong enough reaction that I'd call it shock. She looked as though she was trying to determine how much of what I was saying was true.

"I mean exactly what I'm saying. I'm sorry that I've deceived you. Honestly, I intended to keep on deceiving you. Or, well, maybe I would have told you this after the wind in your sails finally left you. Still, I've never once thought about ending our association. At least, not while you still have that gale."

"...A *gale*."

There was no question in her eyes. It seemed she was merely parroting an unfamiliar word.

"I have a theory that everyone has a wind that blows at some point in their life. You could think of it as something else if you like. Your peak, your greatest memories, something like that. Once we've tasted that in our lives, we're empty without it, simply whiling away the rest of our days with the fond memory of that sensation. It seems to me that that gale hasn't left you yet. I used to think that I was jealous of that, and honestly, I probably still am."

Saitou slowly peeled her pressed lips apart to reveal her tongue, which flicked vacantly a few times as though she were pretending to speak before she declared, willfully, "*This* is the peak of my life? And you don't think this gale has left me yet...?"

"I don't. You still aren't empty, like I am. No matter how empty you might end up after, I feel like everyone has the right to experience that gale at least once in their life."

"Hold it. So why did you even bring this up?"

"Please just listen to what I'm about to say."

I didn't sound like I was getting through to her, but she lowered her eyes to the table and nodded twice.

"I have to tell you this," I continued. Her eyes came back up to me. "I'd always thought that the gale was something you'd get from your work."

"You're saying you think work is the most important thing to me?"

"I did. But earlier it seemed like you were just fine with throwing that job away. Moreover, you were fine tossing it aside for *me*. But there's no chance, not even the slightest, of me getting to feel that gale again."

Her brow wrinkled, perhaps in denial, but I pushed forward, right through whatever it was that she was about to say.

"I mean, even if that's not true right now, I can't possibly risk that possibility. But it seemed you were headed that way, and I couldn't bear the thought, so I *had* to tell you this."

I deliberately hit her with a barrage of assertions, intrusive arguments, and pity, all of which would be hard for Saitou to swallow, given her character. I didn't mind if she got angry at me for this—same if she was sad or spiteful. I didn't even care if how incomprehensible this was had frightened her. Whatever her reaction was, all I cared about was that she distanced herself from me. Having spent enough time with her, no matter how idle, I had some measure of faith that she was wise enough to know when to give up on a relationship.

"Kaya-kun." When she finally broke the silence and said my name, there was neither anger nor sadness in her voice. "What was *your* gale?" she asked as though that was the most important thing, though I couldn't see why it mattered.

Though I couldn't comprehend how she was feeling, I actually had planned to tell her about this, regardless of whether or not she cared. I needed her to know what had shaped me into the person I was today. I needed her to know that I was a unique specimen even among all those who had tasted that gale in their lives. And I needed her to be able to give up on me.

"If you really wanna know, I guess I can tell you."

"Tell me."

I had never told this to anyone before. I couldn't pretend I wasn't nervous. However, there was a reason that I was sharing this special thing that existed within only me to Saitou.

"My gale blew back *then*."

I spoke with placid emotion, falling into the memories of those days that lingered in my heart, as I always did. As I had done so many times before.

"Back then? You mean when we were in high school?"

"Yeah. When I was sixteen, to be precise. I have no idea how others saw me back then, but I was bored with living and always irritable. I was constantly looking for something that would give my life some real meaning." It sounded stupid when I said it out loud. "I spent my time trying out lots of different stuff and getting disappointed with it. Then I met a girl, and I fell in love."

Saitou's eyebrows lifted ever so slightly.

"She lived in a different world. One separate from this one. I could only meet with her at a specific bus stop, and all I could see of her body were her eyes and nails."

Unsurprisingly, Saitou looked at me inscrutably.

"Was she a *ghost*?"

"Not to me. That bus stop connected our world to hers, and I'm 100 percent certain that she existed. I was able to touch her, and I was even able to put things from her world in my mouth."

"That's…"

She appeared to be desperately trying to align what I was saying with her own common sense.

"Are you sure you didn't just dream it? For some reason or other?"

Though she didn't spell it out, it was obvious that she thought I had hallucinated this, whether from an illness or some other foreign contaminant within my body. Though it should go without saying, I was not showing any symptoms of such an illness at the time, nor had I ingested anything strange.

"It wasn't a dream. I saw her lots of times. Whether or not anyone else believes me though, it doesn't change how vividly real it was to me, so much so that I could never forget my memories. So it's fine if you don't believe me."

"…Keep going."

It was probably a point of pride for Saitou that she would never claim to believe something that easily. Her achingly pointless pride—pride that would never accept that all the time she spent with someone like me was a complete *waste*.

"Every night, I went to that bus stop to see her. I'd wait inside the pitch-black bus shelter for her to arrive."

I realized that maybe I should explain that she came down into a basement safe house, but that would have complicated the story a bit, so I left that part out.

"Once every few days, she would arrive from that other world. I couldn't see her whole human form, only her glowing eyes and nails. I thought that she'd have some kind of knowledge, some intel I could get from her that would make my life special, but that didn't go very well. As much as we tried to share our cultures with one another, we couldn't share tastes or smells, and it was impossible to read any writing. The only things we could share were our words, but there's not a lot you can do with just learning rules or customs from another world."

I shared my memories with her, from start to finish.

"What's most important is that we were able to have some sort of real effect on each other's worlds. The same sort of stuff happened in both places, like if you broke something here, something there would break too."

We had now reached an unavoidable subject, something that we could go no further without discussing.

"We tried to find out if there was a way to utilize this connection to help one another."

The next name I spoke was not an accident but fully intentional.

"In the course of these experiments, I lost a dog belonging to Tanaka, the girl who sat beside me in class."

"Hm...?"

As I had predicted, Saitou looked at me suspiciously. She was probably trying to weigh whether my story or her own recollection was more accurate. However, she swiftly demanded an answer of me.

"Okay, sorry if I'm just remembering wrong, or if I forgot something, but..."

"Yeah?"

"...was there ever a Tanaka in our class?"

"Nope."

There was no point in waiting for her to ask the obvious follow-up to that.

"Back then, I tended to just lump all our classmates together, classifying them as 'Tanakas.' A common, average name for the sort of common, average person you'd find anywhere and everywhere. Nothing special about them."

The words seemed to hit her with some measurable force, the impact of which spread across her features. But I wasn't done talking yet.

"Did that include me?"

"No."

Her face immediately relaxed at this, but unfortunately, I had to burst her bubble.

"The ones who conducted themselves a little bit differently from the Tanakas got a different name."

I looked her in the eye.

"I thought of you as 'Saitou' back then, and that hasn't changed one bit. Even now, you're a Saitou to me, nothing more, nothing less."

There must have been a million different emotions overlapping within her, informing her expression. Seeing where her face ended up put me at ease.

"What the hell?!"

That night, for the first time ever, I saw a true despair in the eyes of Saitou Sanae—or rather, *Sunou* Sanae.

"You've probably figured it out by now, but that dog's name was Allumi, and its owner's real name was Aizawa Shihori. In essence, it's my fault that Allumi died."

I continued laying out the facts for her as I prepared two cups of coffee in the kitchen, setting one in front of Saitou.

"Shiori-chan..." she repeated softly, staring at the tabletop. "I never heard about this before."

"That's because I didn't tell anyone."

"...I see."

"Hey," she said, looking up at me for the first time in some minutes as I sat down on the sofa. "Is this all true?"

"It is, all of it."

"Even about you causing Shihori-chan's dog's death?"

"Yep. In essence, anyway. Allumi ended up dead because I stole it away."

For a second, I thought I saw her cheeks droop, but there was no reason for her to make such an expression, so I must have misjudged her reaction somehow. Her face soon returned to the same tint as before.

"Saitou..."

"That's what I call you, even now."

"Was everything you've ever said to me a *lie*?"

I supposed it was important to figure out what specifically she was referring to. I thought hard about all the things I could remember saying to her.

"I don't know if I would say that it was *all* a lie."

This time her face really did loosen up. There was a reason for that: I had purposely chosen my words to make it happen. I knew that if you wanted to really let someone down, it was best to get their hopes up first.

"I picked the words I thought you wanted to hear, the things that would make you like me. I knew that would make things go more smoothly."

I figured that here I would see a more downtrodden expression on her face than ever before, but I only saw her features continue to relax. I wondered if I had not yet done enough and kept going.

"Like I said before, I'm no longer capable of romantic feelings. To be more precise, I left those feelings behind fifteen years ago."

Even after this addition she showed no signs of despair. She just looked down and took a sip of the coffee that I had left on the table for her. "So," she said, as daintily as dropping a sugar cube into a coffee cup, "your 'gale' was love."

As the words hit my ears, I got the sensation of needles being driven into my fingertips. In the moment, I remembered a conversation we had once shared. She had asked me if I ever had an unforgettable love and called me a liar.

At the time, I hadn't been able to unravel the true shape of her feelings, but it had now become clear. She was likely harboring some jealousy, wondering if there was some rival lingering in my heart that she needed to know about.

"So, this girl you liked. What was she like?"

I had to wonder what the driving philosophy might be behind wanting to know more about someone you felt jealous of. Was it so that you could convince yourself to give up? Or so you could snag a victory? Whatever the reason, the only choice here was to tell her the truth.

"I called her Chika, this girl of only eyes and nails."

I pictured those lights floating in the darkness.

"She was always calm in demeanor. She had a lot of interests and loved things like books and perfume. Though, of course, those were all things of her world, so I never got to fully experience them."

"I see," she said casually, waiting for me to continue.

"In terms of species, I don't think she was a human. Though I couldn't see her, I was able to feel her body, and I definitely felt arms and legs and a face there, but her blood glowed, and her hair had a weird texture."

I opened and closed my right hand twice, trying to recall the sensation. In that moment, Saitou took another sip of coffee, clinking the cup back down onto the table. It was as if she was signaling for something to happen.

"So, were you two dating? You and that alien girl."

I sensed a variety of emotions in her tone; fear, astonishment, and hatred for this man who would start talking with deadly sincerity about a creature from another world when we were on the cusp of a breakup. The reservations that those emotions called forth were skepticism—Saitou was clearly wondering how seriously she should be taking me. But regardless of how Saitou felt, it didn't matter to me.

"No, her world had no concept of romance."

"So...?"

"So, I taught her about romance," I said, bulldozing straight through whatever she had been about to say. "I poured everything I had into making this person from another world understand what love was, what lovers were, what lovers do together."

How she understood and pictured my fantastical explanation probably depended on what media she had digested and what sort of romantic experiences she'd had. Either way, I was certain she got the message that it wasn't just some trifling words.

Yes, what Chika and I had was special. The feelings I had for Chika were unparalleled. The light that Chika had shone on me shone nowhere else in this world. No matter how dreadfully basic of a person I was, that alone was crystal clear.

"I have no idea how well Chika actually grasped my feelings, but we worked hard to try to understand one another. No matter what the future held for us, we were happy as long as there were things that we could share."

It was true. That was all I needed.

"The things that Chika gave me, and the things I feel for her, were my everything in this life, in this world. They still are. She was the only one who could ever change me. But that gale left me too soon."

Saitou's lips parted audibly again.

"Suddenly, I could no longer hear her voice, and she vanished right in front of me. I waited and waited, but I never saw her again after that."

I had a wealth of hypotheses about this, but in turning it over so many times since then, I had come to believe that *I* was the reason that I stopped being able to understand her words.

That night, she had rejected me. She distanced herself from me emotionally, and I could no longer comprehend her. I thought about it over and over until the film of my memories started to fray. Perhaps I was mistaken, but at this point there was no possible way for me to confirm nor deny it.

"When Chika left me, my life ended. This time we're spending right now is nothing more than me waiting out the rest of my days. It could end at any time; in fact I hope it ends sooner. I'm just here because I can't bring myself to do something as involved as actively dying."

Sitting here on this couch, facing Saitou, and even talking about Chika were just ways of killing time until my body perished.

"All I can do until I meet my end is to sit here, treasuring my memories of Chika. There is nothing left inside me but the part of me that cares for her. I couldn't possibly give anyone else's life meaning, and no one could ever bring any sort of meaning to mine."

If I were to offer Saitou anything resembling sincerity, no matter how fake, I knew that muddling my words and making her guess at my meaning was not the way to do it.

"Sanae, I've never considered myself in love with Saitou."

From this distance, there was no way she could not have heard me. The thrumming of my words would have carried straight into her brain. She looked at me dead on, falling silent, perhaps processing my words in her own way.

I wondered what reaction she might show me in the seconds that followed. Given it was her, I figured she would do whatever would best let her save face. Wailing or seething with rage would only wound her pride. I figured she would pretend to be calm and then say something dramatic about accepting the particulars of the situation.

As it turned out, my guess was mostly correct.

"I suppose I can imagine things."

I assumed that this was a prompt for me to ask what she meant. Before now, I would have given her exactly what she wanted, but I couldn't bear the thought of her mistaking that for kindness. So I kept my mouth shut, but apparently she wasn't actually waiting for me to reply.

"I wouldn't call it a gale, but I understand the feeling of encountering something that turns you, and your whole world, upside down. Of being held captive by that for the rest of your life."

It seemed Saitou still was not understanding me. I wasn't captive to the feelings. No. Those feelings were my *everything*. I started to try to explain myself again, to chide her, to persuade her, but this ended in failure.

"You and I are alike."

I pondered what she meant.

"We're the same, when it comes to how you feel about that girl."

"...The same?"

Nothing could possibly compare to Chika.

"Back then, I encountered something that changed my life in the way that girl Chika changed yours. Something that has held me captive ever since."

Hearing her so utterly disregard what was special about Chika, I felt an impossible sensation clawing itself up from the pit of my stomach. Yes, I waited for her words, perhaps because some part of me felt there was a possibility that even Saitou might have had some encounter, some feeling, that existed nowhere else in this world.

"For me..."

I waited.

"...it was music."

"That's not the same."

I'm sure that some part of me tried to hold back the words that came spewing out. Yet, fittingly, now that I had spat them out, there was no longer any need for me to keep up appearances for her.

"No, it's not the same," she continued. "But I'm sure that I've felt the same thing you did."

"Don't..."

"Don't what?"

Her expression changed. She had the calm of someone who had seen the monster's true guise and was no longer afraid. What gushed forth from me in the face of this was rage, pure and unadulterated, the first I had felt in so long.

"Don't you *dare* compare her to some meaningless artform...!"

"That girl means just as little to me. But she's someone irreplaceable to you, isn't she?"

"What could you *possibly* know about us?"

The earnest shrug she gave was like nails dragging down my back.

"I don't know anything. I could never understand the things that are important to other people when I don't even really know what music, which I cherish so much, is to me."

"And you'd put that on par with what *I*—"

I coughed, cutting myself off. At first, I thought my own anger had crystallized and torn a hole in my throat. Even in that moment, though, I still minded the engrained societal edict that you should turn away from other people's faces when you cough.

"It's too big for me to really understand, but I've been thinking about it this whole time. How much did you really understand that girl, Kaya-kun?"

"I..."

"I'm guessing you're held prisoner by her because you don't have the slightest idea what she really is to you."

"You're wrong."

Saying that I was held captive implied that if Chika were to vanish from my heart I could actually come to value something else. I could not. I had made it this far only by the warmth of those feelings deep inside me, feelings that nothing else in this world could give me. There was no one more important than Chika. There was no one as precious as her. Only I could fully understand these feelings, entirely unique to me. I wasn't like Saitou, who just had some vague admiration for someone else's creations. I was nothing like someone of that ilk.

How dare she sully my light with her cheap *sympathy*?

"I really thought that music saved me. I thought that as long as I still had a love for it, I would be fine. But when I realized that I didn't really understand anything about it, and that it hadn't been *trying* to save me, it broke my heart. So I'm still trying to determine what it is that music means to me."

I noticed something like joy wrapped up in her expression, which riled me all the more.

"I don't even have to think about Chika and me. I'm not like you."

"What did you like about her, Kaya-kun?"

"All of her."

I didn't have to think twice. I knew just what to say. I adored Chika's very existence.

"I don't mean something that vague. I want to hear it in your own words."

"You..."

Why was she coming for Chika like this? Why was she trying to stand in the way of my light? Did she doubt what I was saying? Or was she just jealous of Chika? If she wanted to know so badly, I would tell her. I searched back in my memories.

"Chika is the only thing inside of my heart that could never fade away. She affirmed the whole of my being."

"And she wasn't just *making* you think that?"

I found myself utterly at a loss for words at this insolence.

"It's impossible to fully understand another person, to affirm them utterly and completely. Basing your feelings entirely on someone else's affirmation of you isn't the same as loving them."

What could have possibly possessed her to keep piling on? I had evolved beyond rage to sheer vertigo. How utterly could Saitou—could this Sunou Sanae—lack any kind of judgment? Had she always been this hopelessly thoughtless?

"People fall in love with even the parts of the object of their affection that they can't see. It's the same whether you love a person or a thing."

Maybe for all of you. I thought. *For you Tanakas and Saitous. But my feelings for Chika are different. They're special.* Special. *No matter how worthless I might be, these feelings matter.*

"I had certain ideals when it came to music, something shapeless, formless. I even thought that it affirmed me to the fullest. But, even with that love, I still have to keep moving forward on my own two feet. Hearing you talk about Chika, you reminded me of how I used to be. Y'know, together we could..."

I heard a switch flip within me.

"That's enough."

It wasn't for dramatic effect or any other particular reason that I cut her off. There was simply no need for me to listen to anything else she had to say.

"You can stop right there, Saitou."

It made sense, if you thought about it. Why was she spewing all these incomprehensible things? How could she be so misguided as to think that her own experiences could apply to me? The things I had experienced were special, something that no one else had ever experienced. She just had no self-awareness. I had always believed myself to be a boring, run-of-the-mill individual, and I suppose I truly was.

But my encounter with Chika was a miracle.

Thus, perhaps it was inevitable that Saitou, who lacked any shred of real understanding, would make logical conjectures from commonplace sources—from the myriad of things she had experienced in her own life or what she had heard from others. What was I even getting so angry for?

What more could I have expected of her?

She was nothing more than a simple Saitou.

She wasn't like Chika at all.

"Just leave, please."

She looked at me, surprised. It was an utterly boilerplate reaction.

"I don't think we should have anything else to do with each other."

I had fully predicted her next reaction as well. Something like anger, a sense of betrayal, crossed her face, and then she said something completely off the mark.

"You aren't going to tell me anything...?"

"If that nothing of a response is the best you can give me, then I don't need to tell you anything else about Chika."

With that, the dam of her anger finally seemed to burst.

"Why would you say it like that?!"

I said nothing.

"Why are you acting like you're the only one who understands *anything*?!"

I wasn't. The only thing that should have read on my face was boredom at having to put up with such drivel from someone who hadn't even yet tasted their gale.

She glared at me. "You arrogant *little*..." I didn't think that I was making a face that would have warranted such hostility. "You're just hung up on some girl from the past!!!"

"That's right."

I could have just sat there and accepted her abuse, but my keeping silent wouldn't be enough to make her back down. I affirmed her assertions as she hurled her insults as though to wash my hands of her, and simply waited for her to fall back on her own.

"You are 100 percent correct. Enough of this already."

I looked away. I figured she might toss the coffee that was

close at hand in my face or maybe sling more abuse in an attempt
to elicit a reaction from me.

"What the hell is this *Chika*?! You say she affirmed everything
about you? She's just as stupid as you are."

See what I meant?

"Maybe."

"You aren't upset that I'm making fun of a girl you used to
love? If you only saw her eyes and nails, doesn't that mean that
you fell in love with your *imagination*? What if you filled in the
rest of her based on what you wanted to see?"

"You're probably right."

"The only thing you actually shared was conversation, right?
You never really saw eye to eye, so you probably just got fascinated
with whatever you selfishly interpreted her to be."

"That's entirely possible."

"And was that girl even actually *there*? It's seriously twisted to
say you'd never forget someone that you just made up in your head."

"That is also true."

"Get *angry*!"

She stood up, huffing through her nose. I saw her hands trembling out of the corner of my eye.

"If this girl was so important to you that you'd say there's no
point in living, that you'd say that all the time we spent together
was a lie, if you'd say that back then was the only time of your life
that ever mattered, then at least have the decency to be true to
your old self!"

Just how mistaken could one Saitou be?

Of course I was being true to myself. Not a day went by that I didn't think about Chika. Obviously, I was being incredibly sincere. I just didn't think there was any use in trying to argue this with Saitou.

"What would that Chika girl think if she saw you now?"

"Who knows?"

It was pointless to even consider, given that I was never going to see her again. And also...

"I don't care about how people see me anymore."

"Just... Jeez, forget it."

With that, she moved away, picking up her coat and shoes and heading toward the front door. I picked up the coffee cup in front of me and took some into my mouth. The taste was weak.

"Y'know something?" Her voice crashed down on my head, making me wish she would just leave. Was she going to give some canned parting remark? Well, this was the last time. I supposed I could at least hear her out.

"You..."

"Yeah?"

"By pinning all your own wretchedness on that girl, all you're doing is *sullying* her."

This time, she actually seemed to leave the living room. I didn't look up, but I could tell by her footsteps. I heard the front door open and then close.

Before I realized it, I had tossed the coffee mug I was holding at the wall. I sat there silent, gazing at the shards of the cup and the dripping brown liquid.

— ✳ —

My life without Saitou—that is, Sunou Sanae—began without issue.

It was nothing more than a return to how my life had been before, which should have been obvious at this point. As far as my life was concerned, Sunou Sanae was just another Saitou to me—certainly no one of any real importance. She was just one of the many people who had passed by me in my days on this earth. That was all I should have been to Saitou as well. There was no reason for her to retain even the foggiest memories of me. There is a limit to how many things we need to retain in our brains across our life spans.

That fact was glaringly obvious. Or it should have been, so *why*?

I felt uneasy. It had stuck with me, her final words that day.

Sullying, she said.

Who was sullying who?

"Morning."

"Oh, good morning, Suzuki-san!"

"I sent you an e-mail with the thing you asked for. You should double-check it."

"Whoa, that was fast! Thank you!"

She had said that I was sullying those memories—that I was sullying Chika.

How ridiculous.

Chika and I were never going to see each other again. That was precisely why I had to keep treasuring those memories, so that I could never forget them. There's no way you could corrupt someone who you would never see again. If anyone was sullying her, it was Saitou. She had sullied our feelings, mine and Chika's. She had left those ridiculous accusations in my home. That foul stench continued to rankle.

"Suzuki, could I ask you to free up this afternoon?"

"Of course. I wasn't especially busy anyway."

"I'm going to have lunch with Kanta-san, so come with me. He seems to really like you."

"If that's enough reason for me to barge in, then certainly."

I wondered if perhaps she was referring to the influence that Chika and I had on each other, but no. I hadn't told her the details of our shared influence, and even now I still bore in mind the possibility that I might have some effect on her and lived my life trying not to make waves. I had tried to eliminate the negative factors in my life as much as possible, not breaking anything, not losing anything, not falling into despair. The idea that I could do anything to harm Chika like that was absurd.

Saitou had said that I was blaming my own wretchedness on Chika. Trying to call me wretched as a criticism was a mistake. If she'd really wanted to hurt me, she should have criticized some particular feature of mine. However, the word "wretched," which I supposed was a dig at the joyless life I led, could have equally applied to so many other people in this world. She had failed to effectively disparage me.

"Hey, Suzuki-kun, brought you a souvenir."

"Thank you very much. I never thought I'd see the day when *you'd* bring me a souvenir, Kudou-san."

"Well, these were *supposed* to be a lovely treat from your senpai, but you can just give it back then."

"Kidding, kidding. I'll gladly accept your gift."

Saying that I was blaming Chika was also way off the mark. I owed a *debt* to Chika for the life I had led so far. For allowing me to be enveloped in that wind. For granting me feelings that I would hold indelibly inside my chest until the day I died. Even if the rest of my days from here on out were hollow, those feelings alone would remain real. Saitou could never understand what that meant when you lived such a meaningless life. For all Chika did for me, I thanked her. I would never degrade her, much less blame the emptiness of my own life on her.

"Hello, this is Suzuki. Thank you for all your help. Yes, as I explained the other day, I believe that will be the case for the rest of the fiscal year. I see, yes, I believe we've met. In that case, I will confirm things with Ueda and get back to you by the end of the day. Will that be all right? Yes. Thank you very much. Have a good day."

Every single remark she had thrown my way was wrong. I should have known that, but it still itched at me. Even now, three weeks after the fact, I could still feel the discomfort crawling down my back.

By the time I had wrapped up some tasks that needed to be finished by the end of the day, it was already 6 p.m. I was dragging on a tasteless cigarette in the company smoking room when one of my coworkers noted, "You're looking a little sluggish lately, Suzuki."

He'd had a kid just the other day. It was probably only because he was right in the prime of his gale, effused with such joy, that he had the leeway to meddle in someone else's life.

"Do I? Guess I've just had a lot on my mind lately."

"That's because you're so serious all the time. You need to go with the flow. You'll live longer if you do."

What he was saying was incorrect. It was *because* I went with the flow, because I hated running into problems or worries, that I appeared so serious on the outside.

"Or maybe it's about time you got married, y'know. Have someone at home to support you."

"I mean, marriage is about supporting each other, so I feel like my private life would just end up tied with my work."

"See? So serious." Apparently my words this time were especially apt, and he laughed, exhaling smoke. "Though I guess having a kid to support gives me the strength to work harder here."

The words of someone right in the midst of his gale, I thought. He was living for the sake of something that he treasured. I once felt that way. That feeling alone makes you feel like you can be anything you want to be. Of course, the fragments of strength, of omnipotence, that you gain from it are all an illusion, and they vanish as soon as your wind does.

"I can't start thinking about kids yet. I don't even have any plans to get married. I'm just looking for a good time."

"No? Wait, so does that mean that girl you were with…"

"Yep."

Now that he mentioned it, I supposed I had once run into him in town when I was out with Saitou. I hadn't remembered us having anything more than a casual conversation though.

I could tell that my response gave him a fair idea of the situation, but I figured I should explain more clearly, lest there be any future misunderstandings.

"We broke up."

"Huh. Shame."

Was it though?

Putting it that way, I guess it was a shame that I had to let go of a fairly attractive person who would readily satisfy my desires.

"She seemed like she was really into you."

I gave a vague smile at this ever-so-slightly surprising analysis. I tipped some ashes into the ashtray.

"I guess maybe she was—when we were together. But that's not always enough."

"Of course, us dirty old dogs need more than just emotional fulfillment, eh?" he said, laughing at his own joke. I laughed right along.

He wasn't quite right. I think that Saitou had been trying for emotional love, and she'd succeeded. If only I had been someone whose gust of life had not passed them by—if only I had been someone who had yet to encounter that one special something in their life. She was mistaken in directing her attentions toward me. There was no place left in my heart for a love of the mind alone.

She probably felt that I was the one in the wrong for dating her without letting her know. Perhaps it was best that I accept this discomfort she had left within me, accept my punishment. Anyone who would steal time away from a girl who had yet to meet her gale deserved to be judged.

That was absurd. There was no need for that. How could anyone possibly possess the right to stone me simply for my silence. Even Saitou...

"What's wrong?"

"...Nothing."

"Anyway, I'm sure you'll find someone else soon."

"I wonder."

"Whoops, if us fellows stand around here gossiping, the folks who don't smoke will have our heads," he said, looking at his watch. Again, he laughed at his own joke, tossing his butt into the ashtray and leaving the smoking room.

Left alone, I took the last few drags of my cigarette. The tobacco flavor that was usually so weak to me was now nonexistent.

I was puzzled. I struggled to sort out whatever had suddenly bubbled up inside my mind. I was so distracted that I didn't notice what my own body was doing, and after I discarded my cigarette I lit up another without thinking, even though I didn't want it.

I thought back on the conversation and the train of thought I had just been going through. My colleague had brought up the subject of Saitou, and I had started thinking about her. When he mentioned that love couldn't come solely from good intentions, it had confirmed for me that I didn't fit what Saitou truly wanted.

This was a correct analysis.

I then wondered if I ought to atone for not telling her how I really felt, but I swiftly dismissed the notion. It was selfish to be angry at someone for simply not sharing all of their thoughts and actions with you, and attacking them for it was clearly not within anyone's rights.

And yet, I had once overstepped in that same selfish way and had hurt the one I cared about most in the entire world.

There was something that Chika hadn't told me, and that fact alone had been too much for me to bear.

I regretted that night with every fiber of my being. And yet, I believed that I had said those things simply because my feelings for Chika were real, because I wanted to know everything about her, and that that alone was proof of the strength of those feelings.

I should have been able to understand how she felt. Yet...I denied it.

It was utterly absurd that Saitou would hate me just for not sharing my true feelings. It was stupid to want to know everything about me.

In other words, I had been blind to my own feelings toward Chika.

If my feelings for Chika were right in front of me, I could have never ridiculed the feeling of wanting to know everything about someone you loved.

Or I shouldn't have been able to.

And yet.

Wait.

Had I forgotten, just for a moment?

Fear coursed through my veins. Ash fell from the tip of the cigarette.

"No," I abruptly muttered, trying to deny what I felt rising up within me. It couldn't be true. There was no way I could possibly ever forget what I had felt for Chika. Feelings so powerful. Feelings so *heavy*. So easily...

And yet, a notion that rejected who I was back then crossed my mind.

"No way."

Could I really have been *that* stupid?

The only thing that had kept me alive was embracing my feelings for Chika. I looked back at that part of my life every single day. I always remembered it. That was what kept me going.

How could I *possibly* ever forget?

That encounter at the bus stop, when there was still a chill in the air.

That time we spent coming to understand one another, little by little. All the words that I couldn't understand. The scents that I couldn't smell. The tastes that we couldn't share. The days when there were wars in Chika's world. How much Chika hated the wail of the siren. Allumi's death. Tanaka, standing in the rain. Chika saving me. Breaking the radio and the school bell for Chika. How happy she had been that the siren was broken. Touching her body. The joy I felt at sharing that first kiss. Spending our honeymoon together. Smiling at one another.

My intellectual Chika.

My imaginative Chika.

The Chika who affirmed me.

That one-of-a-kind Chika.

My beloved Chika.

...Chika.

Why did she leave me?

How could I possibly forget?

The lit cigarette fell from my trembling fingers. Instead of doing the logical thing and picking it back up, for some reason I just took another from my pocket and started to light it—but my hand shook so badly I couldn't manage to ignite the flame, and in the end, I just tossed both the cigarette and lighter in the trash. Smoke rose from the cigarette on the floor, which I had only just started to smoke.

I remembered.

I remembered her clearly.

But I had realized something. The only things that I could manage to dredge up from my mind were the facts. The strength, the weight, the force of those old feelings—I couldn't picture that in the slightest. All I could remember was the *fact* that I had felt quite a lot for her. All I could hear were the words telling me that the feelings had been strong, had been heavy, had been forceful.

My heart didn't leap. I wasn't dancing. I didn't even stiffen up.

In other words, I no longer felt those feelings the way I did back then. I was merely reenacting them.

That was why I was so fine with thinking something that denied the person I used to be.

This fact didn't make my heart ache.

No, this was bad. I couldn't let it happen.

It was all fading away.

Without these feelings, it would all be a lie. *Chika* would be a lie.

Desperately, ever so desperately, I tried to drag myself back to those days. Chika and I had shared songs with one another, hadn't we? I had been so happy to get close to her, hadn't I? But then I thought we couldn't even hear each other's singing and couldn't understand what it sounded like.

No, that wasn't right. We could hear each other, but we couldn't comprehend the melodies.

I started to picture a rot spreading from the corners of my brain. Such fear was inevitable. I tried to figure out why this was happening to me. *Why* was this happening to me? Why had I realized this was happening right now?

I reached into my pocket for my phone. While taking it out, I dropped it once and had to pick it back up, then poked at the screen with my trembling fingers. I scrolled way back in my call logs for a name, which I immediately tapped, and put the phone to my ear. It didn't even occur to me that she might be at work right now or that she might not pick up a call from me.

After a number of rings, she answered the phone with a curt, professional, "Hello?"

"What...did you do to me?"

I was fully aware that this question lacked context. Perhaps the part of my brain that knew how to form sentences had already rotted away.

Sunou Sanae gave no response, so I gathered up what was left of my head to explain.

"I can't remember my feelings for Chika. I remember that I had them, but I can't clearly summon up the emotions. I should be able to, but I can't. I should..."

She remained silent.

"You did something to me that night, *didn't you?*"

I didn't stop to consider how ridiculous this must sound. Deep down, all I knew was that if she had done something to me, cast some curse or some spell or something upon me, it could swiftly be undone.

After some time, I heard her inhale softly. "Come to my place. Nine o'clock on the dot," Sanae said, and then she abruptly hung up before I could agree or refuse.

I stood there frozen in the smoking room until my concerned colleague came to fetch me.

It pained me to just stand around waiting, but I got the feeling that she wouldn't want to see me before the designated time. At nine on the dot, I climbed out of a taxi in front of Sunou Sanae's condo and started swiftly toward the entrance. I had already mailed her duplicate key back to her during our time apart, so instead I entered her apartment number to summon her.

Receiving no reply, I tried ringing her once again. Still nothing. Trying to push down my agitation, I'd just decided to try calling her when I received a text. She was running 15 minutes late.

I waited anxiously for her arrival. I didn't have it in me to wonder how she might treat me after so long apart. There was really no reason for me to wonder about anything. I loitered in front of the entrance, ignoring the suspicious glances from the residents going in and out. Finally, another taxi stopped. I immediately recognized the rider from the side of her face and had to fight my own feet's urge to approach.

After she finished paying the fare, Sunou Sanae walked toward me, dressed in relatively formal attire. I'd planned to greet her depending on how she approached me, but she stalked toward me silently, balled up her fist beside her head, and punched me directly in the face.

A punch from someone of such a slight build was not enough to do much damage, but I was still stunned at the wildly unexpected development. "The admission fee," she stated curtly and unlocked the entrance. Unsure of what I should say, I just followed her inside and boarded the elevator. She didn't say a word. Following suit, I silently stepped out of the elevator and stood in front of her door for the first time in weeks.

Her place looked the same as it had when we were seeing each other. My things were even still there. I wondered at first if she had some lingering attachment to the items, but perhaps if she had actually done something to me, she had also predicted that we would at some point be here together again.

I put down my bag and heeded her direction to "Sit," taking

what had previously been my assigned seat in a chair on the kitchen side of the table. The owner of the home took off her jacket and boiled some water in a red kettle, preparing two cups of instant coffee and placing them on the table.

I hadn't really been craving a beverage, but I thanked her anyway and waited for her to sit down opposite me. By the time her butt finally hit the seat, my patience was already at its limits.

"Tell me," I said. She looked back at me fiercely. "What...did you do to me?"

Not taking her eyes off me, Sunou Sanae breathed in once through her nose, deeply, and replied, "I didn't do anything."

"You must have."

"Seriously, I've affected nothing but my own circumstances. I've performed no hypnosis, nor said any word of a magic spell."

"Then why did you invite me here?"

I leaned forward, my entire body tense. Still, she did not avert her gaze, nor even look surprised.

"*I* haven't done anything, but I know what happened."

"If *you* haven't done anything, then did *he* do something?"

I settled back in my chair and recalled my day at work. Sunou Sanae tilted her head.

"He who?"

"One of my coworkers. But I don't think someone as worthless as him could affect *me* like that."

"Listen," she clipped. "I regret to inform you that *everyone* is special."

Ridiculous.

"Like hell they are."

"They are. Every single person you meet. *You're* the one who decides which of those people can affect you."

"The only one who could influence me was Chika."

She brought her coffee cup to her mouth and let out a long, thin sigh.

"I'll tell you what happened to you."

My heart roiled in equal parts from excitement at finally getting some answers and fear that I might be about to learn something inconvenient. Still, stopping here was out of the question.

"Tell me. *Please.*"

"You forgot."

Before I could even process this bleedingly simple answer, an image popped into the back of my mind: myself, throttling the woman in front of me. In reality, though, all I could do was take one stupid, inaudible breath.

"It's been so long that you've forgotten your feelings for her."

"That's *impossible.*"

"But you have realized that you don't actually have the same feelings for her that you did back then, haven't you?"

She appeared to be waiting for me to reply. I shook my head.

"You're wrong. You're so wrong."

"But you said so on the phone."

"This is just temporary, I'm sure that once I know what's causing this, I'll get it all right back."

"*I've* forgotten." What was she talking about? "I remember in factual terms the passion I felt when I first got into music, and the way that I hated you in high school, but I certainly don't *actually* have the same feelings that I had back then."

"My...my feelings aren't as *half-assed* as those."

I realized that my voice was getting weaker. I wanted to get angry, but anxiety won out, and now I just sounded as though I were asking for help. I wonder how I looked to her in that moment. I got the feeling she pitied me.

"It's fine to forget."

"No, it isn't."

"None of us can remember anything forever."

She was being ridiculous. That couldn't be fine. It couldn't possibly. I searched desperately for the feelings that I knew should have been blazing within me. How often I thought about her at the time, how precious she was to me, to put it in more fickle terms. How I wanted to make her mine, and for her to make me hers. I believed that as long as she was there, I needed nothing else.

I searched. I searched and searched and searched. The more I searched, the more I knew it. I couldn't help but become aware of it, the answer there in the very words that I had dredged up.

Was. Wanted. Believed.

Everything there in my heart was there in the past tense. If I tried to scoop any of those feelings out in their current form, they would crumble and slip through my fingers like sand.

Ah.

"This can't be happening..."

"But it is."

How could she possibly prove that? What could she possibly know?

I was offended. I should have gotten mad and brushed her aside, or simply exited the conversation. But I couldn't. I was standing in my own way.

The amount, weight, size, and shape of the feelings I was once certain I felt no longer existed in present tense. It was like a shed skin, falling from my body, drifting away, vanishing.

No.

No way.

"No."

Not a single grain of sand remained in my palms. It was like a waking nightmare.

"I don't want to forget."

There was nothing to be gained from telling Sunou Sanae that. She couldn't possibly call my feelings back to me, much less summon Chika here from that other world. She had been nothing more than a trigger—a trigger that made me realize that I had been deceiving myself all along.

Yet here I was, shamelessly praying for a miracle. With every fiber of my being, I prayed for this not to end.

She stared at me as I continued to spew wretched, meaningless words. I thought she might laugh at me. I thought she'd lord over me, say that she told me so. However, she just looked at me, biting her bottom lip.

"It's okay to forget how you felt," she said, repeating herself. I shook my head.

"If I forget, then it'll all have been a lie."

This time it was her head that moved slowly back and forth, twice.

"That doesn't make it a lie. We all forget things. No matter how strong our feelings might be, little by little, the memories of them crumble, blur, and fade. But that by no means makes what we felt at the time a lie. None of it is a lie, not how I was so bored in those days that I wanted to die, nor how I found a band that I fell so deeply in love with that it made me want to change, nor the way that you loved Chika."

"But if I forget, then how can I prove it?"

"You still can. *Listen*, Kaya-kun."

She placed her hands over mine, which sat folded on the table. I could never know what it must be like to take the hands of a man whose hands you had let go of just a few weeks prior. The hands of someone she probably hated, was disgusted by, scorned. The hands of someone who had never seriously attempted to face his own feelings.

"I really did think you were a piece of shit."

Wait, what?

"I thought you must be one of the most vapid people I've ever met. You were twisted, drunk on yourself, and only put on the face of a proper working man, and I thought that I must have been a fool to have fallen for someone like you."

She was right. I treated her the way that I had at the time to *make* her feel that way about me.

"Do you know how many times I thought, 'I'll never forgive him'? But still..."

Her eyelid twitched.

"Despite your attitude, you made me think about my own life and uncovered part of my true self."

She was wrong. That wasn't me.

"Kaya-kun, it seemed like you regretted causing that poor dog Allumi's death."

I wasn't that sort of person.

"I thought, this is an idiot who's crying just because he doesn't know the distance from his own humanity." She gripped my hands tighter. "I don't have the slightest idea what's going to happen from here on out, but I can say this much—"

Before I realized it, I was hanging.

"Someday, I'll forget what I'm feeling right now, this feeling of once more wanting to know more about you."

Hanging on her every word.

"So, right now, I have to be true to myself, unashamed of the things I hold dear. I want to be. We can only build up the present through our own toil and suffering. Once you've done that enough, you'll grant yourself a present where you can be certain that the person who loved Chika once existed. I can give *myself* a present where I wasn't wrong to have been so affected by music. And from there, all we can do is it keep living. So, it's all right."

A single tear fell from her left eye. An ordinary, non-glowing tear.

"It's all right to forget me, even."

The remnants of my feelings for Chika, the last embers that smoldered in my heart, crumbled and fell away. On the way to the bottom of my heart, those fragments vanished. But the smallest sliver of my feelings, something that I never intended to share with anyone, slipped out in the form of words.

"I'm sorry."

I hadn't meant to speak the words aloud, much less ever let anyone hear them.

"Chika."

Perhaps I had wanted to tell someone all along.

"I loved her so much. She was the only thing that mattered to me."

Words that would never reach anyone, anywhere.

"I wonder if she's already forgotten me. I hope she at least remembers that we once met."

Only Sunou Sanae was listening. Eyes lowered, squeezing my hands.

The color would never return to my world. It would never get any easier to breathe. I could never be forgiven.

And yet, it was as though I had been given permission to keep on existing in this world.

— ✳ —

It had been about two weeks since the new year began. My world had fully returned to normal, our days back to their old routine as well. Or rather, given that Sanae normally didn't get a New Year's vacation, and I typically didn't do much traveling home to begin with, there were no major changes.

"Let's go to that place again tonight. I want dashimaki."

On Saturday, as I was cooking myself lunch, I received a message from Sanae. I sent right back a simple "OK." I was already in the middle of making some tamagoyaki, but that was fine. Tamagoyaki and dashimaki were different dishes.

She had probably sent the text on the spur of the moment, as evidenced by the lack of any emoji.

I set my finished lunch atop the table and turned up the volume on the new radio I had purchased the other day. The show that Sanae was in charge of was about to begin.

The moment the final digit on my digital clock turned to zero, the radio emitted a mechanical sound that slowly shifted into the pleasantly familiar background music. The female host gave a lively greeting along with the current date and time, followed by her name. I started on my salad as I listened to her opening monologue. I recalled Sanae talking about how much work it was to put together these monologues.

Today's topic was a friend who had gotten back together with a former boyfriend. As I listened, I half wondered if this had been inspired by Sanae—but was embarrassed by my own self-importance when this didn't seem to be the case.

As I listened to the love lives of complete strangers, nibbling on some boiled broccoli, I thought about how many things were going on everywhere in the world. A lot of things were going on with us too, now that we were dating again. Our story wasn't interesting enough for us to submit to a radio show, but after some discussion, things had ended up this way. Everything seemed to be going pretty smoothly for us on the surface, but Sanae continued to tease me relentlessly with, "Um, so tell me about this Saitou again?"

Obviously, in getting back together, what was most important was how Sanae felt about me. Just as she had said to me that night, she still wanted to see more of me. "You're so stupid it's cute," she added.

I wasn't merely going with the flow this time when I swallowed my guilt and accepted her proposal. It wasn't a lie that I enjoyed seeing Sanae at her fiercest, nor a lie that I found her attractive as a member of the opposite sex. I had started to think that, if there was any point from now to the end of my days, it was the simple fact that perhaps I could become someone meaningful. Even if it was for a brief, fleeting moment, it would at least be while I was together with Sunou Sanae. I'd thought that this was an awfully self-centered point of view, but when I told her, she was surprisingly thrilled.

"People can change," she said, though I still couldn't fully believe it myself. I didn't think that my own bland life could change that easily after so many unremarkable years, but I planned to keep building up a present where I at least *wanted* to believe it.

"Speaking of people changing..."

As I wallowed in a rather strange mood, Sanae made a face like she wanted to reveal something to me, perhaps to clear the heavy atmosphere that had taken over the place. I was looking forward to this reveal, but at the same time I was nervous. It was the same sort of face she had when she told me how much she had hated me.

"Did you notice I got some work done on myself?"

"H-huh?"

I made an odd noise. I stared at her face but could see no stitches or seams. I hadn't noticed.

"I hated my face. I got a bit done before I started looking for work. My parents still keep sniping that if they don't see me regularly, they'll forget what I look like."

"I hadn't noticed, but uh, I guess I actually didn't recognize you at first."

"Yeah. I figured that you wouldn't remember me regardless, so I had to push pretty hard."

To my surprise, she revealed that she had in fact recognized me at the station back home, but she couldn't work up the courage to speak to me, so she had just ridden the train the whole time in silence.

I didn't feel bad in the slightest that she had kept this from me. She was grasping her own path with her own two hands. That was a wonderful thing. Just as she had changed her own face because she hated it, I now believed that it was fine if I one day became someone who could no longer face Chika.

Even though I might forget that feeling too someday.

378

When I finished lunch, it was still early in the radio show. After cleaning up my dishes, I opened my laptop and began working on the task I had been assigned. My job transfer ended up getting postponed, and Sanae was still working at the station. She said that she intended to keep this job until she found an answer that she could accept. Wherever she ended up, she hoped to walk in the direction that her own determination pointed her.

After the radio host finished reading e-mails that had been sent in, it was time for the music requests. In between were some commercials and pre-recorded interviews with artists, but for the most part the program was made up of messages from listeners. Now and then I thought about writing in to hear some song I had heard long ago.

"Up next is a request from a listener who calls themself 'Look Look.' *Hello, Himura-san!* Yes, hello there! *I'd like to request the new song from 'Her Nerine,' called 'Silhouette.' This song is the best; it always feels like there's suddenly this great big hole in my life. It makes me wanna cry to think that there's someone in this world who could sing a song like this. You've gotta play it!* So actually, we've gotten a lot of requests for this song. Obviously, I'm a huge Nerine fan, but I seriously can't wait to hear this one live. All right everyone, listen up! Here's 'Silhouette' by 'Her Nerine.'"

I didn't think much of it when the music started playing, nor when the lyrical intro kicked in. It wasn't especially good or bad. I still wasn't capable of making much more than objective judgments about music. I figured it was something I would have to grow into, like a baby would.

That was how I listened to this song, "Silhouette." It was when the female vocalist started singing that the problem occurred.

When I say that there was trouble with this radio show, I don't mean that there was interference in the radio waves or anything. It was me. The problem was with me. When I realized it, I stood up, staring at the radio, almost forgetting to breathe.

I knew those haunting lyrics. I knew not a single thing about this band or this song, but I knew those words with all my heart.

It was a song that had once been breathed into my ear in a dark bus stop.

Hearing the words, all I could think of was that song.

What was going on? They had just said that this was a new release, hadn't they? Wasn't this...a song from Chika's world?

I stood for a while in stunned silence, thinking for the first time in so very long about the connection between her world and ours.

"You want to meet Nerine? What's this about all of a sudden?"

As we sat down at the usual izakaya, after we endured the usual ribbing from the staff—"What, you two still together? Glad to see it!"—and shared a toast, I broached the subject with Sanae.

"Well, not the whole band per se. I just want to meet the person who wrote the lyrics to the song 'Silhouette.'"

"Oh, well, most of their lyrics are written by their vocalist, a girl named Aki. I'm actually pretty close with her. She's a nice girl, but seriously, how come?"

It'd be a lie to say I wasn't hesitant to explain, but there was no reason to hide the truth at this point. I explained to her what had happened that afternoon, as well as what I remembered.

"I see."

"I mean, I could just be remembering wrong."

"I mean, it's crazy if it is the same song, whether it's a total coincidence or if it does actually mean something. Plus... Oh, wait." She started to say something, then took her planner from her bag on the floor and checked it. "Anyway, that's pretty amazing either way, but actually, Aki's doing a solo performance next weekend. I don't know if she's going to do that song, but do you wanna go? I'm sure I can at least get you in to say hello."

"Th-thanks."

I really was thankful. I had expected a smile out of her at this, but instead she stuck out her lip.

"Or will that not work with your schedule?" I asked.

"No, it's just, well, I get it, and I'm an adult, so I know there are a lot of things I have to accept, but I guess I'm just a little jealous," she said, poking at my gut. I felt a little guilty, but I figured that this would give me some hint about Chika and about how I ought to face my own reality from here on out.

The following week, we met up in front of a station in a busy shopping district. I was told that I would be introduced as a colleague, but when I showed up dressed in an inoffensive suit, she withdrew the offer, saying "No one dresses that sharply at a radio station." I had come here in a suit to keep my back straight and hide how nervous I was, an emotion I hadn't felt in some time.

We moved swiftly away from the station, passing through the crowds toward the venue. We crossed a busy intersection and passed by a large movie theater, listening to warnings directed toward solicitors.

We arrived at what appeared to be the entrance to some kind of cellar, Sanae pointing down excitedly and said, "We're here!"

For the first time ever, I entered a music hall. Thinking of how deeply Sanae liked to immerse herself in music, I couldn't help but remember that bus stop where I met Chika.

We descended the stairs. As we arrived at some sort of reception area, I realized that I had not yet received a ticket from Sanae. As I started to call after her, she held up a hand to silence me.

"Pardon me," she said to the receptionist. "I'm Sunou. Shinkawa-san invited me."

"Of course. Could I get you to sign in here?"

After a brief exchange, Sanae received two stickers from the woman at reception, one of which she passed to me. I don't think my face conveyed any particular opinion, but Sanae entered the main area and headed to the nearby bar counter to grab two beers, giving one to me.

"There are a lotta ways to drop money on music. Cheers."

I took the plastic cup and clinked mine to hers, when, as though awaiting our arrival, the room lights lowered. The place wasn't packed, but there were a fair number of attendees. We moved to a spot it would be easier to see from.

The crowd broke out in scattered applause and cheers as someone appeared on the stage. I could tell it was man by his appearance. I'd heard there would be two performers today, so that meant Aki would be the second.

The man, who looked to be around twenty, gave a bright smile to the crowd looking up at him. He had a rather delicate air to him, but when he picked up his guitar and sat down in his chair, the atmosphere in the room shifted. His voice was relaxed but powerful, and the thought crossed my mind that if I had been born with a voice like that, it wouldn't have been wrong for me to think of music as *my* gale as well.

There was applause after each song, and once he had finished eight of them, it seemed his time was done. He gave another brilliant smile, bowed, and disappeared into the back. As the last smattering of applause faded, the lights came up. I happened to glance at Sanae, who stood beside me. She raised both the corners of her mouth at me, then started entering something into her phone. I thought she might ask me my impression, but she was already aware that I was incapable of being moved by others' creations. So her not asking me wasn't for my sake so much as out of consideration for the others around us. Any fans of the singer who was just on probably wouldn't enjoy hearing that.

I wondered if one day I would learn to be moved by books and music so that I could share in Sanae's joy. Even if that day did come, it might be far off in the future; I might not even see that day before I died. Still, it wouldn't be such a bad thing if there was a future where I could shed tears alongside her in the cards.

About ten minutes passed as they changed out the equipment on the stage. In the interval, Sanae shared some memories of this venue with me. She told me how nervous she was coming to this town for the first time in high school and walking down the road to this place, and how moved she was to step across the threshold of a spot that she had heard the name of so many times before. How countless emotions raced through her head the moment the music started and how she ended up crying her eyes out. She came here many times after, and of course, given that it was a place where people gathered, there were some bad memories as well, but even now she looked forward to these visits.

"Obviously, it's impossible for me to experience the same burst of emotions that I did the first time, but there are plenty of new things for me to be impressed by now that I know more."

So, it's fine, she didn't say, but I got the impression that was what Sanae was trying to tell me. It could have just as likely been directed toward me as toward herself. It might have even been directed toward all the people here.

Finally, the staff finished their preparations and cleared the stage, and the lights dropped again. I was nervous. Who was this person we were about to see? What connection did the girl who sang that song have to Chika's world? In direct contrast with the wild racing of my heart, the girl called Aki moved languidly onto the stage.

In the dim light, I saw her hazy form sit down in the chair, guitar in hand. There was a single round of applause, and as she moved closer to the mic, the lights on stage slowly raised.

"Good evening. I'm Aki from Her Nerine."

Her expression was much more sullen than I had seen it in the photos on the band's homepage. After greeting the audience in a tone that could be called neither genial nor amiable, she immediately launched into her first song.

As with the last performer, the moment she started to sing, her entire aura changed. You could scarcely have imagined it from her narrowed, sleepy eyes or her sullen expression, but the voice that flowed from her lips made the whole room vibrate. I had heard her on the radio before, but I was stunned at the difference when hearing her in the flesh.

After finishing two songs, she took a drink of the water that sat beside her, returned her guitar, and brought the microphone to her mouth.

"Next up is a cover of a favorite of mine, 'Fifteen,'" she said briefly, then again began singing in a voice that it seemed she was pouring every fiber of her being into.

I listened closely to the words, thinking about myself at fifteen years old. Perhaps Sanae was doing the same. Many of the people present here today were probably in the same boat. I wondered how many people lament having grown into the sort of adult they never thought they would be when they were younger. I wondered what you were supposed to do once you were done crying over it.

The end of the song brought more applause, through which Aki casually said, "Next up is a new song. It's called 'Silhouette.'"

I noticed Sanae straighten up beside me. I held my breath. Ignorant of whatever was going on with us, Aki started into the song she had written. It was the first time I had heard an acoustic arrangement of it. Hearing it with just guitar really highlighted the unique qualities of her voice. Sadly, I couldn't clearly recall Chika's singing voice. If this song was the same one that she had sung, how would she have sung it?

Still, as I listened to the words, I was filled with something like conviction that I did, in fact, know the lyrics. I felt them tracing the scars left on my heart.

After "Silhouette," Aki sang three more songs, stepped off the stage, and then returned again amidst cheers and undying applause. The man who had performed first appeared with her, and the two did a song together before the concert finally came to an end with the distinct air of a curtain falling closed.

Sanae and I looked at each other. We waited for most of the other attendees to clear out before heading to the green room to say hello.

"So you know that song 'Fifteen,' right?"

"Yeah, I think she said it was a cover."

"Mm! I met Aki when a colleague of mine told me that there was a girl doing a cover of a song that features the vocalist of my favorite band."

I wonder if this means something, she muttered and then looked at her phone. It appeared she had gotten some message from one of Aki's staff, and we moved locations.

I followed behind her, smiling and bowing my head as she

called out to a male staff member, exchanging a cheerful greeting. We stepped through a door that would typically be off-limits for anyone but staff. It was surprisingly cramped back there, and among a crowd of several older people performing various tasks, we found Aki, holding a bag of ice to her throat and staring at her phone.

Sanae slipped past, greeting the various staff members. When Aki looked up, her wholly sullen expression from onstage suddenly burst.

"Oh! Sunou-san!"

"Long time no see!"

"Looked pretty cool up there, didn't I?"

"Yeah, you were super cool!"

"I'm glad."

"I liked that arrangement of 'Silhouette.'"

"It's a good song, yeah?"

In her smile, there was a measure of youth that had been present on her face onstage. I'd heard that she was currently twenty-one.

I wondered how I should broach the main topic. I stood idly at attention behind her until there was a gap in the conversation, and she swiveled back to me, pushing me toward Aki.

"Sorry for the surprise intrusion. This is a colleague of mine. He heard 'Silhouette' and immediately fell in love with your work. I figured it'd be nice to at least give him a chance to say hi, if that's all right with you?"

"Lovely to meet you. I'm Suzuki Kaya. Your performance was wonderful."

Somehow, I managed to hide my nerves in front of her and give her my prepared greeting with the appropriate air of excitement. I couldn't say that I wasn't thankful for how long I had spent living with my true feelings kept under wraps. Aki gave another sunny smile.

"Oh, thanks so much! Pleased to meet you. I'm the vocalist of the band Her Nerine. You can call me Aki."

I fought back my nerves as I received her cheerful greeting. What could I say to confront her? What could I ask to learn about the connection between the song that Chika sung and this Aki? I had considered a million different ways to go about this up until now.

I wanted to ask what had inspired her to write the song. It wouldn't be an unnatural question since she had already heard that I liked it. I wanted to know about Aki herself as well, but it'd be weird to ask her that out of the blue. I knew from her official profile that she had started the band with some friends from her hometown. I supposed the conversation could expand from there. I wondered if she knew anything about Chika or about Chika's world. Aki. *Aki*.

When I tried to convey all my muddled thoughts to her, all that came out of my dry mouth was, "Aki... Is that *aki* like autumn, the season?"

I couldn't believe what I was hearing from my own mouth. What the hell was I saying? My nerves and a multitude of intertwined thoughts had made me ask something utterly meaningless. The time I had here was probably limited. As I sat there suffering—though I didn't let it show on my face—Aki looked briefly surprised. But then she gave a warm smile and said, "Not quite," drawing something in the air. "It's written A-ki, with 'a' like the first character in *yasui*, and 'ki' like the 'gei' in *geinou*," she explained.

"...Oh, is that your surname?"

I needed to change the subject, and fast. I didn't feel good about this line of questioning. I would get nothing meaningful here.

"It is, yeah. I don't like being called by my first name, so I started using my last name. This is my first name." Again, her finger danced through the air, a habit of hers perhaps. Her finger drew one straight line, then two identical sets of five strokes, followed by a set of four. I couldn't read what she was trying to write. *"One song,"* she offered, the name of a person who was practically born to sing. "That is, Ichika."

At first I thought I had misheard her.

"Aki...Ichika."

I remembered chanting that sound over and over in my mind more times than I could count. I probably forgot to even arrange my face.

"Kind of a showy name, huh? It's *sooooo* embarrassing!" Aki Ichika laughed amiably.

I looked briefly at Sanae, who knew exactly what was going on. She gave me a small nod as though she was holding something back, then swiftly broke into a smile.

"Should you really be giving your real name out to folks you've just met? Someone might abuse that."

"I mean, what's a colleague of yours gonna do, Sunou-san?"

The two women joked and laughed together like kindred spirits. I watched them and listened to them.

Or I should have been listening.

Without realizing it, my consciousness had drifted somewhere else.

My heart plunged into that old, familiar darkness.

Then, I noticed. There seemed to be two glowing eyes there. There seemed to be twenty glowing nails there.

No, they *were* there.

I heard a voice.

It wasn't just some crumbling memory. It was like she was really there. No, she *was* there.

"My voice and appearance would be different in a way I might not even recognize at first."

I'd had no idea what she meant back then.

"There are things deeper down, immovable things that we can't choose."

I see.

"If I had been born into your world..."

Chika had vanished. The bus stop was gone. The war was over.

I'd thought that there was nothing left.

"...I still would have met you."

I understood now. We knew how to meet each other.

"How do you write 'Kaya'?"

Aki's voice drew me back, and my heart returned to my current location in the concert venue. I swiftly started to adjust my face when I realized it wasn't necessary. I was already wearing a genuine smile.

"'Ka' as in *kaori*, 'ya' like the 'ya' of *yayoi*."

"Oh, how stylish!"

I wondered what I was supposed to do here. How should I interpret the existence of the girl Aki who stood before me, and what was I supposed to tell her? A number of thoughts ran through my head. Given that this world and Chika's were connected—and that we never did determine what influence they had on each other—it was neither absurd nor impossible to think there could be an equivalent to Chika in my world. Given that, I probably should have conveyed all this to her somehow. Maybe there was something I could do for her.

I thought about it, but the answer I came up with was so simple there could not have been any other.

Our conversation proceeded smoothly, with Aki imploring us to come to her band's next show. I told her sincerely that I was looking forward to it. When we parted ways, the two women shared a friendly handshake, and Aki bowed politely to me.

In the end, there was only one thing that I wanted to do, to say to her.

"I pray that we can both be happy."

Aki looked at me curiously, as she'd probably rarely heard something so emotional from a person she had just met, and returned a joking, "Sure. Thanks, bud," with another quick bow.

After sharing a few more quick greetings with the staff around us, we returned to the main floor. We left the now mostly empty venue and climbed the stairs. Once we got to the top, I looked at Sanae. I saw several emotions float across her face in turn, then her lips parted.

"Are you all right?" she asked kindly, and I in turn replied, "Thank you."

Though there were probably a million things she wanted to say, she held them back and smiled.

I looked up at the sky.

The final thought that ran through my mind was: *I wonder if Chika ever met me over there.*

As per usual, at the end of February, I celebrated my birthday. I had no particular feelings about getting older, but this year's birthday was going to be a little bit different from the previous.

"Yo!"

I looked over at the source of the distant voice to see my brother waving at me from near a station wagon. Sanae and I approached from where we'd been standing alone in front of the local train station, cringing at my brother's enthusiasm.

"Sorry to keep ya! Pleased to meet you, I'm Kaya's big brother."

He offered me a half-baked apology and greeted Sanae with a smile. Sanae, a well-rounded member of society, put her bag on her shoulder and clasped her hands together in front of her, bowing deeply.

"Pleased to meet you. I'm Sunou Sanae. Thank you for coming out here to meet us."

"Not a problem at all," said my flirt of a brother, escorting her to the back seat. As his younger brother, I was horribly embarrassed, but I climbed obediently into the car as well.

As it happened, the actual day of my birthday fell on the weekend, and it was also one of Sanae's days off, so we decided to drop in at my family's home for a visit. The purpose of our visit was to introduce Sanae to my family and to pay my respects at my mother's altar since the anniversary of her passing was the week before. I told Sanae that she really didn't have to come, but it was of her own volition that this day had become our shared reality. The two of us had work first thing tomorrow, so we weren't staying the night, just having lunch with the family. All I really needed to do was put on a vague smile and survive this encounter, but all day she had been ribbing me, "None of your business smiles, Kaya. When I see that face it makes me feel like you're about to call me *Saitou* again." There was really no arguing with her.

My brother chatted with Sanae for the whole car ride. Sanae indulged him in her cheerful Sanae-like way: "We were classmates in high school." "I work at a radio station." "I can't believe how easy you are to talk to! Not like *this* guy." I had no idea what face to make that wasn't a forced smile, so I just watched the scenery rolling by.

When we arrived at the house, my father, who had been waiting goodness knows how long, was out front, holding a cat he had recently adopted. Sanae received a warm welcome from my smiling father and was led down the path to the front door like some kind of princess.

We took off our shoes, washed our hands, and moved to the living room, where I was taken aback to find my maternal grandparents waiting. My father's parents had already passed, so they of course weren't here.

Sanae greeted both my grandparents, then asked if it would be all right for her to pay her respects at the altar as well. Naturally, she wasn't refused, and the two of us went to the altar together.

I felt no particular sadness about my mother's passing, but thinking about it, I wondered what sort of different conversations I would have with my mother now if she were still alive.

On the low table in the living room was more food than six people could feasibly eat. There was sushi that was probably takeout and a large platter piled with vegetable nimono and karaage that my grandmother had probably made. The minute that Sanae and I took our seat on one of the sofas that surrounded the table, my father started fidgeting with something.

"Sanae-san, do you drink?"

"Like a *fish*!"

At her enthusiastic reply, my father happily produced a bottle of liquor from somewhere. Though I rolled my eyes at this, wondering if he had mistaken this for a marriage announcement, I partook as well.

The luncheon proceeded without a hitch. At least both Sanae and my family seemed to be having fun. The conversation jumped back and forth as we talked about our work, life in the city, my mother, and what Sanae thought of me.

"He's as cute as a baby."

My family grinned in delight at this evaluation, which felt half like an insult to me. *Please look after our boy,* my father said, bowing his head. I really should've just let the whole conversation slide past my ears, but there was one thing I couldn't ignore; heartfelt words from my father that sounded as though they referred to both Sanae and perhaps my mother.

"You've gotta cherish a good woman like that, Kaya."

"...Yeah, I do."

I swallowed the food that was in my mouth and then gave a proper reply.

"I hope that I can spend my time doing something for Sanae, no matter how little."

My father, brother, and Sanae all appeared shocked.

Once the meal was over, we enjoyed some coffee with teacakes that my brother had brought. As it turned to evening, we informed them that we were going to stop in at Sanae's house, and the day's meeting ended.

I received some simple souvenirs, was made to promise that I would bring Sanae back again, and together, the two of us left the Suzuki household. There was a fair distance between my family's home and hers, but we decided to walk. Sanae politely declined my brother's offer to drive us there, saying it would be nice to walk around our old streets while we were here.

Sanae's home was in the so-called former foothills. The place was completely built up now, leaving no traces of the old days no matter where we looked.

"Is this where you used to go running?" she asked as we walked side by side. I nodded.

"Yeah. There were some nice slopes."

"Was the bus stop out this way too?"

"Yeah, it was."

With only that, the two of us walked in silence. After a little while, we came to a group of condos that had not been there in the past, passing by a group of frolicking children who probably lived there. We stepped into the empty street to avoid a woman coming toward us, pushing a stroller down the narrow sidewalk. As we passed her by, I happened to glance at her face and froze, but I didn't call out, nor did I even let my face show that I had noticed anything.

Deep down, ever since that day, I had thought of her by her real name. I prayed in the bottom of my mind that this girl, who in some ways resembled me, was doing well. I practically heard a "God, you're gloomy," from somewhere.

"Hey, Kaya-kun," Sanae said to me as we passed through the complex.

"Yeah?"

"What was that about? What you said earlier?"

I looked at her as we walked and saw her looking back at me.

"Don't go thinking you're gonna live for me just because you've got nothing left. I don't want that."

Sanae kept walking. I kept in pace with her, as I had been.

"I can't hope to understand everything about you, and I can't affirm every part of you. All I can do is walk beside you."

She stopped, the corners of her mouth raised. I halted as well, looking her firmly in the eye.

"I want us to live just looking at one another like this, sometimes holding hands, occasionally even sharing the same thoughts. And then, someday, we'll die. I realize now that that's not so bad," she said, and she started walking again. I followed behind her, then moved up to her side.

So many thoughts ran through my head as I thought about what she said. Perhaps there was a version of me who wasn't ashamed of the things he treasured, somewhere down the road she described.

"This is where the rest of our life starts, after all."

"I sure hope so."

I nodded. She poked me in the side, and I turned my head to look at her, simply glad to see that she didn't seem sad. As long I could be happy about that, I prayed, everything would be all right.

I finally realized that I wasn't yet ready to give a name to those days ahead.